THE

ISLAND

WALKERS

JOHN BEMROSE

THE

ISLAND

WALKERS

EMBLEM EDITIONS
Published by McClelland & Stewart Ltd.

National Library of Canada Cataloguing in Publication

Bemrose, John, 1947-
The island walkers / John Bemrose.

ISBN 0-7710-1112-1

I. Title.

PS8553.E47185 2004   C813'.54   C2004-902326-8

We acknowledge the financial support of the Government of Canada through the
Book Publishing Industry Development Program and that of the Government of
Ontario through the Ontario Media Development Corporation's Ontario Book
Initiative. We further acknowledge the support of the Canada Council for the Arts
and the Ontario Arts Council for our publishing program.

I wish to thank the Ontario Arts Council for a Works in Progress grant, 2000.

The stanza from Johnny North's poem, page 310, is taken from a poem by
Bobby West, eccentric, riverman, and entertainer of Paris, Ontario, who died in
1941. Originally published in the *Paris Star*, it was reproduced in D.A. Smith's
superb local history, *At the Forks of the Grand*, privately printed for Paris's
centennial celebrations in 1956.

SERIES EDITOR: ELLEN SELIGMAN

Cover design: Kong
Cover image: Charles Klein
Series logo design: Brian Bean

Typeset in Sabon by M&S, Toronto
Printed and bound in Canada

This book is printed on acid-free paper that is
100% ancient-forest friendly (40% post-consumer recycled).

EMBLEM EDITIONS
McClelland & Stewart Ltd.
The Canadian Publishers
481 University Avenue
Toronto, Ontario
M5G 2E9
www.mcclelland.com/emblem

3 4 5 6   08 07 06 05 04

For Cathleen
and for Alix

THE

ISLAND

WALKERS

A TOWN OF TWO RIVERS, its plunging valley an anomaly in the tedious southwestern Ontario plain.

Bridges. Water at dusk. The play of ghosts on the sloping face of a dam.

High windows shot with gold, glimpsed among maples. Streets that beckon and disappear. The traveller, coming across this place, might be forgiven for imagining that life is better here.

The Victorian facades of the downtown stores, the deep centre of town. The backs of these buildings fall straight to the Shade River. From the Bridge Street bridge, you can savour the Old World atmosphere conjured by their wooden balconies, perched randomly above the water, above the cut stone of foundations, which seem to move upstream as the Shade brushes past through a flecking of shallow rapids. The cries of gulls.

Farther south, under the steep, wooded bulwark of Lookout Hill, you can make out the gap where the Attawan River enters the Shade. Just now, a shaft of light, playing from the hills to the west, kindles the vicinity of the forks. But even as you watch, the conflagration fades, saturating the air with the melancholy of an early dusk.

In the opposite direction, a hundred yards north of the bridge, a dam has stilled the river to a dark lake. Two tall stone abutments rise from the water, to support a rail trestle that disappears among the trees on the west bank. Higher still, just visible among pines, the severe windows of the Bannerman mansion look down the valley with an air of confident, hard-earned plenty. Hidden behind it are the middle- and upper-class houses of the North End. There, a late sun still pours its ripeness down treed boulevards, across spacious lawns, into verandas shaded with striped awnings and trellises of Dutchman's pipe.

But down here, at the bridge rail, all is water and failing light. A lone fisherman in hip waders casts towards the dam. Eastward, on the Flats, the small houses huddle against the coming night. They seem not so much poor as crammed together, and somehow hastily assembled, as though their builders did not make the same claim to permanence as those of the North End.

On the edge of this neighbourhood, you will find a forest of sorts, sumacs and scrub maple forming a patch of wilderness in the heart of town. Much of this wilderness, curiously, has a cement floor, littered with broken liquor and wine bottles that glint in the dimming light, the blackened remains of bonfires. You might make other interesting discoveries: rusted, nondescript bits of machinery, a few soot-stained bricks. It seems, almost, that by some scarcely imaginable act of violence, an entire building – a vast complex of buildings – has been torn up and carried away.

Nearby, the Attawan Historical Society has established a small park. Tidy beds of petunias and a couple of benches uphold an air of beleaguered propriety, under a solitary street light. An asphalt path leads to a metal plaque supported by a cement base.

BANNERMAN'S MILLS

On this site stood Bannerman's mills, in their time the largest knit-goods manufactory in the country. The mills were built by John Bannerman (1850–1932), a native of Boston, who arrived in Attawan in 1876, establishing his first mill on the Attawan River. In 1892, he built these larger premises to take advantage of the greater water-power potential of the Shade. At the height of its fortunes in the 1950s, Bannerman's Knitting employed more than 900 people out of a total population of 5,200. The mills turned out socks, stockings, sweaters, T-shirts, and underwear, including the famous #99 long johns, popular in the hills and forestry camps of Canada's north. In 1966, the mills were destroyed by fire.

Little of importance is now made in Attawan. It has become a bedroom town, a place for strangers, where tour buses stop for half an hour and ladies with tinted hair take quick shots of the older houses, the popular view from the bridge.

At Willard and Bridge, the little park continues to dream in a kind of bland, perpetual Sabbath. On its benches, a few old-timers linger. Some, no doubt, are veterans of the mills and the great work that went on inside. But you will find them reluctant to talk about the past. Ask about the fire, or the investigation that followed, and they will look at you, an outsider, with the rheumy far-sightedness of the old and murmur that they really don't know about that, no, they can't remember. You would almost think they favoured the argument suggested by the maples thickening each year towards the river: that Bannerman's mills had never been.

THE SMALLEST OF ATTAWAN'S working-class neighbourhoods, the Island lay tucked behind the downtown Business Section, separated from it by an old, disused millrace that formed a kind of watery shortcut across a bend of the Attawan River. This sluggish canal was shaded by black willows and bordered by a narrow trail that ran past vine-freighted fences and decaying sheds. The Island contained about two dozen houses, crowded along its two intersecting streets, Water and West. For several generations, the people of the Island – mostly mill workers and their families – had considered themselves quite sepa-rate from the town's other residents: a state of mind most pro-nounced among the children, who conducted ongoing crabapple and hockey wars with their enemies on the Flats or in South Ward and the North End.

The Walker house sat at the bottom of West, overlooking the cul-de-sac where the street met an earthen flood-dyke. Nearly a hundred years old, it had walls of plastered lath-work, with shuttered windows and a front door of solid oak boards. The unstable ground of the area – which was still, in some sense, the province of the river, still prone on occasion to floods that topped the dykes – had over the years skewed the frame of the house and tilted its floors. But it was a well-kept place, the walls cleanly whitewashed, the shutters and doors painted a deep forest green.

One Saturday in the summer of 1965, Joe and Alf Walker climbed onto the roof and spent the better part of the morning stripping the old shingles. By eleven they were busy nailing down the new ones. Joe, who had turned eighteen that July, worked on the slope overlooking the backyard. He sat shirtless, on his duff, and hammered sullenly between his legs, aware of the sun-baked expanse of tarpaper stretching up the slope behind him. From beyond the peak, his father's hammer thundered without rest. It seemed crazy to try to keep up.

He shifted his weight, placed the next shingle, and looked across the yard with its picnic table and apple tree, its narrow lawn and rows of vegetables – beyond the flood-dyke blooming cheerfully with his mother's flowers, to the Atta, flowing through the shadow of Lookout Hill. Under its far bank – a dim cave of limestone and darkly rippling water – it looked cool and inviting: another world. He was labouring under protest, under a sense of injustice that drove him on in angry spurts then dragged him into a sloth so deep it was like a spell. Why were they doing this today? Today – as he'd mentioned to his father last Wednesday, he was sure – he and Smiley were planning to go hunting with Smiley's new .22. His friend had gone on without him. A few minutes ago he'd heard a shot echo down the valley.

He dipped into the bag beside him and the sharp nails bit his fingers. For weeks the shingles had sat beside the house in their paper wrappings, under a paint-spotted tarp. A dozen times at least his mother had said, "Alf, I am getting so tired of that *heap* out there. You'd think we were living in the Ozarks." His mother's idea of the Ozarks came from television, but she used the phrase to convey a sense of social embarrassment, of appearances that were not up to the mark. He always thought it sounded funny in her English accent. His mother was a war bride. Hearing the words as a young boy, he had imagined her striding off to battle in skirts and helmet. The vision had made him slightly wary of her, as if she could lay claim to secret, irresistible powers. Yet there had been nothing but weary exasperation in her complaints about the roof, the mechanical recitation of an old war cry that no longer frightened anybody: an act for tourists. She had grown up in a finer house than this: she'd told him many times about the books, the grand piano, the holidays in

Normandy. "Your father's uniform fooled me completely" – this was another of her stories – "For all I knew he was a millionaire's son." It had become a family joke, told at the right time at parties: her coming down in the world was a mistake, based on her inability to read his father's status by his accent or his clothes. It was not until after she'd arrived in Attawan in the spring of 1946 that she realized what she'd done. She hadn't given up, though: getting the roof shingled was only one in an endless series of assaults on their rough edges – on their house that, by her standards, was too small and, despite their relentless improvements, still too shabby, not to mention situated in the wrong part of town. Joe looked back to the river. Such thoughts were troubling, leading to shadows, sadness. Better to hunker down like his father and pretend he wasn't affected.

Yet his father wasn't impervious. His wife's complaints might seem to sink into him without a trace, snow into dark water, but they could achieve a critical mass. This morning he had roused Joe early and announced that today they were shingling the roof. But why today, Joe wondered, the hottest so far of the whole summer? At breakfast, over a trembling forkful of fried egg, he dared to question the decision – maybe they should wait till it was cooler, he said, thinking the whole time of Smiley's gun, of the wafer of silver light at the end of the scope and even of the word "scope" itself, so pleasing and final, like a bullet smacking into mud. "It's gonna rain," his father said, and when Joe said, "It's rained before," meaning *and you never bothered then*, his father had said quietly, looking at him with those ice-blue eyes the colour of Lake Erie in spring, "No arguments."

He thought there was something fanatical in his father that came from a place of silence and brooding Joe couldn't read: something extreme and overbearing and violent that thank God was not there all the time but that could leap up like a blade you hadn't been careful with and nip you. Now it was his arbitrariness that bothered him most. What gave *him* the right to decide? Why did he have to obey? Why didn't he just throw down his hammer and leave the roof? He suspected that if he did, he would have to leave the house as well.

He had absorbed some old notion that work was something you did for everybody, without complaint. He had worked for as long as he could remember, washing floors, washing the car, digging gardens, stacking cans at the A&P; this summer he was at Bannerman's. He expected to work, but this morning some remnant of an ancient grievance had surfaced: the need for unquestioning obedience was an injustice and so was the loss of his day. He felt, irrationally, as if his entire future had been torn from him.

The hammering from the other side had stopped. A moment later he heard his father's heavy, braced steps come down the slope behind him. The pack of shingles slammed into the roof-boards like a body.

Then the labour of his father's breathing as he surveyed Joe's work.

"Good," his father said curtly, and Joe knew he was disappointed. "Pete's coming after lunch. We should be through by three or four."

The steps went back up the roof. It was then, as a breeze touched the trees across the river, showing the light undersides of their leaves, that a voice called his father's name. Joe looked around but could see no one. The voice had seemed to sound from the blue sky, or in his own head: a husky baritone he did not know, calling, "Alf Walker" on a cheerful, interrogative note.

He looked back up the slope. His father stood at the peak, against the burning sky. His greying hair had collapsed from its place over his ears and was hanging down stiffly, like drooping pennons. He was staring into the front yard, at someone Joe could not see.

"Malachi Doyle," the voice barked, and for a moment it seemed to Joe to speak in a foreign tongue, or a code. Then he realized that the man had spoken his name.

"I'm from the UKW," said the voice, which had the trace of a lilt. "United –"

"I know who they are," Joe's father said.

"Like to have a word or two. Only take a few minutes."

Joe's father did not reply but went on gazing into the yard as if all that had spoken was an echo.

To Joe, his father's silence was excruciating. He had never got used to this habit of his – this habit of saying nothing, so that you wondered if he had even heard your remark, or (meeting the candid stare of those pale-blue eyes) if he had found it too stupid or trivial to merit a response. His father dealt in silences. When he spoke, he seemed to rise out of silence as a fish might rise from the water, its natural element, soon returning to it again. Even though Joe had heard him tell stories in his droll way, and laugh and talk as any ordinary man might, these moments seemed exceptional. His father existed at a distance from him, and the distance was reinforced by silence, as though there were simply too great a space for a voice to carry over: only a fool would stand there shouting what could not be heard.

Now his father looked away, over the rooftops of the Island. Joe licked his lips. Mere seconds passed, but to him they seemed like minutes. He was expecting something even more embarrassing to happen. For the last two weeks, at the mill, a rumour had been circulating that an organizer was in town. Joe had heard the other workers talk about him during break, joking about his presence, or alleged presence, with a skittish indirectness, as though it had something to do with sex. He had not heard his father, who was head fixer in Number Six knitting mill, comment on the subject. Then one evening, walking home with his father and Art Johnson, Joe listened as Art began to chat about the organizer. Art had fallen silent, as if sensing disapproval. After a few seconds his father had said (and it was all he had said), "The bastard better not show his face at my place."

Now here the bastard was, apparently. Joe watched his father briefly touch the back pocket of his trousers, where the bulge of his wallet rode. Then he climbed over the peak and began to sink out of sight: the soiled factory greens, the heavy shoulders in their filthy undershirt, the head with its drooping strands of hair, its bald spot.

When Joe heard the ladder rattle, he got up and climbed swiftly to the peak. Down the steeply sloping roof, he saw the top of the ladder shake a little. But on the sidewalk that ran past the house, and on the small front lawn burned the colour of straw, he could see no one.

2

THE ORGANIZER WAS WAITING at the foot of the ladder: a short, thickly built fellow, perhaps ten years older than Alf, with grizzled flyaway hair and a face so red Alf assumed he was a drinker. He wore a madras sports shirt, darkened over the massive chest with sweat, and shapeless trousers of an indeterminate colour. He watched Alf descend with an ironic but not unfriendly glint in his small eyes, as though he sensed some hostility but wasn't offended. It was part of the game.

"Doyle," he said, holding out a large hand.

"Maybe we could go for a walk," Alf said, aware of Margaret somewhere in the house behind him. Across the street, a sprawled cat twitched its tail; a window looked out with self-effacing curiosity. The whole world was watching while pretending not to.

He took Doyle down the sidewalk towards the dyke at the end of the cul-de-sac. They passed the organizer's dark-green Edsel – a '58, Alf thought – its horse-collar grill and protruding headlights circled in rust. Alf chuckled gloomily to himself. It seemed somehow fitting that Doyle should be driving this unholy relic of a car, a car so bad Ford had stopped building it after three years. The UK-whatever-it-was can't be up to much, Alf thought, sending him out in a car like that. Despite what he'd indicated on the roof, he hadn't heard of Doyle's outfit. He supposed it was one of those small, bottom-feeding unions that lived off what the larger ones had missed.

Doyle was chatting away gruffly at his side, as if he were used to being smuggled out of sight like some disreputable relative. "Had a helluva time finding you," he was saying. "Went to one place across town there, they told me I had the wrong Walkers. 'You got the Flats Walkers,' they tell me. 'You want the Island Walkers.' The Island Walkers," Doyle repeated. "A name like that, I thought I was back in Ireland. Everyone had their queer little monikers. The back-street Kellys, the side-hill Corcorans. I sort of miss it."

Alf gestured ahead of him, indicating the path that saddled the dyke. Doyle jogged up with a burst of energy, his heavy haunches churning through goldenrod. They descended to a foreshore of loose, clattering rock where puddles of stagnant water lay, frowsy with scum. A few stunted willow bushes sat around watching them like dogs. Doyle walked on a few steps and stood with his thick arms akimbo, gazing at the river. Above, the shelving foliage of Lookout Hill hung motionless in the heat.

"Grew up on a river like this," the organizer said. He seemed pleased to remember.

"In Ireland," Alf said wearily. He felt he was taking up a role.

"A salmon river. The fish that used to come up it as long as your feckin' arm."

"Well there's nothing like that here," Alf said. Downstream, a fisherman was casting into the tunnel under the Shade Street bridge. Alf hoped the man – it was Del Featherstone – wouldn't turn and see them.

"I remember my dad and I went out this one time, early morning." Doyle's red face shone. There was something of the child in him, an astonishingly ugly eight-year-old. "We took our bikes. Oh, it must have been three or more miles we went, to a new river. At least it was new to me. Dim. Dyne. Something like that. We fished for two hours and got nothing. Then my daddy made one last cast – you'd have thought all creation had erupted. I mean, the thing was like a bar of silver . . ."

His blackberry eyes gleamed, and a kindred memory – fishing, a river coppered by dusk – slipped through Alf's mind. He let it go.

"Well," the organizer said. Groping at his breast pocket, he plucked out a sorry-looking pack of Macdonald's. Alf waved the cigarettes off and waited while the man hunted for his matches, scraped up flame.

"You're not going to get anywhere here," Alf said.

"You mean with you?"

"With anybody," Alf said. "We aren't in the union way here."

"And why would that be?" Doyle said, blowing a leisurely plume. He looked as if he had all day. He looked, Alf thought with despair, as if he were in a bar somewhere, with a pint at hand and a small one at the side, preparing to enjoy his companion's story.

Alf frowned. He wished he was back on his roof.

"Let's just say we've been through it before."

"Ah yes, the famous strike of '49," Doyle said, taking another drag.

"Bugger the fame," Alf said, with real heat. "It tore this place apart." There had been a wildcat strike, entirely unsuccessful. The new union had been crushed, wounds had opened that still hadn't healed. The only way people tolerated them was to keep silent.

"Tell me about it," Doyle said. Alf shook his head in disbelief. He didn't want to think about the strike – it was the habit of years – let alone tell this stranger about it. He looked away, to the edge of the river, where the corpse of a big carp had been picked over by gulls. All that moved now was flies.

"I take it you went out," Doyle said quietly.

Alf glanced at the other man: how had he found that out? He supposed he'd been talking to people in town. He supposed that he, Alf, still had a reputation as a troublemaker, even though he'd left the strike weeks before it ended. Even though it had ended sixteen years before. They didn't forget in a place the size of Attawan. They didn't change their minds about you, either, he thought with bitterness, at least not very easily. That was how it was in a town where everyone knew everyone else. Or thought they did.

"The more fool I," Alf said.

Doyle chortled and went on watching him as he smoked. He seemed comfortable with the silence, as Alf did not. Alf was torn between going into the matter and simply walking away. But he felt he had to warn Doyle off. It was why he had brought him to the river.

"Look," he said, fixing on the other man. "No one – I mean no one of any account – is going to be interested in your project. You might get a few of the malcontents. There's always some of those. But the great majority – you start pushing them and they'll run you out on a rail."

Doyle's big chest and shoulders heaved, as if he relished the idea.

"Actually, Alf, there's more than a few." The organizer spoke quietly, confidentially, sorry to have to contradict him. "Wrote me quite a letter," he said and, leaning forward, tapped his nicotine-stained fingers on his chest pocket, where apparently the letter lay, nested with his cigarettes.

"Don't even start," Alf said, shaking his head. "You won't believe the trouble you'll cause." He stopped. There was so much more he might say, so much more he wanted to say, pressing its inchoate dark weight on his mind. He stared off towards the dead carp, and the inheritance of 1949 was there, as real and palpable as its rotting carcass, under its boiling cloud of flies. But he did not know how to put it into words.

"I've got to get back to my roof," he said.

Suddenly Doyle snapped away his butt. His eyes had narrowed on Alf, through smoke, and there was a sudden sense of attack.

"And Intertex," he said sharply, "how do you feel about *them*?"

The first time Alf had heard the name, he hadn't quite taken it in. It seemed more properly the name of a machine, or a process, than a company. It was Johnny Carruthers, Bannerman's assistant general manager, who'd told him one evening in May – this was in the parking lot of the beer store – that Intertex had "picked up"

Bannerman's. Not only did the word "Intertex" put him off balance, but there was Johnny's "picked up." What had happened? "They've bought us," Johnny explained in an overly loud voice, as if speaking to a child. "International Textile – big firm out of Montreal. Picked us up last week." Alf had an image of the new company plucking Bannerman's from the ground, like the big hand in the insurance ad. "Picked us up for a song," Johnny said, shutting his trunk. There was a cockiness in his manner, implying that he dealt in this kind of high-stakes activity every day: it was nothing a real businessman couldn't handle. "They're into industrial wovens: car-seat coverings, commercial drapes, that sort of thing. But recently they've been picking up knitting mills, mostly in Quebec."

Alf had experienced a faint vertigo, as if the ground had shifted beneath his feet, for hadn't he been "picked up" as well? Later, he sat at the picnic table in his backyard, under falling apple blossoms, and read about the sale in the *Attawan Star*. Under the headline "BAN-NERMAN'S SOLD" was a head-and-shoulders shot of a bald, handsome, heavy-jawed man in a suit, his shoulders slightly tilted, as though he were leaning out, a bit mischievously, from behind a tree. The caption identified him as R.J. Prince, an Intertex vice-president. The accompanying article revealed that Intertex owned plants in Canada, the United States, Britain, Italy, and France, and quoted Prince as saying how proud Intertex was to acquire such a venerable company as Bannerman's – "a real slice of our national history." He looked forward, he said, "to working with all the good people who made Bannerman's such a success in the past." Alf lowered the paper to the picnic table. A petal, like a tiny silk hat, fell across Prince's head. Alf brushed it off and studied the man's face. Everything about it, like everything he had said, seemed polished with an eye to public consumption. On the whole, Alf approved.

The next day on the fire escape outside the sixth-floor knitting room, where the knitters and fixers took their breaks, all talk was of the sale. Alf sat sipping from his plastic Thermos cup and listened to the eruption of speculations, rumour, fear, along the long iron balcony. Some of the workers remained silent, like himself, but most of the others agreed the sale was a bad thing. It might mean layoffs, Pat Kenner said. He'd heard from his brother-in-law in Quebec that Intertex were "real sons of bitches. They'll take an axe to the place."

Through the deep millyard below, a pigeon glided on taut wings, fleeing from sunlight to shade.

Alf said, "Come on. You'd think the mills had never been sold before."

He spoke so infrequently that all turned to look at him.

"When John Bannerman was an old man, back in the Twenties, they were sold then," he said. "Everybody was worried then too, but it turned out to be the best thing that could have happened. The next twenty or thirty years were the best we ever had."

There was silence after that – he'd given them something to think about – and a minute later as they trooped back in to work, someone clapped him on the back. But he was uncomfortable with congratulations. He had his own worries about Intertex. Two weeks before the announcement of the sale, a notice had appeared on the knitting-room bulletin board, asking for applicants for the position of foreman. He'd applied, feeling the whole time it was an indignity. He'd worked in the knitting mill for eighteen years, worked his way up from knitter to head fixer, and had come in recent years, as everyone said, to pretty much run the place. Increasingly it was he, and not the foreman, Matt Honnegger (who was due to retire that winter), who made out the knitting schedules, hunted down lost orders, and expedited rush ones. He was more than a foreman-in-waiting, he felt. In some sense he *was* the foreman, and any suggestion that he had to take a step back and ask for what was his infuriated him.

The notice had asked the applicants to submit ideas on how operations in Number Six knitting might be improved. Alf had delayed for days, but finally filled several foolscap sheets with drafts of possible answers. In the end, he'd presented Joe with two paragraphs of tight script and stood by, as thin-skinned as any schoolboy, while Joe read it over. When Joe had suggested changes, Alf barely managed to keep civil. It was hard to be reminded that he, Alf, had only Grade Eleven, and that his son would soon be in his final year of high school, on his way to the distant planet of university. But he accepted most of Joe's suggestions (and worried later he should have accepted the rest), and Joe typed up his proposal. The next day, handing the letter to May Watson, the receptionist at General Office, Alf felt a piece of his life pass out of his hands, as though he were releasing into the sea a bottle with a note for help inside. It seemed impossible that so tenuous and haphazard a signal could find its way to the right place.

Spring became summer, the flood-dykes turned pink and blue with dames rocket, and there was no response. On the fire escape, the talk turned to softball and the summer holidays. Bannerman's had changed hands, but the mills, it seemed, were entirely unaffected. The steam whistle above the boiler plant continued to howl up the dawns, calling the workers from sleep. The tall machines continued to pour out their rivers of soft, fragrant cloth. It's like the phoney war, Alf thought, remembering the fall of '39. Canada had declared war on Germany, but when he'd looked up at the sky, suddenly thrilled and frightened by the thought, We're at war, the huge, white clouds had moved on with an unruffled stateliness, declaring all earthly business an illusion.

On the bulletin board over the washing-up sink, the notice faded under its blue-headed tacks. Every morning as Alf climbed the stairs to the sixth floor, he looked for it in trepidation. Its continuing existence seemed a judgment, an unfavourable one that said, "We've considered your application and found it wanting. We continue to search."

"Everything's up in the air with this Intertex business," Matt Honnegger told him one day, his fleshy face expressionless. "It'll be a while before they get around to the likes of you and me." Matt's resignation put Alf off even more. He wanted to be used. He imagined his letter waiting under a mountain of hundreds of others, while men he did not know, in offices he would never see, ignored his fate. And what did it matter, he thought bitterly. Wasn't he a fool to depend on something like this, over which he had no control, depend on it to the point of sleeplessness?

Then in mid-July an earnest young man in a yellow hard hat appeared in front of Alf carrying a clipboard and demanding answers in a shouting voice to such questions as "When you go to the yarn room, how many bobbins do you bring back, on average?" Alf looked into the evasive eyes swimming behind thick glasses. "I'm a fixer," he said. "I don't go into the yarn room." This was not, strictly speaking, true, but he couldn't resist a poke at the automaton. He was rewarded with a brief flutter of panic – something human – but the young man quickly found another question on his board. "How many times a day, on average, do you go to the washroom?"

The place was crawling with them – young men whose excruciatingly detailed questions and bright helmets spawned a bitter hilarity among the workers. Hard hats in a knitting mill! What were they afraid of, falling threads? The hard hats measured, they watched, they timed, they noted down, they disappeared, they came back for more measurements, they disappeared for good. A month later the layoffs began. Twenty from the night shift, an additional sixteen from day. Three from Alf's floor alone, including his young friend Rick Stevenson, who had two kids to support and a wife going crazy with migraines. Those who were left were working harder: Alf often wasn't home till eight o'clock. The political discussions on the fire escape resumed. Time to look at a union again, a few workers said, breaching a taboo. But most, perhaps remembering 1949, argued No: at this stage a union would just act as a red flag, it would bring on more firings. Better to hunker down, ride out the bad times, and (though this was never openly expressed) hope it was your neighbour who got hit, not you.

Alf had kept silent. The firings troubled him a great deal. He lent money to Rick Stevenson and spoke his concerns to Matt Honnegger, hoping that Matt would pass them up the line, up the chain of command that led, through ever more comfortable offices, to the holy-of-holies where someone with half a heart might be listening. At the same time, he tried to grasp the rationale behind the turmoil – tried, as a foreman-in-waiting, to see things from management's point of view. He felt that, as foreman, he would bring a special understanding to the situation – that he could bridge, somehow, the gap between what the workers needed and what the company had to do. How he would manage this remained unclear to him, but he felt it was more urgent than ever that his letter be attended to. He felt the new men, whoever they were, needed him.

"Intertex is doing what they have to," Alf said, stubbornly defensive. He had lost his taste for argument. The sun seemed to be tightening an iron hoop around his head.

"You *like* what they're doing here?" Doyle said, not bothering to hide his sarcasm.

"Of course I don't like all of it – I know these people. But the place was slipping. Something had to be done."

"Still making a profit, though." The organizer had pounced gleefully on "profit," as if it were evidence that refuted all arguments. His black eyes shone.

Alf turned to look back towards the stark slope of his roof, floating tentlike above the dyke. His son was there, a slim, tanned figure standing on the peak. The boy seemed impossibly distant, like youth itself. A panel of shingles hung from his hand like a broken wing.

3

THE FAMILY SAT FOR LUNCH at the picnic table, in the flickering mesh of light dropped by the dwarf McIntosh that leaned from the base of the dyke. Twenty feet away, in full sun, Red, their malamute, lay on his side in the dirt, panting heavily, his lolling tongue like a piece of raw meat speckled with dirt. Margaret had asked Jamie to say grace. The eight-year-old was peeking over his clasped hands as he listed the things on the table. His thick, sun-bleached hair stood up here and there in tufts. "Thank you for our milk, and our water, and our pickles –

"Don't!" he cried suddenly, jabbing his elbow at his sister.

"I didn't touch him," Penny complained to Alf. The ten-year-old's eyes – pale blue like his – were huge with protest. In her pink T-shirt, her shoulders jerked up, declaring her innocence.

"Come on," Joe urged, "the sandwiches are getting stale." Alf's older son had put on a shirt, at Margaret's insistence. Beside his place was a paperback, turned face down. Another book about the war, Alf noted wearily, glancing at the flaming swastika on the cover, the Moloch head of a tank swivelling among ruins: *The Anvil of Stalingrad.*

"I don't like tuna fish," Jamie said to his mother. "Do I have to –"

"There's peanut butter for you," Margaret said coolly, sounding very English. She was wearing her seersucker housedress, the one that left her slender arms bare. Her dark hair, still damp from washing, clung to the side of her head, leaving the tips of her ears exposed and, to Alf's eyes, oddly vulnerable. She was singing at a wedding that afternoon at the church. "And anyway, you don't have to thank God for individual items."

Penny snorted, which brought another murderous glance from Jamie. But he went on with his Great Enumeration. High overhead, a cicada drilled through the heat of noon. Alf looked over at his wife. Her closed eyelids were trembling, as though animated by a subtle electric current. Her face with its pale forehead and fine brows was lifted slightly as she listened to Jamie's prayer.

"Make us truly thankful, inChristnameweaskit –"

"Thank you," Joe said dryly, reaching for a sandwich.

"Wait!" Jamie's brown eyes – copies of his mother's – struck out at his brother. "I'm not done."

"I don't believe it!" Penny cried.

"Penny," Margaret warned. The girl looked at her father, her court of last appeal. Alf had always felt they shared secret, unspoken things about the family, which were rarely made specific: *they understood*. He looked tactfully away.

They waited again with bowed heads, stoically. The cicadas whined, and in Lions Park across the river, the merry-go-round screeched with a sound of metal on hot metal.

"Amen," Jamie said finally.

"I think I'm going to kill him," Joe said.

"He did very well," Margaret said as she drew the platter of sandwiches towards Jamie. On her own plate was a lone scoop of cottage cheese and a slab of beefsteak tomato, red as blood. Another of her diets, Alf thought ruefully. She was thin enough, he felt, hardly heavier than when he'd first met her twenty-three years ago, that evening at the servicemen's dance in Henley-Under-Downs. It was something people remarked on. "If only I knew Margaret's secret! I think she's made a deal with the devil!" Her skin seemed nearly as clear as it had been in 1942. Her hair, which she wore in the same style as then, brushed away from a central part, was as dark and wavily vigorous. All the same, he knew she had changed. There was a hint of sallowness in her face. In her eyes, he glimpsed what he feared was disappointment.

Yet all that week she'd been bubbling around the house, in a much better mood than usual. Jack Ramsay, he thought. Jack Ramsay was the new minister at the Anglican church. Jack was from England, like her, a tall young man of thirty or so, with a brightly boyish face and an affable manner Alf found a bit glib. He had a fine tenor voice, though. That afternoon he was not only going to officiate at the wedding, but was going to sing with Margaret. All week Alf had heard her rehearsing her part, the words of the duet wafting through the house in her clear soprano.

The sparrow hath found her an house,
And the swallow a nest
Where she may lay her young:
Even thine altars
Oh Lord of Hosts . . .

Alf supposed she was in love, after a fashion, with Jack Ramsay. He was used to her falling in love – with men and women both, or with singers or authors or symphony orchestras. It never lasted for more than a few days, or a few weeks, and while it was happening she was effervescent and pleased with everything. He had tried to be philosophical about Jack Ramsay – after all, nothing but high spirits came from these infatuations, and her high spirits were a good deal easier on all of them than the grim patches she fell into at other times.

"I think you're an atheist at heart," Joe was saying, looking at his brother.

"No I'm not."

"You don't even know what an atheist is."

"Yes I do."

"What is it then?"

"He doesn't know," Penny said with scornful certainty, biting a pickle.

"I *do*," Jamie insisted, his eyes bulging at his sister. They had been at each other all morning.

"Tell him then," she sang. Jamie stared hard at Joe, as if by ferocious willpower he could force the answer to appear in Joe's face. Jamie had his mother's clear, open face, a believer's face, it seemed to Alf. The boy worshipped his brother, and considered him a source of impeccable truth.

"It's somebody who doesn't go to church."

"Close but no cigar."

"Perhaps you could just *tell* him what an atheist is," Margaret said impatiently while sawing at her tomato. A couple of weeks before, Joe had announced he was no longer going to church. Alf knew his withdrawal had hurt her.

"An atheist . . . ," Penny began.

"I want *him* to tell me," Jamie insisted, pointing to Joe. Alf noticed that Bob Horsfall had appeared in his garden next door. It never failed, whenever they ate outside, Horsfall or his wife would come out and hang around, pretending to be busy, like children hoping to be asked to play. Horsfall – a small man in baggy shorts – scowled at Alf (his face was set in a permanent scowl anyway, he only needed to darken it a little) and gestured violently to something in his garden: some tomato that had rotted, no doubt, or some broken stem, more evidence that the world was going to hell. Alf looked away. Both Horsfall and his wife were deaf. They could speak only after a fashion, in grunts that scarcely resembled human speech.

". . . is somebody who doesn't believe in God."

Jamie's eyes slowly grew bright. He looked at his sister, his quarrel with her forgotten. He looked at his father.

"*I* believe in God," he said almost in a whisper.

"Of course you do," Margaret said, trying to hurry him past this crisis. "We all do."

"I don't," Joe said flippantly. He was staring at his book.

"You *don't*?" said Jamie.

"Some nice big guy in the sky," Joe said.

"That's enough," Alf said.

"The great white father who thinks it's fine if people die of cancer, or starve to death –"

"*I said, That's enough!*" Alf couldn't stand his son's moralizing, that narrow, superior tone he fell into sometimes, telling them all what was good for them.

They continued eating in silence, in a heat pierced by the whine of cicadas. Jamie's shocked gaze kept returning to Alf. Alf winked and the boy's face twitched, but he kept looking at Alf, unappeased. Alf sensed he was hoping for some reassurance in the face of the strange, bleak sense of aftermath that had settled on the table. It wasn't just that he had yelled at Joe, it was what Joe had said, about not believing in God. What do *I* know about God, Alf thought. He went to church, but this was mainly a social thing, a seconding of Margaret's great involvement there. Occasionally he prayed. But to Whom, what Power? Waist deep in his tomato plants, Bob Horsfall grunted at him, his face twisted with emotions he couldn't speak. Alf stared at his plate. He couldn't imagine Horsfall's life of total, enveloping silence, a life underwater. Sometimes he heard Horsfall's wife shrieking in the house like an animal in pain.

A large ant crawled up Red's tongue. He gulped wetly: gone.

Margaret said, "Joe tells me you had a visitor?"

Her tone, at least on the surface, was casually interested. But Alf knew her too well. He heard buried criticism, alarm.

For a moment their eyes met. Some recognition was there, some quickening, beyond the scope of their daily lives. But it was unsustainable. He looked away and frowned at Joe, who kept reading *The Anvil of Stalingrad*. Why had he told his mother about Doyle's visit? Surely the boy had some notion of the trouble he would cause.

"From a union?" Margaret persisted, in her tone of cheerful innocence.

"Ah, just doing his rounds," Alf said, reaching for another sandwich. "He'll be on to some other town by now."

As he said this, he realized it was probably not true: the man would not retreat so easily. But he wanted to placate her.

"I was surprised you talked to him."

"You'd prefer me to throw my hammer at him?" Alf said, and was gratified to hear Jamie laugh.

"Well, *no*," she said, as if he actually might have. "I just thought, with the foreman's job still up in the air . . ."

"I think that's why Dad took him down to the river," Joe said. Alf glanced at his son, not his usual ally in these quarrels.

"To keep him out of sight," Joe added.

Margaret cut into her tomato.

"I just think we have to be careful," she said.

"I *was* careful, Margaret," Alf said in a soft voice, suppressing his anger. She did not meet his stare. He looked down at his plate smeared with crumbs and pickle juice. The cicadas drilled through the heat, his brain. Some large emotion, who knew what it was, seemed in the offing, but distantly, immured in ice, shining like a sea he could not reach. He was sorry he'd told his wife about applying for the foreman's job. It clearly meant as much to her, perhaps more, than it did to him. Sensing he was being watched, he looked up and saw Penny gazing at him with infinite seriousness, her eyes locked on his. She might have been reading his mind, reading some obscure current of thought he could hardly make out himself.

Sickened by the hatred and violence boiling through the town (one worker had died of a heart attack after his family had been threatened), Alf had left the strike a few weeks before it finally limped to its ignominious conclusion. Margaret had inherited a few thousand dollars from an aunt, and she urged him to use it to start the carpentry business he'd been talking about for years, talking about, in fact, from the first weeks of their courtship, in England. Walking with her on the downs above her house (the air trembling with the drone of bombers setting out for Germany like a swarm of dark bees flooding towards the distant Channel), he had discovered his calling. "I'm going to build houses," he told her in a rush of excitement. In Attawan before the war he had apprenticed with the town's finest builder, Bute Erikson. He'd learned how to build houses from scratch: he could do carpentry, electrical work, plumbing, cement. But it was not until he met Margaret that he glimpsed his future whole. "I'll build *you* a house," he promised her. "We'll pick out the best lot in the North End. Whatever your little old heart desires."

In France, sitting with his back to some ruined wall, with black smoke leaning off the horizon, he had amused himself by sketching out various versions of their future house, tucking the sheets into letters he sent to England. Margaret made drawings too and mailed them on. The house became part of their mutual dream, a shield against the war.

Back in Canada, he found there wasn't enough money to set up on his own, not right away. And Bute Erikson was dead, so he went to work in the mills. To save money, he and Margaret lived with Alf's parents, in their brick cottage on the east side of the Island. But Margaret and Mabel – both of them English, but from different classes – got along like oil and water. His nerves strained by the war, Alf thought he would go mad with their bickering. He and Margaret soon moved out to a rented place around the corner, at the bottom of West. In 1948, he got involved in the movement to bring a union to Bannerman's – involved with Cary Winner, the organizer from Montreal who charmed him into thinking that socialism was the only way forward. Yes, he'd bought it hook, line, and sinker – the vision of a world where all were equal, all shared. But after months of preparations, the strike had faltered in just a few weeks. ("Nothing worse than a strike gone bad," Cary had told Alf, not long before the organizer washed his hands of the whole business.) Margaret's money arrived in the nick of time.

Alf bought second-hand tools, and a Ford pickup truck with a stake box he sanded and varnished to make look like new. On the doors, he stencilled ALF WALKER AND SON, BUILDERS. (Joe was just a baby at the time, but Alf had been thrilled to include him, as though he were creating not just a business but a dynasty.) He papered the town with advertisements. But the business had not come. His part in the strike had sabotaged him, he believed, his reputation as a trouble-maker had ensured that no one with enough money to build a house would hire him. After two years he'd built only one – and been left holding the bills for more than five thousand dollars when his client skipped town. The bank took his truck and most of his larger tools. He managed to keep a few screwdrivers and saws. They still hung in their neat, graded rows above his basement workbench, a reminder of his failure. There were other reminders, like the plans for the Cape

Cod–style house he'd never built for Margaret. They'd had them drawn up by an architect in Johnsonville, in the first heady days of the business. He'd noticed them the other day, rolled in oilcloth and stuck up in the cellar joists with his father's old fishing rods. He hadn't had the heart to take them down.

A manager at Bannerman's – a fishing crony of his father's – had wrangled Alf's old job back for him, and he climbed again to the sixth-floor knitting room where the tall machines waited for him in a familiar, mocking stillness. For all his efforts, it seemed, nothing had changed.

Thirteen years passed. The previous summer, his mother had died of cancer. They had buried her, a stick-woman with an expression of long-set unhappiness the undertakers had not been able to soften entirely, under the red granite stone where twelve years earlier they had buried his father. George Walker had drowned in 1952, while fishing from Bannerman's dam. There were no buffers now, between Alf and the place where time, his time, simply stopped, like a field that stops in the distance, its sheer edge cutting the blue of the sea. He could see that sea's blue haze getting steadily brighter. Where had his life gone? It had gone up in war, in anger, in hope, in the years of raising children, in the churn of knitting machines, in the lick of water on stone. And now he was forty-seven, with a sore back, and less than half his hair, and only one chance left, maybe, to prove to himself, to Margaret, that he was more, better, than a fixer in Bannerman's mills.

Pete arrived while they were eating dessert. Alf heard the throb of the Sarasota and saw the big, two-toned Chrysler swing into the drive behind his Biscayne. The car had fins like the Batmobile in Jamie's comics, so tall they looked on the verge of flapping. The Sarasota was eight years old, and second-hand. Pete preferred to drive the more expensive cars, even if he had to wait five years or more to be able to afford them. His friend strode across the yard, a case of Carling's Red Cap under his sinewy, tattooed forearm.

"I see the party's underway," he sang out. And with a courtly, ironic nod, darting a wary glance from under the peak of his ball cap: "Margaret."

"Pete," she said, putting down her spoon.

"I guess you guys have been busy."

"Well you can take over now," Alf said, glad of his old friend's arrival. With Pete, there would be jokes, stories: he would forget.

Margaret stood up.

"Don't get so drunk you fall off the roof," she said dryly, reaching for Alf's plate.

"Don't worry. I'll keep an eye on them," Pete said, shooting Jamie a wink. The boy's face swam with pleasure. Pete was "Uncle Pete" to him and Penny: since their grandmother's death, the closest thing they knew to a relative.

Margaret did not deign to reply. She only tolerated Pete for *his* sake, Alf felt. Years ago, she had asked Alf why he considered Pete his best friend. "I just think you might do better," she'd said. "I wouldn't say he was my *best* friend," Alf had said, wounded and on the defensive. But whom was he closer to, really? Yet he knew what she meant: there was something of the lost soul about Pete, with his broken teeth and fixed stare, his Grade Nine education.

Margaret lingered with a stack of dirty plates in her hand, asking after Pete's wife, May.

"Oh Jeez, she's not fit to live with these days." Pete's eyes with their look of innocence-protesting candour had settled on Alf, even though he was technically answering Margaret. "I can't do anything right. I put my glass down, she says, '*Don't put it down there!*'"

Jamie laughed at Pete's mocking falsetto. But Penny was watching him soberly, as if unaware of any joke. On her plate was an apple with a slice cut off its side, the white flesh turning brown.

"Well I'm sure she has her reasons," Margaret said. "Penny, you haven't eaten your dessert. Bring it in with you, you can help me with the dishes." Moving as if hypnotized, Penny swung her legs over the bench and sat staring at the grass.

"You heard about Timmy Morton?" Pete said to Alf.

Alf murmured that he hadn't and looked away, hoping to dislodge his friend's gaze, hoping Pete might at least once address Margaret, who in the past had complained that Pete ignored her. "Is it just me," she'd asked, "or does he do it with everybody? Sometimes I get the feeling he's afraid of women." Alf had hastened to assure her Pete was like this with everybody, at least when Alf was around. And it was true, Pete always directed his attention to Alf, as though that were the only comfortable place he *could* look. They had been friends since childhood.

"Guess he got so lubricated he went home to the wrong house," Pete said, still fixing on Alf. "You know those houses on Gold Street: they all look the same? Guess Timmy pulls in the drive, thinks it's his place, but he's actually next door!" Pete grinned around at Joe and Jamie, but his gaze quickly returned to Alf. "Sly Callum's place – Timmy goes right inside like he's in his own kitchen . . ."

It was a good story – Pete was always up on the latest scandal, which he usually dramatized with a few twists of his own – but Alf was distracted by Margaret's departure. She and Penny had gone off across the grass, picking their way over the scattered reefs of old shingles to the back steps. A few moments later, Alf glanced around and saw his wife's dark hair reappear at the window, as she clattered at the dishes in the sink.

"So he's in the wrong bedroom," Pete was saying. "He's taking off his clothes in the wrong bedroom! So then Sly wakes up and says, 'Who in hell's that?' And Timmy thinks, That don't sound like Jean! So then Sly jumps on him, starts pounding him out –"

"Sly's just a little guy!" Joe said, relishing the story.

"Yeah," Pete says, his eyes growing huge. "But don't cross him, eh? So I guess Mary finally turns on the lights and they get it sorted out." Pete was focused on Alf again, his eyes wide with amazed disbelief, as if Alf and only Alf might have the answer to the wonder of human behaviour he was expounding. "I guess Jean was so mad at Timmy when she found out – made him spend the night in the car!"

Hearing the laughter of his sons, Alf grinned. But he was somewhere else, thinking of the woman moving through the dim house behind him.

4

SANDY CLIMBED INTO THE BISCAYNE. Her new cat-woman eyes met Joe's.

"Wow," he deadpanned. Eyeliner. Mascara. He wasn't sure he liked it.

"If you don't like it, I can take it off."

"Take it off?" His gaze slipped to the tops of her breasts, white as scars above the dipping edge of her halter top. A thin silver chain fell out of sight. At its weighted end, he knew, down there between her breasts, hung Christ in his agony.

"Dirty mind," she said, lifting her chin to the windshield.

West Street lay deserted. They drove off the Island, past small plaster houses, small frame houses, past Bannerman's old hosiery mill with its decapitated bell tower and up the broken asphalt road wedged into the hillside. At the hump of the level-crossing he glanced left and saw heat shimmering in the distances beyond the town, over the oily bed of the empty tracks: the eternal absences of Sunday.

She took a small, spade-shaped bottle from her purse, removed the top with its little brush, and with great concentration began to paint her nails. Irritated, he watched the way she curled her tongue over her upper lip and held her hand away to examine her work, an artist enslaved by perfection. It was his notion of her that she was too absorbed in trivial things.

"Why do you do that?"

"Do what?"

"Paint yourself up like that?" He had nearly said, Tart yourself up. Sometimes, and especially now, in the daylight, he was ashamed of their connection.

She gazed frowning at her hand. The bright-red polish suggested to him a cheap carnival gaiety, a violence.

"You don't like it?"

"It just seems . . . I don't know."

"I could take it off if you don't like it."

"No, no," he said, and a moment later: "Anyway, once we get in the water, it's not likely to last, is it –"

"The nail polish?"

"The stuff on your eyes."

She adjusted the mirror and studied herself, worriedly. In profile, her face was almost flat. It had been her father who, years ago, had begun to call her Monkey.

"It's just for *fun*," she said, pulling down the skin of her cheek-bone.

"Look at me."

There *was* something attractive in her makeup, almost primitive, like a mask that made her new. Behind its drama she might be anyone.

"It's growing on me," he said.

She was a year younger than he – his best friend Smiley's little sister, or at least that was how he'd thought of her until a school dance in May, when in the heat of the spring evening, among bodies turning in the pulsation of the speakers, she had tugged him onto the gym floor for a Ladies' Choice. And in the slow maelstrom of couples, with Paul McCartney wailing like there was no tomorrow, they had drifted into a swaying intimacy so easy and natural he felt he had been preparing for it all his life.

They had been steadies all summer. She wore his school ring, taped to make it fit. His mother disapproved. He'd overheard her responding on the phone to a friend who had apparently seen him and Sandy together in the Biscayne. "It's only one of those summer things, quite temporary. I mean, they've grown up together – hardly a seedbed for romance." Then his mother's friend said something, and his mother had replied, in a tone of infinite knowing and scorn, "Yes, *exactly*. She's not really up to his mark at all." Later, Joe had upbraided her. "She's a wonderful girl," he said angrily, wanting to hurt her, "and it's not temporary." In fact, he knew it was. His mother's judgment of Sandy and his own, secret judgment were uncomfortably close. But he hated it when his mother anticipated his thoughts: it made him feel she had stolen a piece of him.

Sandy slid over, burrowing a place for herself under his arm. Her hair yielded to the pressure of his body like a basket of woven grass. In its teased, complex, slightly sticky depths was mostly air. Her breasts pressed together, their tops rising above her halter: stacked goudas. Under the seat he had brought a flashlight. Later, after they'd swum at the bridge, after they'd eaten a hot dog at the Rendezvous, they'd drive out to their parking place above Coles Rapids. He was planning to leave the flashlight on in some place where it would shed an indirect glow, softer than the overhead light, easier on the batteries too. For him, Coles Rapids was the focus of their date, the exciting endpoint of a journey without which the journey would hardly be worth making.

At the Fairgrounds, he accelerated. They crested the new bridge, with its fleeting view of the gravel pits that surrounded the town: turquoise, spring-fed craters, too cold for swimming, and farther away, the conveyor belts leading like little elevated roads across a sad, desert landscape littered with boulders and rusted equipment. Finally, they broke out among the farms: the old houses flashed behind windbreaks of poplar and spruce, while the great, weathered barns held their course like ancient galleons riding the seas of green and bronze crops – the long, patrolling wave of summer.

By four-thirty they had had their fill of swimming and retreated to the flat limestone of Turtle Rock. They lay on their stomachs, on Sandy's pink beach towel, facing upstream towards the iron span that stamped the sky with its dark trapezoid. Chunks of collapsing roadbed hung beneath it like the innards of a disintegrating mattress, suspended by tortured strands of rusted steel. The bridge had long been closed to cars. Only the pedestrian walkway remained open.

Directly below, a little rapid flickered and hushed where the river entered the calm of the pool. The water in the pool was opaque, the colour of creamed coffee, brimming with the soil the Atta had picked up in its long, meandering journey through the farmlands to the northwest. The surface scarcely seemed to move, though here and there bits of weed or grass floated along.

There was only one swimmer in the pool now. Her head moved slowly, edging into the current below the bridge. To their left, the abrupt, sandy bank and the massive, corrugated trunks of the willows lay in shadow. From deep in the recesses among the trees, over the cooling sand littered with the remains of fires and picnics past, voices could be heard. A bottle popped as it broke on a rock. There were almost twenty people on the river this afternoon, but except for the cars ranged along the sand-flats on the opposite bank, there was little sign of them. They had retired to escape the heat, to neck, to drink. By now their activities were all but enveloped in a drowse of silence.

Sandy rolled to her back, wriggled against him. Her hair had collapsed into a stringy mass. Most of her makeup was gone, save for a blotch at the corner of her right eye, as if she had been weeping tar. He licked his finger and cleaned it off. Her face was broad and child-like, her mouth wide and thin-lipped and supple. But what took him aback just now were her eyes, gazing at him with such unguarded affection he had to look away.

"Think we'll get married?" she said.

"*Married?*" he said, suddenly grinning.

"I don't mean *now*, but maybe –" Her finger traced something on his bare arm. "You know – someday."

"I got university," he said.

"I could work, help put you through. Lots of gals do that for their guys."

Her "gals" bothered him. As her makeup bothered him, her too-bright clothes. Sandy might live on the Island too, but their families couldn't be more different. He thought of her house: the ugly wall-paper, the mess of clothes that never seemed to get cleared up, the absence of books, of decent music.

"How do you know lots of girls do that?"

"I read about it," she said, sulking. "I do *read*, you know." She gave him a little shove. But what she read mostly were romances with titles like *April's Summer* and *Ann Masterson's Only Choice*. He had tried to get her to read something more serious – James Joyce's *Dubliners*, Churchill's history of the Second World War – but she hadn't got very far with them. "Not really my style," she'd said, handing his volumes back. "I'm not as smart as you." She said it happily, as if her lesser intelligence were a relief.

"I don't know," he said, after a while. He meant he didn't know about getting married. In fact, he'd known as soon as she raised the subject that he wasn't going to marry her, if he got married at all. But he was being vague to avoid hurting her. It was the one thing he could give her to make up, at least a little, for the imbalance in their feel-ings for each other: the solicitous tenderness of the guilty.

"We'd have our own place," she said. Her fingertips were moving up and down his arm, brushing the blond hairs against his skin. "Our own *bedroom*."

"Oh yeah?"

"Where we could . . . you know."

Her eyelids dropped, and he glimpsed in marriage possibilities – a silky intimacy – that was more than they had known. They had not made love, not fully, not in the way he craved, and now, in the webbed crotch of his swimsuit, flattened against the warm rock, things were beginning to happen.

"Tell me more," he said, looking at her.

"Well, *you* know," she blushed. He had run up against her natural modesty. When they made out in the Biscayne, she kept her eyes closed.

"You make it sound pretty good."

"It would be good." There was play in her gaze now, he had never known her to be so openly seductive.

"Why don't you kiss me?"

Her mouth had never yielded such softness. All he could think of now was what her kiss promised for later, at the rapids. He kissed her again. Between his body and the rock, a second, tubular rock had materialized.

"So what do you say," she said cozily, as if the matter was all but decided. He was amazed at how tenaciously she could hang on to her original idea.

"Will you show me tonight?" he said. "What being married to you will be like?"

"Bad boy!" she said, slapping at his arm.

"But will you?"

"Bad boy," she said, pushing at him.

He hung his head: he liked being a bad boy.

"Seriously now," she said, "what do you think? A possibility?"

Her eyes held a probing sharpness.

He said, truthfully, "I just never thought about it."

"So you just think we'll go on like this?"

"It's kinda nice."

"But it's *enough* for you?"

He looked across the dimming water. The swimmer – it was Marilyn Truscott – reached the shallows and stood up, water pouring off her shoulders. For a few seconds, as she fiddled behind her neck with the tie of her swimsuit, she was all the girls he hadn't known yet.

"Yeah," he said, "it *is* enough for me."

"*You*," Sandy said. She pushed at his arm dismissively, with a show of good humour, but he knew she was hurt. She lay back and closed her eyes, lifting her chin, as if she had found a superior lover in the sun.

A flat, headachy light was coming off the river. "Think I'll take another dunk," he said. After a few minutes he got up slowly and padded with a show of indifference to the edge of Turtle Rock.

He surfaced just in time to hear Smiley call out, "Ship ahoy!" His friend stood in his plaid swimsuit at the edge of the willows, his pale, hairy gut spilling over the pleated edge of the suit, the iodine glint of a beer bottle clamped in his hand, gazing across the river to where a large, sky-blue car was descending through the pasture towards the sand-flats. It was coming slowly, almost hesitantly, easing over white outcrops of bedrock, brushing weeds, disappearing behind a cluster of wild fruit trees to re-emerge with glare masking its windshield: a Lincoln, and brand new by the look of it. Joe had no idea whose it was.

"Jesus," Sid Kovacs said. Sid had just entered the shallows from among the parked cars, a few yards to Joe's right. He was standing in his slouchy little trunks and black horn-rims, his hair swept up by his last dive like a merganser's crown. His mouth gaped in an expression somewhere between amazement and moronic self-forgetfulness as he watched the big car pause.

"Well, it's Sunday," Smiley said drolly. "It might be Him."

Treading water, Joe watched the great, flat-sided car nose down the slope. Its engine was audible now, a low throbbing hum, a bit ominous, as though it were connected to powers, to purposes, he could not read. In that moment many of the kids on the river felt like trespassers. They had never known who owned this place by the water, perhaps they were about to find out. But whoever was in the car was hidden by the reflections coming off the windows. Then as the Lincoln approached the long earthen ramp leading to the

ruined bridge ("Maybe he'll try to drive over," Smiley quipped hopefully), Joe caught a glimpse of Sally McVey in the driver's seat, her
chinless face lifted like a turtle's. Beside her sat her older sister, Liz,
and in the back seat, a third person, at once lit and obscured by the
sunlight flooding the car.

Sid said, "What the fuck are *they* doing here," and it seemed he
spoke for everyone on the river. They were all watching now, watching from the woods and the water's edge as the big car turned along
the sand-flats and crept towards their parked cars, its power steering
singing and weeping, its engine complaining at having to go so
slowly: watching and wondering with Sid, why *were* the McVeys
here? They *never* came here, kids from the North End just didn't,
they swam mainly at the country club, in a pool Joe had never used
himself, though driving past at night he had seen its turquoise glow
in the hillside, and heard the excited voices of swimmers across the
dark fairway.

The Lincoln crept forward, among the loose ranks of Chevs and
Fords and Plymouths with their rust spots, their reddish, primed
panels where some home-repair job had got stalled halfway. It passed
the Walkers' old beige Biscayne and went on, like a visiting dignitary
inspecting the tatty honour guard of some Third World country,
stopping at last behind Smiley's pickup loaded with furniture he was
supposed to be delivering to his uncle. Then the sky-blue car fell silent.
In the pause that followed, a gull, anguishing, fell away down the sky
and the river shone in its distant, unshaded reaches, far upstream.
Then the doors of the car opened and shut and three figures emerged
to walk swiftly behind the other cars and out onto the sand-flats
towards the bridge. Sally led the way, in her Bermuda shorts and golf
hat, followed by her sister, Liz, with her slightly rounded shoulders,
her ponytail jiggling. A few steps behind came a girl Joe did not recognize, a tallish girl, also in Bermudas, who wore her blonde hair in a
Dutch bob: a blonde helmet whose front edges curved up slightly over
her cheeks. She seemed aware, as the McVeys did not, of the people
watching from the river. Twice she looked over at them, at Sid Kovacs,

gaping back at her from the shallows, and at Joe, treading water in the deepest part of the pool. There was curiosity in her glance, he thought, and a sense she knew her situation was absurd.

The McVeys forged on as if they were on some important expedition, Sally with her usual air of good-natured, slightly goofy self-confidence, her face up, and Liz hurrying after her with her head down. And finally the third girl, taller than either of them and walking more slowly as she followed them up the earthen ramp and onto the pedestrian walkway.

At first it seemed as if Sally was planning to lead the little group across the river and into the woods on the far shore. But about two-thirds of the way across, she stopped abruptly and turned to look over the river. Her sister stopped beside her. The other girl stopped a few feet to their left. She leaned over the rail to look down into the little rapid. The movement lent an inward curve to her wide-set shoulders, bare in their sleeveless blouse, and in the water, Joe was suddenly aware of the nakedness of his feet, bicycling slowly.

It was an odd moment, those on the bridge and those in the water and at the edge of the woods looking at each other without saying a word, looking and perhaps wondering, as if until that moment they had not suspected that the world contained any others but themselves. The only sound was the plash of the little rapid and, briefly, the faint, tearing roar of a high jet as it trailed to the west.

For several seconds, an eon, no one spoke. The sun burned orange on the top girders. The river gleamed distantly, as it descended between the green fields upstream. The distilled, shadowy air held all in suspension. Joe could not take his eyes off the third girl. There seemed to be something on her right cheek, a whiteness, like a dusting of flour, but when she moved her head a little (or perhaps he himself had moved, carried almost imperceptibly away by the current), he could not be sure he had seen anything.

It was Smiley who finally broke the spell, calling up to the bridge that the girls should come in swimming: the water was great.

Then Liz McVey, who in class sounded so icily sure of herself, called out in a voice that seemed oddly quavery – an old woman's voice – that they didn't have their suits.

"Not really necessary," Smiley said in his normal speaking voice, to Joe.

"What!" Liz called, her voice gaining strength. "Can't hear you!"

"What!" Smiley roared to the bridge.

"What!" Liz called. "What did you say?"

"I mean, she can always borrow mine," Smiley said quietly to Joe.

"Ah let up," Joe said.

"What! What did *I* do?" Smiley held out his hands, his beer, in a plea of innocence.

"Stop teasing them."

"Teasing!" Smiley practically shouted it. "I'm not teasing! Why would I be teasing!"

Joe knew they had to have heard on the bridge and that this was Smiley's intent; he was out to embarrass someone, he didn't care who.

On the bridge, the two sisters drew together to confer. The third girl continued to look over the water. At the edge of the woods, someone growled, "What the fuck are *they* doin' here?" It was Marty Cain. Joe watched him step out from behind a tree, his thick body looking white and unhealthy in the shadows. From his hand drooped a twenty-sixer of rye.

Someone else said, "We should *make* 'em go swimmin'." "Ah come on," Joe said again, but he was not sure anyone heard. In truth, he didn't give a damn about the McVeys. It was the other girl he was worried about. She seemed out of place with the McVeys, better than them and, in some inexplicable way, vulnerable. In the space of two or three minutes, he'd become her protector.

But of course there was nothing he could do but watch, in a state of extreme attention, slowly moving his arms and feet to keep his place in the current.

The McVeys looked down the river and over at their car, clearly uncertain about what they should do. Beneath them, the little rapid hushed and splashed.

"Fuck the lot of them," Marty Cain growled, taking a swig from his bottle.

"We're waiting!" Smiley shouted to the bridge.

"Shut up!" Joe said.

"What's eating you?"

"Just leave them alone."

Smiley looked at him, mischief glinting in his deep-set eyes.

"Hey, you in love again?"

Joe turned in the water, furious. On Turtle Rock, Sandy had sat up and was watching matters intently. She sped him a smile of amusement: wasn't this fun?

On the other side of the river, Sid Kovacs shouted up to the bridge, "Who's your friend? The good-looking one?"

"Asshole," Joe seethed across the water.

"Use your eyes, man," Sid squealed back, making no attempt to keep his voice down. "Lookit the body on her!"

"Take off your clothes and join us!" Sid called joyfully to the bridge. "We can have an orgy!" And he let out a whoop and threw himself backwards in the water. His spluttering head reappeared a moment later, minus his horn-rims. "My glasses!"

The sisters were no longer in doubt. They began to walk back along the walkway, with as much casualness and dignity as they could muster. As they passed the third girl, Sally murmured something to her and touched her arm, but instead of following the sisters, the girl turned and looked down over the opposite rail, on the upstream side of the walkway, through the torn roadbed. Joe knew what she was seeing: the speeding water visible through the hole in the concrete, which made you feel the bridge itself was racing upstream. Finally she began to follow the McVeys.

Sally McVey reached the sand-flats and Marty Cain, putting back his big head, bellowed, "Rich bitches out!" Bellowed it with a viciousness that broke from him like a torrent of poison. "All fucking whores back to Snob Hill!" Yet even then the situation might have been salvaged, for at first only a shocked silence answered Marty, as if the others felt he had gone too far. Then Liz McVey began to run, spurting forward suddenly, and in a moment her sister was running too. From the edge of the woods, pandemonium erupted: catcalls, boos, the pack gone wild.

Under a willow, someone beat jubilantly on an oil drum with a stick. The sisters passed the parked cars, Sally leading as they headed for the safety of the Lincoln. Joe smashed at the water and yelled at the others to stop but soon realized he was only adding to the din. Appalled, he watched the third girl walk calmly across the sand-flats. She neither hurried nor looked as if she wanted to. The abuse from across the river might have been only a breeze.

Then she did something extraordinary, she stopped and looked at them. She looked first at Sid Kovacs, tilting her head a little as if she were wondering what kind of odd beast this was, sitting up to his chest in water and braying like a five-year-old. Sid fell silent. Then she looked at Joe. He said, "Sorry" to her but, with the din still going behind him, was not sure she heard. He saw there *was* something on her cheek, at once whitish and pinkish and in the dimming light oddly elusive, changeable: a dusting of snow, the imprint of a tiny hand.

The others, too, had fallen silent. It was odd, as if they were expecting her to make a speech, or lead them towards some other, more interesting activity. Someone, a girl, laughed sharply, perhaps in embarrassment. The mad tattoo on the oil drum had stopped.

Down the shore, the Lincoln gunned into life. As Joe turned in the water to watch, the girl walked calmly towards it, her white tennis shoes lifting and falling on the packed sand.

It was late when they got back to town and gently raining. They came down West, past the crouched, jammed-together houses of the mill workers. Beyond, the Atta and its valley made an unfathomed darkness, stretching for miles into a countryside that was a misery to think of: wet woods and mud and huddling animals. Sandy sat next to him, her hand with his school ring resting on his thigh. It was how she always rode, but something had changed. There was a sense of distance, disjunction, a sadness that seemed to flow from some irrevocable and inexpressible failure. At the same time, a new idea was beginning to course through him, with an excitement that made him blow suddenly through his teeth.

"You okay?" Her voice small.

"Fine. How about you?"

"I'm fine." She did not sound fine. Expansively – and to forestall any serious talk – he swept his arm around her shoulder, gave her a squeeze. The black road shone like a pelt.

Stopping in front of her house, he watched as she got out and went up the drive. When she turned on the porch to wave, he had already started to pull away. As he swung east onto Water, the white-washed, foreshortened facade of his own house flashed and dropped behind as, with deepening anticipation, he accelerated through the rain-sweetened air. The Biscayne charged up the long hill past King's Park and Central School and the railway station, flying over the hump of the bridge into the North End. For a moment, as if a spotlight had found him, questioning his right to exist, he was aware of the condition of the car: of the rust eating its way around the fenders, of its old car smell, the dust on the dash. His shirt prickled at his back, another flaw: it was a hand-me-down from his father.

The rain had stopped. He prowled the streets in a hush of tires, passing under ancient trees where solitary street lights burned in nests of wet, shining leaves. Across vast lawns, the big houses peered darkly from their porches. Every object – those paired Muskoka chairs, glazed with rain – seemed about to disclose some secret. He turned onto Robert and the McVeys' house reared up among its maples: a neo-Georgian place with banks of shuttered windows and a wide front door. All the lights were out, save one on the second floor, glowing between slitted drapes. Slowing as much as he dared, he glanced up the drive and saw the Lincoln nested in shadow, its big, low-slung body alive and, it seemed to him, ambiguous, its properties only to be guessed at.

5

MOST MORNINGS, Alf walked to work. And most mornings, when he reached the corner of West and Water, he glanced left to see Pete striding off the footbridge from Lions Park, lunch pail swinging. Pete lived on the other side of the park, in a small clapboard bungalow he had built with Alf's help in the early Fifties, under the wooded flank of Lookout Hill. Pete worked in Bannerman's dyehouse, which explained why his hands and arms were often stained with streaks of Persian red or navy blue, and why even his clothes sometimes looked (Alf thought) as if he'd been painting a barn with a shovel. He wore a baseball cap, tilted well back off his narrow forehead.

This morning they met as usual. Pete's thin face lit up as he saw Alf, his eyebrows rising in humorous acknowledgment as though the two of them shared an ongoing joke they need not explain.

They fell in together, striding at a good clip along Water. Fifty paces ahead of them, Joe scraped along in his jeans and T-shirt, armoured, as it seemed to Alf, in the trappings of his secret life. What was the boy thinking about? Alf had no idea. Six forty-five. A torrent of light rushed the trees on Lookout Hill. Birds sang like mad from maples shrouding the small front yards. They passed the brick cottage where Alf had grown up – the same ragged cedar hedge, the same balding lawn – under the maroon leaves of the maple Alf's father had planted in 1939, when Alf's brother had gone off to war. He always sensed a presence here, as if his parents were alive still, peering out from the curtained windows, waiting for them to come back. But he gave the house scarcely a glance. He didn't want memories now, any more than he wanted talk. Enough to be awake in the flooding light. Mercifully, Pete was keeping quiet.

The main street still lay in shadow. Others were travelling with them, on the opposite sidewalk, or gliding past in cars: all headed for the mills, all wrapped, still, in the solitariness of their recent sleep. They passed the white pillars of the war memorial: Alf did not give it a glance, though he was aware of it, of the names carved in its stone, a chorus breathing, it seemed, with a nearly inaudible hush, under the stir of leaves. Then past the hardware store with its display of powerful lawn mowers, the tiny office of the *Attawan Star*, where the show window featured a large aerial photo of the town, the forking rivers a dark, inverted Y. High overhead, the eastern face of the post-office clock met the assaulting light.

Pete tugged down his visor, to shield his eyes from the sun streaming down Bridge Street. Bannerman's whistle gave a warning howl. I better get that old Jacquard going, Alf thought, and felt the sudden shock of cool air as they advanced over the Shade.

Pete gave a tap to the bridge rail, as though for luck. "Alf, I just put this out to you –"

Something in his friend's tone alerted him. Far ahead, Joe reached the end of the bridge and abruptly pivoted towards the path that ran along the dyke. His sudden movement shocked Alf, as if the boy had simply flung himself away.

"You might have heard. There's this organizer in town –"

Overhead, gulls screamed.

"A bunch of us have been meeting with him. Nothing's settled, like. We're just checking out our options."

"Doyle," Alf said, half to himself. He hadn't heard anything of the man for a couple of weeks. He'd begun to believe, to *hope*, that he'd left town.

Pete gave a little laugh that to Alf sounded guilty. "I guess maybe he's talked to you."

"I think maybe you know he's talked to me."

"Yeah, yeah, well actually –"

"Well actually what?"

"I said I'd speak to you."

"About what?" Alf said grimly. Of course he knew. He glanced sharply at his friend and Pete's nervous eyes fled under his visor.

"Like I said, we're just checking out our options."

"You don't have any –"

Pete fell silent. Alf knew he was being remorseless with him, unusually so. And still he had anger to burn: he tried to put it into walking, as if he could simply leave Pete's news behind. Up ahead, Joe had already disappeared from the dyke. There was a stink of decaying river weed. And the screaming gulls.

They were not used to major disagreements. They might argue about who was the better hockey player, Pulford or Baun, but their friendship was built on an easy amiability – an understanding they would avoid anything that roused strong emotion. It was no preparation for this – the air bright with danger.

Pete tried again, on a placating note: "A union can do things, Alf. These layoffs – if we had a union, there'd be seniority, like."

"You always said you were anti-union."

"I mean, they wouldn't be able to treat people like they do. There'd be protocols."

"Protocols," Alf mocked. He was sure Pete had got the word from Doyle. His friend, after all, had barely graduated from public school, and he had never cared about current events or political matters, as far as Alf knew. He never read a newspaper. "You know what happened the last time we tried this?"

"I know it was bad. But we gotta move on –"

Gotta move on. He suspected that was Doyle's argument too.

"You don't know," Alf said grimly. "You weren't here." Meaning: you were still in the navy in '49. You have no right to speak about what happened.

"Different circumstances, Alf."

Alf threw up his hands in anger and despair. They had nearly reached the end of the bridge. Pete had to hustle to keep up. "Malachi's a good guy, Alf."

"A good guy," Alf seethed. The very mention of Doyle made him want to hit something. He felt as if Doyle and Pete had been conspiring behind his back. He spoke with angry sarcasm: "So Malachi's a good guy. A nice guy to have a beer with. Is that any reason to follow him? Hell, good guys have been screwing up the world since it began."

He swung onto the dyke-top path. Pete kept right behind him, down the dirt incline that led onto the playing fields behind the arena. Two hundred yards away, sunlight boiled in the upper storeys of the mills. At the lip of the stack, a rag of smoke flapped.

Pete said, "I mean, hell, if you think a union's such a bad idea, why don't you come out to one of our meetings and tell us why?".

Alf stopped. Pete's eyes met his frankly from under his visor. There was a plaintiveness there, a beseeching. But at the same time, over a nervous smile, Pere was challenging him, and this was new. Alf was startled.

"You're a fool," Alf said. "You follow this guy and we'll all live to rue it. Honestly, Pete, you're a bigger ass than I thought."

Something changed in Pete's gaze, something went bright and at the same time seemed to burn up in its own brightness. It was as if he disappeared. His face was still there, grinning as if he believed Alf was only joking, but Pete had gone away, sunk beneath his features like a drowning man beneath the surface of a pool. Alf turned away, joining the crowd streaming into the deep canyons between the mills.

The stairs of the knitting mill were a mass of people, a steady thunder of shoes climbing the filthy treads. He put his head down and trudged. He had done this for eighteen years, all told. The thousands of mornings seemed to have become one morning, *this* morning, an eternity he was condemned to spend watching, a few inches from his face, the wide, labouring bum and knotted calves of Millie Jennings.

He was still furious. How many of these people had talked to Doyle? Who was taking the organizer seriously? What he could see told him nothing. Yet everything he looked at – Millie's ugly legs, a discarded gum wrapper – seemed a clue. Every face in its bland, dreaming thickness had turned treacherous.

The knitting room was on the top floor, the sixth. He walked towards the bench where his tools were kept, noting with disgust that someone had failed to put one of his wrenches away. A faint, chortling murmur made him look around. Sun slanted among the rows of tall machines, each bearing its circular rack of bobbins. Against the far wall, the knitters sat on their long bench, looking back at him with blank, unreadable faces. He was swept with distaste at their sullen immobility. Just then, the buzzer gave out its nasal command: seven o'clock. It was time to go to work, but the knitters did not stir. Their tardiness – it would last only a few seconds – was meant to declare that they were their own masters, even here.

Hearing the sound again, he looked up. Under the high ceiling, a drive-belt hummed, awaiting the moment when its power would be channelled to the machines below. Inches above it, on a sprinkler pipe, sat the trapped pigeon. Alf could clearly make out its slender head, cocking sideways to look down on him with tiny, burning eye.

The next morning, when Pete didn't show up on the Lions Park footbridge, Alf went on by himself. It was the same the next morning, and the next. Pete was driving to Bannerman's now. Each day, arriving at the mills, Alf saw the Sarasota's towering tail lights parked in the dead-end lane beside the dyehouse. But he never managed to run into Pete himself.

He felt he really *should* call his friend. Pete was prone to these withdrawals. Once, years ago, Alf had criticized Pete for something, and Pete had vanished from his life for nearly a month. Then one day he'd just showed up again, acting as if nothing had happened. Alf supposed that's how it would go now. One morning Pete would come striding off the Lions Park footbridge, grinning his gap-toothed grin, telling some funny story, and they would go on as before, without a mention of their quarrel. He was worried, though, and sorry, yes definitely sorry, for some of the harsher things he'd said.

Twice he picked up the phone to call his friend. Twice he put the receiver back down, with a sense of confusion and defeat. He couldn't sort out apologizing from admitting he was wrong.

One hot afternoon in the midst of this standoff, he was sitting on the floor of the knitting room, among the parts of a knitting machine he'd spread on newspapers, when the freight elevator floated into its bay. Behind the safety gates, Alf caught a flicker of bodies moving. Then the gates were flung back and a group of men stepped out. Their dress shirts, turned up crisply at the cuff, broadcast a shock of white into the room. There was a young woman with them: tall, in an extremely short skirt, her long legs stalking forward in black mesh stockings. A bald, tanned, handsome man touched her back and leaned over to whisper something into the teased cloud of her hair. She put back her head and opened her mouth in a silent, cheerless laugh, showing a wealth of teeth.

Twenty feet away, Alf instinctively drew up his legs, a man exposed in the bath. They had stopped outside the elevator. The bald man, who stood well over six feet, seemed oddly familiar. But the only figure Alf recognized was Gordie Henderson, the assistant manager of the sweater mill. He looked around anxiously, as if searching for shelter in a thunderstorm.

Spotting Alf, Gordie hurried over.

"Alf, I need Matt."

"Think he went down to the dyehouse," Alf said, glancing up. Tufts of black hair blocked Gordie's big nostrils. In truth, Alf had no idea where Matt Honnegger was. The soon-to-be-retired foreman was just as likely to be in the can, relaxing.

"These people are from Intertex," Gordie said in a tense undertone. "Top guns. They want a tour."

"I'll see if I can find Matt."

"Maybe you could take us around –"

Gordie had already decided for him. As he waved the others over, Alf struggled to his feet. Unable to find a rag, he hurriedly wiped his hands on his trousers.

"Alf, this is Mr. Prince –"

"Bob Prince," the bald man said in a low, rich voice: a heavy load on casters. Alf remembered where he'd seen him – that photo in the *Star* the previous spring. It was a bit like meeting someone whose fame had preceded him, a little whirlpool of excitement. Alf was on edge, aware that these men were perched high on a ladder he wanted to climb himself.

"Mr. Prince is vice-president of ah –," Gordie faltered.

"New Acquisitions," Prince said. He put out his hand.

"I'm a little dirty," Alf said, dragging his hand again across his shirt front. The others were watching blankly.

"A little honest dirt," Prince said. The hand remained in place: it had become an order. Alf took it. For a lingering moment the other man's glowing eyes – they were a pale, icy blue, almost exactly the same colour as Alf's – reached into his with a searchlight's candour. Alf experienced an obscure shame.

"Alf's our head fixer," he heard Gordie say. "There isn't anything he doesn't know about this place." Alf wondered if Gordie was about to leave him with this bunch.

Prince introduced the others. Their names and faces flashed by him. Jacobson. Martin. Raleigh. Macrimmon. Each of them leaned forward, following their boss's example, to take his hand. A thin man with rimless glasses looked at him more directly than the others. Then the green eyes fled.

"And this is Shirley," Prince concluded, with a hint of affection- ate condescension. He offered no last name, as if like a child or a mascot, the young woman at his side did not need one. Shirley preened in her heavy makeup, smiling at a place beside Alf's head.

To his relief, Gordie stayed to conduct the tour. The assistant manager led them into the first aisle of machines. Unsure what he was wanted for, but relieved at no longer being the centre of attention, Alf tagged along.

They stopped by the first machine, a Richardson. In a circular drum, hundreds of latch needles made a soft hushing sound as they worked in rapid synchronization while, above, bobbins swept around and around on a carousel, wafting a faint breeze over their sweating faces.

"If you could stand up here by me, Alf."

His mouth suddenly dry, Alf took his place beside Gordie. To his relief, the assistant manager seemed determined to do all the talking. Alf thrust his hands in his pockets. His fingers found a key, the teeth of which he raked absently with his thumb. A bit of lint drifted across the floor, and on a distant window ledge sun glinted on a pigeon's neck. Gordie's high, frantic voice scissored the close air. He was explaining how the mill was organized: knitting at the top, cutting just below, all the stages stacked over each other so that, at the end, the finished sweaters could flow out the door. Alf cast a glimpse at Shirley's bodice, the artfully undone button there an undoubted happiness.

Out of nowhere, his father's drowned body rose. He saw the pale head laid back on the metal table in the back room of McArthur's Funeral Home, saw the deep, nearly bloodless gash crossing the shoulder and chest like a bandolier. The wound had not killed him, Rick McArthur told Alf. He had drowned first. Then sustained his injury while turning in the currents under the dam. "The old timbers down there," Rick told him, "they're thick with spikes." He had never forgotten that phrase, "thick with spikes." He would think of it as he crossed the Bridge Street bridge and happened to glance upstream at the dam, foaming benignly across the river. *Thick with spikes*, as if some monster were down there, bristling with spines: an unimaginable power.

Momentarily, he felt adrift in space, a ghost among the humming machines. Brushing the sweat from his brow, he looked up. Prince was listening to Gordie in a fume of impatience. The executive's heavy jaw worked frantically at a piece of gum, and he was casting hard glances around the room. The other men seemed to have caught their boss's unhappiness: their frowning faces fed off it like scavengers off a half-eaten kill. Only Shirley seemed unaffected. Her girl's eyes, alive behind the mask of her makeup, had been drawn to the machine working in front of her. She seemed hypnotized by the streaming threads, which raced from the bobbins to be consumed by the drum of pullulating needles. But what mainly fascinated her was the place below the drum, where the tube of patterned cloth appeared as if out of nowhere, inching down between the machine's iron legs like something newborn.

They moved deeper into the room, down the aisles of tall machines, under the drive-belts thrumming near the high ceiling. Most of the machines here were older than the Richardsons: with their stationary racks and dark metal they had been churning along since Alf's father had started as a fixer here, back in the Twenties. The knitters took care to keep clear of the visitors. Occasionally, a hand reached up to place a loaded bobbin on a spike or a face drifted briefly in a distant aisle. But the executives from Intertex might well have had the impression that the machines were running themselves.

Gordie was not doing well. Sweat poured off his high, bony forehead, dripped off his nose into his plaid tie with its red ensign clip. He had been all right describing the overall operations of the mill, but when it came to specific machines and routines, he was out of his depth. And Prince knew it. The executive was watching him coldly now, snapping questions at him like pucks. And when Gordie managed to send back a coherent answer, Prince chopped another at him mercilessly. Gordie – he was the only one of the party wearing a jacket – mopped compulsively at his face and repeated, "Right, right" over and over.

It was a display of cruelty on Prince's part, for by now the executive wasn't even giving Gordie time to answer. The other men stirred uneasily, averting their eyes.

Finally a question came that Gordie seemed not to hear. The little man stood with an odd half-smile on his wet face, gazing at a place below him as if at his own impending doom. He half-seemed to welcome it.

"Sorry," he said, looking up.

Alf said quietly, "Mr. Prince wants to know how we handle rush orders."

Prince said, "Maybe you could tell us, Alf. I think it's time we heard from the man on the floor." Prince's gaze, in all its remorselessly shining insistence, had swung to him. The others, too, looked at Alf, perhaps with a touch of hope, like a crowd looking at a new challenger, a new victim.

Alf told them about rush orders. Remembering how irritated Prince had seemed with Gordie's meandering, he kept his answer short and to the point, and when he had finished, Prince had another question ready and he answered that too, snapping it back as efficiently as he could. Prince glowed. He cast a knowing glance at the others, as if to say, There, that's what we want – as if he were taking credit for having created Alf's answers and maybe creating Alf too, shaping him up out of the chaos of this hot, almost-wasted afternoon. They went on down the aisle, stopping at another machine. Alf tried to turn Prince's next question back to Gordie, but Prince said, "No, no, you've got the ball now," and of course there was no choice. He was leading the tour.

He expected that at any minute a question would come that he could not answer, or that Prince would throw him more questions than anyone could answer, but the attack never came. Prince had turned genial, interested. His blue eyes shone as he listened to Alf with a proprietorial enthusiasm. It was as if another man altogether had appeared in the white shirt and faultless tan trousers. He even began to make jokes. The others responded with an exaggerated, relieved hilarity, and after a while Alf relaxed too. He realized that Prince had no intention of humiliating him. He realized he was on home ground. He'd tended these machines for years, he'd taken them apart and fit them back together and knew them as well as the heavy Lee-Enfield he had once lugged around Europe, the parts of which he could have assembled blindfolded. But he had never put his knowledge into words before, not to such an extent, and now, a new thing, he saw his years of experience transformed, almost effortlessly, into the currency of language, and it was exciting to him, liberating.

Prince stopped abruptly. Everyone else stopped too, as the boss gazed around with a self-satisfied smile. "Shirley," he said, "I've been thinking," and it was evident his words were meant not just for her but for the whole party. His voice held an invitation to them to prepare the tribute of their laughter.

"Don't you think it'd be a good idea to get one of these things for the apartment?" He indicated the tall machine churning away beside him, disgorging its tube of soft white cloth. "Save you all that shopping."

Even Gordie laughed. Alf saw him at the rear, grinning like a kid desperate to be one of the gang.

Before he left with his party, Prince paid Alf a compliment that made Alf's face burn. "This is the salt-of-the-earth sort," the executive said, looking around at everyone, "that keeps a company going. Without the Alf Walkers, you might as well call it quits." The tour had cost him an hour he could hardly afford, but he was cheerful enough about having to stay late. The future was suddenly looking awfully rosy. It was nearly eight before he left the mill and made his way along Bridge, stopping by the plate-glass windows of Bud Mackie's Motors.

In the showroom, a navy-blue Impala rotated slowly. One door was open, revealing the instrument panel, seats swathed in creamy leather. And what clean lines the car had, compared to his old Biscayne! Yes, fins were definitely out – even the snug, horizontal fins of his Biscayne seemed clumsy and old-fashioned now. He gazed at the flawless, flowing surfaces: the deep-blue panels disappearing and reappearing endlessly, as in a dream.

6

"I SUPPOSE HE'S ALWAYS buttering people up like that. Saves having to pay them more."

"Don't be so modest," Margaret told him. "You deserve it, Alf."

She was sitting opposite him, while he shook HP Sauce on his dry chop and tried to suppress the tide of his excitement. He hadn't meant to tell her about Prince's compliment, he felt too much like a schoolboy bringing home news of some minor triumph, but it had just popped out.

Through the screens came the distant cries of children at play in the park across the river. Backlit by late sun, Margaret was sitting forward in her chair, with her elbows on the table, her forearms crossed, her hands spread on her shoulders in a way that made her seem young, eager.

"I'll be happier when I see it lead to something definite."

"I don't know why it wouldn't –"

"It all depends whether Prince remembers me. I mean, when they get around to deciding on the job. If he has anything to do with it at all –"

"Honestly, love, I should think you'd get it with or without his help. If they want the best –"

He frowned at his plate – it seemed to be tempting fate, to be talking like this – but he was pleased at her support. How long had it been since she'd looked at him as if he were her beau again, his head full of plans? He kept frowning, but he was irrepressibly buoyant. When he'd finished eating, he went out to the garden. Dusk had sifted from the opaque, shadowy mass of Lookout Hill. The sharp, earthy scent of tomato was in the air. He cupped his hand under one of the great lobed beefsteaks, hefting its coolness, and to his surprise it released itself into his palm.

Later, in bed, he sat listening to the thin cry of his wife's zipper from the walk-in closet where she undressed. Slipping from under the covers, he crossed the floor and peered around the door. She was just bending to step out of her half-slip. He gazed at her wide upper back, cut by the stark white statement of her bra.

"Would you like a cuddle?" It was their word for making love. They had not made love for weeks, there hadn't seemed time or energy for it, the feeling.

She hesitated, and he seemed to hover over an emptiness. The worst of it was, he felt he was asking her for his reward, for bringing her good news.

"Well I was *counting* on it," she said, giving him a smile over her bare shoulder. He wasn't sure he believed her. But he crept back to bed, satisfied enough.

He waited for her under the sheet, already hard, waited as she went down the hall to the bathroom, waited as she turned on the taps and flushed the toilet and squatted to put in her diaphragm with a sound of cracking knees, waited as she came back up the hall, detouring to check on Jamie and Penny, waited as she closed the door and slipped out of her dressing gown in the dimness that allowed him a brief, thrilling glimpse of her small breasts, waited as she slid under the sheet beside him, her hair dark on the pillow as he reared on one elbow to begin his courtship, waited another moment or two to let her settle, in the near-dark where she waited, as always, with a stillness that moved him.

A curtain belled from the window as he bent to kiss her. Her lips picked softly at his.

His hand crept over her stomach, where the skin was extraordinarily soft, slack, discoloured, he knew, with marbled streaks: it was what having children had done.

She grasped his wrist.

"You know I don't like that."

"Right. Sorry."

He moved his hand to the bottom of her rib cage, under her breasts. There was a tension in her, which seemed to evaluate his every move. He had noticed it the first time he had ever touched her, dancing together that night of the servicemen's party in Henley-Under-Downs: an electric pulse that seemed to push him away as he struggled to lead her. They had fought each other around the floor.

But he had loved her that first night, the clear, vibrant openness of her face and wide-set eyes, which seemed to look towards the future, towards him, with an adventuring gladness ready for anything, *anything*. And her air of refinement – that trim, high-shouldered dress, cinched at the waist, the sharp plunge of her bodice over a chest of pale, unimaginable smoothness. She seemed so much finer than any of the other girls in the crowded hall. So he learned to put up with her strangeness, her physical wariness. In a way, he felt he had been stalking her, courting her, ever since – still trying to come close.

Her lips touched and tempted his with a bird language of their own. And she had learned how to hold him, her slender fingers firm. He found her exciting, and her physical elusiveness had become part of this, an infinite tease.

When he was in her, he moved slowly, postponing his own climax in the hopes he might help her to her own. He wasn't actually sure she *could* come, though she insisted she did, or at least insisted she had pleasure enough. She was working hard beneath him, her long body trembling with that high-strung alertness, that almost negative magnetic force. He sensed she was pushing herself harder than usual, hungering perhaps for some kind of breakthrough, and he stayed with her. Finally she told him she was getting sore. "You finish, dear," she whispered. "Are you sure?" "Yes, yes." But he was so numb himself he had to work a good while longer before he finally crested and passed quickly, too quickly, through that place where he had never been able to stop.

7

JAMIE WATCHED ANDY WILSON slide his bike into the stands and walk away through the crowded Boys' Yard, throwing back his orange mop of hair with a jerk of his head. Moving in closer, Jamie touched the racing tires thin as snakes, the cherry-red frame, not a scratch. Andy Wilson lived in the North End. Snob Hill, some of the boys called it, not the boys who lived there, but the boys who lived lower in the town, where the rivers were, the brown and misty rivers that smelled of mud and rotting things. His mother had bawled him out when he'd said Snob Hill. She said she was sure people up there wouldn't like it. She said they were no more or less snobby, no better or no worse, than anybody else. Maybe. But they were different. When the Grade Three boys from the North End played tag, they didn't ask anybody else to play with them. They ran back and forth between the fences of the Boys' Yard, shouting each other's nick-names, Pud and Clumbs and Schooner and Drums. It was like a private party, a party where everyone pretended to have a good time, even if he wasn't. There was a lot of *pretending* about the boys from the Hill, he felt. They were always together, talking loud, getting something organized.

His own bike – he didn't ride it to school – had once been Joe's, a CCM with a banged-up maroon frame and no fenders, which meant you got sprayed when you rode through a puddle. Andy Wilson's bike was different altogether, with its silver handbrakes and the swept-under handlebars that reminded him of the horns of the mountain sheep in *Animals of the World*. Looking at the racer made him happy, like looking in the windows of Eaton's that time his family had gone to Toronto, all the little elves working away in Santa's shop, and the electric train chugging through the tunnels in the mountains, a happiness for looking only, you couldn't touch.

He drifted away from the stands and through the yard, lingering for a while to watch several Grade Six boys play conkers. A chestnut flew down and struck another chestnut, hanging on a string. There was a loud crack and a cry from the boys as the struck nut swung crazily in an arc. When it settled, they saw that a bit of its shell had come off, revealing the yellowish meat inside. "Mick's gonna have a ten-kinger," a boy said.

Jamie went over to the chainlink fence that surrounded the yard and stood with his back to it, hooking his fingers in the wire and leaning out. Behind him, on the other side of the fence, an enormous elm tree rose, its great branches drooping over the yard "like a giant umbrella," his new teacher, Miss Wayne, had said. She had showed the class the leaves of the elm, pointed like spearheads. He gazed around the milling yard, where boys ran or gathered in groups. Some were trading or flipping cards, or rough-housing, or talking in bragging, shouting voices. A few stood alone, like him, but these boys were too old, or too young, to be friends. Last year, in Grade Two, Johnny Simms had been his friend. But Johnny's dad had been laid off at the mill, and in August the whole family had driven away, Johnny's mother and sister in the car, and Johnny and his dad in the cab of the truck with all their furniture, and Johnny's face had looked down at him, Jamie, from the high cab, and Jamie's heart had gone No no no under his T-shirt because he'd heard his dad say that they, the Walkers, would probably never see the Simmses again.

He looked up into the elm arching like a vaulted roof over a third of the yard, and remembered what Joe had said about not believing in God. When he'd said that, Jamie had sensed something leave with extraordinary speed, *woosh*, like the wings of the ducks that time on the river. Everything looked the same as before – the backyard, the picnic table, his daddy's face – but something had emptied, as if his own insides had poured out. *I believe in God*, the voice said.

Jamie looked around, half-expecting to see somebody. He never did, though. Whoever spoke in that voice – that voice that was so close to him, it seemed to have slipped into his own head – was gone. Gone or invisible, like the Invisible Man.

Once, driving after supper in the country, he and his family had got lost. On both sides of the road, green water shone among trees. An old man on a horse had come by, sauntering along beside the car with a slow clop-clop. He wore a slouchy hat, bronzed like his face in the thickening light, and he drew to a halt as the car stopped and pointed back up the shadowy road to show where they should go. Sometimes, in the early morning, Jamie woke to a sound he did not understand: a faraway cooing that filled him both with sadness and a happiness that was even deeper than the sadness, like a lower note. Looking out the window, he could never see exactly where this sound was coming from – it seemed to come out of the hill and the trees and the river, and yet from none of these things. And once, looking for its source, he had seen the old man in his slouchy hat, standing under a tree across the river. He had nodded to Jamie, and Jamie had nodded back. Later he wondered if the old man had been God. Or perhaps he was an angel, and God was nearby.

You can't see God, the voice said. *He's shy.*

"Hey stupid, where'd'ya get those pants?"

Tommy Leach, from the Flats. Tommy had a large face, from which his bony nose stuck out like a fin. He was in Grade Five, two grades above Jamie, a fleshy boy several inches taller than he was, with pale-white skin like the belly of a carp. Jamie followed Tommy's sneering gaze to his pants, which had once belonged to Joe. On one pocket was stencilled the picture of a bear, rearing up on its hind legs, its big head roaring. On the other pocket was Davy Crockett in his buckskins and coonskin hat, aiming Old Betsy at the bear. Down the outsides of the legs ran a brown plastic fringe.

It was the first time he'd worn them.

"They're not stupid."

"Sure they are. You look stupid in them. What's that stuff sticking out?"

Tommy's upper lip had curled up, showing two big teeth. Jamie had noticed that Tommy was one of the boys in the yard who had no friends. He had watched him hang around other boys, but the boys ignored him. Lately, he'd taken to carrying a little horseshoe magnet. He'd stick it to the fence, then look up with a smirk to see if anyone was interested.

Tommy reached out and began to pull at the fringe.

"Hey don't!"

"Gimme a piece of your pants!" Tommy cackled.

"No!"

"Just a little piece!" Tommy was snorting with laughter. Little pearls of snot appeared under his nose.

Jamie's hand slapped at Tommy's, where it was tugging at the fringe.

"Hey, you hit me!" Tommy cried. His eyes had lit up, as if he thought this was a good thing, good and funny.

"Just leave me alone," Jamie told him. His heart was knocking.

Tommy shoved him back into the fence and held him there with one hand while his other hand tore off bits of fringe, sprinkling them around like grass. "Look! His pants are coming apart!" he called over his shoulder to whomever would listen. No one was even looking.

His nose. Grab his nose, the voice said.

Startled, Jamie looked and saw Tommy's big, thin nose. He seized it.

"Hey!" Tommy shouted. Now he sounded like a duck.

Tommy's mouth was open, showing those big teeth, and he flailed at Jamie, striking his head, his shoulder, but Jamie hung on for dear life. He was in an odd state, almost calm, knowing only that he had to hang on to the slippery thing between his fingers. Tommy lashed out with his foot, in its high black running shoe. Jamie dodged it and kept tugging on his nose, this way and that, like the string of his kite when he made it dance. Tommy sank to the ground. And still Jamie wouldn't let go, even though white stuff was seeping from the nose and Tommy was starting to sob with a hiccup sound. Others had gathered around, laughing and yelling, "He's got him by the nose!" One boy got down and put his face right up to Tommy's, as if to see if it was true.

Tommy tried to get up, but Jamie put him down with another tug and sat on him. Finally a big boy from Grade Eight said, "I think you've beaten him, you better let him go." When Jamie released his grip, Tommy lay blinking up at him. On his upper lip was a moustache of bloody white stuff. Jamie barely had time to look at him before the others had picked him up – lifted him right into the air. At first he thought he had to fight them too. But then he realized they were cheering. The big boys from Grade Seven and Eight were calling his name as they carried him around the yard, chanting, "Jamie Walker, Jamie Walker!" and other boys were running over to see. Soon there was a great gang moving through the yard, with Jamie perched awkwardly on their shoulders, holding on to someone's head, worried he was putting Tommy's bloody snot in his hair, feeling he was going to slip off at any minute. And it was then that he looked towards the corner by the bicycle stands and saw Billy. And even at that distance he knew Billy was looking right at him, following him with his black eyes around the yard. And fear went through him like cold water, because he knew what Billy was thinking: knew what he, Jamie, was going to have to do.

At recess, he went downstairs to the boys' washroom. He was standing in front of the urinal, which was taller than he was, watching his pee spread over the cracked porcelain into the sick-smelling drain, when he heard someone walk up behind him. Zipping up, he turned. Billy's black eyes fixed on Jamie's nose.

"So I guess you think you're the best fighter now."

"No."

"I guess you're gonna have to prove it."

"I don't think I'm the best fighter. You're the best fighter." Jamie believed this. He'd once seen Billy fight a boy a foot taller than himself. He'd leapt on him, biting and scratching like a wildcat until the boy, Dickie Collins, had run bawling into the school.

Billy's eyes were still on his nose. Jamie wanted to hide his nose, put his hand over it. It was as if, because he'd twisted Tommy's nose, his had to get twisted too. It was as if Billy really didn't see *him* at all, only his nose, which suddenly felt as big as his face.

"I don't wanta fight you," he said.

In a cubicle, someone farted, a real good one. Jamie grinned, thinking he and Billy might share the joke, but Billy didn't smile back.

"After school," he said.

After recess on Friday afternoons, they always had art. It was Jamie's favourite class: the smell of paints and glue, the rattle of the big sheets of paper, white as new snow, where you could do anything, anything you could think of: a happiness you could touch. The previous week, he'd started a picture of Indians attacking a covered wagon train. The wagons were racing along the prairie, and the Indians, mounted on their spotted ponies, were shooting flaming arrows. Their camp was up in the hills: lots of teepees (easy to draw) and a fire for dancing around, and lines going up and down like waves, for the hills. Ever since Joe had told him about Geronimo and Crazy Horse, he'd always been on the Indians' side. When he took his bow up the river, he pretended he was Crazy Horse, spying on the people who'd built their homes on his land. He went secret ways, so no one could see him.

But today, thinking of Billy, art wasn't so much fun. He drew in a couple more Indians, on their horses, and looked out the window. The great, frowsy head of the elm was there, filling the sky. Once, he'd seen it in a storm, all grey and tossing and lit by lightning: a huge, living head, tossing its wild hair. Was that God? Silently, he said to the tree, "Please help me," but the tree went on hanging, like a great, sad old umbrella with holes in it. Maybe it would rain and he wouldn't have to fight. He'd never seen anybody fight in the rain. He thought Billy might, though.

Billy was his age, but he was in the special class for slow learners, along with the retarded kids like Dougie French – Dougie with his big, slobbery lips and happy eyes. Billy wasn't retarded, but the previous year he'd been in Jamie's class and he was always in trouble. Once he'd got the strap for sassing Miss Bell. The dark leather strap, thicker than a belt, had smacked down on his hand four, five times and Billy had laughed a strange gurgling laugh while Miss Bell, her face getting redder, had hit him three times more. When Billy came back down the aisle to his desk, his cheeks were shiny with crying but he hadn't made crying sounds: he was grinning, as if it were all a joke.

When the bell went, Jamie stayed behind and asked Miss Wayne – he *loved* Miss Wayne, with her broad, happy face and kind voice – if he could help her clean up. But she said, No thank you dear, and smoothed down his hair a bit. He went out into the hall, with his rolled drawing in his hand. From the landing, he could see out the window above the door, see clear through the empty Boys' Yard all the way to the gate and the park across the road. And Billy was there, sitting on the curb, poking a stick at something in the gutter as if, maybe, he was torturing an ant. Looking at him, Jamie felt alone, maybe more alone than he'd ever felt. Billy was alone too. The two of them were more alone, it seemed, than if there had been only one of them.

Jamie went downstairs to the washroom and tried to pee. But there wasn't any pee to come out, so he went to the fountain and let its clear water bubble up like little silver balls for a while before he drank. When he went back upstairs, Mr. Small, the janitor, walking with quick steps behind his wide broom, called out that he shouldn't be there.

He went out. Walking across the Boys' Yard towards the gate, he thought of a plan: when he got to the gate, he'd run – tear away like blazes down the hill and hope he could make it home before Billy jumped him. But for some reason he didn't run. He walked past the elm to the gate and looked across at Billy, who dropped his stick and stood up. Jamie had a strange feeling that all this had happened before, and there was nothing he could do about it. He didn't feel afraid any more, just lonely, like that time when he was little and his mom had forgotten to pick him up at the babysitter's.

"Come over here," Billy said.

Jamie hesitated. Somewhere nearby, a whisper in the trees, the voice said, *It's all right*.

Clutching his drawing, Jamie crossed the road.

"What's that?" Billy said, scowling at the tube in his hand.

"My drawing. Indians."

Billy looked at him. Not at his nose this time, but at him. There was something sleepy in his dark eyes, and bright too, as if he were peeping out of a fog.

"Show it to me."

Jamie unrolled his drawing on the grass. Billy got down beside him, on his knees. There was a hotness coming off him, as if he'd been running.

"These Indians are attacking the wagons," Jamie said. "It's because the white people are taking their land from them. This one with the red feather, that's Crazy Horse."

"Crazy Horse," Billy said. The name sounded hard and queer, stuck somehow in his throat.

"He was the greatest Indian leader. He was a friend of Geronimo. They used to live around here, a long time ago."

For several seconds neither of them spoke as they looked at the picture.

"I'm an Indian," Billy said.

Jamie went on staring at the picture, but he wasn't seeing it any more. He was feeling the still, blank space where Billy's words had gone, like a pebble when you dropped it off the bridge and it hits the water and disappears. But the rings are there, spreading out, and something else: a feeling in your body.

"My mother's Indian. She don't like me to tell anybody."

"I won't tell."

They looked at the picture.

"This is a good drawing," Billy said.

"I'm gonna put more Indians in."

"Scalps?"

"Yeah. I could show them scalping somebody."

Jamie rolled up the drawing and they got to their feet. He was looking right at Billy now, seeing the black hair that came down in a mop almost to his black eyes, and the skin that looked brown, tanned maybe, and maybe a bit dirty, and his heart was going again, under his T-shirt, but it wasn't because he was afraid. It was because this was all new. He was somewhere he'd never been: he was with an Indian.

8

A TUESDAY: BURNT GRASS under a cloudless sky. The Grade Thirteen boys plucked lacrosse sticks from a cardboard drum and played a game – shirts versus skins – between the towering white H's guarding the ends of the football field. In the distance, across waves of goldenrod and the low darkness of a marsh, rose the faultless green – an Island Eden – of the golf course. Joe flung a long pass to Bobby Merchant and remembered he'd forgotten to study for his French test. Later, he skipped his shower and walked quickly through the crowded halls to Mr. Kay's room. He'd bone up before the others arrived.

Flooded with indirect sunlight, the first-floor classroom held thirty desks of blond wood. Along the walls hung framed posters depicting the Place Pigalle, the Eiffel Tower, and the ruins of the Roman theatre at Orange. At the front, Mr. Kay stood with his back to the blackboard, talking to someone sitting at the desk before him. The teacher was speaking French, pushing out the sounds with an exaggerated earnestness in a big, hollow voice. He wore a short-sleeved nylon shirt, a narrow wool tie, and black horn-rims whose bridge he kept nudging up his nose with the middle finger of his right hand.

She sat in the first desk of the window row: a girl in a light-green sleeveless dress, her slender right arm lying on the desktop, motion-less except for a small stroking movement of her fingers on the wood. As Joe flung his gym bag under his seat, the teacher offered a bland hello and the girl turned to glance at him. The shock hit him before he knew what the shock was for, as if his body had recognized her before he did, recognized the face whose details he had pretty much forgotten, under the thick bangs.

He opened his book and stared into it, seeing nothing. At the front of the room, their conversation ran on. Joe looked up again and saw, on her cheek, that pale dusted whiteness, a burn, or a birthmark: the brand of the evening on the river.

She, too, was speaking French. He thought she *sounded* French, the way she rounded the sounds, savouring them before she sped them on their way with protruding lips. Mr. Kay's wide, grinning face – at the moment it seemed an overgrown boy's face – had reddened.

Joe turned a page. But it was all a charade now. He might have been an actor pretending to read while he waited to say his next lines. He kept looking up at her, at her dress cut in a low square at the back, exposing tanned, ideal skin; at the thin silver bangle she toyed with at her wrist. Her light voice had a trace of something low in it, an impure chest note that thrilled and obscurely frightened him. He listened to their conversation with dry mouth, half-resenting her arrival: he had been happy with his life.

What were they talking about? Though he'd always done well in French, he was lost before the effortless flow of their talk: it was something about France, he thought, or was it Switzerland? Something about picnics and cheese and the price of coffee – or was it cafés? In the street, Vern Melling's truck rumbled by, carrying a small mountain of fly-circled trash, and from a juniper bush below the window a bee floated up, testing the flow of cooler air along the glass.

The rest of the class began to arrive, a hubbub of voices and flung gym bags and books slapped down on desks. The girl in the light-green dress looked around, curiously. She did not see – though Joe saw – how in the aisle behind her Elaine Brown hugged her books to her chest and directed a tolerant smile at the interloper who had stolen her desk.

"Bien!" Mr. Kay said loudly: their signal to quiet down. "Alors mes amis," he said. A book dropped, and through the open window the bee floated in, drifting upwards towards the fluorescent lights.

The teacher discovered Elaine, waiting.

"Ah Elaine! Ton banc!"

"C'est votre banc?" the girl said. Silence was spreading through the room as the others became aware of her.

The girl started to rise, but Elaine said she was happy to sit at the back. "You're sure?" the girl said. In her voice was a hint of laughter, as if she were secretly enjoying this bit of confusion. Hugging her books, Elaine walked to the back, smiling a prim, self-congratulatory smile.

Speaking in French, Mr. Kay introduced the new girl: Anna Macrimmon. The name sounded odd to Joe, a patch of rocky land amidst the smooth lawns of the French. She had turned to the class and Joe looked again into her face, drinking every detail: the birthmark on her cheek, the faint Asiatic slope of the eyes, a pale, unusual

green under her dark and well-defined brows. Her bobbed hair with
its thick bangs gave her a tomboyish look, he thought.

"Bonjour," she said to the whole class.

One or two ragged bonjours answered back.

"Non, non," Mr. Kay admonished. "Encore! Plus fort!"

They managed it better the second time. Joe was chagrined, on
her behalf. Their welcome must have seemed childish to her, he
thought, like something in grade school.

Mr. Kay handed out scrap paper. The test was about to begin.
The teacher's brogues squeaked as he paced slowly at the front of the
room, reading out, *en anglais*, the sentences they were to translate.
"He will have come. You ought to stay. She will have been there."
Pens scratched and tapped in the pauses. Anna Macrimmon tilted her
head to the side as she studied what she had written. The wing of her
hair fell forward, and she tucked it back behind her ear. He saw that
her ear stuck out a little, a flaw of sorts. Above, the bee followed the
fluorescent lights and then abruptly glided down to touch the poster
of the Roman theatre at Orange: the golden ruins under their blue,
savage sky.

In small groups, the students of 13A walked along a sidewalk white
as bone and as straight as a runway, between the carports and burnt
lawns of the new housing development known as the Shade Survey.
Every year, Mr. Mann invited his senior history class to lunch at his
home. Joe trudged along beside Smiley, who was telling some story
about how he and Freddie Farmer had been nearly killed on the
weekend. They'd been driving along the Johnsonville Highway, going
almost ninety, Smiley said, and it wasn't only dark, it was foggy, and
suddenly they'd noticed the road curving away to the right and they
were headed to the left, into God only knew what. "Shit, man,"
Smiley said, and a great happiness shone in his deep-set eyes, "I
thought we'd bought it."

line of the dam's edge. Beyond, the Bridge Street bridge and the backs of the downtown stores seemed at once to move and to remain fixed above the metallic glint of the rapids. But what predominated was the vast, ecstatic light itself, a presence that seemed to lean off the still-hidden reaches of autumn.

"Try to imagine," Mann said, "another day like this. A hundred, five hundred years ago. Some things don't change, at least not very quickly. This kind of light. The crickets. This has always been a good place to be. There are springs in the hillside, hardwood trees for timber and shade and fuel. Good soil. This view of the valley where you can see your friends or enemies approach.

"Of course, other people knew this place before Shade did – Indian people. I've found arrowheads in the hillside, bits of pottery. We call our town Attawan, after these people, but in fact we have no idea what they called themselves. It was the Hurons who called them the Attawan – the full name, the correct name, is actually Attawandaeron, quite a mouthful. The word means, 'People who speak a slightly different language,' and it tells us that the people who lived around here spoke an Iroquoian dialect, not too different from the Hurons' own. Anyway, these people, the Attawandaeron, disappeared about four hundred years ago. Disappeared completely," Mann added, and paused. A cricket went on turning its squeaky wheel. Faintly, mournfully, a diesel horn sounded beyond the town. With Mann's word "disappeared," some profound absence had been summoned. All felt it, and were held by it.

"What happened to them?" someone said finally, unable to bear the tension. There was a stir among the others, a deepening of attention: they had to know if they themselves had survived this absence.

Mann shrugged, and shook his head. "We don't really know. They may have been wiped out by disease, or by Iroquois raiders coming up from the south. Maybe they made some bad political choice, you know, allied themselves with the wrong power. Maybe they didn't keep up technologically – were too slow to get guns or other things made of iron. In any case, they're gone, and we've inherited these late-summer days of theirs, which they must have found as lovely as we find them."

Mann paused, frowning at the ground as if slightly chagrined at his outburst of poetic sentiment. His audience remained still. He went on: "When Abraham Shade came here, in the early 1820s, he fell for this place immediately. We have his diaries' word on that. He always said the place felt haunted to him. He and his family were the first whites to settle here, but he claimed he could sense the people who had lived here before, even though they'd been gone for, oh, two centuries or more at that point. It was his brother, John – John was a bit of a scholar, in an amateur nineteenth-century way – who told him what we know of the Indian people in this region. Shade decided to call the town after them. A lot of people didn't like it at the time. There was quite a debate. But the name stuck . . ."

By moving his head slightly, Joe could see Anna Macrimmon. She was sitting on the ground, under an oak tree, with her hands clasped around her shins, her chin lifted a little as she listened.

They crowded into the long living room lined with books and comfortable-looking couches and chairs. Over the massive fieldstone fireplace hung a small, framed painting of mountains falling sheer to a glacial lake. In a corner sat a spinning wheel like some strange, upended wooden bicycle.

It was the first time Joe had been in Mann's house, the first time he'd looked into the teacher's private life, and he was alive to every object. At the same time he felt uncomfortable and rushed, aware of his stinking shirt, and of the others who, with no idea how important this all was, crowded around Mann like cattle. He hated having to share Mann's house with them, hated that Anna Macrimmon had come on this day of all days, when he wasn't ready for her. He could sense her, somewhere in the hot press of bodies behind him.

Mann said, "If you look down at the floor."

Joe looked down miserably at the wide, darkly gleaming boards. A drop of his sweat fell.

"Usually, you'd expect pine floors in a pioneer house like this. But this is oak, two-inch oak laid across oak beams. In fact, again unusually, almost all the wood in the house is oak. Can anybody tell me why that might be?"

Silence met his question. The brown eyes in the expressionless face swept slowly over them, challenging. While the pendulum clock ticked from the mantelpiece, a faint nervous urgency spread among the students: they knew the teacher was capable of waiting minutes for an answer.

Joe put up his hand. Mann nodded at someone else.

Brad Long spoke in his deep, pleasant voice, which easily filled the room with its usual hint of happy scorn – surely it was all so obvious! "There was lots of oak around here – it was handy. And also, being the kind of guy he was, he knew he wanted to be number one, so he put in the best."

"Good," Mann said.

Joe burned at the lost compliment: he knew as much. But Brad wasn't through.

"I guess he wanted us to stand here one day and admire him." Brad raised his large hands and looked towards the ceiling, as if addressing a gallery of ancestors, looking down appreciatively on the scene from heaven. "Great floors, Abe!"

The class laughed. Joe thought he heard Anna Macrimmon's voice behind him, silver among the rest.

They ate lunch outside. Joe took a sandwich and paper plate from the long table Mann had set out under the locusts and retreated to a shady spot near a concrete birdbath. Anna Macrimmon was still moving through the line. With her were Liz McVey and Sheila Benson, a pretty, sharp-featured girl with bouffanted hair and a hard, snorting laugh. They carried their plates to a little knoll under a tree and sat on the ground, tugging their skirts over their knees. A few minutes later, Joe watched as Brad Long joined them. He lowered his rangy frame onto the dry grass at their feet, stretching himself out with all the ease in the world – a Roman at a banquet – before the prim statuary of their folded legs.

Brad raised his arm, gesturing lazily to make some point, and Joe saw how the cuff of his pale-blue shirt was turned back with a pleasing yet casual exactness, turned back once and kept there by some magical, gravity-defying power, unlike the cuffs of his own sad shirts, which fell down constantly unless they were rolled up several times. Now Brad's laugh came, tolerant, self-enjoying, warm. Joe saw Anna Macrimmon shake her head in disbelief or denial, saw the heavy silk of her hair move like something alive. But she was smiling too, or fighting back a smile, as if to say, Go on with you.

A little way off, a group of Brad's friends – boys from the North End gang – were watching Brad with barely suppressed merriment, as if he were doing what they hadn't the nerve to try themselves.

Joe picked at his tuna-fish sandwich. Ever since he'd seen Anna Macrimmon that first afternoon on the river, she had seemed to exist for him only. And now she had become the property, in a sense, of everybody who cared to look at her, including Brad Long, *who had no idea who she was, what her true value was, not really.*

"Yugga."

Smiley. He sat down cross-legged beside Joe, his plate loaded with booty.

"Food," he grunted, playing the caveman. Joe looked away.

Mayonnaise leaked from Smiley's mouth. "That new girl," he said, "I keep thinkin' I've seen her somewhere."

"How could that be?" Joe said coldly.

Smiley ate with hunched, predatory enjoyment. "I dunno. It's weird. She's pretty good-lookin'."

Joe said nothing. Smiley looked up with staring frankness, his mouth open.

"Don't you think she's good-lookin'?"

But a lane had appeared in the headlights. They'd run over a gate and smashed the grill on Freddie Farmer's dad's car, but otherwise no damage done.

Thirty yards ahead, Anna Macrimmon was walking between Liz McVey and Elaine Brown. Joe caught the back of her head, vanishing and reappearing among intervening bodies. Even when he lost sight of her, or looked elsewhere – at the sidewalk, or into Smiley's tiny eyes, racooned with fatigue – he could sense her presence, a peculiar, magnetic darkness in the blazing sun. He had failed his French test, and had an intimation that worse lay ahead. His lack of a shower had left him sweating, a disaster when he considered that he was also wearing his red-and-white-checked sports shirt. The cloth was cheap, and stank as his sweat reacted with the dye.

They went up the narrow drive between high cedar hedges, past the plaque that told them that Abraham Shade, the founder of Attawan, had built this house in 1823. Then the house itself appeared, a long, low cottage with unshuttered windows, surrounded by tall locusts. Patches of sun trembled on its walls of whitewashed plaster. The blue door stood open.

They sat on the parched front lawn, under the huge, arthritic locusts, while Mann talked to them with his back to the valley of the Shade. The teacher – Joe's mentor and favourite – was a slim, rather short man, his heavy eyelids pouched with melancholy, his thinning white hair combed forward in points like Julius Caesar. He spoke more quietly than any of their teachers and, on the whole, said less. Yet there was something in his slow, abraded speech that held them, a kind of casual sincerity, as though it would be impossible for him to say anything but what he actually thought. He was retiring at the end of the year.

Mann spoke of Abraham Shade and his house. Behind him, the valley floated in late-summer sun. Details were visible, miniaturized by distance: the webbing of the CN trestle and, glimpsed through its stone legs, the brown water of the Shade, easing towards the sheer

"She's all right. I haven't really noticed."

"You should. She's right over there."

To Joe's horror, Smiley pointed.

Joe looked off miserably across the lawn, over trembling islands of shade and sun, into a lilac bush. He wanted to start the day, his life, over again.

"Not there. Over there."

"For Christ's sake, I *know* where she is. Stop pointing!"

After a moment Smiley said, "I wonder what that thing is on her face – you see that?"

"No."

"Look at it. It's like some kind of burn."

Joe lurched to his feet and started to walk quickly towards the house, picking his way among groups of students. Just then Mann emerged, carrying a pitcher of ice water. Normally Joe was happy to see the teacher. He liked to stop after class to talk with him, finding in his power of listening – that stillness – something that made his own thoughts rise and come clear. But he wasn't ready for Mann now. He asked where the washroom was.

Mann put down his pitcher and led Joe through the house, which sprawled to the rear through a series of additions. The teacher moved with surprising swiftness, his small feet in their worn, pointed shoes pattering on the tiles. The bathroom was behind the kitchen. "The old summer kitchen," Mann said, and as he stepped back to let Joe pass, the teacher touched him lightly on the back.

Joe closed the door, fit the bolt, stripped off his shirt, and began to wash his face and upper torso, sloshing up water almost wildly. His face in the mirror seemed an assembly of imperfections. Under his right eye, a pimple raised its minaret of shame. Patting himself dry, he studied a framed photo hanging beside the window. Two young men, both wearing shorts and white shirts, their arms draped loosely over each other's shoulders, grinned back at him with abandoned smiles of pure happiness. Behind them soared the white, tentlike summit of a distant mountain. He saw with a start that one of the men was Mann: Mann with dark curly hair, his eyes less pouched, Mann in the bright disguise of youth. The other man had the kind of smooth, almost feminine face Joe remembered from a painting he'd seen in a book: the unearthly face of an angel by Raphael. This is crazy, he thought, breaking suddenly from the image with a sense of alarm. I'll speak to her. I have to speak to her.

He passed through the house with a feeling that he was living under a sentence, a feeling that he was being dragged forward in a kind of dream-state by his decision. And yet, the whole time, he told himself he was free: maybe he'd speak to her, maybe he wouldn't. He was afraid of his own cowardice, and half-looking forward to its intervention. When he reached the front step he glanced across the lawn and saw with thudding heart that she had got up, that she was moving away from the others with a paper cup in her hand, following the hedge that ran from Mann's yard into the adjacent property.

And then Mann was there. The teacher held up an old-fashioned-looking camera, with an accordion chamber of black fabric, and asked if he could take Joe's picture. He'd taken every graduating class for years now, he said, candid shots, it had become a tradition. He positioned Joe against the door, softly gripping his biceps to move him back a little. As Mann frowned into his viewfinder, Joe watched Anna Macrimmon drift down the line of hedge, her head raised and tilted a bit to one side, as if skeptically.

"There we go. Handsomest fellow in the class," Mann said with a grin. A moment later, laconically: "I see we have a new girl."

"Yes." Joe evaded the teacher's eyes.

"Why don't you introduce me to her?"

"I don't really know her. She just came."

"Then we'll introduce each other."

Walking with Mann under the locusts, he was under sentence again, marching out to his execution. They passed Smiley, who looked up from his sandwich. "Yugga," his friend said quietly. As if he knew.

She was walking along the other side of a large garden, towards a belvedere on the brow of the hill. The untended garden belonged to the old Bannerman estate, which was now a nursing home: a tangled place where the surviving flowers fought silently with the weeds.

Mann was going on about the arrowheads and other artifacts he had found in the hill. Someone from the museum in Toronto was coming to have a look at the site. Joe nodded automatically, scarcely hearing.

Now she was in the belvedere, kneeling with one knee on the narrow wooden bench, looking into the valley. As they approached, she turned. Each time Joe saw her face it seemed new to him, a revelation. Again he saw that dart of amusement in her eyes, as if their arrival were the beginning of an adventure she had half-expected. But there was also a candour that chilled him. He wondered if she remembered him from the river.

Mann introduced himself and shook her hand. "This is Joe Walker, one of your classmates."

"Yes," she said, putting out her hand. Joe took it, and was conscious of its firmness in his, and of the coldness of his own.

She looked back to Mann. "I was just thinking about what you said. About how Shade fell in love with this place. Do you think certain places call to us?"

"I suppose it depends to some degree on your individual psychology," Mann said, "and of course there's the general human need for shelter. But there's also something beyond those things. People, at least most of them, don't like to pitch their tents just anywhere."

She was watching the teacher with her head a little to the side, ignoring Joe. He stood like a servant, miserable and grateful.

"Take this place," Mann said, gesturing to the valley behind her. "There's something about it that satisfies a need."

"Beauty," she suggested.

"Yes, maybe it's as simple as that," the teacher said, his eyebrows going up.

"Or as complicated." She was looking at Mann with a kind of fencing irony, clearly enjoying herself.

"Indeed. I wasn't born here, not like Joe," Mann said. Her gaze flicked over Joe and returned to the teacher. "But when I came – well, I was rather like Shade – I felt I belonged here."

"It reminds me a little of Europe," she said.

"Oh yes? What places?"

"Oh . . ." She trailed another, idle look over Joe. He had never in his life heard people discuss beauty as a thing in itself, as though it were possible to meet Beauty walking down Bridge Street. "The Dordogne, maybe, bits of Italy. You know, limestone and bridges. That *old* feeling."

"Yes!" Mann said, with a sudden outburst of enthusiasm. When he smiled, which he did rarely, his face was radiant. "I've often felt that myself. The feeling of lives that have gone before. Of course the spirit is different here, and I'm afraid the food isn't as good."

"I don't suppose," she said.

"Where are you from?" Mann said. He glanced at Joe, as if inviting him to participate.

She gave a short laugh at that, as if this were at once the most simple and most complex question in the world: really, it had no answer. "I was *born* in Montreal," she said, with an arch emphasis, as if getting born were a kind of joke, "but my father's worked all over the place. Abroad mostly. I've lived almost as much in Europe as here. My mother's French."

"Aha," Mann said. He looked again at Joe, with a kind of shining blankness. Joe felt he was invisible to them both. He had never been to Europe, which was a mythical land to him, a land of wars and towers. He felt completely out of his depth. He shifted and smiled vaguely as they talked, and hoped she couldn't smell his shirt.

"So what brings you to Attawan?" Mann said.

"Oh, my father's working here now. He's an accountant. His company's just bought some mills here."

"Bannerman's," Mann said. "Joe's father works there too."

"Really," she said, sounding not at all interested. But at least she looked at him again.

"He's in the sweater mill," Joe said, his face heating. He wished Mann had never mentioned his father. He wanted no past just now; he just wanted to stand here, as new as she was.

There was a pause, excruciating to Joe, who felt he should keep the conversation going. He grinned but could think of nothing to say.

"Say, listen," Mann said, rousing himself. "I'm taking a picture of everyone here, it's a tradition with my graduating classes. If you wouldn't mind –"

Anna Macrimmon stood with her back against the dilapidated belvedere. Her playfulness had suddenly evaporated, replaced by a kind of moody tolerance of the process, as she squinted against the sun, turning away the cheek with the birthmark. When it was over, Mann said, blushing inexplicably, "Well. Good. I'm sure Joe would like to show you around." He left within seconds.

Anna Macrimmon looked at Joe.

"I've seen you before," she said flatly.

He thought of denying it, but with a nod his admission escaped him.

"Where?" she said rather grimly.

"That –"

"No, no, let me guess!" She went on looking at him, as if his face were a painting. He *knew* he was blushing, knew the pimple under his eye was getting bigger, knew his smell must soon reach her, if it hadn't already.

"The bridge," she said. "That time with the McVeys –"

"I didn't yell anything," he said.

"You were in the water," she said, squinting at him.

"I was telling them to stop –"

"*Were* you!" she cried skeptically.

"Scout's honour," he said, raising two fingers.

She was looking at him mischievously now. "You know, the McVeys were *quite* upset."

There was a hint of accusation here. He nodded.

"So why were you doing it? Why were *they* doing it?"

He shook his head, as if to say, Stupid kid's stuff, who can explain it? But she was not going to let him off so easily. "Walk with me," she said. "Tell me."

They went down the wide, grassy path. The back of her hand brushed his.

"I'm waiting," she said.

He knew perfectly well why the others had taunted the McVeys: they disliked them for their wealth, their snobbery, for the fact that Doc McVey was landlord to several of their families, for the fact that they'd come down to the river to gawk.

"There's too much history to it," he said.

"That sounds fascinating –"

"It's sort of a neighbourhood thing. Stupid, really."

"You mean like a class thing?"

He thought she meant "class" as in school.

"Most of those kids weren't in their class, the McVeys' class."

"That's what I mean," she said. She looked at him, wondering. "They're what? Working class?"

He was sure he was going to burn up in front of her. He never used the term "working class," though he knew perfectly well what she was getting at. Working class was lower than middle class. His father was working class; his mother was, or had been, middle class: what did that make him, a kind of mongrel?

"It's stupid, really," he said. "It's because Doc McVey owns a lot of houses. Some of those people pay rent to him. They think he charges too much."

"Aha!" she said. "And does he?"

"I have no idea. We own our own house."

She studied him as they walked along.

"I'm sorry, I'm embarrassing you. We'll talk of something else."

"Not embarrassed," he lied. But he was relieved when she turned her attention to the outbuildings of the Bannerman estate. They moved towards the great house, its high-pitched slate roofs looming over the treetops, passing by an assortment of sheds, and the gardener's stone cottage. She peered in the windows, where glass shelves held African violets and knick-knacks, into the gloomy little rooms beyond. Her forwardness amazed him. He knew they were trespassing but did not say so. In her curiosity she seemed unconscious of such concerns, and he felt he should be too, as if she were teaching him about some wider form of freedom.

That evening after supper, Joe climbed over the dyke and stood watching the river. Upstream, a small rapid turned its liquid body between rocks: a flashing of white in the dimness. Everything had changed. Because of the half-hour they had spent together, everything he looked at – the hill lifting in darkness, the ghostly band of children traipsing noisily over the footbridge to Lions Park, the sky's last, red wound – bore her sign.

She was not in class the next day. Taking attendance on his clipboard, Mr. Kay glanced over his horn-rims at her empty desk and hiked his eyebrows slightly – a mere twitch of surprise before his round face subsided into the stoic blandness behind which adults lived their remote lives. To Joe, it was as if the teacher had passed nonchalantly by a burning building.

That morning, everything was saturated with her absence: a deserted classroom, the jumpers of the girls phys. ed. class as they flowed across a sun-beaten field, the tribal echo of laughter from a washroom, an absence that still contained the promise of her, for it seemed possible she might materialize unexpectedly, as she had the first time, and the second too. He wondered if she had decided not to come back at all. Her powers in this matter seemed absolute, she was everywhere and nowhere, as fluid and invisible as his mood, a clear sea on which he drifted, becalmed. In biology he sliced his finger on a scalpel. The blood, a small red sac at his knuckle, surprised him, because it *was* him. It was a shock to remember that he had his own body, his own separate life.

At noon, Sandy waited for him in the little park across from the school: a waif in a shapeless plaid dress, coming forward with a hopeful half-smile, from under the caved shadow of a maple. He was appalled by her ordinariness, by her very existence, so small and finite and limited. Her powers touched nothing beyond her, not a single blade of grass.

He fell silent as they trudged along Shade Street, past mansions presiding with humourless reserve over long, sloping lawns. Overhead, a cicada poured its electricity into the late-summer heat. He felt the past had reached out to claim him. He had become someone else with Anna Macrimmon; now he was his old, humdrum self again, sweating and disconsolate in his best shirt, a dark-green corduroy that was too hot for the day and not nearly good enough for his purposes. What had happened with Anna Macrimmon had been a dream, an illusion. This was real: the armhole of Sandy's sleeveless dress, where the band of her sweat-stained bra showed; her bright, chattering voice saying nothing he cared about.

They passed the mouth of Senator's Lane. Boys were flinging sticks into a tree. Clumps of leaves fell, chestnuts in their spiky rind like the heads of medieval war clubs. She said, "I guess I was expecting you last night?"

Her very gentleness, her care for his mood, irritated him.

"What for?"

Her flat face lifted to him, an offering of herself.

"My essay?"

"What essay?" he scowled, trying to evade his rising guilt. It reached him anyway. "I'm sorry. I forgot. I was busy." And a moment later, more gently: "Did you finish it?"

She shook her head, like a child, he thought.

"It's not due till next Monday."

"Maybe we can do it on the weekend," he said. Immediately, the thought of even a few more days with her oppressed him.

Anna Macrimmon returned the next morning. Joe was sitting at his desk in Mr. Kay's room, waiting for the class to begin, when on some instinct he turned to see her making her way among the students who had not yet taken their seats, threading a course with her books held, in that way girls had, to her chest.

Her face restored itself to him in a heart's leap of glad recognition: of course, *that's* what she looked like! In the intervening day, so many particulars had slipped from memory. Now her face reclaimed its own reality: the neat helmet of her ash-blonde hair, her dark brows, and of course the mark on her cheek, which appeared just now like the image of a small, pale, half-ruined flower.

Yet she was different. It was her clothes. The green sheath had been replaced by a crisp white blouse with sleeves that ended partway down her forearms, a full skirt in some rich shade of green, threaded with hints of other colours, with a broad belt. He watched in astonishment as she came closer. Her change in appearance seemed like the evidence of some mysterious fecundity, like the flowering of day lilies in his mother's garden, each morning new blossoms in new places, lifting their trumpets on the still air.

After the class, he caught up to her in the hall.

"Hi there," he said casually, falling in beside her.

There was something unsurprised and wholly accepting in her glance, as if his arrival were nothing special. He was put off balance.

"Hi *there*," she said, with an irony he could not grasp.

"Were you sick, or –"

She was searching his face with a simple calm.

"Or what?"

"I missed you," he said, and blanched at his mistake.

"Thank you," she said quietly, looking away.

It was hard to keep beside her among the jostling, streaming bodies. A locker clattered shut, and someone nearby growled in an undertone, "Eat your nose!"

They went into the biology lab, with its black desks and deep sinks. A smell of formaldehyde penetrated everywhere, from vats at the front of the room. The class was dissecting cats. Joe pulled out his stool, aware that Anna Macrimmon had stopped several desks behind him. He kept playing and replaying his appalling gaffe. He felt like pounding his head on the desk.

Smiley had fetched their cat. Lying stiffly on its side on a metal tray, it looked drowned, the eyes crimped shut, its soaked, matted fur standing up in points. Joe turned the page of his notebook, looking bleakly over his drawings. The previous week they had cut up frogs: the yellow skin of the bellies pulled back like waistcoats; the gum-wad hearts turned grey by the preserving chemical. Such knowledge had nothing to do with Anna Macrimmon, it seemed. She was behind him now and somehow, in her power, she had withdrawn meaning from everything, from his carefully drawn pictures, from Smiley, bent with his knife to the cat.

He let Smiley do most of the dissecting, while he half-heartedly made notes and diagrams. Mr. Brunt drifted by, an intense little man with an oversized head, like a baby bird's. He chewed a pencil and shouted instructions in an almost incomprehensible, chastising way. It was like being harassed by a barking dog, though one whose bark was far worse than his bite. Joe looked out the window, across the burnt playing fields towards the huddled ranch-style houses of the Shade Survey. A black cat was slinking across a lawn.

From the back of the room, over a low murmur of voices, a girl's voice spoke up clearly, saying she couldn't do this, she *wouldn't* do this. Anna Macrimmon.

He saw her looking across the desks towards Mr. Brunt. Her face had coloured, filled with an expression of disbelief sharpened by anger. She was demanding that the teacher give an accounting of himself.

"This is *disgusting*," she said for the second time. "Where did you *get* these cats?"

Mr. Brunt removed the pencil from his mouth, gave a hollow chuckle. "You going to faint?" he said. He seemed hopeful she *might*.

"That's not the point! I can't do this, not to *her*!"

She was holding up her hands – a scalpel was in one – and looking down at the grey, soaked form in front of her. Everyone watched in amazement. She had spoken to the teacher as if he were an equal, or even an inferior: it was unthinkable.

"Lie down if you're going to faint," Mr. Brunt said. His face had grown tomato red.

Anna Macrimmon shook her head. She bent down behind her desk – Joe wondered if she *had* fainted – and a moment later popped up with her books and went swiftly from the room, leaving the door ajar. Liz McVey hurried after her, a silent helper.

"Meatheads," Mr. Brunt said. It was his favourite phrase of disapproval. He put his pencil back in his mouth, like a stopper into the vial of his fury. "There's always one," he mumbled, forcing a grin. No one laughed. No one understood what had happened, but the breaching of the usual borders of obedience and decorum had touched them deeply, as if they had witnessed an act of violence. Only they did not quite know, as they turned back to their trays, where exactly the violence lay.

That night Joe dreamed of a cat. It lay on its side, under a clear, shimmering bath of formaldehyde, not moving. There was a sound of quick, shallow breathing, as if someone were labouring in a high fever. It was not the cat that was breathing – it was still, or almost still, under the warping shine of the chemical. The nightmare did not change focus, or show him anything else. It was like being shut in a brightly lit room hardly bigger than he was.

Anna Macrimmon was excused from dissection and allowed to learn anatomy from her textbook. The next day she sat at the back of the lab by herself, working at her books with a peculiar, private intensity that made him sad and wistful. She wore a thick, black ribbon bound over her hair. The change seemed to Joe to have something to do with the events of the previous day, as if she were in mourning for the cats, though at the same time there was something sharp and aggressive in the new look: she did not smile, not that he noticed. It was clear he scarcely existed for her.

One morning – it was a week after the cat incident – he was walking by himself through the North End, on his way to school, when he saw her coming towards him down Senator's Lane, down the deep, sun-splotched cut between two big Victorian houses. She was wearing a sand-coloured dress with a shallow V-neck and was walking with her head down, her books cradled loosely in her arms. She was quite close before she broke from her daydream and saw him, saying his name in a friendly enough way, but with that hint of flatness that had so discomfited him before.

He had picked up a chestnut in his nervousness, and now stood rolling it in his fingers.

"What's that?"

He gave the nut to her, and she examined it with obvious pleasure, putting it to her face to smell it. "It's like mahogany. And what's this?" She picked at the bits of sticky white stuff that clung to it. He noticed that the skin around her nail was shiny and red.

"I'm not sure. All the new ones have it when they come out of the shell."

He helped her find a couple of others, which she put into the pocket of her dress. "This is one of the best trees for them," he said, and watched her intently – her throat, her hair – as she gazed up into the foliage.

"Do you live near here?" he said.

"Over on Banting. I haven't walked this way before."

He nearly said, I'm glad you did, but managed to hold back. They walked together up Shade.

"Too bad," he said, "about that cat business."

She did not immediately respond, and he wondered if he'd made a misstep. He did not seem able to be natural with her. She said, "I'm probably too sensitive about some things. It just occurred to me that that cat hadn't died of old age."

"He gets them from farms," Joe said. "Barn cats."

"Barn cats?"

"They live half-wild in the barns. They keep down the mice."

"A good and useful life," she said. "I don't know why they have to die. It's not as if we don't already know about cat anatomy."

"No," he said with a nervous laugh. There was a quickness in her, a quick, tart opinionatedness, a little intimidating.

"Does he kill them himself?"

"I don't know."

"I'll bet he does. The man gives me the creeps."

A bee skimmed across the road, passing them at knee level. A red Studebaker swished down the tree-shaded street, and a woman in one of the large houses on the embankment to the east paused in the sweeping of her porch to look at them. Late summer had brought everything to perfection, though the autumn was present too, a honing of the air.

Anna had stopped to fumble in her binder. She extracted a paper, shaking out its folds with one hand and offering it to him. "I wrote a poem about it."

He took the page in the glare of light. What did he know about poetry? Tennyson's "Ulysses" – he liked that one – "Daffodils," bits of Hamlet's soliloquies, they knocked around in his head and sometimes, at odd moments, they'd pop out. "To be or not to be." "Now, fair Hippolyta, our nuptial hour draws on apace." He looked at the page with its column of typescript and suddenly, the slight touch of a breeze, he sensed her vulnerability as she waited for his reaction.

The cat is not dead.
That is only the illusion of her wet, spiked fur,
Her stillness
Her buttoned-down eyes
Her last, desperate run stiffened into an emblem
Of former cat.

The cat is not here.
What you see in these packed organs
This grey waste of cells
Is only a trace of cat –
Cat-tracks
Printing the snow of our notebooks.

The cat has gone elsewhere.
Once again
The cat has eluded us:
A whisper in dry grasses,
A howl of dismay
From the country of her other lives.

Reaching the last line, he felt something. He wasn't sure it was his
nervousness around Anna Macrimmon, his terror springing a trap
door to new depths, or if it was the poem itself, its strangeness, like
a bullet severing water.

"It's good," he said, and coloured at the appalling inadequacy of
his remark. "It's very good – wonderful! That last line." He shook his
head, stymied by his amazement.

She took the page back from him, and they went on without
speaking. Just knowing her the little he did, he had been pitched into
new country. But this, her country, was stranger than he had realized.
There were huge, shadowy regions, tricky paths, a wilderness. He
was lost, and he didn't like it. At the moment he felt he was failing
her, in his silence.

"You're a poet," he said to the space in front of him. "I mean, I don't know about poetry. But *that*!"

He glanced at her suddenly and found her looking at him; there was something alert in her eyes, searching, but he couldn't decipher it.

"Do you have more?"

"A few," she said.

"I'd like to see them some time. I mean, if you –"

He thought she was blushing.

"I'm sorry, Anna, if you don't want to –"

"No, I'll show you some time. I want to."

"Good!"

"Good," she said, a dull echo. He felt she was slipping away. Desperate, before his advantage disappeared entirely, he said, "There's a dance next week, Friday. Maybe not the greatest dance in the world, but I wonder if you'd like to go with me."

She looked up the street. "I don't think so, Joe."

Her voice sounded muffled. Not for the first time, he felt she was older than he.

"Or we could go to a movie, or just . . ."

"Don't take this the wrong way, but I'm just not up for that sort of thing."

"What sort of thing are you up for then?"

She smiled faintly, shaking her head a little, as if she found him incorrigible and a bit amusing. She did not answer.

He felt as if she had taken him very gently and put him aside. She was friendly enough afterwards, so that he wondered if she had dismissed him at all. But no: it was done. He licked his wounds for a day or two and then – he could scarcely help himself – began to shadow her again. He contrived meetings in the hall, and a couple of times ran into her on the way to school. He was careful not to force anything, to pretend to be at his ease, camouflaging his true feelings. Once or twice he tried to push things further, but she rebuffed him. He understood it was a matter of trust. If he did not chase her, then from time to time, for a little while, they could be together. Watching her, laughing at some joke she'd made, pretending she was only one of a dozen girls he liked, he drank her in secret, deeply and gratefully.

And if there had been only two of them in the world – this was a fantasy of his – then friendship might have warmed to something else. But others were present: the North End kids had closed around her like a herd welcoming their own kind. She was often alone – it seemed to him her natural state – but when she wasn't she was with Liz McVey and Diane Cochrane and Sheila Benson and Carol Jeunesse – all the reigning clique of girls. To his eyes, they were her inferiors. Walking with her down the halls, holding their books to their chests or under their arms, in their plaid skirts and neat blouses, their cardigans and blazers and cropped or bouffanted hair, they seemed her attendants only, ladies to her queen.

And Brad Long was clearly in the picture. Brad Long with his easy ways and fine clothes – those always-new-looking shirts, their tab collars left so deftly open, the soft cardigans, the neatly creased khakis, the chocolate Hush Puppies – Brad was paying a lot of attention to Anna Macrimmon. His locker was beside Anna's – damnable luck – but Joe thought there was more than coincidence in the number of times he saw Brad leaning there, leaning over her as she bent to select something from the narrow cupboard or simply listened to him, held in the protective space his tall body made, held by his low voice that surrounded her with a chuckling casualness, everything easy and smooth and carrying them on together like two idling lovers in a canoe.

Once, too, he saw them walk away together after school, up Angle Street, which was telling: Anna Macrimmon lived in that direction, but Brad didn't. He wondered if she'd asked him to her house. He followed them, at a distance, and saw them turn up Cairn, but after that, wary of being seen himself, he lost them. They could have gone into a house (he didn't know which one) or turned down another street. He was too upset, too aware of his own pathetic absurdity to follow farther, but that night it seemed to him that he had certainly lost her, friendship was surely the most he could expect. And yet there was an anger in him, with her, with Brad Long, for he felt he was better than Brad, *and better for her too*, and it seemed a major fault in her, the first he'd discovered, that she could not see this for herself.

One day soon afterwards, he and Anna Macrimmon came to the fountain in the hall together. She bent to the silver knob – it seemed alive under its quivering beads of water – holding back her hair with the tips of her fingers.

"So good," she said, wiping her mouth with her hand as she turned to him. "Cold."

"It's from springs outside of town," Joe told her. "They get it before it even comes out of the ground." And remembering dimly something from their first conversation, at Mann's house, he added, "From the limestone."

Something sparked in her green eyes; he felt quickened by the sudden, stark watching at their centres. "I love the word 'limestone,'" she said, studying his face, his mouth. "It's such an odd word. There's lime trees, and the colour lime, and the lime they used to throw on dead people."

"Quicklime!" he said happily.

"Yes! And then there's the stone," she said. "All those things shouldn't go together, but they do, because of the word. The word melts them, fuses them, somehow."

She seemed almost intoxicated with their wordplay: he felt challenged.

"It makes me think of secret things, deep in the earth," he said, still held by her gaze. He felt half-drunk himself, beyond the bounds of his usual nervousness. His mind was dancing. "Underground rivers. Caverns."

"*Caves,*" she said ominously.

"I know a cave near here," he told her. "It's not very deep, really, but it's made of limestone."

She looked at him brightly: she liked the sound of *that*.

"What's this?" Brad Long said.

He had approached them from behind, grinning.

"Oh Brad," she said, glancing back to Joe with an air of complicity. "We were making poetry. You wouldn't understand."

"I *love* poetry," Brad protested, in his joking way.

"I know you do, poor boy," she said, patting Brad's cheek. Joe, who had been feeling wonderful about his exchange with her, was appalled at their familiarity.

The three of them went into English together. Ahead of Joe, Brad brought up his hand behind Anna to the place where her blouse met her skirt. Joe couldn't tell if Brad was actually touching her, or simply coming close, in a gesture of protection and ownership meant as much for his eyes as for her.

9

WHEN THE PHONE SHRILLED, Alf had his hands in the innards of a knitting machine. Quarter to nine. The lights were on in the deserted mill. In a nearby window, a yellow sky hovered behind the reflections of the machines. He had often complained to Margaret about having to work late, but the truth was he liked the quiet and isolation of the mill at his hour, when the knitting machines stood silently in their rows and he could concentrate on one thing at a time. He ignored the ringing and it stopped abruptly. Two minutes later it started again. Wiping his hands on a rag, he hurried up the aisle into the stark cubicle that was Matt Honnegger's office. It was Margaret, gasping out his name as if she'd just been running. Jamie hadn't come home, she said. He'd gone out after supper by himself and now he was an hour late. Joe had already searched the Island and the park.

The fear he experienced seemed small and faraway, as if a fish had jumped out in the centre of a calm lake. "He'll be along," he told her. "He's just traipsing around with one of his friends. Probably out in the woods."

"All his friends are at home."

Hesitating, he thought of the night outside, the long shadows of woodlots edging across fields, the cold, remorseless fret of water as it undermined banks, frothed over stone. He intuited all this in a flash – the wild lands to the northwest of town – and it woke him to a sudden, plunging loneliness, as if it were himself who was lost.

When he swung into the driveway, the headlights of the Biscayne caught Margaret and Penny, turning on the top of the dyke to look at him. Behind them, Lookout Hill loomed darkly. His daughter's white socks flashed and criss-crossed as she ran suddenly towards her mother. Below, Red's tawny eyes burned. A few minutes later Joe appeared and the family stood by the picnic table while Alf tried to calm them and make a plan. They were all looking to him for a solution, he could feel the pressure even from Joe, as if in this hour of crisis some atavistic instinct to turn to the oldest, strongest man had pushed aside all the usual subtle and not-so-subtle challenges to his authority. But Margaret was only giving him this authority provisionally, he knew, sensing an impatience in her that verged on fury. "We'll go up the river," he told them. "We should check that fort he made with Johnny Simms. He's always talking about going out to Devil's Cave," Joe said. And so they turned their guesswork into a kind of certainty. But Alf knew the boy might be wandering anywhere. He might (he pushed the thought away, but its essence remained) be miles from town. If someone had taken him, missing him by thirty seconds was as bad as missing him by a day. It might already be too late. In the light from the house, Penny had lifted her face to him. He could hardly stand the way her big eyes took in his every movement, his every word, as if she could conjure up Jamie out of his body. Alf swept her hot cheek with his fingertips. "Hey there, girl. He's going to walk in here and wonder what all the fuss is about."

"This will teach you not to tease him," Margaret said to her.

"I *never*," Penny said and burst into tears.

Alf shot a glance at his wife. "This isn't the time for a Sunday-school lesson."

"Well, I'm just *saying*, this will teach us *all*," Margaret said defensively. She could change directions as swiftly as a politician.

Alf nearly said, That's not what you meant. But this was not the time for a game of deny and accuse. He could never beat her at that game anyway.

"What about Red?" Joe said. "Maybe he could find Jamie."

The big dog had been trotting up and down the yard in a frenzy of impatience, whining and yelping, his ears pricking and laying back.

"More likely to find a skunk," Alf said. "Better tie him up."

He went into the house for his flashlight. When he came back out, Margaret urged him to call some of the neighbours. At first, Alf resisted. The prospect of a search party made his fear seem melodramatic. He didn't want to look a fool in front of the Island men. "At least call Pete," Margaret said.

"We're losing time," he said, still irritated with her.

"Alf, there's so much ground to cover out there."

"Call him," Penny said. Everyone looked at her, startled by something in her voice. She was staring with perfect calm at Alf, and for that moment she had more authority than anyone in the family.

Alf went in to phone Pete. They hadn't spoken since their quarrel.

"Pete," he said, starting right in, "we've lost Jamie. I think he might be up the river."

"I'll be right over."

They gathered in the backyard. Their neighbour, Bill Olmstead, had arrived too, drawn by Margaret's shouting from the dyke, and Bill's oldest son, Dick. Alf disliked both of them, fleshy, overtalkative men, the son a taller copy of the father. They were brimming with high spirits, and gave the impression that hunting for Jamie was some kind of adventure. Pete, though, was subdued. He had brought a rope.

Margaret and Penny came with them as far as the footbridge. They were going to stay at the house in case Jamie showed up. "Or if someone calls," Alf said. He wouldn't let himself think too clearly about who might call or for what reason. He knew the police wouldn't call, they would arrive at the door.

"We'll get him," Alf said, and for a moment met his wife's gaze. It was too dark to see her clearly, but something in her face seemed to reach towards him, and in an instant his hostility towards her evaporated. More than anyone, she – the two of them – knew what was at stake.

At the edge of Wiley's farm, the men split up. Alf took the low trail, which followed the bends of the Atta through the woods. Over the high pasture to his left, the sky carried a last faint streak of iodine. He lashed his beam at the shrubs on the bank and out over the river, unable to resist the call of his fear. Of course, he wasn't going to see Jamie floating down the middle of the Atta (he told himself), but it was the river that worried him. A night in the woods wouldn't hurt the boy, but the water was the unknown factor here, the water jumping now in his beam, hurrying on with a purpose of its own. High in the south, a chalky, flat-sided moon had escaped the clouds.

He could hear the others shouting out Jamie's name from the hills of the farm. He resisted shouting it himself, though the word "Jamie" kept rising in his throat. To shout seemed an act of desperation, and he was fighting desperation as though, once set loose, it might generate what he feared most. Then he heard Pete shout again, and almost as an echo, he shouted too: the word "Jamie" broke from him, leaping into the night sounding hoarser than he'd intended. He collected himself and shouted again, as his beam penetrated the saplings that had grown up at the edge of the dam. There was no response, or at least none audible over the steady bass hush of the water. For a few minutes he explored the neighbourhood of the dam, playing his light over the wide sweep of concrete, shiny with the water that skimmed down its steep face, and into the mildly boiling pool at its base. He found the dam disheartening. It was so huge, the volumes of dark water packed behind it so great, that he was glad to continue on up the trail. In a grove of dead saplings he darted his light at a sudden gleam and saw the metal basket of an abandoned shopping cart.

He had walked on these paths all his life. He had played out here, fished, swum, he had even worked for a couple of summers for old man Wiley, at a dollar a day, weeding turnips, mucking out barns. Yet tonight the place seemed entirely new to him, as if he had never seen its true aspect, the malevolence lurking in a darkness that closed around his beam with a catlike swiftness, as though seeking to hide what he had narrowly missed. He wasn't even sure what he was looking for. If the boy was conscious, he would surely hear their cries and call back. And if he wasn't? Alf's beam leapt between the trees, combed the undercover of tangled weeds, looking for a small, huddled body. Perhaps Jamie had knocked himself out, trying to climb a tree. Perhaps he had fainted with the pain of a broken leg. He tried to make orderly sweeps with the flashlight, but the density of the woods made a mockery of his system. He trekked through ferns – their brown, dying fronds flattened to the earth – and climbed the little hill to the swinging vines. There were footprints here, made by several shoes. Some seemed about the right size for Jamie, but he couldn't be sure. He studied them, trying to force himself, unsuccessfully, to remember the pattern on the soles of his son's shoes. The tracks seemed somewhat fresh, made in the last day or so. A little encouraged, he went on, under huge, leaning oaks. They had been giants when he was a boy. To his left the fields of Wiley's farm – fields where he had once picked rocks and walked behind the hay wagon – had turned grey in the moonlight.

Again his light swept over the river. Sluggish water gleamed in its covert, alien life. Jamie could swim, but Alf's father, too, had been able to swim. And so it came back to him, despite all his efforts to keep it at bay: that Sunday afternoon in June of 1952, when he'd looked out the front window and seen Gerry Milton, the Town Yard foreman, pacing on the sidewalk as if he were undecided or lost, his rubber boots leaving faint, wet tracks on the concrete. They met at the front door. When Gerry told him, his face plaintive under his rumpled hair, his eyes boring into Alf's as if he, Alf, might save *him* from this distress, it seemed to Alf that he had always known that his father was dead. He had known it for time out of mind, it was part of who he was and who his father was. Gerry was not giving him news, but only forcing his gaze to the side, towards a blackness that had always existed.

He had had to tell his mother. He led her to a chair while she cried, *What! What!* And he understood that she, too, already knew, had always known. Perhaps it was the war that had given her fore-knowledge: she had already lost Joe, Alf's brother. And now she knew, or had come within a hair of knowing, that her husband, too, was dead. He had been dead through all the forty-six years she'd known him, dead through their courtship on these same paths where he, Alf, was walking now, playing his feeble beam ahead of him, dead from the first moment he had taken breath and dead for a billion years: dead was inscribed in the bone, in the minuscule, pushing seed, in the whirling atom.

When he told her, her right arm flailed with a life of its own, as if she might push away the knowledge falling into the light. He had hated life at that moment, and he felt the same hate sickening in him now as he stopped and looked up through the treetops, where a few faint stars pulsed, to calm himself. He was in a rage against life, because this was what it came down to: the fear, and the fear entirely justified, because somewhere out there your own death, and the deaths of those you loved, was waiting for you. Life enticed you to love it. It lured you on with the sweet, terrible music of happiness. Life told you: Love, Get Married, Work, Hope, Pray, Put Everything on My Altar. And in the end it abandoned you without a backwards glance . . .

He followed the trail along the edge of the woods. He felt calmer now, and ice cold, set against life, determined to pluck his son from its trap. He would find the boy if he had to die doing it. Beside him, the rough, weedy fields moved past in the moonlight. Then the trail descended to the bottomlands of the Atta. The area had changed since his boyhood. Then cows had grazed here, and kept the land clean and open. Now it was thick with wild fruit trees. Pale, narrow paths ran everywhere, a confusion in the grey, metalled moonlight.

"Jamie!" a voice cried distantly, and hope flared in him. Had they found him?

No one cried again. He went on. The little trees, like rough bouquets, seemed to stand in his beam as if expecting something, stupidly. Then the brush exploded beside him, and he whirled to meet the attack, his heart slamming. His beam just caught the fleeing deer, its white tail uplifted, bold as a placard, as it bounded away among the trees.

"Christ," he said, and regretted swearing. He felt he had to keep himself pure or Jamie would not appear. He had to be clean, silent, calm. He went on, aware he no longer had a plan. He was simply following his instinct, following the paths to the north, searching in the mud for more running-shoe marks (he found none) through the great plain made by the oxbow, trekking on with a grim alertness. He could no longer hear anyone calling. Perhaps they had found him? "Jamie!" he cried, and his own voice came back to him, a much smaller cry from the wall of the valley.

Again he reached the river, and stood playing his beam over the grey water. There was something sinister about the water, furtive and scheming and hurrying to escape. A little rapid surfed along like a tribe of small water creatures, making their desolate way upstream. The air smelled of autumn, of decay, a chilling emptiness.

Upstream, a bit of the rapid seemed to detach itself: a scrap of whiteness moving erratically in the dark. He shone out his beam and it stopped. Jamie was there, in his white T-shirt and shorts, his eyes glassy, blinking in the light like an animal caught drinking. In a moment he would vanish.

"Jamie!"

"Dad!"

"Stay there! Jamie, don't move! I'll come to you!"

He moved around the edge of the black inlet that separated them, stumbling through thickets and water, the beam of his light darting back to Jamie continually. Then they were together, the boy in his arms.

His beam swept over a second pair of legs, also in shorts, standing about twenty feet away. There was a boy there, a dark-haired boy about Jamie's age, his arm raised against the light. His little body in its red T-shirt was pulling slowly back, as if he meant to run away.

"Who's that?" Alf said. He had let Jamie slip to the ground. The other boy, still held by the light, had put a start of fear in Alf, as if he were in some way involved in the danger to Jamie and was a threat yet; as though he had found only half of Jamie, and the other half remained to be brought to safety. He turned his beam back to his son, who was waving the other boy over.

"*Jamie! Jamie!*" voices cried from the hill.

"I got him!" Alf yelled.

A silence, then: "He's got him! He's got him!"

"Is that the Boileau boy?" Alf said.

"Billy," Jamie said to the boy. "It's all right. It's my dad." The Boileau boy was peering to see past the light, his black eyes fiercely suspicious. Alf was surprised to find the two of them together. The Boileaus were tough, poor. The boy's uncle – or was it his cousin – had been in jail.

"He lost his dog," Jamie said. "We tried to get it. We went up past the cave. We got lost."

"Come here, son. It's all right."

The Boileau boy grinned a wooden grin and did not move.

The searchers returned in a group, jubilant under the lopsided moon. Jamie rode for a while on Alf's shoulders. Pete offered to give

Billy a ride, but the boy shook his head and moved away, walking a little way off from the others and saying nothing, though from time to time he grinned that painful automatic grin, as though he thought it was required of him.

Beside Alf, Bill Olmstead was going on about how he had never had any doubt they'd find the boy. He branched into other stories, about lost children and lost dogs and the time he'd got lost himself, in the bush behind some cottage up north. And not one of those episodes had turned out badly, Bill declared, as if good fortune were only a matter of having a positive attitude.

Ahead of them, Pete was walking with his head down, the unused rope swinging in a coil from his hand. The sight moved Alf: the guy had come through for him, without a moment's hesitation. Well, of course, he'd have done the same. Catching up to his friend, Alf put his hand on his shoulder. "Pete – thanks." "Okay, buddy," Pete said, avoiding Alf's eyes and blurting out the words, as if they sprang from an emotion too powerful to be safely acknowledged.

Alf drove Billy home. The boy sat alertly on the edge of the Biscayne's front seat, grunting yep or nope to Alf's questions and watching every turn of the road. His hard little voice sounded trapped in his throat. There was something of a queer little man about him.

The Boileaus lived on the Flats, on the east side of town, in a plaster-and-lath cottage overshadowed by the rail embankment. One of the supports for the front porch had been replaced by the trunk of a birch tree. Pulling up at the curb, Alf looked at the curtainless front window and saw the flickering of a small television, the top of a couch, and a hole in the wall that showed the lath-work beneath. He wondered if Billy had even been missed. But then he saw Lucille Boileau trudging along the street from the direction of the river. When she saw the car, she stopped. Getting out, Alf shouted to her, "It's all right, I've got him," and watched as she buckled, as if struck in the stomach. She was still weeping when she came up to him.

She crushed Billy's head against her. Then thrust him back abruptly, giving him a sharp slap on the side of the head. "You had me worried sick!"

"Don't be too hard on him," Alf said. "He was with my boy. They got lost up the Atta."

"You never told me you were going up there! Where's Fuzz, eh? You lost him again?"

"The rope broke."

"*The rope broke*," Lucille said to Alf, with heavy sarcasm.

"They were doing their best to get back," Alf said.

"You get inside," Lucille said.

Billy shot up the walk.

She turned back to Alf. She was about thirty-five, Alf guessed, beautiful in a severe, threatening way, her long black hair escaping its pins in wisps and collapsing waves, her high, plush cheekbones shiny with tears. There was something shy in the smile she offered him, he thought, and something evasive and cunning. For years – he saw her often at Bannerman's, where she worked in the sewing department – her mouth had fascinated him, it was so wide, the lips so large and mobile, a freakish mouth, like some odd sea creature come to live on her face.

"I'd die if I lost him," she told him, her eyes fixing blindly on his shirt front.

She lunged up at him, catching the back of his neck with one hand and putting her mouth on his. It was more than a kiss, it was as if she had leaned up to take a large, soft bite out of his face. Driving over the bridge, he was still thinking about it, an electric excitement flaring across his chest where she had pressed against him. He felt twenty again, everything vivid: the damp, rancid air over the river, his hands tingling on the wheel, and there, past the traffic light, past the Baptist church and the library, the high, lonely, crumpled moon.

THE LIGHT IN THE BATHROOM had a greenish tinge. Jamie's mother made him sit on the toilet, with the seat down, while she perched on the edge of the tub, one knee in its brown stocking touching his, her eyes looking straight into his. In Jarrod's Shoe Store was a machine you put your feet into. Then you looked into a viewfinder and saw the bones in your feet, all pale and strange like little ghosts. He felt she was looking at his bones.

"What were you doing with that boy?"

"Nothing."

"You weren't doing *nothing*."

She tapped his leg with the rubber spatula. It was what she used to spank him. Her anger was huge, it filled the green light and shone off the tiles behind her head, but he didn't know what he'd done to make it happen. He watched the flat rubber touch his knee and looked back into her eyes. Usually there was help in her eyes, but now there was none, though he couldn't help looking for it.

"We were just playing."

"I don't want you playing with that boy again."

"Billy?"

"I don't want you to have anything to do with that Boileau boy. Do you understand me?"

The spatula tapped again on his knee.

"Why?"

"His family are not our kind of people. Do you understand?"

He looked at the faucet in the tub, where a big drop was swelling, getting ready to fall.

"We were just having fun."

"Jamie!"

"We *tried* to get back!"

He was crying now, and when he cried, his thoughts started to slide around, he couldn't keep track. What was our kind of people? Kind was good, wasn't it? His teacher, Miss Wayne, was kind, and his mother was, usually. Now she was not kind – was she not his kind of people?

"Look at me!"

He tried to meet those black eyes, which were looking at his bones.

"Dad wasn't mad," he whimpered.

"He doesn't want you playing with that boy either. Promise me you won't play with him again."

"Mom!"

"Promise me!"

The spatula tapped. He was crying, he hardly knew why, except that something was not fair. What had he done wrong? When you did something wrong you were punished, but why was he being punished for just doing what he thought was right? He had tried to help Billy find his dog, and he had tried to get home as fast as he could. Only he hadn't been able to find the trail.

"Jamie!"

"I promise! But, Mom, why are the Boileaus our kind of –"

"Why are they *not* our kind of people? Because, they're just not nice, good people. They've been in trouble with the law."

"What trouble?"

"That doesn't matter. The point is, we're done with them. Right?"

"Yes."

"That's my boy."

She gave him another tap with the spatula and stood up: the matter was clearly finished as far as she was concerned. He watched her peer at herself in the glass. She put a finger to a place on her cheek and pulled the skin down. Inside the pouch under her eye it was red, like the inside of a fish's gill.

On Monday Jamie stayed home from school with a touch of the flu, his mother said, feeling his cheeks. He sat in bed sipping ginger ale and looking at his books, especially the Tim stories, and at his Superman and Donald Duck comics. On Wednesday his mother announced he was well enough to go back. He went up the hill and found Billy waiting for him at the gate to the Boys' Yard, grinning so widely – so clearly glad to see him – that Jamie felt sick to his stomach.

"Hi."

"Hi."

"Look what I got!" Billy said. He looked over his shoulder, then put his hand in his jacket pocket and pulled out a little cardboard tube with a brass cap on one end. It rolled in his palm.

"A bullet," Billy said in his strange, throat-gurgling voice.

"For real?"

"Shotgun."

"Where's the point?"

"They don't have points. You put in gunpowder. Then you put in other stuff, like marbles or rocks or BB's. We can make gunpowder after school. Okay?"

"I dunno. I promised I'd help my mother."

Liar, the voice inside him said. Jamie blinked.

"You grind up coal and put other things in."

"I dunno."

"We can go to my house," Billy said.

Liar, liar, pants on fire.

"Shut up," Jamie said to the voice, and felt his face burn. "Not you," he said to Billy.

Billy put the bullet back in his pocket. Some Grade Five boys went by with their heads back, howling like wolves. Jamie walked off abruptly towards a group of boys who were playing conkers. Billy came with him. Jamie stood pretending to watch the nuts as they swung and smashed, but all he could think about, really, was Billy, who pushed another boy out of the way and stood beside him. He walked away again. Billy came again. He stopped and Billy stopped.

He tried one more time: walked over to the wall of the school, where Fattie Lonsdale and Mike Harms were down on their knees, tossing cards into a corner with quick flicks of their wrists: baseball cards and hockey cards and flags-of-the-world cards and car cards, covering up the asphalt in the corner like leaves. Billy arrived beside him. He grinned at Jamie with his brown-edged teeth: this was fun!

The monitor shook her bell and the boys in the yard began to drift towards the school. Billy fell in beside Jamie, in the line going into the south door.

"You better get to your door," Jamie said.

"Oh yeah!" Billy said, and he clapped his hand over his head and pulled a face, as if to say, What a goof I am, and Jamie laughed in spite of himself. Then Billy started off, but he came back almost immediately and told Jamie to hold out his hand.

"What for?"

"C'mon, just hold it out."

He put out his hand. Billy laid the empty shotgun bullet in it.

"It's a present," Billy said and ran off.

During spelling, Jamie felt a little queasy, and then just as he was putting his speller away under his desk, vomit shot out of his mouth. It slapped onto the hardwood floor and lay there in a big brown pool with flecks of yellow in it. He couldn't believe it. He'd seen other kids throw up in school, seen them taken off to the nurse's room while Mr. Small, the janitor, came in and spread sawdust on it, and scraped it up, and washed the floor, though for a long time afterwards no one would step there, on the vomit-smelling place that made you feel like vomiting too. And now *he* was that kid that had done this stupid, smelly thing. They were all looking at him now, up and down the rows, some of the boys grinning, or craning to see, or saying Wow, and looking at him like they didn't know him any more, just like they looked at Hel Grimm, the German boy who couldn't speak English and who had come to school one day wearing leather shorts.

BEHIND HER DESK in General Office, the receptionist, May Watson, lifted her sagging alcoholic's face. "They want you in the board-room," she droned, her heavily lidded eyes fixed on Alf's chest.

"Did they say what it was about?"

They: like a creature with twenty heads.

Mary's right shoulder twitched, a faint shrug.

He went through the office, up the carpeted stairs and on through a murmur of voices, the machine-gunning of typewriters, conscious of the stains on his factory greens. The last door on his right bore a small brass sign: BOARDROOM. He paused, imagining a dozen men waiting for him on the other side, their heads turning as he knocked. But the room was empty. He went in, leaving the door ajar. Chairs of yellow oak surrounded a long table of the same wood. On a corner of the table, someone had left a napkin and a half-eaten Digestive biscuit.

He sat, but after a few seconds got up again. On the wall by the door, the grave features of former Bannerman's executives, in photo-graphs and paintings, gazed past him with a serenity that seemed fixed on some distant, finer future. On the opposite wall hung several historical photos. He roamed past them with his hands in his pockets, glancing at women in long-sleeved, high-necked blouses with elaborately piled hair, looking up from their sewing machines. Men posed stoically by trollies and drive-belts. He recognized several of his parents' friends. They looked younger than he was now: Mary Plumstead, Vickie Short, Johnny Bickersteth, Al Partridge, so many of them English. Yes, when he was growing up, Midlands accents had been as common in town as Canadian ones. His mother had come out in 1910 on the *Empress of Ireland*, a girl of twenty-three with a ten-pound note pinned inside her blouse and her mother's best silver teapot riding in her trunk, knowing no one. He searched for her in a large photo of the 1927 Bannerman's staff picnic. He might have been there himself that year: he would have been what, eight? A great mass of people in summer whites stared from a bleacher. Their unsmiling faces seemed to squint into the glare of an immense imposition.

He moved on to the next photograph: The Bannerman Stingers, Ontario Senior "B" Champions, 1938. He had a smaller version of the picture at home. All the same, he had to look for Joe, had to make sure his brother was in it, as if Joe, the wild one, the one who always did the unexpected, might have slipped from the frame when no one was looking.

And there he was, in his place in the first row, kneeling with the other players in his striped Stinger uniform, his curved stick slanting towards the enormous silver cup that flowered in front of them. He wore his blond hair slicked straight back, suggesting even in repose, speed, his genius for attack.

"Found someone you know?"

The rich, genial voice startled him. Masked by the drone of the air conditioner, Bob Prince had materialized across the table. He held a manila file folder against the breast of his light-beige suit. His bald, deeply tanned head gave him an oddly foreign look – Italian or even Arab.

"My brother," Alf said, glad to see the executive. No matter what this meeting was about, he felt he had an ally.

"Oh yes? Let's see –"

As Prince rounded the table and leaned to examine the photo, the air was suddenly brisk with his aftershave. In profile, his heavy jaw jutted out a little, with an exaggerated aggressiveness. "A hockey player!"

"He was pretty good. Best player on that team, anyway."

"Ontario Champions," Prince noted approvingly.

"After that series, the Leafs scouted him."

"And did he go to the pros?"

"No, ah –"

"He had better things to do," Prince said, with friendly conde-scension.

"I guess you could say that. When the war came he signed up right away. My mother didn't want him to go, but we couldn't keep him out of it."

The pale-blue eyes were watching him guardedly now. A note of respect entered Prince's voice. "And after that, did he –"

"He was killed," Alf said, turning away. He felt ashamed, but of what? Of the dead place, the silence, he felt, when he said the words "He was killed"? Or of the emotion he knew lay trapped behind them, like an animal in a too-small cage?

At the same time, he knew he had struck a blow at Prince. And that he had used his brother's death to do it, like a stick he had found in the street.

"I'm sorry," Prince said in that beautiful voice. The air conditioner rattled. Behind smeared glass, sumacs drooped in the heat. "We left behind some of the best, didn't we?" The executive shook his head, letting a beat go by.

"I was air force myself," he said. "Not that I saw much flying. I wanted to be a pilot, but I kept getting airsick, so they shunted me over to Intelligence. We went ahead of the Spitfires, in France, looking for new airfields as the front moved forward." Prince rounded the table, gesturing at a chair for Alf. "Bert Hatch tells me you were army."

"Yes, did the walking tour."

As he took his seat, Alf glanced at the file folder lying before Prince. He couldn't read the tab.

"Well, I got to ride in a jeep," Prince said. "It's funny, I always felt I'd missed something, like I hadn't really done my part. I mean, no one ever shot at me."

"It's not all it's cracked up to be," Alf said.

Prince released his brilliant grin. "I don't suppose," he said, and in an instant the smile was gone. "So," he announced, frowning at the file folder: a change of mood, direction. The war, Spitfires, Joe's death, were swept aside. "I called you over to talk about a problem I have. I think the thing to do is give you a bit of background first."

Prince leaned back in his chair, a big man trying to make himself comfortable, his jacket open, his rich-looking brown tie with its gold clip buckling over his white shirt. Alf glanced at the shut door behind him – apparently no one else was expected.

"We're determined to get Bannerman's back on its feet," Prince said. "New lines, new machines, new accounting – we're planning to put a computerized order system in. All this costs a lot of money, of course, more, really than Bannerman's is earning. And we're willing to invest it, providing we don't think we're going to get any nasty surprises."

His gaze fixed Alf for a moment, as if *he* might have something to do with nasty surprises.

The executive frowned and tapped his fingertips together. There was a weight about the man, a sense of grave and important responsibilities. Alf was flattered at being taken into his confidence. He was also mystified. Surely it wasn't Prince's job to tell him he'd been made foreman? But what else could this be about?

"You've probably heard, Alf, that there's been a union sniffing around."

"I've gathered," Alf said, shifting in his chair.

"Well, I've nothing against unions in the abstract. But the thing is, with all the investments we're making here, we really can't afford one."

"No," Alf said. And Prince said, shooting him a meaningful glance, "I mean, we *really* can't afford one."

"No," Alf repeated.

"If I can share a confidence with you, Alf. If Head Office – I'm talking about *my* bosses now – thinks there's going to be labour troubles here, they could pull out just like that. I mean, they feel it's a gamble coming in here anyway. They're nervous."

The executive winced as he put his hand into the breast of his suit coat. He might have been feeling for a pen, or touching a sore.

"Have you seen any sign of the union yourself?" he asked. The blue eyes flicked back to Alf. Alf understood why he had been summoned. Prince felt he could trust him; he needed information.

Alf sat forward in his chair. There was danger here. He felt it would only increase if he wasn't candid with the man.

"Actually, an organizer came around to my place. I set him packing."

Prince did not return his smile.

"Ugly bugger with a red face?"

"That's right."

"Doyle," Prince said.

"That was the name," Alf said, nodding. "I'm afraid he didn't –"

"We've had a lot of trouble with his outfit, in our plants down east," Prince said, cutting him off. "He doesn't look like much, but he's dangerous. What did he say?"

Alf shrugged, eager to dismiss Doyle as inconsequential. "The usual. Sign on the dotted line and your worries will be over." He glanced at Prince, who was clearly waiting for something more substantial. "He said Intertex had such deep pockets it was a crime they didn't pay people at Bannerman's more."

"These *socialists*," Prince said, shaking his head. "They're all alike. They think we're just walking treasure chests. They have no idea what it takes to run a company, to *keep* it running. No idea where wealth comes from –"

"No," Alf said.

"And that's *all* he said to you? Did you get any sense he was making progress?"

"He wasn't with me."

"You said that," Prince said, with a touch of impatience. "I mean with others. How many has he signed up?"

"He didn't say," Alf said. "But I wouldn't think he's got more than a few, if that."

"And why is that?" Prince said, leaning back in his chair. There was something remorseless and searching in his look.

"Well, we tried the union route before. 1949. People got burned, badly. I don't think there's many who'd like to try it again. Truth is, they don't even like talking about it."

"Yes, I've heard that," Prince said. Behind his tanned, handsome face Alf sensed a pressure, as if some emotion had been so long contained there it had solidified. "Let's hope you're right. I gather you went out yourself."

Alf's face was fairly burning up. He could not stop glancing at the manila folder. He knew what was in it now. His whole life was in it.

"I was young and foolish," he managed.

"Tell me about it."

"Oh." His mouth had gone dry; he had never explained these things to anyone, and doubted he could do it. He was half-afraid of condemning himself. "I'd seen things, in the war. I guess you'd say I had a chip on my shoulder. If it hadn't been the strike, it'd have been something else. I guess life seemed simpler then."

"What did you see, in the war?"

Alf shook his head: it was indescribable, really. "Lives thrown away. My brother. I guess I had it in for authority. Some of that left-wing stuff sounded pretty good to me. Get rid of the bosses and do it ourselves, if that's what they were saying. I was never very good on the theory."

"I had some of the same feelings myself," Prince said.

Alf looked at him in surprise.

"The fuck-ups you saw come out of headquarters: they were enough to make you sick. But anyway, we won," Prince said grimly. "I guess that's the bottom line."

There was a pause. Prince frowned and looked at the palm of his own hand. The air conditioner clattered.

"Alf, look, I want you to help me. This is something you can do now, before you're made foreman. Oh, I should've mentioned that," Prince said, showing his smile for a moment. "We're so behind on some of the housekeeping stuff. We won't have the new promotions figured out till November, but I think I can reassure you that you're in."

Alf nodded, and a small airplane did a loop in his stomach.

"Oh yes, you're definitely in," Prince murmured. "But before then, I want you to have a look at this union. Go to some of their meetings, if they're having any. See if this Doyle fellow's making any progress. I don't need to tell you, Alf, that a lot depends on this. Will you do that for me?"

Prince was looking at him keenly, with just a hint of a brotherly smile, a neediness. Alf said, "You mean, just take the lay of the land."

"Go to a few meetings. Make some notes. You can report directly to me." Prince took a card from his jacket and scrawled something on it before handing it to Alf. "That's my phone number at the Executive Motel, over in Johnsonville. Call me as soon as you've got anything." Prince nodded at the card. "'Fraid I'm living out of a suitcase these days. My wife's not too happy about it." They shook hands. "I know I can count on you, Alf." The pale-blue eyes held Alf's in a glow of sincerity. Alf was the first to look away.

12

"YOU MENTIONED A BUNCH of you guys were meeting with an organizer?"

Silence came back to him, down the line. To Alf it sounded conspiratorial, as if the others were with Pete even now, listening in. Out the kitchen window he could see Margaret's dark head, the hissing spray of silver as she watered her garden.

"I'm not saying I'm on board. But I'd like to – see how the land lies." He was trying, scrupulously, not to tell a lie.

Someone was coming down the stairs. He seized gladly on the interruption. "Look, it's kind of difficult to talk here."

"This is good news, Alf."

Alf peered around the corner into the hall. Penny, in her shorts and halter top, was trailing one hand along the wall, singing softly, tunelessly to herself.

"So when can I –"

"I've gotta check with Malachi first," Pete said. "If it was just me, Alf, but we're worried G.O.'s found out. We have to be careful."

Alf thought, Anybody could have seen me go over to G.O. Maybe Pete knows I was there.

Already he regretted calling. This mutual suspicion was giving him a terrible sense of déjà vu. It was the atmosphere they had breathed in '49. Then, though, he had been excited by their cloak-and-dagger games. Now this manoeuvring seemed juvenile, poisonous.

Penny entered the kitchen, glancing at him as she crossed to the sink. In the weak light the whites of her eyes shone, her sandals scuffed the linoleum.

"Tell me at work, will you? It's a bit difficult just now."

"I'm really glad to hear this, Alf. Malachi was saying just the other day how much he'd like to have you aboard."

"I'm not saying I'm –"

"I was telling him what you and Skinny Jones did during the strike. Putting that flag up. We had a good laugh."

With a fresh pang of regret, Alf remembered the bedsheet, dyed red, they had raised over the post-office clock. He said thickly, "We didn't know what we were doing."

When he had hung up, Penny turned to him, her large eyes watching as she drank. She lowered the glass with a little explosion of breath. "What didn't you know what you were doing?"

"Oh nothing. Something a long time ago."

"When you were a boy?"

"A little older than that."

"Tell me." Anticipation lit her face at the promise of a story she hadn't heard. He felt almost compelled to tell her. He could talk to her more easily than anyone, even Margaret, it was like talking to himself. Now her pale-blue eyes – Penny's got Alf's eyes, they said in the family – seemed to be drawing out his secrets. He had to be careful.

"Did you do something bad?"

"No, just kind of stupid."

"Tell me."

"Some other time."

She continued to gaze at him. There was something blank in her, open and clear and blank, like a calm sea. It seemed capable of waiting forever – for what, he couldn't be sure – waiting with a simple, troubling absence of judgment or expectation for whatever might fall into it. Deep in the house a pipe whined as Margaret turned off the outside tap.

"You said we could skip stones," Penny said. The previous summer, the summer of his mother's death, his daughter had been diagnosed with diabetes. Every morning she gave herself a needle. Alf found it hard to watch, less out of squeamishness than because it – the diabetes – was something he hadn't been able to protect her from. Alf's great-uncle, John, had died of diabetes as a boy, so the disease, the doctor had said, had likely come to Penny through him.

They went down the brick path through the dripping tomato plants, over the dyke to the river. The flat water in the bend gave off a dim light of its own. Mechanically, he began to hunt for a stone. He felt detached from all activity, detached from himself. In the thickening dusk, the substance of things was washing away.

Penny handed him a piece of slate. It seemed unreal in his hand, and he had to toss it a bit, press his thumb on its sharp edge to make it come alive. It seemed – he knew this was pure superstition, and ridiculous – it seemed she was posing him a test, a test he felt he'd already disqualified himself for.

He sent the stone down the gleaming river: a path of little white nicks erupted in the dimness.

"Seven!" Penny cried.

She handed him another.

Two days later, Pete phoned back: "Tonight at eight. My house."

At a quarter after eight, Alf crossed the footbridge to Lions Park and made his way past the deserted swings and empty bandstand, climbing the embankment towards Pete's ranch-style bungalow, tucked into the wooded hillside. A bird chirped sleepily, silver in the night's purse. A dozen cars were parked in the drive and on the shoulder of the road that descended darkly from the flank of Lookout Hill. With a start he recognized Doyle's heavy Edsel, abandoned on a tilt, two wheels in the ditch.

Pete's wife, May, met him at the front door: a tall woman in slacks and a sleeveless blouse with an anxious, searching quality in her slightly protuberant eyes. She and Alf had been lovers for a few weeks in the Thirties. Ever since, he'd felt a yearning coming from her, as if she was still waiting for him to do something, say something, that would assuage the churn of unfinished business. Slipping her gaze, he kissed her on the cheek, and for a moment their intimacy came back to him: her cries in the hotel room in Johnsonville, under horrible wallpaper with its purple roses as big as cabbages. From the back of the house came a tribal bray of laughter. "I better get in there," he said. But she had caught his arm. "Alf, I'm worried about this union business. If G.O. finds out."

"It'll be all right," he said, and felt he was assuming more responsibility than he'd meant.

He went down the hall to the kitchen. Beyond, the porch was a cave of shadows lit only by the pale light flooding through the screens and the light from the kitchen door. Around the perimeter, in the murk and glow of cigarettes, fifteen or twenty people lifted ghostly faces.

"Alfie!" he heard Pete say. Others, too, caught up the welcome. They seemed glad to see him, he heard his name tossed out by several voices, both male and female, heard, "Hey, buddy, good to see you!" and "Here's blue eyes!" and "You can sit next to me, Alf." He was taken aback. For a moment it was 1949 again, in the early days of the strike, when they had called each other brother and sister without self-consciousness.

Christ, don't get sentimental, he thought. But he was shaken. Something old, forgotten, had come and touched him in his isolation.

May brought him a chair and he sat near the kitchen door. Near the far end of the porch, in the faint light from the yard, Doyle's pitted face glowed like bronze.

"Glad you could make it," the organizer growled. A note of irony? "We're just going through the mills, one department at a time. Trying to get an idea of who's likely to support us."

"Who's solid and who's kind of wishy-washy," Ed Berry said, from his chair beside Alf. The tiny planet of his cigarette reddened under his downward-tilting face.

At first, Alf had trouble concentrating on the discussion. He was preoccupied with the emotion that had taken him unawares, the uncanny sense that this was not 1965 but 1949. Sitting across from him was a little owl-faced woman called Margo Love. She'd been one of the most violent of the strikers, in '49. He remembered how she'd followed every vehicle that broached the lines, pounding on the hood and screaming obscenities. When the police had tried to drag her away, she'd lain on her back kicking in the air so that her underwear showed, threatening to impale all comers with a hatpin. She looked a little heavier now, but it was still the same Margo, quick to take offence, and challenging the other speakers so often Doyle had to tell her to wait her turn. Rebuked, she scowled at the wall over Alf's head.

As Alf listened, he couldn't help remembering how, sixteen years ago, there had been an excitement in the air, a sense that they were not just making a union but reshaping the world. This lot seemed depressed, by comparison. They seemed isolated from each other, as if they hadn't fully made up their minds to be here at all, slow to offer suggestions, letting two or three people carry the ball, while Doyle, smoking and cajoling and glowering at his clipboard, seemed to get more irritated by the minute. Already – a secret sigh of relief – Alf saw himself reporting back to Prince: You've got nothing to worry about. This bunch isn't going anywhere.

The discussion turned to Number Six knitting. The organizer's gravelly voice came down the porch: "All right, Alf, you see any possibilities there?"

Before he could answer, Woody Marr broke in. "You can put down Sid Queen and Ellie Snider right off the top," the knitter said, raising his bulldog face and stabbing with a thick finger. Woody was a short, powerfully built man who, Alf felt, had always been resentful of him, for reasons that were never clear. Perhaps it was simply that Woody was resentful of *everyone*: there was an anger in him, a bitterness, that seemed to flow not from any discernible cause but from the depths of his personality. Woody had gone out in '49, and got fired for it. Like Alf, he had returned to Bannerman's after an absence of a few years.

Doyle tapped the bottom of his pencil on his clipboard. "You agree with Woody, Alf?"

"I'm not so sure about Ellie Snider," he said.

"Why not?" Doyle said sharply.

"Hell, she's *solid*," Woody growled as he watched them both.

"What are your reasons, Alf?" Doyle said.

"Well, she might be sympathetic, which I doubt. But she's got three kids to look after, and no husband –"

"This is bullshit," Woody said.

Doyle made a note. "Anyone else," he said, looking straight at Alf. Alf shook his head.

The porch fell silent, though there was a covert restlessness, as if people were disappointed by his response. "Hell," Doyle said suddenly. "It's like a bloody dungeon in here. Could we have some light?"

The weak overhead bulb flooded the porch with a sickly light. Eighteen washed-out faces blinked and avoided each other's eyes, as if they had been exposed in some private, vaguely shameful act. The woods up the hill had disappeared. Looking around, Alf was startled to see Lucille Boileau in the corner behind Doyle. His heart leapt, for she was leaning out to look at him, her black eyes lit with recognition.

"The overall picture," Doyle was saying, "ain't very good, brothers and sisters. In fact, it stinks. The for-sures don't add up to more than ten per cent of the total. We're really gonna have to do some persuading, folks. Really go after those maybes."

"So is there any hope or what?" someone said.

"There's always *hope*," Doyle said abruptly, as if hope were a weak ally it was best not to depend on. "The thing is, we have to build, get thirty or forty per cent of the place signed up before the suits find out. And they *will* find out, believe me. Then the bloody horserace starts. We might have to sign the last ten per cent, to take us up to fifty-five, in a weekend."

"So is it worth going on?" Rob Cole asked, a young shipper Alf knew. He had a wife and God knew how many kids. "I mean, I don't mind takin' the chance if there's decent odds."

The porch went still: there was intense interest in Rob's question. No one wanted to get fired for trying to start a union; everyone knew there was a risk. Doyle stared at Rob as if he hadn't heard him, his pencil twitching in his fist like a little orange tail.

"What this company's doin' to you here ain't right," Doyle said at last, and his voice was low and threatening like something in the back of a cave. "It isn't *just*. It may be legal, at least as the world stands presently, but that's a different matter. Slavery was once legal too.

"These layoffs: I know many of you are worried it's gonna happen to you. Some of you are running twice as many machines as before. You know, in your hearts, that this isn't right. It's no way to treat people. It's just a backdoor way of cutting your pay. And there's signs they're gonna cut your benefits too, such as they are. Without a contract, you have no protection against that –"

Doyle paused, melodramatically Alf thought, to light another cigarette. Everyone watched as the flame lit his pitted face.

"What you're asking for – to make a union – it's only what's yours by law," the organizer continued, under a spreading cloud of smoke. "You understand that, that's why you're here. All we have to do is bring some of the others to the same place of understanding. Then they'll act, they'll join us. I remember a mill in eastern Ontario, Dempsters Mills, we started off with a smaller group than this. There were ten of us, a band of ten. By the time we'd finished, we'd organized a two-hundred-man shop. Two hundred and seventeen. 1959. And still goin' strong."

Doyle's tiny eyes nearly closed for a moment as he took another draw and sent the smoke on its way. He had presence, Alf would give him that. What he did seemed important. What he said, in that raw, earthy voice, seemed worth listening to, and not only that, it seemed true, or at least truer than the common run of talk. If I hadn't been through it once already, Alf thought, I'd be half-ready to sign myself . . .

"This isn't just about money," Doyle said. "We're making something here that has to do with justice, security, decency. This is a rich country. Ordinary people worked hard to make it that way. Why shouldn't they have a fair share of what they've made? Why should the rich get to keep their jobs and their privileges, while all the 'cost-saving' is taken out on you? It's the same question people were asking in the Depression, and it hasn't gone away. If there's enough for all, why are some forced to make do with so little?

"The rich think they have the right to forget the rest of us. They think they have the right to take and take, even if it means pushing us down. They don't call it pushing us down, they call it the laws of economics. They call it freedom. They call it the market. They say that the best way for the market to work is for them to get as rich as Croesus, and somehow, magically, we'll all be taken care of. Well it ain't true, brothers and sisters. They're playin' a game with the rules rigged their way. And no matter what they call it, it isn't right –"

Afterwards May served cookies and fresh coffee. Alf found himself standing next to Ed Berry.

"Thought you were dead set against this union stuff."

"Not me," Ed said, struggling to raise his head. Years of working over flatbed knitting machines had left him preposterously stooped, his face nearly parallel to the floor. Alf wondered how old he was –

sixty-three, -four? – not far from his pension anyway. And putting it at risk by being here.

"I mean, you didn't go out in '49."

"I wanted to go out," Ed said. "My wife said she'd leave me if I did. Regretted it ever since."

"You could take that more ways than one," Alf said with a laugh. Ed didn't smile, so he switched to a more sober tack. "So even after what happened, in the strike, you're still willing to try it –"

"I want another chance," Ed said softly, with great dignity. His grey eyes – a young man's eyes – glanced up with sudden vividness.

"So your wife has changed her mind, has she?"

"Edna's no longer with me."

Chagrined, Alf remembered the car accident: the newspaper flash-photo of Edna Berry's crushed car, like some dark, shapeless meteorite.

"Ed, I'm sorry. I forgot." They stood uneasily, nibbling at their cookies. And then Lucille Boileau was there, her wide face smiling up at Alf. She seemed extraordinarily pleased to see him, as if their encounter the night he'd brought Billy home had ignited some sense of loyalty or friendship or simple liking out of all proportion (it seemed to him) to what he'd done. "Wasn't that some speech?" she said, her gaze assaulting his. Choking on a piece of peanut-butter cookie, Alf couldn't answer.

"He's overcome by your beauty," Ed said to Lucille.

"Go home with you!" Lucille said.

"Only if you'll come with me," Ed said, heaving a little.

"You liked that speech, did you?" Alf said when he'd recovered.

He was watching her sharply, and for a moment something passed between them – he couldn't have said what – an acknowledgment, a fear.

"You didn't like it?"

"Well, these old lefties," he said. "They know all the tricks –"

"You don't sound very keen," she said, perplexed.

"Oh Alf's keen," Ed said. "Back in '49 he was one of the keenest."

"He helped my father," Lucille said. She had recovered from her moment of doubt and was glowing at him again. He saw the gap in the side of her teeth, which gave a hint of the hag to her smile, and was aware of how the white cotton of her blouse swelled over the shallow V of her bra: another world.

"That wasn't really the strike," Alf said, a bit embarrassed. He'd forgotten all about the incident.

Lucille told Ed, "A bunch of guys started pushing Dad around in the hotel. Alf stepped in and stopped them."

"He'd do that," Ed said, nodding.

It was another half-hour before he could get away. Catching him in the kitchen, Pete slapped him generously on the back and drew him into a conversation with two women from sewing. Alf kept glancing at the clock over the stove. The sense of his own fraudulence was overwhelming. He felt he was in a bubble, with his oxygen slowly running out, and no real connection to anyone.

13

OVER THE NEXT WEEK, Alf slid Prince's card from his wallet so many times it was soon covered with the grey smudges of his fingerprints. But each time he picked up the phone, something stopped him: the memory of the faces at Pete's house. If he did what Prince wanted, he'd be putting those people in danger, no question. And he was resentful that he had to do *anything*, let alone something distasteful, to get the foreman's job. Of course, Prince hadn't *said* that one thing was dependent on the other, though the implication had been there: a smiling understanding, a glance towards the manila folder where his past sins lay entombed, the suggestion he might move on, move up, if he atoned.

The following Monday, the phone shrilled through the kitchen, where Alf and his family were eating supper. A few minutes earlier, he had quarrelled with Margaret. She had asked him, innocently enough, if he'd heard the rumours about a union organizer living at the Vimy House: "I wonder if it's the same one who came here?" He tried to avoid a direct answer, and when she pressed him, he snapped back at her that, hell, he couldn't go around checking every bloody rumour that came through town. In truth, he suspected her of suspecting him, though of what exactly he wasn't sure. He felt he had done nothing wrong, not yet, and yet a vague pressure of impending guilt, a foreknowledge of what he was going to do, or might do, had made him see criticism everywhere.

His outburst had spread a bruised, isolating silence in the room, which the phone now interrupted. Penny answered.

"Daddy, it's for you."

As he crossed the room, she kept her eyes fixed on his.

"Alf. Bob Prince here."

The "Bob" took him unawares, postponing for a moment his understanding of "Prince." Whom was he talking to? Then he lurched forward, obscurely thrilled, into the intimacy offered by that rich, confiding voice, as if, already, he were being offered membership in those places where the powerful met in affable familiarity: on the greens of private golf courses; in elevators flashing up towers of light and steel.

"Have you got any news for me on that matter we discussed?"

"Ah yes, yes, I think so."

The silence over the line demanded more.

"It's difficult for me to talk now. Could I see you at G.O. tomorrow?"

"I'm not sure that's a good idea, Alf. Too many curious eyes. Could you come over tonight? I'm at the Executive. Room 226."

When Alf hung up, his family was staring at him: four faces backlit in the receding light, watching him with the stillness of grazing animals interrupted in a field, as if mystified by the very fact of his existence.

"Is there something wrong?" Margaret asked.

"No, no," he said, touched by her note of concern. "Mr. Prince wants to see me – company business." As soon as he'd spoken the phrase "company business," he felt reassured. It was as if he'd cited "state secrets" at a time of national emergency. Company business was not always nice business, though it was necessary. The awards, the beaming honours, would come later.

It was a twenty-minute drive to the outskirts of Johnsonville. In fields sprinkled with garbage, the hulks of closed and decaying factories drifted under the elongated pink islands of the sunset. Smaller businesses still clung to the edge of the highway. The Biscayne passed an auto-glass outlet, several fast-food restaurants, and a sprawling store that sold wooden lawn furniture, the unpainted Muskoka chairs and lounges crowded right up to the shoulder.

The Executive Motor Lodge formed a square C, two storeys high, around a central courtyard where a swimming pool gave off a clinical glow. He parked near the office and climbed metal stairs to a long exterior balcony that ran past a series of identical doors and picture windows. A pretty young woman in a short dress marched crisply towards him, her high heels ringing on the metal gangway. Her gaze, like a disapproving restaurant hostess's, swept coldly down his canary-yellow polo shirt (one of Bannerman's, four years old), his too-short, synthetic, navy-blue slacks, his black church shoes. He had put on the wrong clothes, he saw that now, though he didn't suppose there was anything better in his closet. Margaret had picked them out for him, discarding nearly everything she unearthed with an impatient brusqueness, kneeling to sponge vigorously at an ancient mustard spot on the trousers, as though she had guessed how much was riding on tonight and was angry with him, with herself, for not being ready.

The drapes in the window of Room 226 had been drawn. From the back of one, the lining hung down like a discarded undergarment.

Beyond the door, a man's nasal voice climbed in excitement: "He's going for it! Look out! Oh!" The TV, Alf realized, a football game. He had to knock twice before the door opened and Prince's brown, rectangular face loomed.

"Alf. Good to see you. Come in."

Prince offered him a chair near the window, then padded away in bare feet to stand by one of the twin beds, arrested by a collision on the screen. "Toronto and Hamilton," he said, mesmerized. In his large hand, a glass contained ice, a smear of amber. Alf smelled again the atmosphere of his aftershave, at once brisk and suffocating, saw the heavy, slightly protruding jaw open in a smile that tightened into a wince.

"You a football fan?" Prince had not taken his eyes from the screen.

"You bet," Alf said. In truth, he never watched it. The repetitions of chaos along the line of scrimmage, the frequent stops, bored him. He was a hockey man.

"I got ten bucks riding on this with my son."

"You've got kids?" Alf caught hopefully at the domestic detail, a hint of normalcy, of something he had in common with Prince. He was trying to relax, to adopt the air of someone who'd dropped by a friend's place: for wasn't Prince's casualness with him – the bare feet, the game – a signal they'd moved onto a more intimate plane?

"You don't mind if we watch for a while?"

"No, no, great."

Still riveted to the screen, the executive climbed onto the near bed. He was wearing faultless tan slacks and a white sports shirt with buttoned pockets, open at the throat to reveal a fine gold chain that disappeared into the first shadowy hint of chest hair. Alf crossed his legs and surreptitiously eyed the spot on his trousers. It had dried, but the mustard stain had survived Margaret's attack: a rude little splotch shaped like a pike's head.

To the screen, Prince said, "You want a drink? I got a Scotch going here."

Prince poured his drink on the little table between the beds.

"Ice?"

"That'd be great."

Alf sat with the heavy glass, trying to lose himself in the game. Bodies streamed together, collapsed in a writhing heap. The referee ran up in his prisoner's stripes, waving furiously.

"Ho-ho," Alf said with enthusiasm, "he really ran into it that time."

"Patterson didn't give Clarkson his block," Prince said with disapproval. "He'd have been away." Alf realized Prince was pulling for the Argos and adjusted his comments accordingly, for in truth he hardly cared who won. Half an hour went by. Sitting with his knees up, the executive picked absently at a corn. The ball-carrier dodged under the uprights, raising both arms.

"Yes!" Prince cried, with a shocking fierceness. There was a huge fund of energy in the man, of willpower. He wasn't just watching the game, he was trying to make things turn out the way he wanted.

Alf looked around the room. Prince's suitcase lay on the far bed, like a giant clam opened to reveal a mass of neatly packed clothes. There was a shiny gold package in it, beside the rolled socks: like a gold brick, with a frilly bow.

On the shag carpet, just past the TV and inside the closet door, sat another suitcase: small, square, powder blue. A woman's, Alf realized, a makeup case. Did Prince have his wife with him, or – what was her name – Sharon? Shirley? Those long legs. He looked at the closed bathroom door and bleakness went through him like a cold wind. He sipped his Scotch and stared at the far wall, where a painting of sailboats hung: vague impressions in yellow and pink, leaning in the curve of a tropical bay. Prince roared his approval at a play. Alf had the feeling he'd been here before, exactly like this: waiting for someone who scarcely knew he was there. He wondered if Shirley, or his wife, whoever she was, was waiting too, behind the closed bathroom door, maybe, or downstairs in the bar with its neon palm in the window.

It was almost an hour before the game finished and Prince got up with a tired groan to turn off the TV. "Guess I owe the kid ten bucks," he said, and he flashed Alf a brilliant smile. There was something so open, so boyishly charming in it – it was the thought, it seemed, of his son – that Alf instantly felt better.

His ankles cracking, Prince padded over to the closet and reached inside a hanging suit jacket. As Alf watched, the executive looked down and discovered the makeup case. His bare foot nudged it discreetly out of sight. Then he sat on the edge of the farther bed, facing Alf. In his hands was a small spiral notebook and a fountain pen, which he pulled apart, fitting the cap over the other end with surgical fastidiousness.

"Okay, tell me what you got."

Alf had tried to imagine this moment. He was still not sure what he would say.

He chose his words carefully, frowning at the rug that looked like turquoise grass that had lain uncut for weeks. "I don't think you've got a thing to worry about. This union – Doyle's not going anywhere. There's only a small band that's interested – and they tend to be people no one would follow. Malcontents, I'd call them. They're a pretty sad lot."

The word "malcontents" pleased him. He had been saving it.

"Who are they?" Prince said flatly.

Alf rubbed his shoe on the turquoise grass.

"I mean," and he cleared his throat as he prepared his lie. "Their own leader, this Doyle fellow, told me he wasn't at all pleased at the prospects."

"They may be malcontents," Prince said, "but that's how it usually starts, with *malcontentism*." He delivered the word with cheerless irony.

"I went to a meeting," Alf said.

"Where? Whose house?"

Prince made a sharp stroke in his notebook.

"Not a house, not anybody's house," Alf said. "It was, ah, out in the country. By the river. They had a fire," he added, absurdly. He was describing a meeting he'd been to in the fall of '48, when they were just starting the union. They had roasted wieners, and it had been a happy time, an exuberant time, a time beyond Prince's reach.

Prince looked at him with bemusement. Alf felt his lie was obvious.

"All right," Prince said. "A fire. Who was there?"

"Only a few. Doyle. A few others."

"How many?"

Alf shrugged. "Half a dozen or so."

"You didn't count?"

"Six," Alf said, "not including myself."

The tip of the pen made a small mark in the notebook.

"So who were they?"

"You have to understand," Alf said, "some of these people I've known for years. They may be misguided, but they're –"

"This will be confidential."

"It's not that. I've grown up with these people –"

For a few seconds Prince's eyes met his: they seemed to contain no emotion at all, just a long, chilling evaluation. Alf might have been a post, or a piece of paper. Then the executive began to speak. He was all concerned seriousness now, confiding and almost gentle. "Alf. You've been picked out as one of the people who has a future in this company. But if you're going to succeed, you're going to have make up your mind about which side you're on."

"I'm with you," Alf said.

"Once we have confidence in someone – well, the possibilities of moving up in Intertex are excellent. We pride ourselves on being a meritocracy. There are executives in this company who began as office boys, as ordinary workers. We gave them a chance, and well, they knew what to make of it." Prince paused, letting Alf take *that* in. When he spoke again, it was on a whole new level of intimacy. He seemed, almost, to be confessing. He seemed weary, and more human. "Look, I sympathize with what concerns you. You're loyal to these people, and that's a fine thing. I'm loyal myself. I mean, hell, I came from a poor family. My father worked in a mattress factory all his life. Never made foreman, though he deserved to. And there were seven of us to feed, including my mother, God rest her. I know what it's like, Alf. I know what it's like to wear hand-me-downs and sleep under an old overcoat because there aren't enough blankets. I have every sympathy for the working man. But the only way the working man's going to be taken care of, the only way things are going to improve for him, is if the company he works for does well. That's the *only* place the wealth is gonna come from. It doesn't come from the sky. It doesn't come from *good intentions* . . ."

Prince took a sip of his drink, frowned at the floor before going on. "Textiles isn't steel. It isn't General Motors. The margins aren't big, the competition is ferocious, every penny counts. Every *quarter-penny* counts. We can be good guys, and sign a nice fat contract, and three, five years from now, we wake up and realize we can't compete any more because we've been too generous – I put that word in quotes – in fact we've priced ourselves right out of the market. So, the company goes under, and where's your working man then?"

Prince leaned forward. "I don't wanna hurt these people, Alf. They're my people too. I haven't forgotten that. And I'll do everything I can to avoid hurting them. But better a little blood now than a lot of red ink down the line . . ."

The silence lasted for several seconds. Now Alf felt patronized – he knew these arguments, and had even used some of them himself. But at the same time he felt he needed to be reminded of them. He'd slipped back from a point of understanding he'd reached before. He looked at the sailboats on the wall, he looked at the carpet. All right, he thought.

"If I give you their names," he said, "what will you do with them?"

"Bring them over to G.O., one by one. Give them a good scare, frankly. Tell them we know what they're up to and imply – this is not something we can come out and say, in any case – that they better get back on the straight and narrow or risk losing their jobs."

"So you won't fire them –"

"I find that's rarely a good tactic. As far as it lies within my power, no."

"As far as it lies within your power."

"I'm not here to split hairs with you, Alf."

Alf got up and turned to the window, parting the curtains a little. Across the highway, the spotlit image of a beautiful blonde gazed from a billboard. She was expelling smoke from her cigarette, her heavily lidded eyes smiling with a carnal suggestiveness over the frail thrust of headlights.

"Woody Marr," he said, turning back to Prince.

Prince hesitated, then wrote.

Alf experienced a strange, plummeting absence. It was like being at a memorial service. All that is read out is a name, and yet somehow the whole life is there, its dark parade.

"Next."

Alf said nothing. He was staring at the bed with its flowered spread: its rumpled pattern of twining brown vegetation, huge pink flowers – a nightmare jungle repeated in a million rented rooms like this.

"I have to go," he said.

Prince's grin flashed.

"You've only given me one name."

"I shouldn't have. I'm not on the union side, but this is – I know these people."

"Alf, as I've said –"

"When I'm foreman – then I'm on your side. But I can't do it this way."

"So you're putting the gears to me."

"This has nothing to do with you. It's them –"

The blue eyes had fixed him with a disbelieving smile. *Oh come on*, they said. *You and I know what's going on here. I can't believe you'd be such a fool* . . .

Outside, the pool lights had been turned off. Above, along the rails of the balconies, a heaven of small white lights had come on, twinkling around the courtyard.

The next day he watched Woody climb the stairs to the knitting room with a start of dread and relief. Relief that he was still here, and dread that he, Alf, had hung the other man's life over an abyss. All that morning he kept glancing over at the knitter. The powerful little man with the straight back and the pug's face moved quickly around his machines, tying up threads or replacing bobbins with brusque, angry gestures, just as he always did: a man perpetually pissed off and apparently liking it that way. Just before noon Alf walked down the aisle to Woody's stand.

"So how's old number eleven going?" Alf had fixed the machine two days earlier.

"Hey, buddy," Woody said, his ugly face lighting up. He had never called Alf buddy before: evidently he suspected nothing. "She's goin' like the hoor from hell."

That afternoon when Alf took his break on the fire escape, Woody sat where he had rarely sat before, beside him. There was something deliberate, almost ceremonial, about the way the knitter poured coffee into his Thermos cup, his breathing coming with a slow, laboured huffing. He sat erect, his back not touching the warm brick, and put one big, scarred hand on his knee. Then he raised his cup in a way that seemed extraordinarily dignified, like a stout Japanese warrior.

Along the balcony the other knitters smoked, talked, drank coffee or tea as they gazed out through the bars of the railing, over the deep millyard. Through a distant gap between buildings, golden-rod gilded the face of the dyke that hid most of the Shade.

"Best season of the year," Woody growled. His blunt face had lifted, scowling to the sun: even his praise was defiant.

"My old man used to go deer hunting," Woody said, "up on Manitoulin with the Indians. Had a bit of Indian blood himself."

Alf didn't suppose Woody could actually remember his father, who had been killed in the Great War. He kept silent. He didn't want to encourage Woody, didn't want to know any more about him. Yet Woody was determined to talk. He told Alf about Manitoulin Island: a hunt camp on an inland lake, a story about his father's prowess with a rifle. "Went up there myself a few times. They remembered him in Wicky."

Six floors below, a cart rumbled across the asphalt floor of the yard. Woody took out a package of Craven A's and offered them to Alf, who felt compelled to pluck one out, though he had stayed away from cigarettes for ten years now. He bent to the flame dancing in the chapel of Woody's hands and dragged smoke into his lungs, sitting back to expel it with the sense it no longer mattered what he did, watching the smoke's pale body twist and disintegrate on the blue air.

Three days later Alf crossed Willard to the flat-topped building that held General Office. May Watson's chair was empty, which was just as well: he didn't have an appointment. He went swiftly up the stairs and down the carpeted hall, past the boardroom where he'd had his first meeting with Prince, searching for Prince's office. But his name appeared on none of the brass nameplates marking the doors. Just as he was about to retreat, he heard a toilet flush. A few seconds later, Judy Stackhouse, Prince's secretary, stepped into the hall, smiling warmly as she saw him.

He stood behind her in her office as she leaned into an inner room. The brief factual rumble of Prince's voice answered her. "Send him in."

Prince was standing with his back to him – pointedly, Alf thought – looking out the window behind his desk, one hand in the pocket of his trousers as he surveyed a thicket of reddening sumacs. Without turning he told Alf to sit. Alf slipped warily into an armchair covered in green leather. On Prince's blotter was a paper napkin and a half-eaten Digestive biscuit.

Prince took his own chair. "So," he said, dusting at some invisible particles at the edge of his blotter. When he finally looked at Alf, his face was void of expression, as if Alf were no longer worth even the minimal trouble of courtesy.

"I think we've got off on the wrong foot somehow," Alf said, his voice suddenly parched, breaking. "Somehow you've ended up teed off with me, and maybe I'm a bit teed off myself. But the thing is, I'm loyal to this place –"

"You have the names then."

Prince cleared another particle: the last few grains of the time he had to spare. One more sweep and all his patience would be gone.

"Well, no. That's not why I –"

"Then why are you here?"

"I – I thought we might start over, you and me."

"And how would you propose that we do that, you and I?"

"I want to bury the hatchet. It's just that –"

"I hadn't realized the hatchet was out."

Alf stared back at the man regarding him, it seemed, with utter frankness. Had he misjudged something? Was Prince offering more leeway than he'd imagined? Encouraged, he went on: "The thing is, that name I gave you, I've had it on my conscience. I'd just like to say: he's a good man, a good worker, and I'd hate to feel I'd put him in danger in any way. Especially since, like I said, this union business is going nowhere."

Prince swept once more at his blotter. "I know you like to tell yourself that, Alf. But it's actually not the case. We have evidence that it is going somewhere. Those names you have are critical."

Alf looked away. He had a cutting sense of letting the side down. What was the matter with him? And yet, his chance still lay before him. He was still in Prince's motel room. All he had to do was say a few names, and he would be back, instantly, in Prince's good graces. He would resume his progress along the upwards-climbing road, the road that led, by degrees, out of the world of sore backs and time clocks. He stared at the rich wood of Prince's desk.

"Alf, I fear you may be a little sentimental for this business."

Prince's voice seemed to arrive across a great distance, as his father's once had, calling him out of a daydream.

"Business, Alf: it's war, really. I mean, it's played within the law, more or less, and people try to be gentlemen about it, even buddies. And that's all necessary – oil for the wheels. But to be frank, it takes a certain bloody-mindedness. You can't worry about other people too much." The cajoling drone of Prince's voice went on. Remotely, Alf heard separate words and phrases, floating sedately by on its tide. He stared past the smooth head in front of him, into the jungle of sumacs behind the office. What he saw was a wine cellar in France. In September of 1944 he had killed a German soldier who had ambushed him. The fellow had leapt over some barrels and Alf had whirled just in time to take his weight on the barrel of his gun and fire. A few moments later one of Alf's mates had flung back a door and light had flooded the body at his feet. It was a boy, not more than fourteen or fifteen. Above his grey army uniform the startled eyes had already fixed on nothing. His mouth was open in a small, rabbity smile, as though he'd intended only a joke. In his hand was a broken wine bottle. Feeling light-headed, he left immediately. In the outer office, Judy Stackhouse looked up brightly. "Alf – are you all right, Alf?" She stood as he leaned for a moment, planting his hand on the edge of her desk. "Would you like a cookie?" Smiling hopefully, Judy nudged the package of Digestives towards him, across her scarlet blotter.

14

SMILEY PHONED. Did Joe want to go hunting?

"Come over to my place," his friend said, and hung up.

For weeks Joe had avoided Smiley's house because he was avoiding Smiley's sister. He had told Sandy they could still be friends, but seeing her was painful: painful to have his guilt aroused by the way she clung to him still, by the way she looked at him, as if there were a debt he owed her, though of course she never said what it was. She gave the impression she was willing to go on waiting, patiently, willing to do whatever it was he wanted, even if it was going to be years before he asked her. One morning he had walked to school, knowing she was following a block behind. He had refused to turn and wait for her. Then at the rail overpass he had looked back, in remorse, to discover she was no longer there.

He followed the path along the top of the dyke, with its view over the Island yards, where people were raking leaves towards spindling fires. The smoke rolled across the dyke, flattening over the dark water of the Atta.

Sandy's father was kneeling on the back porch, prodding with a screwdriver at a small electric motor. His round face with its shiny cheeks glanced up at Joe.

"Joe," he said flatly, looking back to his work. Almost casually, a judgment had fallen.

Joe lingered, watching, held by the hope of reprieve: held by the chance Charlie Richards would say something that would allow them to go on as before.

"What's that for?" he said.

Charlie Richards worked on without answering: he who for years had treated Joe with such friendliness Joe had felt like one of the family. In the summer, waiting for Sandy to come home from her waitressing job at the Oasis, Joe used to sit with him on the patio

under the Manitoba maple, sharing a lemonade, while he talked
about the war with an air of humorous disbelief, so unlike Joe's
father, as if the whole thing were a bit of rollicking bad luck he'd been
fortunate to have escaped: that time in Italy, when a sniper had kept
him pinned against a rock for an entire day . . .

And then Sandy would arrive, swinging around the corner of the
house in her beige Oasis uniform, her eyes going straight to Joe's, her
lips suppressing a smile that emerged anyway: their happiness a
secret, though he saw now it must have been plain to everyone. All
that was gone now, a summer, an eon, ago. Watching her father's
prodding screwdriver, he was filled with regret.

"I found it in the cellar," Charlie Richards said. "It's a good little
engine. Seemed a shame to throw it out."

Smiley carried the .22, its barrel pointing towards the ground as if it
were scenting a trail. They left the grass of Lions Park and entered
the cleft in the cedar bush. Then the borders of fields, woods, the
path weaving in and out of the light, past an old hay mow rusting
into a heap of rocks spotted with the golden suns of lichens. He
wondered if his father had ridden it. His father had worked on
Wiley's farm as a boy, and its fields were saturated with the stories
he had told Joe: unharnessing the draft horses, King and Maud,
riding them bareback into the river in a time before time when
actions seemed larger than life, and so powerfully etched they could
almost be happening still, just out of sight – his father and Pete
Moon still racing the heavy-shanked horses through the gleaming
shallows. He had a sense that little had happened in his own life, by
comparison. His father, in a way, owned the land he was walking
on, just as he owned the Depression, and the war, all the great
adventures of the past, and now nothing was left to Joe but a kind
of ordinariness, a sadness.

Across the sloping field stubbled with the pale, chewed-off stalks
of corn lay small heaps of earth – groundhog mounds – as if

someone had dug random postholes. Joe and Smiley watched them keenly, looking for something to kill. A blue jay flew towards a pine, and Smiley followed it in the scope, his heavy face grimacing against the stock.

"*Pow*," he said softly, and the jay both died and lived.

They settled into a hollow, on dry, pressed-down grass, looking back over the field they had just skirted. Distantly, across the river, they could see the heights of the North End, above the severe gash made by the CN tracks. Joe scanned the backs of the big houses, their roofs and second storeys visible over the edge of the precipice. It was possible Anna Macrimmon lived there, just there, behind the green awning; or there, where a huge beech had shed half its gold.

"Give me the gun," he said.

The tunnel of the scope took him closer. He planted its thin cross on the naked limbs of the beech, on a dilapidated gazebo where an orange towel hung from a railing.

Swiftly he lowered the .22 and sighted into the field. His shot raised a puff of yellow dust that drifted away.

"Hey!" Smiley said.

"I thought I saw one," Joe said, lying. He had *had* to fire. He handed back the gun with trembling hands.

After an hour they had seen no groundhogs, so they went on, following the trail where it descended through trees into the bottom-lands of the Atta: the savannah of grasses and weeds and wild fruit trees where a few weeks earlier Jamie had been found. After a while they came to a sandy beach by the river and sat on a great, silvered log, looking out at the beer-coloured water where it spread towards a rapids.

"So," Smiley said.

Joe waited for the blow: he was sure his friend was going to lay into him about Sandy.

"So I guess I'm droppin' out," Smiley said.

"Dropping – you mean, out of *school*?"

Smiley's deep-set eyes scanned the water. There had been no hint of this.

"Smiley!"

His friend shrugged, as if the whole matter were beyond explanation and even comprehension: it was just something that had happened to him. Joe was on the verge of laughing. Surely Smiley was joking in his deadpan way. His friend was one of the best two or three math students in the class. He had talked of going to university.

"I thought you were going on. I mean, what are you gonna do, go into the *mill*?"

He didn't bother to hide his sarcasm. Smiley sat with his head down, twisting a bit of stick.

"With your abilities, you could be a teacher. Some kind of scientist –"

"Thought maybe I'd join the Marines."

"The *Marines*?"

"See the world," Smiley said with a bleak giggle.

"Tell me why you wouldn't go on. Seriously."

Smiley looked at the stick in his hands and said, "It just seems pointless."

"What does? Getting up in the world? Not having to work with your hands?"

"I sort of like usin' my hands."

"So you're going to join the Marines and" – Joe gestured angrily at the river – "kill people."

"I wouldn't stay there for long. Just for a year or two, for the fun of it –"

"They shave your head and call you an asshole. You call that fun?"

Joe could get no more out of him. He looked at his friend: at the snub nose plastered with coppery freckles, at his eyes flicking back and forth over the sand, his smile secretive and angry, as though he were enjoying the destruction of his own life. Joe got up and moved towards the water, picking up a stone and flinging it hard, watching it enter the river and standing with his hands on his hips, watching the water change and not change, sliding towards the churning catastrophe of the rapids.

"I love Anna Macrimmon," Smiley said.

Joe turned back towards him. What Smiley had said seemed so preposterous, so *impossible*, that it had already become incomprehensible.

"The new girl," Smiley said in a choked voice, looking at him miserably. "I love her."

It *was* impossible. Smiley never spoke like this, never revealed his feelings, straight out, about anything. There was always a joke instead.

But Smiley was looking towards the water with such desolation, Joe knew it was true.

"You're friends with her," Smiley said. "Maybe you could speak to her for me."

"Speak – what would *I* say?" He was just starting to experience outrage at what he felt was a trespass.

"I dunno. Find out how she feels about me."

"She's not your type!"

"How do you know? What's my type?" The small eyes flicked at Joe, hostile.

"She's a poet. You don't like poetry," Joe said, grasping at straws. He couldn't come right out and say, She'd never love you. You're a slob, it's unthinkable.

Smiley looked back at the river, unmoved.

"I mean, hell," Joe said, walking back towards the log, "she's – you know, the way she is, the way she dresses, she's –"

"What – better than me?"

"I wouldn't say that exactly –"

"It's what you meant." And to the river: "You're saying she's too good for me." After a moment he added, "I know she is. I know I won't ever get her. But when she – all I have to do is see her, and I know she's the only one I'll ever want."

"You'll want others," Joe said.

"Fuck off," Smiley said.

"Oh come off it."

Smiley exploded from the log. Joe had no time to react before his friend was shoving him backwards, shoving and straight-arming him with a cold fury in his shrunken pupils.

"For fuck's sake, what are you doing?" Joe yelled, shoving back. In a way, he was not surprised by what was happening. What was coming out of Smiley now – he had the feeling he'd always known it was there, a resentment that had become more tightly packed with every year, awaiting a spark like this. He was frightened, not so much by any physical danger as by the sense of vast emotion running amok. With pounding heart, a little desperate, guilty too (he knew he'd spoken in a superior way to Smiley, knew that he'd always felt secretly superior to his friend, and sensed that now he was reaping his punishment), he pushed back. They were slapping at each other, on the verge of punching, when Smiley strode back to the log and picked up the .22. He turned and sighted the gun at Joe's forehead. The eye Joe could see was closed, while Smiley's other eye was buried behind the glass porthole of the scope. Smiley's finger held motionless on the trigger, and still Joe didn't believe he'd pull it. He stood watching, alert but not really afraid as Smiley sighted the gun down his chest.

"Pow," Smiley said.

15

BILLY WAS WAITING for Jamie under the elm. Yellow leaves were falling, one and two and three at a time, twirling and wafting and setting down, soundlessly, on the asphalt of the empty Boys' Yard. Every day Billy's class for slow learners was dismissed fifteen minutes earlier than the other grades, and every day when Jamie's class got out, Billy was waiting for him. Several times, Jamie tried hanging back inside the school, but Billy went on waiting, sitting under the elm, looking up at the doors. Jamie always had to leave eventually, driven out by a teacher or the janitor, and always he told the same lie to Billy. "I have to go home and help my mother." Billy usually walked home with him, though his own house was in another direction, on the Flats. Jamie would say, "Don't you have to go home?" and Billy would say, "My mom ain't home from work yet," and go on scuffing along beside him, grinning that brown-toothed grin whenever Jamie looked at him, as if there was nothing better in the world than scuffing along in the leaves – the piled and drifted leaves whispering and swishing around their knees – in the smell of bonfires. The first time, he had come right up to the door of Jamie's house and would have come in too, if Jamie hadn't blocked his way. "I have to help my mom," Jamie told him while Billy peered past him into the kitchen. Jamie was afraid his mother would see them together. Then there would be the spatula to deal with again, the bone-looking in her black eyes.

Billy stood up and came towards him through the yard, smiling that blazing smile that made him, Jamie, feel bad, knowing he was going to lie to him again, lie to him and disappoint him and – after they'd walked down the hill together – leave him standing on West Street while he went into the house. The worst thing was that Billy would wait outside the house, sometimes for a long time. Jamie would look out and there he'd be, sitting on the curb, poking at something with a stick. Once, his mother had seen Billy waiting. "Is that the Boileau boy out there?" Jamie had shrugged and said he didn't know, and his mother said, "Just wait in here till he goes away." No, he couldn't go out and play until Billy went away, and when it was finally safe to go out, there was nobody to play with. The lonely feeling he got – the sad, lonely feeling – was not just in him. It was in Lookout Hill, rising yellow across the river, and in the river, the colour of old metal, chopping away among its scummy stones. He'd float sticks and bomb them with stones, or go over to Lions Park and swing, until he was called for supper.

"I know," Billy said in his flat voice, with a hint of a sneer. "You have to go home and help your mother."

"No I don't," Jamie said.

Billy was walking beside him now, towards the gates. *No I don't* had just popped out. He was sick of telling the old lie, but now that he'd said something else, said the truth, he felt like he didn't know where he was any more. He didn't know what to say next.

Across the road a black dog with a white streak between its eyes was lifting its leg to pee.

"We could go to the Indian Trail," Billy said, after a moment.

"All right," Jamie said. But he felt like running away.

It's all right.

He looked up, startled.

"Really?" he said, questioning the voice. He had stopped at the gate. The dog was by another tree: a squirt of yellow and it trotted on.

Sure, the voice said. *Go ahead.*

"What?" Billy said.

Praise the Lord and pass the ammunition!

Jamie laughed. The voice had tickled him.

"What!" Billy said, dancing around him.

"Praise the Lord and pass the ammunition!"

Billy was dancing from foot to foot while he held his crotch with one hand like he had to go to the bathroom.

"We could make gunpowder!" Billy said.

They crossed the park and went down the road that led to the Indian Trail. The trail ran through woods on a steep bank, so that you could look down and see a road, rooftops, far below you – or up and see the fences straggling along at the end of people's yards. But the trail itself (which was really many trails, interwoven) was a secret place, and they went along hidden from view, with sticks for spears, a raiding party that had snuck into town to burn and steal things and kill people. They were on horses now, little Indian ponies that neighed and stamped and sidestepped down a slope to a clearing. On the far side of the clearing was a smooth, rounded rock, like the half-buried shell of an enormous turtle.

"My grandfather's buried there," Billy said. "Underneath the rock."

"For real?"

"He was a chief."

Jamie looked around. He had forgotten the spatula and his mother's eyes. The motionless yellow trees around the stone (they were standing on it now, as on an island in a rising flood) seemed to know they were there.

16

TALK OF LIZ McVEY broke out one day after gym, when the boys of 13A were dressing in the locker room. Dick Osborne said he'd heard that Liz had broken up with her boyfriend, Bobby Tanner, a salesman three or four years older than she. Bobby, someone else said, had been "banging her." This set off a spirited discussion about who might get to bang her next, a happy prospect since Liz was generally agreed to be one of the best-looking girls in the class. Brad Long – idly drying himself in the doorway of the shower – shamed them all into silence by announcing, with an air of melancholy authority, that Liz was a "classy lady." There was something in his reputation as a ladies' man that took the ground from beneath their feet, for if Brad, who was generally thought to be "doing it," spoke up for a girl, it reminded them of their own pitiful lack of experience. The "classy lady" was out of range of most of them, anyway, because of her looks and because she was the daughter of the town's richest man.

When Liz stopped Joe in the hall, all this was in his mind. You couldn't hear that a girl had been doing it and then forget all about it as she stood not two feet away, gazing at you with those large, beautiful, yet somehow frozen eyes. She wore her curly hair cropped short, and her full mouth was crimped a bit on either side, pushing out the underside of her top lip. It was a babyish kind of mouth, with a look of having just been pulled off the bottle. Joe was attracted to her, yet didn't care for her habit of putting on airs, especially an air of languorous boredom. She was a star actress with the Drama Club. A year before, he had watched her play the lead in *Deirdre's Island*, a murder mystery about a vengeful society lady and her guests. An entirely different Liz had emerged: taut and feline and astonishingly mature. The critic from the *Johnsonville Gleaner* had gone off his head about her, but at the same time she had given Joe the willies, there was something so repulsive about the atmosphere of controlled hysteria she conveyed.

Now she was asking him to a party at her place, the following Saturday night. This was so unexpected – he was not a member of the North End gang – that he hesitated. She seemed provoked by this, for staring at him with those too-bright eyes, she purred, "*People* will be disappointed if you don't come," with such an insinuating emphasis on "people" that he felt pierced by some as-yet-undeciphered message and said, Sure, he'd be glad to come. After she'd trailed off, he stood dissecting that cryptic "people," coming almost instantly to the conclusion that she was referring to Anna Macrimmon.

In the next class, English, he watched Anna reading her copy of *Macbeth*. For weeks now he had been aware of a deepening connection between them. Their conversations seemed to carry a more complex load of emotion. Their glances, he felt, increasingly hinted at the possibility of a mutual future. He was *almost* sure this was real and not just something he'd dreamed up, but he didn't speak about it in case he was fooling himself. Now he watched her as she read with deep focus, that absolute self-containment she seemed able to summon, to fall into, at any time. He had seen it during an assembly, while a comic skit was being performed on stage. He had looked over at her and discovered her – amid an entire gymnasium roaring with laughter – simply looking, neither amused nor disapproving nor oblivious. There was some force of calm in her, some mindfulness, that he admired and was in awe of, for he had never seen such a thing in anyone, except perhaps in Archibald Mann, though in Mann's remoteness there was always something stern, as if he were dissecting or even judging what he saw. But in Anna Macrimmon there was no judgment: she was simply looking, her head a little lowered in that way she had, and in that looking, he felt, was more seeing than he could himself imagine. What was she thinking? Did she think them all fools? He had come to the point where she seemed superior not just to all the other girls but to himself as well. This was daunting – what could he possibly do to deserve her? And yet he pressed on, in his secret way, pursuing her.

He let two classes go by before he contrived to meet her in the hall. She seemed no more friendly than usual, chatting to him as they moved through the crowd, though when he asked if she was going to Liz's party, she sent him a brief sideways smile, past the pale wing of her hair, and said, in a whimsical, sing-song voice, "Oh, I think so." There was a flirtatiousness here, he thought, woven with shyness, at once hiding and disclosing something deeper.

Liz's invitation tipped him towards buying the coat. He had been eyeing it for weeks, fearful it might disappear from Art Blostein's show window: a windbreaker-style jacket with a body of rich choco-late suede and beige, knitted arms. Propped in front of the headless torso that wore the jacket was a little card carrying the silhouette of a rabbit's head and the message: AS ADVERTISED IN PLAYBOY. The coat, when he tried it on, seemed too large for him, but Art Blostein assured him that was the style, and as he gazed at his three selves in Art's triple mirror (each looking a little different, each claiming to be genuine), it seemed he had changed: he looked bigger, more relaxed, more in the know. "It's you!" Art said happily, and his rubbery clown's face sent a laughing smile of approval over Joe's shoulder.

He crossed Shade to the bank. At the wicket, he couldn't help looking around, worried his mother might come in. He had never taken money out of this account before, not since he and his mother had opened it ten years before. Wearing her best coat, a heavy English tweed (he could still see its houndstooth checking, its infinite repetitions like the interference swimming up a television screen), she had announced to the teller and anyone else who cared to listen (it had seemed to him that the whole bank was listening) just how well Joe was doing in school, how someday he'd go to university: that's what this account was for, to save up all his allowances and gifts and payment for small jobs. Afterwards, she'd practically made a ceremony of handing him the little book with its stiff red cover. "This is your future," she'd said. "Take good care of it." He'd carried his future through the streets of Attawan, his hand sweating, it seemed so important. When they got home she'd relieved him of it and put it in her dresser drawer.

According to the book – which he now kept in the battered blue dresser wedged beside his desk – the account contained more than a thousand dollars, most of which he'd earned himself, working summers in the mill and filling shelves at the A&P after school. He took the money – four new twenties and a ten – back to Art's, and Art folded the jacket into a box, turning two wings of tissue paper over it with the tenderness of someone burying a baby.

That evening, after he got home from the A&P, he smuggled the box up to his bedroom and hid it in the back of the closet. It was critical that his family not see the coat, which was like a new skin to him, tender and vulnerable. After supper, he felt he had to look at it again. His parents were watching television – the rumble of canned laughter was floating up the stairs – so he opened the box, slipped on the coat, and went swiftly down the hall to his parents' bedroom, where a full-length mirror hung on their closet door. In its icy rectangle, the coat looked fine, too fine, with its bulky arms like knitted chainmail. It outshone everything else: his green slacks with their shiny, shapeless knees, his tired desert boots, even his face. Yes, the coat was perfect, but his mouth was too thin and his ears stuck out. He gazed at himself suspiciously and disapprovingly, as if he had run into a disreputable cousin.

Leaving the room, he met his father in the hall. As they passed, his father threw out his hip in a friendly bodycheck.

His father seemed not to have noticed the coat at all.

"Say, Joe," his father said. Reluctantly, Joe turned back to him.

His father looked tired these days, hollow-eyed – Joe's mother had mentioned he wasn't sleeping well – and now he drew back his lips in a kind of wince, as if his words had to be tugged from his flesh, like a sliver.

"You're going on to university –"

The coat suddenly felt huge on him, almost clownish.

"That's right."

"I was wondering," his father said, as he drew his hand over his balding head, "are you doing it for the money? I mean, is money your main purpose for going on – to make a lot of money?"

"Not really," Joe said, bewildered. In truth, he had never thought about money per se. What he thought about, in that line, was a different way of life: a house with a library, maybe. But even *that* wasn't the whole story.

His father's eyes flashed out at him. There was something shy in his father, a youthfulness that had never grown entirely used to the world's light. "It's history, I guess, that attracts you?"

"That's right."

His father motioned with his hand, as if tossing away a fistful of sand.

"You love it, I guess."

"Uh-huh."

They were both uneasy now, at this mention of love. Joe was reminded of the time, years ago, when his father had tried to tell him about sex. They had both been mortally embarrassed by his "And you put your body inside the woman's" delivered with grimly set jaw and averted gaze. Joe had already known *that*.

But now his father looked at him directly, and for a moment the blue eyes blazed out not in shyness but in strength and glad discovery.

"Good," his father said. "That's good." And he nodded and nodded, in awkward, fond approval. "You keep on then."

Joe went back to his room and stripped off the jacket. He did not understand what had just happened, but he felt like weeping. He felt like a fraud. His jacket was a fraud, and he was a fraud for thinking it might make a difference. His dad loved him. He hated to be reminded of it. The knowledge of this love flooded through him like a weakness, dissolving everything that a moment before he had been reasonably certain of. Who was he? What in hell was he doing? He stared at the new coat with remorse and hatred.

Two days later he went back to Art Blostein's and bought tan slacks, a pale-blue, button-down shirt with faint pinstriping (just like the shirts Brad Long wore, he noted with satisfaction), and a soft, navy-blue cardigan. At Jarrod's, down the street, he bought a new pair of Hush Puppies in chocolate suede. He hid these items in his closet, and on the evening of the party smuggled the new jacket, still wrapped in its box, into the trunk of the Biscayne. Then he went back to his room to change.

At nine o'clock, he was ready. Wearing his old poplin windbreaker over the new sweater, he crept down the stairs. But his mother must have been listening. She came down the hall in a fluster of excitement to see him off. A week before, when he'd told her he was going to the McVeys', she'd barely been able to contain her pleasure. A day later, she'd announced that she'd washed his best slacks and shirt; she'd even cleaned his church shoes.

And now she would see what he had done. He stood in the little entrance hall and watched her eyes – her wide-set eyes in which he could read every nuance of her inner weather – watched them brighten as she took in the new slacks. And the cardigan, peeking out below his jacket.

"Joe, what have you done? Let me see!"

He was ready to do battle, to tell her, It's my money, I earned every penny, but she was delighted.

"Oh Joe, open the jacket! Let me see!" She stood back, her gaze roaming and glowing.

"Yes, that's wonderful, you've got wonderful taste. Where did you get them?"

He told her the story. She stood close to him, too close, really, for comfort, gazing at him in a fever of admiration and picking microscopic bits of lint off his sweater, pushing his hair off his forehead. "I got a new jacket too," he told her sheepishly. She made him fetch it from the car. She seemed less delighted with the coat – he thought her face darkened when he told her the price – but the tide of her enthusiasm could not be stopped. Suddenly leaning up, she planted a kiss on his cheek. For a moment, smelling her familiar smell, feeling her lips brush his skin, he sensed the vanished world of the 1930s come flooding up in her. His mother, too, might have been eighteen.

The streets of the town were lit with bonfires, where householders had raked leaves to the curb. Some of the piles flared as he passed in the Biscayne; others smouldered till the gust from the car fanned them, sending bright sparks tumbling across the road. Occasionally, a heating chestnut popped. Smoke rose in tottering pale columns, and the smell of it at his open window was the joy of the world burning, life-giving and sharp. He parked on Robert and walked past a dozen other cars towards the McVeys', glancing at the open garage where the windshield of the Lincoln gazed out with imperial calm. The car was one of the chief shrines of the many he had created wherever Anna Macrimmon had sat, walked, spoken to him. In his chest another fire burned.

A small window gave a view into a large hall covered with an Indian rug. He saw the flowing, curving base of stairs carpeted in deep green and a long, panelled hall leading towards the arctic glow of an empty kitchen. Music pulsed distantly – he thought he heard Diana Ross's voice cakewalking to heaven – but no one answered the rap of the heavy knocker. He was wondering if he should try the back of the house when the door opened and Doc McVey stood before him in a silky black-and-red dressing gown, worn – Joe found this odd – over his shirt and trousers. At his throat was a dark-blue ascot, in his hand a glass filled to the brim with ice.

"A late reveller," Doc said in his mild, slightly fey voice as he peered with cheerful irony through his round glasses. He was a tall man with a babyish face and a habitual look of playful bemusement, slightly scornful. He was a doctor, and though he no longer practised, he kept his old office downtown at the head of steep stairs over Maggie's Beauty Parlour. He had inherited money – Joe had this from his father – and made a great deal more investing it in the stock market, as well as buying and selling properties in the area. For several years – this was an open secret in the town – he had been having an affair with a woman called Babs Wilcocks, who worked as a secretary in Bannerman's General Office.

"Aren't you Alf Walker's boy?" Doc McVey said, ushering Joe in.

Suddenly his past, his family, seemed all too vividly present, as if they had trudged in behind him. The music was much louder now, but he could see no signs of a party.

"Your dad and I went to school together. He was very fast on the track, your dad. He gave me a lot of trouble in the hundred."

"Is that right?"

"Oh yes, he was fast," Doc McVey said suggestively, as though some scandal were associated with his father's speed. As his large eyes – magnified, it seemed, by his glasses – fixed Joe with a look of amused watchfulness, Joe had the sense he was being tested, as though Doc McVey were waiting to see if this interesting creature, *Alf Walker's son*, might perform a trick or two. Joe looked away down the hall. Sally, Liz's younger sister, was approaching with a bowl of popcorn. She acknowledged Joe with a shy smile and, sticking her neck out awkwardly as if to facilitate her escape, started up the stairs, followed by a fluffy white cat. Doc McVey was still looking at Joe. "Down there, through the kitchen," he drawled, gesturing with the ice.

As Joe reached the kitchen, Liz McVey climbed from a dark room sunk beyond it – from a babble of voices and the wail of Dion complaining, once more, about Runaround Sue.

"Joe! I was afraid you weren't going to make it!" She came towards him with that overly intense look of hers, almost tragic, and leaned up to kiss him on the cheek. He caught a whiff of something musky, arousing. Taking his coat, she tossed it over several others on a chair; as she turned away, the pile toppled to the floor. "Can I get you a drink?"

While she rummaged in the fridge, he restored the coats to the chair, hanging his own over the back, and turned to the doorway that led, he saw, to a large room packed with shadowy bodies. The only light came from the kitchen and from the outdoor lights shining through a wall of French doors, from the deserted patio. He could not see Anna Macrimmon.

They lingered talking in the kitchen. Liz stood with her back to the counter, with one arm planted on her hip, the other stretched along the counter. It was a bold pose, and it suited her, suited her look of blazing candour. Below her knee-length skirt, maroon stockings complemented the deep cherry red of her blouse. She wore more eye makeup than usual, a touch of Cleopatra. He found her attractive, in a provocative, almost vulgar way.

"I *liked* what you said yesterday in Mann's class, about war not being good for anybody. *Very* beautifully put."

He muttered his thanks. He'd been rather embarrassed by his own comments at the time, his argument with Brad Long in front of the whole class, in front of Anna, about the benefits of war. Brad had bragged that his father, an officer on a destroyer, had gone away a boy and come back – this had raised a laugh – "a real cool guy."

"War must be so horrible," Liz said, looking at him with deep concern. "Don't you think?"

He said, "Did *your* dad go overseas?"

"Oh heavens no!" Her hand with its three rings splayed over her chest. "They would never have had him, not with his *eyes*. My God, he couldn't have told which end of a gun was which. Oh no, he missed it all, thank God. Or I think, thank God," she added ominously. He glanced at the dark door to his right. He was expecting Anna to appear at any minute. Someone turned up the music. In the cupboards, glassware was beginning to dance. Liz said, "Why don't we go somewhere where we can actually hear each other?"

Reluctantly – yet half-glad of the distraction – he let himself be led through the dining room, where a vast table gleamed in the dimness. Then into a large living room, past a long couch with carved, shapely legs, upholstered in some striped fabric. Two identical, moss-green wingback chairs faced a fireplace with a marble mantel. There were Indian rugs scattered over the broadloom, while oil paintings glinted under little tubular brass shades: bright, ornately framed landscapes showing winding autumnal rivers, a red northern sky stamped by a V of geese. He had never been in such richly decorated rooms before. From this moment on, he would never think his own house anything but shabby and second-rate.

But the living room was apparently not to Liz's taste. She led him on, through the hall where he'd first entered, through a heavy door into a den. This room looked more lived-in. Photographs in gilt frames hung over a carved desk where a stack of papers was pinned with a rock of raw glass. There was a small television and a wide couch covered in a beige material, with throw cushions in green and blue. Liz curled up at one end of it, drawing up her legs in their maroon stockings. He sat at the other end, but had difficulty finding the right posture. To match hers would have committed him to a directness and intimacy he did not feel. He sat at an angle to her, his attention diverted by a large book resting on the coffee table. On its cover, a racing yacht tilted under full sail.

"So," Liz said, as if they were two old friends who at long last had found time to talk.

"Your dad likes sailing?"

"Oh yes," she said, a bit impatiently. "He's already got one boat, up at the cottage. But he's threatening to get one he can go around the world in –"

"Really?"

"I hear you broke up with Sandy," she said, ignoring his question. "Or do I have that wrong –"

"No, you've got it right," he said, a bit surprised. He looked into her face, all sympathy and concern, though in her eyes the brightness danced: wasn't life hard and wasn't it fun?

"A *very* pretty girl," Liz said. "I hope it wasn't too painful."

"Well," he said, shrugging. It had been painful, but not in the way she perhaps meant.

"When Bob and I broke up – this was over a month ago – well, it's not something you want to go through every day."

"No," he said. It occurred to him she might be vetting him, for Anna. Anna would have to know whether he was free. "No," he repeated, more strongly. "Not every day."

Behind him, though the closed door, he heard someone come into the house. He looked around.

"Just ignore them," Liz said sharply. "They can find their own way."

"Is Anna here?" he said.

"She *was*," Liz said, without missing a beat. "She and Brad got here first. They went off about twenty minutes ago –"

"Oh they're here together?" he said, feigning a mild interest.

"Together!" she cried. "The original Bobbsey Twins! We were running out of beer and Brad said he could get some from a friend, although of course knowing Brad they probably went by way of the gravel pit." She was watching him with a straight-on innocence now. The abandoned gravel pit to the east of town was a favourite parking spot. There were nights when the spring-fed lake at its centre was completely ringed with cars.

Later, she drew him onto the dance floor for a slow one. Her hand was cool in his, and as she snuggled in, her pelvis brushed against his thigh. His own excitement – the stirring in his trousers – seemed a distant thing, a nuisance, really, and he pushed her back a little. It was clear now that Liz had never been fronting for Anna, she was only fronting for herself, and though he found this flattering, he could not stop thinking about Anna, Anna out there in the night somewhere, Anna with Brad Long. He refused Liz's view of them as inseparable, because it didn't square with what he knew. It was true, Anna and Brad had gone out together, at least once, but to Joe's mind she was more at ease, more content, with him. He didn't trust Liz. All he needed was to have Anna find him all wrapped up with Liz and he could kiss his chances with her goodbye – which, maybe, was Liz's plan.

After three dances he left her on the excuse he needed a washroom. The one off the kitchen was in use, so Liz directed him to the second floor. Returning downstairs, the sound of a cabinet door squeaking in the den tempted him to look in. Anna Macrimmon was there, leaning forward to peer into a tall bookcase. She wore a rather short, pleated skirt of green plaid, which he'd never seen on her before, green stockings, and a tight-fitting white blouse with long sleeves.

"Anna," he said, going right up to her. Beer had given him confidence. "I thought you weren't coming. I was heartbroken."

"Go on!" she cried, catching his bantering tone. But she put her arm through his and drew him to the books. He was suddenly giddy and, at the same time, stone-cold sober. She had never been so physical with him. His right arm weightless.

"Look at this," she said. "They've got Shelley's poems –"

"Jeez, do you think we better tell him?"

"Oh you're as bad as Brad," she said, giving his arm a squeeze.

"Don't say that," he said, keeping up the levity. But her reference to Brad had stung. "I'm far worse."

"Then I'm *really* in trouble!"

She squeezed his arm again before releasing it. He watched her take down the ancient-looking volume in its faded leather cover. He was drunk on her now: her smell that was scarcely a smell but a freshness, a space: her shoulder brushing his as they leaned over the musty-smelling pages. He read:

The awful shadow of some unseen Power,
Floats though unseen among us . . .

Her attention to the brittle page was all-consuming, it drew the whole room towards Shelley's words: the furniture, the photographs, the other books, all found their centre in the packed lines of verse. But *he* couldn't concentrate on the poetry. He kept looking up at her, at the way her lips moved slightly as she read, at the way her hair fell across her birthmark, white burned below brown.

She uncovered a picture of the poet, under a tissue overlay. Shelley's huge eyes were trained upwards in anxiety and exaltation. "I've been in his house," she said, "on the Gulf of Spezia – the Casa Magni. You can feel him there. He was only thirty when he drowned."

"How did he drown?" he said, for something to say. His eyes went on roaming her face, her hair.

"He was sailing and – he put out in a storm he shouldn't have put out in. Maybe he thought it was time."

She looked at Joe now, with a meaning he could not decipher: a probing seriousness and, far away, a hint of gaiety, of cold, bright gaiety, sun on a cold sea.

"I wonder what year this is," she said suddenly, turning back to the book.

She found the date on the last page, and they struggled with the Roman numerals.

"I'm no good with these things."

"Eighteen fifty-six," he said at last, "the year the Crimean War ended."

"You love it too, don't you?" she said. And when he looked puzzled, "The past."

"Sometimes I feel like it's still going on," he said. He had once tried to tell this to Smiley, and Smiley had mocked him mercilessly. He had not told anyone since.

"Yes!" she cried. "You think that when you turn a corner, you'll run into women with long dresses. You'll run into Shelley!"

"You've been in his house," he said, wondering.

"Yes, I went there with – a friend. It was hard to find. But the people around there all call it Shelley's house. There's not a plaque up or anything. They just remember. You get a feeling they're proud to."

"Where is it again?"

"In Italy, near Leghorn. It's on the sea. You know, the last anyone saw of Shelley he was laughing as he went out to meet the storm."

For a moment, beyond speech, their gazes remained locked. She was the first to look away. He saw colour flood her neck, saw it change the mark on her cheek: the white becoming pink.

"Let's go out," he said.

"Where? Out in the cold?"

She had her head down, evading him.

"I mean, let's go out on a date. Let's go for a walk."

"I can't, Joe."

"Why can't you? You go out with *him*."

"I *like* Brad," she said, lifting her face in defiance.

"You don't like me?"

"You know that's not what I mean. I like you very much."

She was riffling quickly through the Shelley now. She put the book back on the shelf.

He touched her hair, tried to tuck it behind her ear, as he had seen her do, so many times. She pulled away.

"Just go for a walk with me sometime," he pleaded.

"Of course I will – a walk."

She had turned her back on him, and her voice sounded muffled, miserable.

"Anna," he said.

Liz came in.

"There you are," she said. "We've been looking all over for you!"

Brad, grinning, towered behind her.

17

IN THE OLDS' SPEEDOMETER, the green ribbon grew longer, extending to seventy-five, eighty, as Brad floated them past a string of slower cars. He steered with one hand, his arm straight to the wheel, and kept glancing over his shoulder at Joe, chatting with his happy, boasting mixture of enthusiasm and disbelief, as if the world were full of marvels he could scarcely credit.

"Too fast," Anna said from the seat beside him. Her dark glasses gave her a convalescent air. She had a headache, and for the last half-hour had kept mostly silent. They were on their way to Niagara Falls. The trip had been Liz's idea: Anna, unlike the rest of them, had never seen the Falls, and wouldn't it be nice for the four of them to go down? So here they were, on the day after the party, in Brad's father's black 98, watching the oncoming lane where a tractor and wagon had just pulled into their path.

"Brad," Joe warned from the back seat.

"I got it," Brad said, and at the last second, while fascination hovered at the edge of horror, he tucked the Olds behind a station wagon.

"You see," Brad said cheerfully, "if we'd been going any slower we'd be dead." In the filthy window of the station wagon a child was waving frantically.

"If you'd been going any slower, we wouldn't have been out there," Anna said dryly, and Joe, sitting directly behind her, thought, How can you go out with him?

Through gaps in the trees, Lake Ontario gleamed dully like sheet metal. Their near-miss had filled the car with silence. The bitter, devouring land fled past in its post-harvest brownness. A dog ran down a hedged drive, its bark small and faraway. On a porch, a carved pumpkin scowled. After their exchange over the Shelley, Joe had not been able to talk alone with Anna again. He felt there was unfinished business between them. He'd asked her to go out with him, and in that moment felt he had brought her, her head bowed away from him, to the edge of a response that would reveal something new, that would break them out into new territory. Perhaps his doom lay there, but he was more inclined to think her answer would favour him, for he clung to a conviction that they were bound at a level she must eventually acknowledge. The centre of his awareness was the soft helmet of her hair, not two feet away, and her face, looking straight ahead, alive with expressions he could not see. He felt he was alone with her – the others in the car were no more important than strangers – and that she felt this way too.

They came down through the city of Niagara Falls, past the empty motels and cavernous eating joints, past the low hall with its shadowy bumper cars, huddled together for the winter, past a ten-foot-high picture of a bearded fat lady: Rasputin with breasts.

"God, isn't this *awful*," Brad said happily. No one answered him. A Sunday bleakness had settled in; it seemed a mistake to have come.

Just ahead, across an area of parkland, the tops of the two great Falls came into view: a shredding whiteness, slightly unreal amidst the clouds of mist rising from the gorge and filling the air with moisture. Brad set the wipers going.

"Stop!" Anna cried suddenly.

"There's no parking here," Brad said, grinning across at her.

"Stop, stop!" she ordered. Sitting forward, she was pounding her hand on the dash like a child in full tantrum.

"Brad, stop!" Joe shouted. He thought she was going to be sick. When Brad pulled over to the curb, Anna got out immediately. Joe followed.

"Joe, please, I have to do this alone –"

"Are you all right?"

"Yes. Please – I have to see the Falls alone."

She hurried across the road without looking back, the collar of her camel-hair coat up, and passed among a series of shrubs wrapped head-to-toe in burlap: a procession from the land of the dead. On the far side of the park, she crossed another road and disappeared behind a tour bus.

Her sudden desertion left them stunned. "We should wait for her," Joe said, but when after several minutes she had not come back, or even reappeared, Brad suggested they go and park. They drove on, behind the dolorous thump of the wipers, to the public lot near the Canadian Falls.

A few minutes later, Joe looked down the length of the stone safety wall, which snaked along the rim of the gorge through the mist. He could see tourists, gathered here and there on the wet pavement, peering over the railing that topped the wall, but there was no sign of Anna Macrimmon. On the other side of the wall, the shallow water of the Niagara raced over limestone towards the brink. There, the edge of the bedrock was a wavering shadow under the turning water. The river at this crucial juncture was green, an extraordinary, livid green, shining and flickering like a living jewel, and for a moment it cleansed his mind of all but itself. Far down, on the black shifting marble of the basin, the *Maid of the Mist* looked like a toy, its decks crammed with yellow-suited ants.

Desultorily, they debated whether they should look for Anna. Above the Falls, the wide river descended through its rapids, where a rusting barge had stuck on a reef: a pivot for circling gulls. In Anna Macrimmon's absence, the Niagara had grown cold and desolate. They had come here to show her the Falls, and without her, the water seemed to lose its meaning.

"If she wants to trek around out here, that's fine," Liz said. She hadn't bothered to look into the gorge, and she appeared miserable, her hands buried in the pockets of her fur jacket. The mist and cold and raging river seemed an affront to her, an unnatural habitat she had to endure between the comforts of more sheltered places. "I'm going into the restaurant."

"I'll go have a look for her," Brad said, gazing down the gorge.

"She hasn't had enough time," Joe said, meeting Brad's eyes.

"Oh really?" Brad said, bemused. Joe found his air of superiority maddening.

"She's never seen the Falls," Joe said. "This is important to her, seeing them for the first time. She doesn't want to be disturbed."

"I'm not gonna stop her looking!" Brad laughed.

"She's a poet," Joe said, with real anger. "She can't look at something if you're there jabbering beside her."

"Who says I'll jabber?" There was a knifing seriousness in Brad's look now – he didn't always play the joker.

"Come on, boys," Liz pleaded, a bit wearily. She took Joe's arm and tried to draw him towards the restaurant. He broke away.

Joe was prepared to do anything to keep Brad from going after Anna. He knew he looked ridiculous, knew that, in the end, he couldn't stop Brad, but he hung on stubbornly, with his hands jammed in the pockets of his new coat, glaring at everything that moved.

"Joe, *please*," Liz begged softly.

"You don't know the concentration it takes, to make a poem," Joe said and felt colour flood his face, to find himself defending poetry. "She has to really look at the Falls. She's told me about it," he added, half-lying. She had told him about "looking exercises" she did, when she'd stare for minutes at a time at a leaf or an insect, to train herself to see what was actually there. But he didn't really know about the connection between this activity and the making of poems. "It's important that she be alone, because even to have another person around distracts her."

"Okay, okay," Brad said, raising his hands in sarcastic surrender. "I'll tell you what. I'll walk along here – is that okay? I'll walk along here, and when I see her, I *won't go up to her. I'll hang back, okay?*"

When Brad trailed off along the wall, Joe was tempted to go after him. For a furious moment, he wanted to grab him, start a fight, throw his joking, lanky body into the gorge. But Liz was tugging at his arm again, and this time he allowed himself to be led into the restaurant. They sat at a linen-covered table behind tinted glass, which made the Falls outside seem doubly gloomy, like an old photograph. A waiter brought them water. Liz ordered soup and a sandwich. Joe, who was not hungry, and who was still conscious enough of his surroundings to be appalled by the prices, ordered soup. He was furious with himself for exposing the depth of his feelings about Anna. What had he gained but the mockery he'd seen dancing in Brad's eyes?

"Anna's a strange girl," Liz said dryly. The soup had left a red mark at the corner of her crimped mouth.

Joe mucked with his spoon in his bowl.

"I guess you've seen her poetry," she said, trying again. "She never shows it to me. Is it good?"

"It's better than good," he said. "She's a poet: it's what she wants to do. It's what she *does* do," he added defiantly, pushing bits of cracker around. Anna had told him one afternoon when they were sitting together in the school library that she hoped to publish books one day. She had said, "I think my life would be well spent if, at the end, there were a hundred pages of poems that people still

wanted to read when I was gone." He remembered the iron wistfulness of her voice, the sun falling across their scattered books,
remembered how the inside of his foot had accidentally brushed
hers. Remembered, too, the strange wave of sadness that had over-
whelmed him, when she'd revealed her ambition: as if giving your
life to poetry were some heroic but ultimately doomed act, like
setting off to cross the Atlantic in a boat too small. He had experienced the same feeling while defending her to Brad by the barricade.
Her task seemed hopeless, and yet it made him want to protect her
all the more. Her ambition was her place of vulnerability, and there,
somehow, he felt he could help her.

"So tell me about it – this poetry of hers –"

He met the overly frank gaze of those violet eyes. Liz had made
poetry sound like some childish indulgence.

"You can't tell somebody *about* poetry," he said angrily. He was
quoting Anna, *If you could say what it was about, there'd be no need
to write it.* He looked away, to the sepia Falls, toiling unreally past
the distant safety wall. He felt half-drugged by the warm restaurant,
and half-furious with frustration. His body needed to act, to dispense
its seething energies. He kept tearing open packets of crackers and
crumbling them in his soup while Liz watched.

"You like her, don't you?"

He blew out dismissively and looked past her to the Falls.

"Because I'll be straight with you, Joe, she's with Brad. She's in
love with him. And anyway, I don't think she's really for you. You're
too much like her. Too moody. She needs someone like Brad, to keep
her spirits up. I mean, Brad makes her laugh."

He looked into Liz's cool, almost beautiful face, and hated her.
He felt she had put long, cold fingers inside him and grasped some
essential organ and squeezed it. But he sat perfectly still, not speaking while she ate her sandwich and sipped her coffee. He looked
again past the dark, curly mass of her hair to the distant Falls. A
dreariness was overcoming him, an exhaustion. The world was not

as it should be, and yet the world was here, as unchangeable and for-midable as bedrock. He went on watching the shredding water, sitting in his restaurant chair. It was as if he and she had been together for years: she, his wife, calmly eating, accustomed to his sullen refusal to talk, his wandering eye.

A few minutes later, Brad and Anna came in, their faces pink with activity and excitement.

"She wants to go everywhere now," Brad announced tri-umphantly. "The *Maid of the Mist*, the whirlpool –"

"I'm drunk on this place!" Anna said, stripping off her coat as Joe, suddenly self-conscious, grinned at the tabletop. "It's cured my headache."

Later, they drove to the whirlpool, where the Niagara coiled against itself in a great elbow of the gorge, about a mile downstream from the Falls. A steep, forested path led down through a break in the gorge wall. At the edge of the water, Anna stood on a low rock and looked out over the wide, green pool, where whitecaps charged this way and that and chewed-up logs circled endlessly, unable to escape the sucking power of the whirlpool. Beyond, where the river entered, were rapids: white giants in perpetual frolic.

And perhaps Joe's argument with Brad bore some fruit after all, for without speaking of the matter, the three of them left Anna alone. But Joe watched her: she was more fascinating to him than even the surging water, though in a way she seemed part of it, its focus and intelligence. She stood absolutely motionless, with her head a little down, her sunglasses pushed back onto her hair, her hands in the pockets of her coat, confronting the whirlpool. He wondered what she was experiencing, and was moved to think that this was her work. It was her job, as a poet, to open herself to the river. He was envious that, already, she was practising her calling. She was older than he, she was farther down the road that led on through life.

He could feel the force of her concentration. Once, she reached up to keep her glasses from falling. But otherwise she was still. She had forgotten her friends completely, she had forgotten *him*. He watched her deep gaze travel out, across the powerful river, the shifting slabs of water, the eruptions of liquid bedrock, and at the same time in, as if the whirlpool were inside her. At that moment, perhaps sensing his attention, she looked over at him, though he was not at all sure she actually saw him. Her eyes, he thought, seemed oddly blind.

18

ANNA FELL ILL AGAIN – her headache coming back – and on the way home lay in the back seat with her head in Liz's lap and Joe's new coat pulled up to her chin. From the front seat, Joe could sometimes hear her let out a long sigh, or a whimper of pain. Mostly though she was silent, and this silence suggested an act of concentration, as if she were trying to accomplish some delicate, difficult task, like threading a needle in the dark. He had never witnessed such a severe reaction to a headache before, his mother simply took an Aspirin and turned grim. But this, it was as if Anna Macrimmon had been flung violently to the perimeters of existence. Yes, for all her calm, all her maturity, she harboured a sensational vulnerability, a secret dialogue of extremes. In some way he could not fathom, her headache seemed connected to her excitement in the gorge, to the way she had looked so steadily at the river. It was as if she had looked too long at the sun.

The headlights of the 98 ploughed up the highway, briefly illuminating the windows of anonymous villages. Everyone had fallen silent, out of respect for (and perhaps oppressed by) the suffering in the back seat. Joe felt he had failed the promise of the day. Perhaps Anna Macrimmon had taken something from their trip; perhaps she kept some precious fragment that might become a poem. But he felt his outburst at Brad had corrupted their time together, encasing him in an isolation and jealousy from which he was unable to fight free.

Only one thought consoled him: his new coat on her body, as if he were secretly holding her. When Brad let him out at the end of Water Street, he left it in the car.

She was not in school the next day, Monday, nor the day following. As in the past, her absence had a palpable quality, as though it were part of her, the part she was showing him now. In phys. ed., he stopped on the playing field to watch some sparrows blow downwind, the whole flock pulsing and flooding along almost merrily, their tiny lives somehow at home in the vast, stone-coloured sky. In a few seconds they were gone, vaporized by the distances over the empty fields. Her absence was there too, in the brown fields stretching towards a distant stand of pines; in the dreamlike progress of a white truck, making its way down the Golf Links Road. All this purified him, in a lonely way, of his sense of failure around Anna. Away from her, he gradually felt ready to meet her again. Each time he saw her she was new: but so was he.

On Wednesday, she was back. She seemed under the weather still, Joe thought, pale and a little remote, but warm enough as she smiled at him and touched his arm. Clearly she considered him a friend; and though he thought friendship a dead end, he was reanimated by her touch. In English class, Mrs. Fraser asked her to read her essay on the Romantics, which the teacher said was the best work she'd seen in years. Joe watched as Anna stood hesitating beside her desk, frowning at the loose sheaf of foolscap in her hand. Two rows over, Elaine Brown lifted her small head and gazed stoically into space. Until Anna Macrimmon's arrival, she had been accounted the best English student. Now, it seemed to Joe, with every essay returned to them, with every answer Anna made in class – though she never volunteered one and always had to be asked by Mrs. Fraser – Elaine seemed to be mourning her fall into second place.

"Aspects of Romanticism," Anna Macrimmon read in a voice that to Joe was touched with doubt. "Among people who read poetry, the Romantics seem to have fallen out of favour. Where once young men and women read Wordsworth or Shelley or Keats to each other, now we prefer 'tougher' or more 'modern' writers such as T.S. Eliot, or W.H. Auden, or Dylan Thomas. In one way, this is good and natural, for those more recent writers catch the flavour of our troubled times, when two world wars have shattered some of the cozy certainties society once rested on. But we are in error if we think that Wordsworth and Shelley and their company have little or nothing to say to us. In fact, they understand the modern world as well or better than many of the writers who followed, for they were there at its birth, when the first factories and industrial towns were creeping across the English countryside, and science was beginning its long undermining of the Christian Church. They received the shock of the new in their souls, and while they still looked to the future with confidence, there is a shadow aspect to their work that presages, profoundly, our modern skepticism about the phenomenon of so-called progress. I believe that their analysis of the situation is the deepest we have, still, and that, in a way, we have yet to catch up to them.

"Take Wordsworth, for example. In his sonnet that begins, 'The world is too much with us . . .'" She read on. They listened, they who for the most part did not read poetry, for whom Wordsworth was only the author of "Daffodils," which they had had to tediously memorize – they listened with a quietness that was rare for them. Perhaps it was her voice that held them, more than her ideas: a light voice, almost a woman's, yet breaking at times like an adolescent boy's in little patches of roughness. A few of the students seemed to listen to every word. Others slipped into daydream, into the bare trees branching into the cold blue sky outside the classroom windows.

When she sat down, the silence continued. A radiator clanked in solitary appreciation. Then applause rippled briefly through the class.

After school, Joe turned past the trophy case and saw her in her brown cloak and tam, pushing open the glass doors to the street. In seconds he was beside her.

"Your essay was wonderful –"

Immediately, he felt the poverty of the word "wonderful." She used language so well that when he tried to speak, he felt like a complete amateur. Yet the irony was that around her, or even just thinking of her, he seemed about to say everything he had always wanted to say but lacked the words for; he seemed about to relieve the pressure of all the confused ideas and feelings he had carried with him all his life. Once, when he was very young, he had known things, but no one wanted to hear about them – not his parents, who never had patience or time, or Smiley, who had made fun of him for trying. So he had fallen into the habit of silence, and into the deeper habit of not paying attention to what was stirring in the shadows: his intuitions about the beauty and ugliness and truth and strangeness of things. Yet whatever was there, was still alive for him. Instinctively, he knew she was his chance to speak.

She was walking quickly, as if fleeing something, her face cast down a little, sheltering behind the erect collar of her cloak. She thanked him for his compliment but in the same breath added, "I couldn't help thinking how simple-minded it was."

"Oh no –"

"By the time I was through, I even doubted I agreed with it, with most of it."

She seemed genuinely dismayed. He did not know what to say. If *he* had written such an essay, he would have strutted for weeks afterwards. But to her, it seemed a defeat.

"I mean, how can I say that life has got more regimented than it was then? I wasn't alive then – and I don't have that much experience now. It was all wrong –"

A car went by, full of students, honking as if coming from a wedding. Davy Mackelroy thrust his freckled face towards them and screamed. Joe watched Anna jump back and glance quickly at the car, and in that moment he saw, again, her vulnerability. He had once thought of her as immune to such things, as she had appeared that first afternoon on the river: remote and superior and somehow unblemished. But since then he had seen a great deal more: her headaches, the red places on her ink-stained fingers where she'd torn her cuticles – and now this reaction to the kids in the passing car. He saw she was immersed in the thousand particular details of life – all that misery he knew himself.

And this gave him hope that he had a place by her, as her help-mate at least.

"Factory life," he said, and suddenly he was swept with tenderness for her. His fear and self-consciousness had vanished. "I liked what you said about that –"

"I've never worked in a factory," she said. There was laughter in her voice, dismissive, and hinting at despair. "What do I know about factory work? It's ridiculous that I stand up there and tell people about it. Half of them probably know more about it than I do –"

"But you got it right," he said.

She looked at him.

"I've worked in a factory, in Bannerman's." He could feel his face heat at his admission. Before, he had done everything to hide his background from her. But now, he was willing to risk exposing it. "It's no fun," he said, "watching machines go around all day. Putting socks in boxes. It sort of drives you crazy. You go numb. Nobody likes it. I mean, people write things on the walls, in the washrooms, about how much they hate it. The management keeps painting them over and putting up signs not to do it, but it doesn't help. The writing always comes back."

"What work did you do?"

"Lots of things. For a while I was a knitter."

"A knitter!"

"Sure, I sat in a rocking chair and knitted," he said, joking. "There was a whole roomful of us –" When she laughed, it was the girl in her who laughed, sunlight on a wave. He walked her home. She lived on Banting Street, in a large house of weathered brick, with a small white porch supported by four pillars. For a while they stood at the curb, in the drifting smell of bonfires, talking. She seemed in a better mood now, holding her books over her chest, smiling at the stories he told her about life in the mill. But he wasn't simply telling her stories. He was watching her, calculating when to make his next move. He couldn't help himself.

Stepping up on the curb – a sudden hot rush of courage – he said, "So when are we going on our walk?"

She looked at him. "Did I promise to go for a walk?"

"At Liz's party. I wanted to take you out to Devil's Cave. It's a cave in the limestone, you'd love it, what the river does there. It sort of slides in, you know, with these little whirlpools in it – they pop up and go spinning away –"

"It sounds fascinating," she said, still looking at him; he felt he had moved her. But then she added, "Maybe Liz and Brad would like to go –"

"I was thinking, just the two of us."

"Oh, Joe," she said quietly, a note of alarm.

"I don't think they'd mind. Heck, we don't need to tell them." He half-hated himself for pressuring her – surely he was being boorish and insensitive – but he couldn't seem to stop. She was looking askance now, into the road.

"If I tell you something," she said, "do you promise to keep it to yourself?"

"Yes, of course!" Unexpectedly, she was presenting him with two of his most fervent desires: she was opening herself to him, and she was asking something of him.

"And not ask me any more than I want to tell you?"

"Not a word," he said. He was watching her eagerly now, loving every movement of her eyes, her face.

"I – this sounds so melodramatic. I made a promise to myself. A couple of years ago, I – well, something happened. I had a pretty bad time. And after, I promised myself I'd – I'd take things easier. I'd live a more ordinary life."

"Ordinary –" He did not see how anything about her could be ordinary.

"I just wanted to be, I don't know, like most people my age. I wanted to, you know, do my schoolwork, have fun, have a boyfriend, and not get too serious about it – just ordinary things." She was deeply flushed now, watching him, and her eyes seemed to be begging an understanding for what she could not express.

"So I guess what I'm saying is, let's just be friends. You're very special Joe, very – special, but I can't – I guess what I'm saying is, I need some room."

"I'll give you room," he said and couldn't help adding, "I'll give you anything you want."

She let out a little explosion of breath. Abruptly, she turned from him and hurried up the walk.

That evening after supper, he crossed the dim yard and climbed the garden steps to the top of the dyke. The Atta gleamed like oil, under ghostly limestone. He turned and looked towards the North End, hidden by trees and houses. She had pushed him gently away, and at the same time she had given him a secret, or at least a piece of one. How could having a bad time make her want to be ordinary? Had she told her secret to Brad? Did Brad know he was part of the ordinary life she wanted, or in this ordinary life was there no room for the telling of her secret? Did Brad know, how had she put it, that she wanted to have a boyfriend *and not get too serious about it*? And where did that leave him, Joe? She had said he was special: did being special disqualify him for the ordinary life she wanted? He walked along the path on the top of the dyke. Someone was riding a bicycle across the footbridge to the park. He could see the spokes flash, behind the wire mesh fence, and hear the planks rumble, each one speaking out in turn as the wheels fled over it.

19

MID-NOVEMBER. Lookout Hill a grey cloud looming over the Business Section and the Island. Alf was walking home from work when Pete's Sarasota drew up beside him.

"Hey-yoh," Alf said, stooping to peer inside. Pete held his cigarette like a pencil in his crimped fingers, turning from the wheel to look unhappily at Alf. His hand, Alf saw, was stained red with dye.

"You get it too?"

"What?"

"I just got laid off."

A sudden nausea swept him, at the smell of stale smoke and sour, ancient seat covers. And Pete, Pete just went on looking at him, accusingly it seemed to Alf, with the butt smoking in his fingers, his eyes hard. It had been a couple of months since Alf had given Woody Marr's name to Prince, months of worrying what the result would be. But nothing had happened to Woody, or to anyone else. He had begun to think he was home free.

"They didn't lay you off?" Pete said. And still his eyes held Alf's, with their look of pain and accusation and, under it, something of his old plaintiveness, his old hopefulness, hanging in gamely.

"No, no. Pete, this is terrible."

"The scumbags said there wasn't enough work. Complete bullshit. Somebody squealed on us –"

"How do you know?"

"Everybody's who's been let go was at my place that night."

"There's more?"

"Eight I know of. I'm gonna phone Doyle," Pete said, finally releasing Alf from his gaze. He ground out his cigarette with a sharp twist.

"Who else?" Alf managed.

"Get in," Pete said. Alf got in and shut the door. Ahead, a few snowflakes drifted across Water Street. He felt he had passed a subtle border into another world. Everything looked the same, and yet he knew it wasn't. The sign hanging outside the Royal Hotel, the orange cloud of willows above the millrace bordering the Island: they seemed hollowed out from the inside, less themselves. Pete put the car in gear and they drifted down Water.

"You're sure it's just union people?" Alf said, rousing himself.

"Every one of them was at my place."

"Who?"

"Terry, Lucille, Ed –" Pete ran through eight or nine names. He glanced over at Alf. Alf found it awful, the darting of those wounded eyes. He felt Pete suspected him. What else could he think, given that he, Alf, still had his job?

"How about Woody?" Alf said, as casually as he could. He had worked it all out before, tossing in bed, imagining the worst. Woody was the key. He had given Prince Woody's name: if Woody had been fired, it meant Woody had not talked. But if Woody still had his job, it might well mean he had given Prince some names to save it. And if Woody was the *only* person to keep his job, other than himself, it meant he had talked for sure. And in that case, though Alf hadn't given up the names directly, he might as well have. He had knocked over the first domino, which toppled the rest.

Pete looked away into the falling snow.

"Well?"

"What?"

"Was Woody laid off?"

"I dunno," Pete said dully. His voice held a note of despair, as if something had just collapsed inside him. "There's a few I ain't heard about."

When they got to Alf's place, Alf insisted that Pete come in and have a beer. Mercifully, Margaret and the children were out, but all the same Alf immediately regretted having Pete there, regretted his thin figure hunched at the table peering bleakly through the smoke of his cigarette, gesturing with his red hands, bad-mouthing his foreman and everyone else on management he could think of. He wanted to get on the phone to Woody – no, not to Woody, that would give the whole business away – but to *somebody* and find out if the knitter had been laid off. He was smoking now too. Blue uplands of smoke hung in the kitchen, drifting in the snowy light from the window. Ever since he'd taken Woody's cigarette on the fire escape, he'd been smoking on the sly and hiding the fact from Margaret. Now he no longer cared.

That evening he was unable to use the phone: someone was always in the kitchen. At eight o'clock he put on his coat and drove over to the Flats, glancing at Woody's stucco bungalow as he floated past. Woody's brown Ford with the Magnetic Hill sticker on the bumper sat in the drive. A minute later, approaching the arena, he saw the jammed parking lot and remembered the game: *someone there would know*. He parked the Biscayne on the edge of the baseball field, near a grove of oaks. Behind the trees rose the mills, a watery sheen in their dark windows. Ahead, a muffled chanting sounded in the pale, round hill of the arena.

He slipped down a corridor and emerged in the open space at the end of the bleachers. And Woody was there, standing by himself near the corner boards, watching the game through the wire mesh. Alf found himself moving towards him. This is stupid, he thought, all you have to do is see if he's at work tomorrow. But he couldn't help himself. On the back of Woody's sweater-coat the image of a pheasant had been knit. The bird was beating up on sharp wings, its head like a hood pierced by a red eye.

He stood beside Woody. Just then, the puck caromed into the corner in front of him, and in a moment several players thudded into the boards. Sweating faces grimaced through the mesh as they battled for the puck. A whistle blew and they skated calmly away.

"So," Alf said. His heart was slamming. "You still have your job or what?"

Woody went on looking at the ice, where the green and white uniforms milled. It was as if Alf didn't exist, as if he were a ghost making sounds the living could not hear.

The cold air smelled of rotting wood, of winter.

"Yeah, I still have my job," Woody said. "Can you think of any reason why I wouldn't?"

Alf met Woody's tiny, flinty eyes, like flashes of metal, of pure hatred in the podgy face. Around them, the crowd bayed.

20

WITHIN ANOTHER DAY, he had the full picture. Everybody who'd been at Pete's that night had been laid off, fourteen people in all. Only Alf and Woody were unscathed.

It seemed to Alf his involvement must be obvious to everyone, at least to everyone who had been at Pete's, though by now, surely, word had spread. He couldn't go out without the sense of being watched – watched and commented on, as if his guilt were indicated by a mark on his face, or by one of those signs the mill workers sometimes stuck on a fellow's backside for a joke: PLEASE KICK HERE. But hell, he told himself, he'd only given up one name, and that man still had his job. He couldn't really be blamed for the others, could he? And besides, the union was finished: so some good had come of the dirty business, hadn't it?

But he kept thinking about the laid-off workers, especially Pete, and was unpersuaded by his own arguments. He traipsed down Shade Street, avoiding people's eyes. Entering the A&P, he tripped on the step. A moment later he pushed through swinging doors into the odour of fresh-ground coffee.

His cart had a squeaky wheel. He pushed it past one aisle – too many people – and turned it, squeaking faithfully, down another. Joe was there, in a long white apron, putting up cans of peas.

They made small talk, awkwardly.

"I was thinking I could get some tickets for the Gardens," Alf said. He felt an urgent need to give his son something, to fill his sense of a looming emptiness. The boy's cheeks flushed.

"That a good idea?" Alf asked.

"Sure."

"Great."

"Good."

Over Joe's shoulder, Alf caught sight of Dick Forsyte, his small face grimacing as he studied the label on a can. Dick was one of the laid-off. The sight of him – so casually looking up from the can to the shelves – momentarily paralyzed him. Dick's presence seemed large, radiant: he might have been famous. Alf shifted a step, concealing himself behind his son. "Forgot to go to the bank," he said, swinging his cart away. In the street it was snowing: large, slow flakes falling peacefully out of the darkness.

The bank was overheated. He waited in line, in the solemn, churchlike atmosphere, looking down at the grey tiles tracked with slush. Ahead of him, a woman with her hair in a fraying bun – it was Matilda Squires, the Presbyterian minister's wife – moved forward a step. By the heel of her shoe lay a quarter. Alf shuffled past it.

"Say, is this yours?"

He knew the voice – that compressed, slightly muffled quality, as if it came from underground – and he turned to meet Lucille Boileau. She was holding up the dirty quarter between thumb and forefinger.

"Oh Jeez, Alf, I didn't recognize you."

Her smile with its missing tooth lit her face.

"I'd say it was yours," he said dryly.

She slid the coin into the pocket of her jeans. There was a child-like deliberateness in her movement, which he found pathetic: as if she thought the quarter was really going to make a difference. She was wearing a black leather motorcycle jacket with silver studs on the shoulders, black jeans, and cowboy boots with pointy toes.

"I'm sorry about what happened," he said.

"Well, what can you do, eh?"

"What they did, it was illegal –"

He felt he was about to burn up, in his zipped-up coat.

"I guess you got off, eh?" she said, glancing up shyly.

"For now, anyway."

"Oh, they won't lay you off. Not a good man like you."

He waited for her in the street. She came down the steps counting a handful of bills and scarcely seemed surprised to see him. Snow fell silently around them, appearing and disappearing on her black hair, the black leather. He had a curious sense of their absolute isolation, as if they were meeting in a forest.

"Look, Lucille, I want to help you out." She looked blankly at the folded wad in his hand. "You can pay me back when you get another job."

He looked at her wide mouth, those overinflated lips. Years ago, he had heard a rumour that Lucille Boileau took in men for money.

"You keep that," she said, pushing back his hand. "But tell you what: you can take me for a drink."

They crossed the street to the Vimy House, passing through its low, arching porch, held up by stubby pillars of orange marble, into the dim lobby where a fuzzy grey cat lay curled on the desk. A leather couch leaked hanks of matted wool. He had not been in the Vimy House for years. His distaste for the place was underlaid by a sense of inevitability, as though the intervening time had been a kind of illusion. This was what had been waiting for him, and this was real: the smell of smoke and stale beer and longing, the dregs of a happiness that hadn't lasted a single night.

He had abandoned himself to her; he felt he owed her that much, anyway. He traipsed after her black jacket into Ladies and Escorts, letting her choose a way among the small, round tables spotted through the room. She stopped near a large window entirely covered by shapeless drapes. Beside it, in an ornate frame, hung a photograph of the old King and Queen, taken during their brief stop in town before the war. The famous couple were standing on the platform at the rear of their rail car, the King in a double-breasted suit, the Queen in a cavalier hat and white fur stole, waving over a mass of roses. The pale photo was like a reflection of distant sunlight, a lost afternoon.

"I was there," he said, pointing, and knew again the smell of the oily railbed in the heat, the town band playing "God Save the King."

"So was I," Lucille Boileau said. "We walked up the West River Road, all the school kids. They gave us little flags. I was so happy: I was going to see the King and the Queen. But the train stopped too far down the tracks and the crowd got in the way. I never saw them."

"Ah, you didn't miss much," he said. But he could still remember the thrill of seeing those royal faces, so familiar from photographs, smiling over the crowd that had run down the tracks to catch up to them. When the train finally drew away, sliding like a miniature version of itself into the heat-warped distance, it was as if some magic – some never-to-be-repeated chance at happiness – had fled their lives.

In a distant corner the only other customer, Bessie Kinnaird, stared at her wineglass. Behind the bar, Rick Taylor, in a white shirt rolled to the elbows, was working something out with a pencil. The room was quiet, a cave-shelter from the snow, a kind of tomb: Alf was relieved to be here.

Rick brought them four draft, setting each one on the yellow Arborite with a sharp rap. Alf supposed Rick was wondering what he was doing here with Lucille Boileau – he knew tongues could wag later – but for the moment he felt armoured in indifference. He belonged to Lucille now, to the large, dim room where every word and action seem muffled.

Lucille raised her glass. "To all us poor sods who lost our jobs," she said. "No, that's too sad. To the future!"

He threw back the bitter beer, swept by a wave of disgust. He couldn't understand why she wasn't accusing him, or at least acting suspicious. Did she really trust him so much? At her distant table, Bessie Kinnaird raised her glass in a trembling hand and took a brief, wondering sip, like a girl.

"So are you looking for work?" he said sharply.

"Oh yeah, makin' the rounds."

Her vagueness irritated him.

"Where've you been? Up to Samuelson's?"

"Sure."

He didn't believe her.

She shrugged, and he sensed her helplessness. Indians: they were all the same, weren't they? Drifting through life, never doing enough for themselves.

"Have you been over to Johnsonville?"

"I don't really like Johnsonville."

"Why not?" he said. "If you can get a job there."

Again she shrugged.

"What's the matter with Johnsonville?" he persisted. "I would think that'd be a good place for you."

She was staring unhappily into her beer.

"Isn't it?" He thrust his question home, wanting to provoke her. He wanted her to see what he was.

"Why?" she said finally, to her beer. "Because there's Indians in Johnsonville?"

He looked at her remorselessly.

"Everybody hates 'em there," she said, tossing her head. "Anyways, I gotta be home for Billy."

"Well, were you home for him before, when you were at Bannerman's?"

She was silent; her wide face, which had something open and trusting in it, was trained unhappily at the table now. He pitied her and yet he kept the pressure on: he was waiting, half-elated by his own cruelty, for her to attack him. "There must be somebody who could look after him."

"Not anybody I trust," she said.

They drank for a while in silence, and smoked. She took his cigarettes sullenly, and the smoke drifted up from each of them, mingling under the high, pressed-tin ceiling. They had nothing more to say to each other, it seemed, and yet he felt bound to her, responsible. Behind the heavy drapes, cars swept the snowy street.

Alf shifted in his chair and noticed something at his feet: a stuffed animal, a little brown horse with a red wool mane.

"What have we here?" he said. When he tried to stand it up on the table, it fell soundlessly into a puddle of beer.

"Cute," she said. "Rick's little boy."

He spoke in an undertone. "Can you imagine bringing up a kid in here?"

"Sure," she said, as she ground out her butt. "It's warm."

She left to go to the john. Her reprimand lingered in the drifting strata of smoke, a bitterness he could not mitigate. What did he know about keeping warm? Compared to her, he supposed, he was rich. He saw her coat, with its torn, scarlet lining, crushed at the back of her chair, and wondered if he could slip the bills into her pocket.

Amazingly, she came back laughing. She told him she hadn't noticed the toilet seat was up: she'd nearly fallen in. He lit another cigarette for her. Her face descended to his flame like someone drinking light and for a moment he loved her: her broad, foreshortened face with its black eyes shining like pools of oil, the little sickle scar on her forehead. Settling, she told him a story about ice-fishing with her father, years ago on Lake Erie. "I fell in," she said, laughing again. "I mean, I was up to my neck in slush. Just like a bottle of Coke." Her father had pulled her out and carried her, wrapped in his coat, to the nearest house.

"The people wouldn't let us in," she said. "So he had to run to the next house – it was another mile over, just about killed him. Just about killed *me*. They put me on the stove, eh? They had this platform for dryin' boots. I got good and baked."

"What do you mean," he said, "they wouldn't let you in?"

Her pink tongue skimmed her lower lip, and he understood what she meant, in the same moment that he understood he had shamed her.

He couldn't stop thinking about Bob Prince. Whatever his own guilt in the affair, Prince was the force behind the layoffs, he had no doubt: the liar who'd told him he'd only give the union supporters a good talking to. He was in a fury with the man, with whatever fury he wasn't already directing at himself. In a dream, he saw the executive's dark-blue Cadillac Fleetwood patrolling behind him. He ran into a woods, but the car was soon there, above him, descending through the treetops with a thwacking sound, like helicopter blades. Its underside was composed of creamy flesh. In this belly a slit – some sort of mouth – pulsed open and shut, briefly revealing a toothless cavity.

The snow did not stay; the town reverted to the dour emptiness of late autumn. One Saturday, emerging from Tugg's Hardware, Alf saw the Fleetwood moving down Shade. It was definitely Prince, his tanned dome and handsome face lifted a little, with a kind of offhand nobility. The car floated over the Shade bridge and climbed towards the upper town, accelerating so smoothly it seemed to be powered not by an engine so much as a magnetism, a wish. Backing the Biscayne into the traffic, Alf began to follow. He had no plan. He was simply drawn to the other man, half in anger, half in the hope that something might yet be done about the layoffs – that he still had some purchase in the places of power. About a mile from town on the Johnsonville Highway, he caught sight of the Fleetwood just as it turned down a secondary road. At a rail crossing, he lost it again behind the monotonous lumbering of boxcars, and when the caboose finally rattled by, and the clanging and blinking at the barrier finally relented, there was no sign of it in the wasteland of gravel pits and cold grey lakes beyond. But a mile down the road, with the countryside swathed again in the brown tangle of autumn, he glanced between the stone posts that marked the entrance to the Langside Golf Club (Members Only) and saw the car, parked among several others.

He left the Biscayne and walked into the clubhouse, through an empty locker room, up stairs onto a red carpet that led down a pan-elled corridor. A young waiter in a short jacket asked if he could help. Alf brushed past without a word, instinctively heading for the smell of food, the clatter of dishes. The dining room was mostly empty: a scattering of white linen squares across a large space lit by the day-light silvering at the mullioned glass. Prince was at a window table, in a grey tweed jacket, tieless, just pouring beer into a tall glass. As Alf approached, he looked up without expression. He might have been expecting him.

"Have a seat, Alf."

That voice again: freakishly unruffled, the soul of civility. Alf had an urge to throw a chair through the window. He remained standing, in his jeans and windbreaker.

"You said this wasn't going to cost anybody their jobs."

"Would you like a drink?"

"You said this wasn't going to cost anybody their jobs."

"So you said."

"Don't get fancy with me!"

The young man in the short jacket and bow tie was hovering.

"Is everything all right, Mr. Prince?"

"Just fine, Danny. Bring Mr. Walker a –"

"I don't want anything," Alf told Prince. With a gesture from the executive, the young man turned reluctantly away. Prince spoke to the tabletop, gravely.

"As I remember, I was speaking only of the people whose names you gave to me. Or *were* going to give to me. And there, well I believe I kept my word. The man whose name you gave me wasn't laid off."

Alf looked down at the executive in disbelief: it seemed a snake's argument.

"What are you saying? Are you saying if I'd given you all the names they'd have kept their jobs?"

The other man winced, as if at a digestive pang. "As it happened," he said, frowning at the bubbles that rose in his pilsner glass, "I had no intention of laying off those people. But I have my own bosses, Alf. I don't have the free hand everyone imagines I do. There are people above me who are determined to play rough."

Prince looked up frankly now, with coldness in his eyes, a warning that he was barely tolerating this interruption, it had better not go on much longer. Alf fumed, moved his feet. In a company where the line of command stretched out of sight, you could always say it was someone else's fault.

"I hold you responsible," he said.

"So do they," Prince said wearily. "I'm the meat in the sandwich."

"Take those people back," Alf said. "Go to your bosses and beg. Like I'm begging you now. Hell, you know what it's like for them? With Christmas coming on? Take them back. I'll stake my job on their not starting a union. If they do, fire me."

Prince touched the neatly folded napkin beside his cutlery: the peace he was not being allowed to enjoy. The young man came back with a salad. They watched in a trance of blankness as he set it down, left.

"Take back Pete Moon," Alf said.

Prince played with the pilsner glass, making the surface of the beer tilt rapidly.

"As I understand it, he was one of the leaders."

"He didn't lead anything. All he did was have the meeting at his house."

"Oh really?" Prince said, and his eyes flashed up. "I believe you told me the meeting was by the river. There was a fire?"

He spoke with riveting irony. It was clear he had known all along that Alf had lied to him.

Alf stared grimly out the window. A groundsman was trundling a wheelbarrow past the putting green. Beyond, the fairways rolled towards a distant grey palisade of woods.

The waiter reappeared with Prince's sandwich. Alf went on watching the groundsman as he put down the barrow and began collecting the small flags from the holes of the green. He was aware of how much better it would be to be out there, in the cold air, with his hands on honest metal, honest wood. Here, he felt crude, out of place. He did not know what to do with his hands. And he was nauseated: his rage turning sour inside him. He looked at Prince, who pushed the sandwich away from him, as if in distaste. The executive spoke directly to him now, with grim self-containment.

"Alf, I can't give anyone his job back. But I can tell you this. As far as I'm concerned, that foreman's job is still open for you. We've had our disagreements, you and I, but I still consider you the best man for –"

"You can shove your fucking job," Alf said.

Driving back, he pulled up to the shore of one of the lakes in the gravel pit and turned off the engine. His hands were trembling. He buried them under his armpits and watched the grey water, which seemed ominously still, as though it had come to the very point of freezing.

●

A FEW DAYS LATER, Alf sat at his cellar workbench, trying to ignore the commotion of an arrival overhead: the cheerful soprano of Margaret's greeting, the drag of chairs. In his hands was a bit of pine he was struggling to carve into the likeness of a pike. His model was an old Lands and Forests poster pinned on the tool board behind the bench. Caught in the glow of the hanging lamp, the freshwater fish of Ontario swam past in an ordered school. Rock bass. Yellow perch. Pickerel. The pike was the most sinister: a flexible torpedo of pure appetite, its splotched body narrowing to a flattened, evil head. To be that cold, that efficient, and beyond all feelings but the feelings of hunger and satiety: it seemed to Alf an ideal state.

He had taken up carving during the war, for a distraction. He could remember sitting on the bank of a canal, its surface broken by upthrusting pieces of machinery, the bloated belly and stiff legs of a dead cow. In his hands he held a little piece of wood, its dirtiness nicking white with each stroke of his pocketknife: a small sanity. He had carved farm animals and given them away to children.

There had been a boy about Jamie's age with huge, believing eyes, the eyes of hunger. Alf had given him a tin of rations, but the boy's face had lit-up only when Alf offered him the little horse he had not quite finished, its tail still attached to its hind legs. *Un cheval. Pour vous.* Fumbling in his high-school French.

He gaped at the memory, come up after all these years. The boy in his cloth cap. A smell of burning oil and rotting flesh. Alf touched the piece of wood to his nose. Someone else had been there too, a soldier, whom he experienced as a pressure of absence, a shadow without a face, though he could see the man's boots dangling beside his own over the putrid water. He was sure the man, whoever he was, had not lived out the day.

Margaret came down the stairs and stood beside him.

"It's May," she said in an undertone, touching his back. "She's terribly worried about Pete."

He stared at the fish in his hand.

"Alf, I wish you'd tell me what's wrong."

"Nothing's wrong," he said tersely.

Nearby, the furnace blower came on with a soft roar. They had known each other for twenty-three years, and the silence between them could not merely be silence: it was a night cut by the flight of coded messages, the riffling of dog-eared files. He slid her a hard glance and saw her face – those vivid eyes in her porcelain skin – rapt with a pained earnestness, offering him the balm of listening and talk. She loved him, he saw. Often he tried to tell himself it was otherwise, that they had been going their separate ways for years – she with her friends on the Hill, her church interests, her music; he with his work, his fishing, his sports. They had the family in common, but otherwise they might just as well have been living apart. It was convenient to believe this, it set him free, it justified his unhappiness. But he saw it was not true.

He pushed past her and trudged up the stairs. At the kitchen table, May looked up at him and he saw in her darkly circled eyes the shadow of his own malaise.

"I'm worried sick, Alf."

"Hey, it can't be that bad." His voice seemed magnified and unreal to him, like that time he'd acted in a play for the Couples' Club. He had played a gardener, a role with only three lines, and yet he'd felt as false as at any time in his life. "Pete's had rough times before."

"Not like this."

Alf pulled out a chair. Behind him, Margaret filled a kettle at the sink, then turned to the stove. In the soft explosion of little blue flames he sensed the presence of a powerful, saving domesticity. For a moment he believed in their ability to help May. To help themselves.

He said, "You know, when he got out of the navy, he had a hard time then? He was really down. But he got through it, eh? A few weeks?"

May was watching him hungrily, her eyes glittering with unspilt tears.

"Or that time you lost the baby?"

"Yes." Her voice small.

"You know, he's got too much of the devil in him, that guy. He'll bounce back."

Margaret had swept noiselessly from the room. He noted her absence with a slight start of panic. He did not feel up to comforting May alone.

"How long has it been since you've seen him?" she said.

He shrugged, pulling a face. "Oh I don't know. A few days maybe." He was lying: it had been at least two weeks. He had found it unbearable to be with his friend. He had had to move with such careful, guilty deference that he seemed to be holding his breath. "I lent him tools," he said, eager to put in a good word for himself. "He was gonna start work on the rec room.

"He seemed fine," he went on. He felt he had to keep pouring words into the silence. "Practically his old self. In fact, he seemed pretty hopeful." Manic was more like it. Alf had seen his friend in this state before, though never so bad: half-crazy with plans, talking a mile a minute, and still, unbelievably, talking union. Talking about Malachi Doyle as if the Irishman were Jesus Christ himself, as if he were going to save them all yet. Malachi this, Malachi that. Malachi thinks we should lay low for a while. Malachi says that when the union goes in, we'll get our jobs back. Alf hadn't had the heart to contradict him.

"He was looking for work," Alf said. He knew his friend had been out every day, covering the county in the Sarasota. Filling out forms. "Had some good leads too. Up at Samuelson's . . ."

He found himself talking about the places where Pete was likely to find a job. It was as if he had caught his friend's desperate optimism, and was using it to fill the space above the table. But it was no good. May was shaking her head.

"It's different now. He's given up."

"Not for long," Alf said quickly, and saw again the boots of the other soldier, hanging above the canal.

"He just sits in his chair all day, watching TV. He's drinking –"

Margaret returned with a box of Kleenex. May was looking at Alf through her tears with a strange, anxious smile, as though everything she was telling him about Pete was in fact the source of some secret happiness. He could not take his eyes away.

"He hit me," she said in a high, pleading voice. "It's the first time he's ever –"

Margaret leaned over, sliding her arm along May's back.

"I can't *blame* him," May was saying, "Not really. I was nagging him to get out, to see his friends. I told him it wasn't the end of the world, people had lost their jobs before, and he started to swear at me and then he – he's not himself, Alf!"

Tears swam down her face. He watched in dull horror. You did one thing and it made other things happen, like a scattering of billiard balls. And then there was a woman you had known all your life, an innocent woman, weeping at your kitchen table.

Behind them, the kettle had begun to sing.

Alf trudged across the Lions Park footbridge. The Atta fell towards him through shallow rapids: a waste of yellow water he wished he could go on following indefinitely along the muddy trails that accompanied it out of town.

He had to knock twice before Pete's eye and part of his face appeared in the small, round window in the front door. For a second, his pupil regarded Alf with a curious indifference: a specimen under glass.

"Hey buddy," Pete said, bringing him in.

Alf entered the dim, hot room with its reek of stale beer and farts: the compost of unhappiness. Staring at the TV, Pete let himself down into his plaid Easy-Boy.

On the screen, football players broke from their huddle and trotted back to their positions. The screen was full of snow, and from time to time the picture swam upwards, creating the odd impression that the room was sinking.

"American game," Pete said. His gaunt face – thin even for him – was dark with stubble. He glanced covertly in Alf's direction, his gaze briefly brushing Alf's knees. It was the look a frightened man might give, checking out sources of danger.

"Get yourself a beer," Pete said, staring again at the TV. He had his own bottle, he had several, parked on the TV tray beside him. "You know where they are."

To Alf, there seemed a hint of accusation in this. *You know where they are.* As if Pete were calling to account their years of friendship, the years his house had been as open to Alf as his own. As if he were saying, I trusted you.

Alf fetched a beer and sat on the low couch, grateful for the distraction of the game. He needed time to think about what he would say. The announcer's voice, rich with masculine authority, rose and fell with the action. There were other voices too, higher and more nakedly excited, and the crowd roaring distantly.

Alf had the nightmarish sense he had lived all this before. Prince's motel room came back to him with a shock: the sailboats on the wall, the flowered bedspread, the little blue makeup case. And Prince picking his corns on the bed, in the smell of aftershave. There had been a football game on then too: the same soporific blend of voices and crowd sounds, the sense of important, exciting things happening, but happening elsewhere. On the screen, a clutch of cheerleaders shook their pompoms like the heads of vanquished enemies.

The picture swam upwards and went on swimming as the room sank. Though the temperature must have been over eighty, he felt chilled and his throat was sore. Pete did not move.

"I'll fix that," Alf said.

"Just give it a rap."

The picture righted itself. He went back to the couch wondering how long Pete would have sat there if he'd been by himself.

When a commercial came on, he asked Pete how the job hunt was going.

"Had a few nibbles," Pete said, after a while. On the screen, an old man was pouring out cornflakes for a smiling boy. In the land of happiness.

"Oh yeah? Who?"

Pete didn't answer.

"May dropped by our place," Alf said, steeling himself. He did not like to talk about emotional difficulties, his own or anyone else's. Better to be silent and let them solve themselves. But he had promised May. He said, "I guess she's pretty worried about you."

Pete took a swig of beer: he might have been deaf.

"Look, if you don't want to talk, just say so," Alf said, with an edge of irritation. He experienced a thrill of danger: it was the first time since Pete's firing he'd dared to speak roughly to him.

"What's to talk about?"

"Your wife's over at my place, bawlin' her eyes out. She's worried sick."

"She tell you I hit her?" Pete said to the TV.

"Yeah, but she doesn't blame you. And anyway, that's not why I'm here. I'm worried about you too."

Pete said nothing.

"Look, what's going on with you? Is it the job or what?"

He was daring Pete to accuse him. He sat watching his friend, exposing himself like a target. But there was a hostility in this, and more power than Pete could face. Pete flashed another sideways glance at Alf's knees, took a swig of beer, and continued to stare at the screen.

"I dunno," Pete said. He winced and shifted in his chair. "I get these funny ideas."

"What do you mean?"

"I dunno. I can get pretty black. Paranoid, like."

Alf waited.

"Just a mood, you know," and Pete motioned with his bottle towards the screen, where a large Negro with immense, padded shoulders tore off his helmet and began to yell at another player. Pete said, "You have to wonder who your friends are."

"What do you mean?" Alf said, his throat tightening. If it's going to happen, he thought, let's get it over with.

"Just craziness," Pete said, moving his bottle in a dismissing wave. "Not important."

Alf said, "You think I had something to do with your losing your job –"

Pete went on watching the screen for what seemed an eternity. Alf watched the thin face of his friend, laid back against the white antimacassar.

"Not you, buddy," Pete said finally. "Woody's the guy. Everybody knows that."

"Because I wouldn't give your name to God himself," Alf said, managing to produce a rasping chuckle. "Not that He'd ever ask for it."

Pete grinned at the screen.

Alf tried to turn his attention back to the game, but his heart was pounding. *Not you, buddy, Woody's the guy, everyone knows that.* Did Pete really believe that, or was he just trying to let Alf off the hook? His mind raced with a thousand questions, questions he wanted to ask Pete but didn't dare. *I'll never let you down again,* he promised silently. Yes, he'd get Pete through this bad patch and they'd go on together, better friends than ever. Talking – confessing – would do no good at all. It would only cause more pain, and their friendship didn't need more pain. Better to encase what he knew in cement and sink it to the bottom of a deep hole and let it stay down there, forever. Let it disappear, as it surely would, with time. Unless Prince talked, of course. Or Woody. He had stopped breathing. He sucked in air and stared at the screen where the cheerleaders were bouncing in another war dance.

The next program was a Roy Rogers rerun. Cowboys on horseback thundered merrily among the pale hills of California. Pete seemed mesmerized. Alf was moved by the images of foreign sunshine, that rollicking male freedom.

"You gotta get out of the house," he said, with a sudden uprush of tenderness. "You're rotting in here."

"Where would I go?"

"Anywhere. We'll drive down to Port Dover. Pick us up a couple of babes." They had actually done this years ago, before the war. On the pier they had met two girls and driven with them to the sand hills: immense crests of sand, and the greeny-blue of Lake Erie spread below them.

"This time," Pete said, "I get the pretty one."

They went the next day, a Sunday afternoon of brilliant light flooding the brown land waiting for winter. Alf drove the Biscayne. Pete sat in his dark-blue Stingers jacket, occasionally raising his cigarette to his lips as he stared out the windshield. He did not look to the right or the left and did not speak unless prodded by Alf.

They were driving south, towards the Great Lake that had drawn them all their lives. Alf had gone to Erie by train the first few times to attend Bannerman company picnics as a boy. Later, his father had taken him bass fishing at Long Point, and in recent years Alf had occasionally rented a cottage for a week at Port Ryerson. He had never lost his excitement at seeing the lake after a long absence, and now, as they crossed the endless flats of the hinterland, studded with the green and red barns of the tobacco farms, he felt the old anticipation rising in him again, the old freshness of anticipation.

As they drew near Port Dover, little mounds of sand erupted beside the highway, and as they came down the muddy river the sky ahead seemed to change, to grow larger and brighter. They swung on to the bridge and there it was, past the dull little river and the derelict boats and the buildings and the pier: dazzling, turquoise Erie.

They ate lunch in a near-empty restaurant overlooking the public beach, in the full heat of the sun streaming in the plate-glass windows. Pete kept his coat on, zipped to the chin, and left half his whitefish untouched. Out on the lake, a snub-nose fishing boat was ploughing in across the glitter, its shadowy silhouette trailed by a cloud of gulls.

On the way out, Alf stopped off at the washroom. Pete said he'd meet him outside, but when Alf emerged blinking in the glare, the scrap of beach was empty. A cottage with boarded-up windows looked out bleakly to the lake. Alf went back to the street, walking past the Biscayne and along the line of restaurants and tourist shops, most of them closed. He experienced a stab of panic. He realized that, in some way, it made perfect sense for Pete to disappear, to evaporate in broad daylight.

He walked around town, and finally came to the concrete pier with the stubby lighthouse at its far end. A boy on a bicycle came clanking off it, with a fishing pole laid across the handlebars. The pier looked empty, though he could not tell if anyone was standing behind the lighthouse. He started to move swiftly along the pier, fighting down a rising sense of alarm.

He was almost at the lighthouse. And now he was past it. No one was there, on the guano-spotted end of the pier. He looked into the clear water. An oil stain shone on the swell, the body of a tiny fish floated upside down. The sandy bottom was just visible, ten or fifteen feet down – the rippled, empty, sandy bottom, wavering as though alive.

Pete was waiting for him at the car. They'd just missed each other, apparently; Pete had gone into a store to look at some belts, he said. Driving home in the waning light, the long shadows of the tobacco barns reaching over the frozen earth, they talked more easily than they had on the way down. Pete told a story Alf had never heard before, a story that began with Pete's ship putting into Marseilles, a couple of years after the war. He'd gone on shore leave and found his way into a small nightclub where a band was playing jazz. It wasn't like any jazz you'd ever heard, he said, it was faster, happier, one guy was playing a violin. Later in the evening he'd danced with a woman who had taken his fancy. "She was the prettiest thing," he said, keeping silent for a while. "Black eyes . . . God." He'd fallen for her, he said, to the point where he was ready to stay in Marseilles. But he had gone back to the ship. "I still think of her," he said. "Isn't that strange? I think of her like I met her only yesterday. I can still feel the way her back felt. So slim and – makes you wonder what could have been, you know? You do one thing different, and your whole life is different."

Two days later, a Tuesday afternoon, Alf was repairing a machine when Matt Honnegger told him he was wanted on the phone. Margaret, Matt said. Alf left his tools and walked towards the little office that overlooked the gravelled roof of the dyehouse. A pigeon was on the sill, looking in, and for a moment he saw its orange, unblinking eye, which seemed to watch him with naked curiosity before it flapped off. On Matt's desk the receiver lay on its side, looking blacker, heavier, than usual. In the eighteen years he'd worked for Bannerman's, Margaret had called him only twice: when Joe had been knocked off his bike by a car, ten years before, and in September, when Jamie had been lost.

For a moment, her voice saying his name, crying his name, held in the balance the lives of his children. Who was hurt? Who had slipped away into the unthinkable? It's Pete, Margaret said, and he experienced a momentary relief before her voice carried him further, away from safety, away from the world that had existed only moments before. It was the car, Margaret said. She was crying. Pete had shut himself in the garage and turned on the ignition. May had found him.

22

THE MORNING AFTER PETE'S FUNERAL, under a faultless blue sky, each twig and branch bore a delicate slice of snow. There was a sense of hospital stillness, as if the snow or the sender of the snow, conscious of a need for convalescence, had swaddled everything in bandages. Joe dressed as quietly as he could – he needed to be at his job at the A&P by nine – and slipped into the hall. The closed door of his parents' bedroom – nearly as white as the snow outside – met him with a mysterious, oppressive blankness. He went swiftly downstairs, propelled by a quickening expectation of escape. But his mother was at the stove, making breakfast.

She sat opposite him while he ate, from time to time taking long, noisy sips of coffee. He was irritated by this, irritated by the way she put down her cup and sighed with a world-unsettling weariness. Her sighs seemed to go right through him, to touch his every secret dread and doubt. In his silences, his father retreated into the distance, leaving the air cold but clear: a kind of freedom. But his mother had a way of filling his mind with the atmosphere of her own concerns, and it was suffocating. He worked at his food and tried not to look at her sagging gown, where the tops of her breasts rounded, ivory at the frail lip of her nightdress.

"I'm worried about your father," she said.

He hated it when she said "your father," a phrase that seemed to block the light in his sky, as if a mountain had suddenly loomed. Reaching for the ketchup bottle, he shook out the red sauce stubbornly. He did not want to talk, not now; he wanted only the isolation of his sleepiness.

"He hasn't been himself for weeks now."

"He's just sad about Pete," he said quickly, through a mouthful of egg. He felt he knew more, far more, than he was letting on. And suddenly he remembered standing at the edge of Pete's grave, as one of the pallbearers. He'd seen a darkness in his father's face, not only shadowing his eyes but living somehow in his gaze, as he looked down at the box that contained the body of his friend. It had seemed to Joe that his father had a connection to the coffin that superseded all others: a yearning, as if he wished he could go down into the earth with Pete.

Shocked, Joe had looked away, down the wall of the hole, and noticed a bit of root sticking out from the dirt. And this root – crooked and hairy and white at the tip, where the backhoe had sliced it – pierced him with a feeling so wild, lonely, and ungovernable that he had to bite his lip to keep from crying out.

"It started long before Pete," she said.

"Well," he said, shrugging, wishing she'd stop. He sipped at the hot coffee. He found something wrong, even indecent, in his mother's prodding. There *were* times when he talked willingly enough with her about his father, airing his complaints. But just now he felt a powerful identification with his father and his silences. For a moment he understood the deep usefulness of those silences, in which pain and a lot of lesser but still bothersome things might disappear. He glanced at the clock.

"I feel there's more going on than he's telling us," she said. "At least more than he's telling *me*."

At the window, a blue jay blundered into the glass with a soft thud and was gone before they could look.

"Of course," she said, and her gaze drifted into another dimension, "what *has* he ever told me?"

"Don't know," Joe said, lifting his cup.

"You know, he wasn't always like this," his mother said. Her eyes had found him now, with a commanding brightness.

"Like what," he said, frowning.

"So quiet. When I first met him, he was almost chatty."

"Dad?"

"He talked as much as I did, I'm sure. And charming? He could be the life of the party, your dad. I know it's hard to believe, but he was really quite different."

"What happened," he asked, interested now in spite of himself.

"Well, the war," she said, with a long, dismayed glance away, and he felt the word "war" enter the room in all its dark, mysterious glamour: the great event he had not known but which seemed to cast its shadow over everything that came after. He was insatiably curious about the war, all the more so because his father's silences encompassed it so thoroughly. He had never heard his father speak more than a few sentences about his experience overseas, while from an early age he, Joe, had been instructed by his mother not to ask him about it. "We don't want to upset him," she'd say. And so the war had become a presence in the house, a presence he was not allowed to mention, but it lived in his father's face and sat down with them for meals, and hung among his father's tools, and hunkered in the spaces between his father's words. Joe imagined the worst, he couldn't help himself, for what but the worst could generate such a deep, long-held silence? Sometimes he imagined that his father had killed a man, or perhaps many men. He would look at his father's hands and see the backs of them, the strong, nicked-up fingers with their dirty nails, roped with blood.

And here was his mother saying that, before he'd gone off to France, his father *had been a different man* – a cheerful, outgoing person who once came to a masquerade ball dressed as Rudolph Valentino, with his blue eyes shining out of a black half-mask, and charmed every woman there. And after the war, he had come home a moody, paranoid, silent man who would throw himself face down in the street when a truck backfired, who slept badly, and who could not break the habit of crumbling up his cigarette butts so they could not be found by an enemy that still lurked, apparently, in every street. His mother could hardly recognize the man she had fallen in love with, and although she did not say so directly, she hinted to Joe that she had wrestled with the question of whether she still loved him, whether they should still marry. Of course, she had gone ahead, and borne in her life this particular cross of trying to lure (persuade, trick, love) back into the mainstream of life a man who had left it.

"What those boys went through over there," she said to the haunted place above her coffee cup.

"But what happened to him!" he cried, leaning forward abruptly. The gap in his knowledge of his father seemed critical. He was curious about the war, but this curiosity had something to do not only with battles and guns and wounds, but with how to grow up, with how to be a man. And the war seemed the central clue: it seemed to contain some secret of courage or survival or growing older he needed himself.

"I'm sure I don't know," she said, looking at him in a wondering way. "His brother was killed, of course – he wasn't there for that, they were in different regiments – but his mother never forgave him for it afterwards."

"Never forgave him because Joe died?"

"Joe was her favourite. She was always harping at your father to look after him. By the time I met your father, he'd made a kind of joke of it. But when he came home from the war without Joe – I think she felt, well, I probably shouldn't say this, but if only one of them was going to make it back, it should have been Joe."

The next morning his mother asked him to come to church with the rest of the family. He hadn't gone for months, not since declaring his atheism, but he softened in the face of her "I can't do this alone." She did not have to explain what "this" was. There was a sense of unhappy drag in the family, centring on his father's isolation. It had fallen mainly to her – to the engine of her brisk English cheerfulness – to lift them back to normal.

They took their usual pew on the main aisle, about halfway to the altar. When the choir entered in their red robes, Joe looked automatically for his mother – he had done this since he was a boy – and watched as she sat, her posture self-consciously erect. Her air of weary concern had lessened a little, he thought. She had lifted her face and seemed to be listening for something, a kind of call, that came from the old, dark rafters and hanging Union Jack and banner of Saint George, from the altar with its white embroidered cloth and tall candles and fretted golden cross. To Joe's surprise, he found himself moved by all this – first by his mother's bearing, and then by the church itself, warm and welcoming and all but full on this bright winter morning.

Penny and Jamie knelt beside him on the thin prayer-board, worn into shallow hollows by the pressure of countless knees. Beyond them knelt their father. Joe had often felt there was something out of place about his father here – that collapsing hair, his badly knotted tie, his stare of bleak abstraction – but today this quality seemed to have deepened, as if his father, for all his trying, could never fit among the others. Joe felt pity for him, and at the same time, remembering what his mother had said – that before the war, his father had been *a different person entirely* – he kept glancing along the pew, as if he could find in the way his father held the prayer book, or looked blankly beyond its pages, some trace of the happier, more talkative man he had once been. As the phrases of the general confession sounded around them, Penny sang out the responses almost rapturously. But Joe, aware of his father's silence, kept silent too. *Almighty and most merciful father, we have erred and strayed from thy ways like lost sheep. We have followed too much the devices and desires of our own hearts. We have offended against thy holy laws. O Lord, have mercy upon us miserable offenders. Spare thou them, O God, which confess their faults . . .*

Emerging from the church, they blinked in the snow glare. It was as if they had been born to a new world and needed time to get used to its superior brightness. Icicles dripped from the church eaves, and the parking lot was flooded with exhaust fumes, billowing like cumulus in the warming air. At home, he found himself thinking of Anna Macrimmon, though in a way he was reluctant to think of her – it was like bringing her into a sad, squalid room, a room that must make her think less of him. Yet he kept sensing her, up there on the hill, in the house with the white porch, a reminder that his life belonged, or might belong, to places other than this house with its chipped baseboards and stink of Brussels sprouts and deepening atmosphere of defeat. He wanted to be rid of his family, whose troubles were not his. What did he have to do with his father's sadness or his mother's searching gaze that seemed to beg of him a solution he knew he could never deliver? The next morning he put on his best slacks and cardigan, as well as the suede jacket with the knit sleeves (after the Niagara trip it had come back from Anna smelling faintly of her, so that alone in his room he would often bury his face in it, until he could no longer find her in the stronger smells of suede and his own sweat), and climbed the hill to school.

It was another blazing-white winter day, painful on the eyes, and in the dimness of the corridors he was momentarily unable to see anything. The other students drifted like shadows amid the slamming of lockers. But his eyes had adjusted by the time Anna came. Elated, he watched her feel her way down the stairs, in her cloak and tam. "Joe, is that you? This light –" Smiling in her blindness, she grasped his arm.

"I wonder if this is what Hades is like," she said, looking happily around her.

"I don't know," he said, his heart thudding. "I've never been."

She laughed briefly and let go of his arm (the skin of his forearm was on fire) and was about to pass on when she added, in a quieter voice, "Joe, have you given any thought to the Christmas formal?" Her green eyes met his with a merriment he recognized as flirtatious. "Have you thought about taking anybody?"

He shook his head, but he was lying. He had thought of asking *her* but had abandoned the idea because of course she had forbidden any such thing, and anyway, he had to assume she was going with Brad. She touched his arm again, letting her fingers linger on the outside of his biceps. "I was thinking it might be nice if you asked Liz. I know I shouldn't say this, but I know she's dying for you to ask her."

He saw she was manipulating him. She was using her power over him to get something he might not want himself. He was a little taken aback, for he had held her morally above him, above all of them: she might know moments of weakness, but she was good, good all the way through, frank and kind and open, and everything she did, her slightest gesture from smiling to reading an essay, was touched with a rightness. He felt a flash of anger against her, for letting him down. Yet his positive feelings were vast, in comparison, and later in the day he talked to Liz. Her beautiful, madeup eyes fixed his intently. "I'd love to go with you," she said with a quiet directness that surprised him. He was more pleased than he expected: Liz McVey *was* attractive, and besides, by taking her, he would be close to Anna. Even though Anna would be there with Brad, he would ask her to dance. His plan came to him with a leap of excitement: he would take her onto the floor, put his hand into the curved small of her back . . .

That afternoon Anna fell in beside him as they walked to Biology.

"Well, you've made one girl very happy."

"Who, you?" he said coldly. He had not quite forgiven her.

"Well, yes, me," she said, her face reddening. "But you know who I mean." She touched his arm. "I hope you're not angry with me."

"It'll cost you," he said. "You have to promise me at least once dance." And he dared to add, "A slow one."

She stopped abruptly, so that he had to turn back to her.

"I haven't told you, have I? I'm not going to the dance, Joe."

She was going with her parents on a Mediterranean cruise, over the holidays. They would fly to New York and on to Lisbon. Then by ship past Gibraltar and so on to Barcelona, Marseilles, Rome. He listened to her itinerary with a sinking heart. How could he not be happy at her obvious happiness at the prospect of her trip? But she had come from over there, and he had always held an irrational fear that Europe might one day reclaim her. He was almost more jealous of Europe than of Brad Long.

He thought of breaking his date with Liz, but in the end went ahead, in a spirit of defiance. *He would do it, but he would do it his way.* He paid $2.50 for a corsage at Mills', and drove up the hill in the Biscayne, its front left fender bearing a fresh dent caused by his father's having skidded into a tree. He was not in the least embarrassed by the car: something in him was almost daring Liz, the whole world, to find fault with him. She wore a thin-strapped gown of black velvet and long, matching gloves that she peeled off halfway through the evening and stuffed in the pocket of his rented tux. By ten o'clock she had wrapped both arms around his neck. They swayed in place, barely moving, while candles quivered at the perimeter tables and the Morganaires in their baby-blue jackets and frilly shirts stood up as one, their horns filling the dark with a swelling ballad.

Afterwards, in the Biscayne, they necked in the school parking lot until their mouths were sore, and when he moved to touch her breasts, it was Liz who suggested they go somewhere more comfortable.

She took charge so easily, he felt she had done all this before – with Bobby the salesman, no doubt – but he had no jealousy of Bobby for he had no particular claim on Liz other than the claim of pleasure. She guided them to Johnsonville, to a double-decker motel built around a pool filled with logs and snow. He found their room nice, tasteful, far superior to anything he knew at home, with its twin beds, a painting of sailboats on the wall, a single lamp shedding a warm light over the flowered spread. "I'll be out in a minute," she told him, kissing him before she slipped off to the bathroom. There was something theatrical in her look – her eyes flashing meaningfully at him before she disappeared – that made him feel he was taking part in a play. A moment later, turning to undo his tie and stiff collar, he was swept with doubts. What was he doing here? He wasn't sure he even *liked* Liz McVey. Just being with her, especially here, was a kind of lie. He went on undressing, though. From the bathroom came a sound of running water. When it stopped, he heard the familiar words of a Christmas carol seeping through the wall from a TV or radio in the next room. Silent night. Holy night. Sung in a high, clear, inviolate voice: a boy's.

23

"SEE, IT SAYS CRAZY HORSE. 'Crazy Horse grew up in a Sigh-Ox village,'" Jamie read, hesitating only a little on the hard words, "'on the great plains.' Can you read that?"

On the bench beside him, in the Children's Room of the library, Billy was grinning his grin that was not really a grin, showing his brown-edged teeth. They were alone.

"Try to read that –"

"Crazy Horse," Billy said, giggling as if it were a great joke, and his black eyes snuck sideways, as if he wanted to get away. Jamie was trying to teach him to read. One day they had met Billy's mother on the street, and seeing that Jamie had a book and Billy had none, she had said, "I wish you could get Billy here to read – get him out of that class with the retarded kids." So he'd taken Billy to the library. And seeing that Billy just looked at the backs of the books on the shelves and then started walking on the benches as if *that* were more interesting, Jamie thought he'd find him a book he might like. *The Story of Crazy Horse* was one of his favourites. But all Billy did was flip through, looking at the pictures, then he started balancing on the benches again. So Jamie started reading it to him in the hopes he'd get interested and read it to himself. "Read that!" he said, pointing. "Read the next sentence. It's really a good story." Billy stared where he was pointing, and his grin got more fixed and the light in his eyes looked as if it were going to burn him up. He pushed the book away.

"What's the matter?"

"I don't feel like it."

They went outside, into the slowly falling snow. At the corner, Billy said, "I got you a present."

"What?"

Billy wrestled inside his windbreaker and dragged out the Crazy Horse book, in its clear plastic wrapper.

"You took this book?"

"It's for you," Billy said, in his flat voice. "I hooked it," he said, still grinning, and Jamie remembered the chocolate marshmallow cookies Billy had hooked the day before, from Kinnear's store. They'd eaten them at the rock in the Indian Trail.

"You don't have to hook things in the library. They're free. You can take anything you want. You just show them your card."

Billy grinned: Okay, he knew *that*!

Jamie took the book from Billy, explaining he'd already read it, put it inside his coat, and snuck it back into the Children's Room. When he came out, Billy was throwing snowballs at a Stop sign. They started across the road, and it was then, looking south towards Water, that Jamie saw his mother. She was crossing Water, marching briskly along in her grey coat, her arms filled with groceries. All she had to do was glance to her right and she'd see him with Billy. His father had seen him with Billy one day on the main street and had only winked at him as if their being together was a kind of joke. It would be different with his mother. There was a sharp edge inside her, and wrong was on one side and right was on the other, and she never hesitated to tell him which was which. And also, he wasn't entirely sure it wasn't wrong to be with Billy. He hadn't felt too good about those cookies. But he had no other friends, and besides, Billy wouldn't leave him alone. He stuck to Jamie like glue.

He took a step backwards, to get out of her line of sight, then another. Billy grinned.

"What ya doin'?"

"Nothin'. Walkin' backwards."

Billy laughed his gurgling laugh and took a couple of steps backwards himself.

They went along Bridge Street to the bridge and looked down at the steaming black water, at the weeds bending under its surface, and up the river past the dam to the rail trestle, where a string of boxcars was rumbling against an empty sky. "We're Sigh-Ox Indians," Jamie said.

"Okay."

"You can be Crazy Horse, because you're the real Indian."

"You wanta come to my house?" Billy said.

They walked to the Flats, along Willard and Pine to Billy's. The place made Jamie sad with its lonely-echo feeling and no pictures on the walls, just a couch with a rip down the back. Billy's bed was a mattress on the floor, his toys were scattered all over, and there was a smell of pee. After a while Jamie said he had to go: he and his Dad were going to buy a Christmas tree. "Are you getting a tree?" he asked, and Billy said he was going to cut one, right now. They could both go and cut one, okay? And because Jamie wasn't going with his father until that night, and because cutting a tree would get them out of the house, he agreed.

Billy brought up a hatchet from the basement, and they walked up the road under the rail trestle: a web of dark girders through which slits of faraway sky showed. They went up a short street and along another to a forest of evergreens. In the forest, which was still and peaceful, the snow poured over the tops of Jamie's boots and chilled his feet: he was beginning to wish he hadn't come. But they waded on, talking about which tree would be good to cut, and finally they picked one and Billy started hacking at it with the hatchet. Pale gashes appeared, but though he was hitting it fiercely, gritting his teeth, he couldn't get much deeper than the bark. Then Jamie took a try and it was while he was whacking away at the trunk that a voice sounded beside him. He was so scared he dropped the axe. He was ready to run, but Billy just stood there looking at a man – an old man Jamie did not know. He was smiling at them with a mouth that had no teeth. "Trying to take my treesh are you?" he said in a rough but not unfriendly voice. "I know yis one," he said, nodding at Billy. "Who are you?"

"Jamie," Jamie said. The old man was wearing an open coat and a plaid shirt underneath and a cap from which his ears stuck out like handles. He winced and looked at the tree and said they should come with him to the house, he'd get a proper saw. Jamie looked at Billy, but Billy just fell in behind the old man, following in the soft trail his boots made.

The house sat up on a small hill above the forest. Behind it stretched the open space of a gravel pit, where Jamie could see cement towers and a snowed-over line of conveyor belts. Then he was in a big kitchen, not bright and neat like his mother's, but warm, with bare-wood cupboards, a kitchen table painted bright red, and an oil stove with slits in its side that reminded him of catfish gills. The old man told them to take their boots off and sit down at the table. While the old man was rummaging in a cupboard, Billy looked across the table at Jamie and said, "We'll get candy."

"Did I hear something about candy?" the old man said. His hair was as white as the snow.

He came back with a big glass jar full of different kinds of sweets: jawbreakers and licorice and others wrapped in twists of foil. The old man set the jar on the table and looked at Billy and said, "So, shall we tell him our little game?"

Billy looked at Jamie. "You take your pants down and he feels your dick and then you get the candy. Sometimes he sucks it. Then you get three candies."

Jamie wondered, Sucks the candy?

"I don't do anything you don't want," the old man said to Jamie. His smile had changed, he had teeth now, yellow teeth as straight as the boards in a fence. Jamie felt his face go hot and the old man giggled and said, "Now I think Billy here should go first, to show how it's done. Okay, Billy?"

Billy jumped out of his chair and went over to a couch near the oil stove. He lay down and the old man went over and sat beside him on the couch and looked back at Jamie. "It's just a little game," he said. "It feels nice. Why don't you come over here and look?"

Jamie didn't want to go over, but when the old man winked at him and shook his head for him to come, he went. He stood beside the old man as he put out his big, lumpy hands and pulled down Billy's trousers. And he thought of being in the doctor's office when

Doctor Carr looked at his dink, carefully pulling back the skin, and he thought of the time Carol Jenkins and her friend Chrissy Bell had pulled his pants down in Carol's outhouse and they had hardly been able to stop laughing, and afterwards the girls had pulled their own pants down and showed him the place where they had no dinks, just a slot like a piggy bank. All these other times seemed to be with him now, as he watched the old man move his big, crooked fingers very gently over Billy's thing, pulling and stroking it the same way he, Jamie, sometimes pulled and stroked Red's ear, feeling its smoothness run through his fingers. "There there there," the old man said (he had hair in his ears and even sticking out of his nose, Jamie saw), and he seemed almost to be singing, crooning away like a mother to a crying baby though Billy wasn't crying, he was grinning up at Jamie as if he considered the whole business rather silly. Then he stopped grinning and his eyes went far away, blank.

"See, that's all there is to it," the old man said suddenly, looking around at Jamie. "You wanta try?"

"Aren't you gonna suck it?" Billy said.

"Not today, you rascal." And the old man snapped the band of Billy's underwear. "You get yourself a candy or two. Just call me the Candy Man," he winked to Jamie.

Billy pulled up his pants and got off the couch. The old man was looking at Jamie now, looking at him with a friendly smile in his eyes, showing his board-straight teeth. "Nothin' to it," he said.

"He's chicken," Billy said, walking back to the table.

The old man winked at Jamie and patted the couch.

"Just hop on," he said.

Jamie lay down on the couch. He looked at the ceiling and looked at the old man's long chin with its spiky stubble and felt his pants being drawn down. When the old man said, "Just raise your hips a little," he did, and felt his nakedness in the air. Then the fingers touched him, and it felt nice down there, it felt nice and smooth, except the old man's hand was a little cold, just like Doctor Carr's hand, and the old man was crooning over him now, as he pulled his thing just like he, Jamie, pulled Red's ear. "Oh you've got a nice one," the old man said. "That one's gonna be a real beauty," and he bent over suddenly and kissed Jamie's dink. But his stubble scraped Jamie's thigh and made him twist away and the old man pulled him back, hard. In that moment, he knew something sharp and angry in the old man. The old man had jerked him back to where he wanted him, jerked him back like you'd jerk a bag of sand. Suddenly, he wanted to go home. He wanted to be at home, at the kitchen table, drinking tea-milk, and his mother there and all the lights on and the house snug against the cold. But he was not there, he was here, and the old man was bending to kiss him again, and everything that had been so strange and nice – the nice old man, the candies, the touch of his hands and even his lips – suddenly was replaced by a loneliness so strong he wanted to cry.

He heard his voice say, high and strange, that he had to go, but the old man kept his face down on him and he felt his dink in the old man's mouth and the drag of something else that must have been his tongue. The thing was, *down there* it felt good, but down there was only a part of him now, small and far away, and in the rest of him he did not feel good: he felt cold and lonely, and he had the idea that the old man was eating him, eating him bit by bit starting with down there and there was nothing he could do about it. He looked at the ceiling, he looked at the old man's head, balding and covered with scabs. He turned his head and looked at the little table by the couch and saw the old man's teeth sitting there in a jar, grinning under-water. "I have to go," he said again, and the old man lifted his face, which was red now, and said in a coy, pleading voice, "Arn you going to help ush cut the tree?" Putting his hands over his dink (it felt wet, he half-expected it was bloody though he didn't look), Jamie told the old man he was going with his father to buy a Christmas tree. So the old man got up and put in his teeth and Jamie got up and pulled up his pants, not looking at himself down there, not even wanting to know that down there existed. He did not want candies now, but he picked one out of the jar, fake-smiling when the old man made a joke, not wanting the old man to touch him again. Before he could go out the door, the old man bent down to him. He held Jamie's shoulder with one hand and said, "Who's your father?" And for a moment Jamie, looking over the old man's shoulder at Billy, who was poking away in the candy jar, not upset at all it seemed by what had happened, could not think of his father's name.

"Alf Walker," he said finally, and the old man grunted. Then he said, "I wouldn't tell anybody about this if I was you. This is secret, okay?"

Jamie said okay: he would promise anything if he could just get out. He looked over at Billy again, thinking they could leave together. But Billy was chewing a candy and did not look back. "We can go," Jamie said, but Billy did not seem to hear him.

"Because if you tell," the old man said, and his fingers tightened hard on his shoulder, "bad things might happen. Okay?"

"Okay," Jamie said, and the old man said, "Look at me," and he looked at the old man and saw the bad things in his eyes.

Outside, he trekked away through the forest of Christmas trees. The sun was just going down, a fire behind the hill across the river, and the snow was blue, and their old tracks were blue. And though he was headed home, he felt he had no home, he was just here, with a lump in his throat and a wet, loose feeling in his pants, trudging in the blue snow that spilled over his boots and went on forever.

"Course," his father said, and his voice went inside Jamie and filled him so that he seemed, almost, to be listening to himself. "When I was a kid we'd cut our own tree."

Their headlights reached up the steep, winding road of the Mile Hill, through a forest where trees leaned out into the light, from banks of ghostly snow. They were on their way to Gowans' farm for a tree, and the heater was making a sound like a toboggan scraping over rough snow.

A car appeared up ahead, its headlights flicking down.

"How come we don't now?"

His father said nothing, and Jamie knew he hadn't heard. *He's sad about Pete*, Jamie's mother had said. *They were friends when they were boys.*

"Dad?"

"What?"

"How come we don't now?"

"Don't what?"

"Cut our own tree." He thought of Billy's hatchet, bouncing off the tree without hardly cutting it and felt again the sadness of the forest of Christmas trees outside the old man's house, in the blue, lonely snow. It was still with him. He felt he shouldn't have left Billy. He wondered if he was still in the house, on the brown couch, and he saw again the look in Billy's eyes when the old man touched him, his eyes going faraway, not scared, but faraway as if he were in a daydream where no one could ever find him.

"Well," his father said, and again there was a pause. The tires crunched over a patch of ice and up the road, a long shape bounded through the edge of the light. "A deer!" Jamie looked but whatever it was had already vanished into the jail of shadowy trees that fell towards the river. His father slowed the car, and they looked off the road where a cable hung between posts. He couldn't see the ground there, it dropped away so sharply. The deer seemed to have flown away among the trunks of the trees.

"A buck! Did you see that? Did you see the antlers on him!"

His father's jacket smelled of smoke, a good smell. Jamie peered past him out the open window where the cold air flooded in. The trunks of the trees were lit dimly up one side.

"Did you see him?"

"Yup," Jamie said. But he wasn't sure *what* he'd seen.

"A big boy, eh?"

"Yup."

He didn't know if he was the big boy, or the deer was, but he was happy that his father was happy at the sight of the deer. The happiness of the deer had filled the car. He looked over at his father, hoping it would last. His father put the car in gear and they went on, through the high-piled snow.

My love is in the blue snow, the voice said. He sat alert, very still. He hadn't heard the voice for a long time, though he hadn't noticed until now. *My love is in the blue snow*: it was deeper in him than anything, than even his father's voice, or his own voice, and at the same time it seemed to have come from the night around the car, lit by the car's passing lights. He waited for it to speak again, but the only sound was the roar of the heater.

24

MARGARET WATCHED as the Reverend Ramsay, Jack to her, picked up his tea tray by the wooden handles and placed it carefully on his desk, the bone china rattling almost musically. There was also a plate of the biscuits his sister had sent from England: Fortnum & Mason's. Just watching him put out tea, the way tea should be put out, calmed her. She felt it was something people in this country didn't understand: the measure of peace that came with doing things right. Taking the right amount of time. Ceremonious. People here slurped their tea from any old sort of mug or cup, even paper ones, as if all they cared about was slaking their thirst. But tea was hardly about thirst at all, she felt. It was about conversation, and restraint, and good cheer: a bulwark against the failing day.

"What have you got this year – two angels?" Jack Ramsay said, taking a chair near her. He crossed his legs, in their priestly black serge: a tidily good-looking man, with a pleased, suggestive shine in his eyes, as though his occupation as the minister of St. Paul's Anglican were not only a pleasure to him but a bit of a lark. He had the English talent, so welcome to her, of making an instant party, a little conspiracy of merriment.

"Both shepherds. Penny had her heart set on being an angel but –"

"Well, she *is* an angel," he intoned.

"I'll tell her that," Margaret said, "if you don't mind. She's convinced she's quite ugly in her bathrobe. Of course what she'd really like is the Virgin Mary, all the girls want the Virgin. I was the same, back home."

"I never wanted to be anything *but* a shepherd. The angels seemed sissy to me, and as for Joseph – unimaginably embarrassing."

"Why was that?" she cried eagerly. Any talk that led them back to England was a joy to her.

In the main hall outside his door, children were making a racket. In another ten minutes they would begin the next-to-last rehearsal for the Christmas pageant. Besides singing in the choir, Margaret was assistant director this year, which involved riding herd, mostly, making sure the requisite number of bodies was trooping down the aisles at the right times, searching for lost halos.

He said, "Well, if you were Joseph, it meant you were married to Mary. The other boys wouldn't let you alone about it. Reduced more than one Joseph to tears. Married to the mother of God at thirteen, not easy!"

He shot her a twinkling look, lingering a split second longer than was necessary. She enjoyed his flirtatiousness. He was married to a Canadian woman much younger than she. But Helen was childless, and though she was pretty and good-hearted, Margaret found her a bit thick. She felt she offered the minister a taste of something a little more cultured, more in the spirit of his spirit. And it all felt safe.

"We've a lovely Mary this year," she said, looking down, suddenly uncomfortable. In the hall Stella Bridgeman, the pageant director, was shouting for order.

Jack Ramsay's voice came down a tone: "You wanted to speak to me."

"I suppose it can wait . . ." She glanced at the open door.

He got up to attend to the tea.

They had never talked intimately, not really: intimacy had only been implied. Far from ever mentioning her problems, she considered it a point of pride to give the impression she had none. Others might come crawling to him, for help. But she and he were equals, in their English merriment. She no longer wanted to confide in him.

He handed her a cup and saucer, and went to close the door.

The cup steadied her: the creamed tea, its soothing fragrance. She sipped and went into herself, to find the reason, the *feeling*, that had brought her here on an impulse. She was no longer sure of the purity of her motive. Perhaps she had only wanted the distraction of his company.

But he was listening, waiting, only two feet away. The panelled room with its smell of old books and mildewed Sunday-school papers had filled with the pressure of expectation.

"It's Alf," she said, looking at the front of his desk – and immediately felt as if she had betrayed her husband to a process she was not sure she believed in. Already, in her mind, she was backpedalling, portraying matters as less serious than she felt they were. "I just feel, losing his friend and all – he's in a bad way. It's been nearly three weeks since – since the funeral – and he's – he's always been a very private person."

She sipped at her tea, avoiding his eyes. She had no way to convey, did not want to convey, what lay behind her husband's gaze.

"What do you mean – a bad way?"

"It's nothing specific. He's just – well. It reminds me how he was, after the war. Not really himself at all. The children feel it. I suppose it'll be all right."

She shifted in the hard chair. Her time of month was coming on and for a moment her digestive tract seemed crammed with nails. She felt all this must show in a general unattractiveness. Yes, it was a mistake to have come.

"If he'd like to drop by for a talk," he said. His tone had hollowed, professionally sympathetic now. But *he* had actually withdrawn, she felt. It made her feel even more the pariah. "Would you like me to speak to him?"

"No, no. He'd know I – he wouldn't thank me. He's very proud," she said, and a flash of love went through her, for her husband. It was something she did not often think of, but now rediscovered as true. In her husband's isolation, which she deplored, was something else, which she did not deplore at all. He was better than all the rest, better than Jack Ramsay with his endless, friendly chatter.

"No," she said, suddenly protective. "It's all right. Just let it be, for now." And thinking she must give Jack *something* for his time, she managed a smile and added, "It's been helpful, though, just talking to you."

"Not at all," he said. "Grief," he said, and the word sounded theatrical on his tongue, "it can take a long time to work itself out. You just have to be patient with him. Pray for him," he told her. "I'll pray for him."

"Thank you," she said. She *had* been praying for Alf, but this mention of prayer unsettled her. Prayer was such a private thing, the words leaping and stumbling from the heart. She felt that in talking openly about it, he had turned it into something vaguely shameful.

Yet prayer, really, was a joy to her. To feel the leap of her silent words, the leap of them in the dark bedroom, as she lay beside her husband: an electric current of joy, as fine, and finer in its way, than singing. Prayer *was* a kind of singing. What she wanted, almost more than anything, was for Alf to know the same joy. But he had never taken kindly to her suggestions that prayer might help. She suspected he did not pray. Watching him in church, from her place in the choir, it seemed to her that he was set against the place and everyone in it: his mouth not moving during the prayers or hymns, his eyes looking straight ahead without any discernible emotion. And in bed, in the dark, she had no sense of him praying, in the dark beside her. It was disheartening, to think he did not know this joy. But then again, perhaps he did. He was so private, and prayer was the most private thing of all.

She left Jack Ramsay's office feeling uneasy, and followed the mob of children into the church. She separated the angels from the shepherds, the shepherds from the wise men and the animals. A few lights had been turned on against the leaden day outside. She noticed Penny, slumped by herself at the end of a pew. Her daughter looked forlorn. Since getting diabetes, Penny seemed more prey to these moods: Margaret was perpetually wondering if her blood sugar was all right. She picked up a shepherd's crook and approached her daughter. "Is this yours, love?" Looking up out of her abstraction, Penny appeared not to recognize her. Those eyes simply looked at Margaret, out of their alien blue.

Later, at home, she found Alf on the bed, lying on his back with his shoes sticking out from the bottom of the spread. The top was pulled up to his chin. He had been lying there, as the light grew dim, for God only knew how long, in the cold bedroom.

Changing her dress, she snapped on the light on her dresser: an act of aggression, to make him stir. After a while, he threw back the spread and sat on the edge of the bed. He was wearing his trousers and an undershirt and his hair was splayed every which way. She was hopeful, but he stuck there, staring at the floor and scratching at his thigh. It infuriated her, the way he had given in to his sadness – if that's what it was. Even more than she wanted him to talk, she wanted him to bury his sadness, like she did. She wanted him to drive sadness out of the house, by force of will.

"Supper will be a bit late. I just put the meatloaf in." She went past him quickly and out. Turning at the top of the stairs, she glanced back along the hall and saw that he had not moved. He was looking at her now: his shadowed eyes agleam. It was his postwar look, definitely, when he would watch her, backed by such a fund of dark knowledge she had felt she must scream or suffocate. There had been days when she wanted to leave him, to go back to England. One day she actually packed her bags and carried them as far as the front door. But leaving was no longer a possibility. There were the children now, and there was something else: she was married to him, in a way she had never been married at twenty-three. Over the years, like two trees twining together, their trunks had fused. Perhaps they did not belong together, perhaps their natures were all wrong for each other (she had considered all such possibilities), but there it was: their marriage was a fact, a fact that had somehow made its way to the core of her being and lodged there.

She met his gaze frankly. She would not be cowed by his look, as she had been, years ago. Even though she understood nothing about it, about what he was feeling or thinking or remembering, she refused to be cowed.

"Come down soon," she said briskly. "I'll make you tea."

25

DEEP IN THE LINCOLN the transmission shuddered gently and they were floating, Joe and Liz, past the parking meters and the strolling pedestrians and the show windows with their banners announcing post-Christmas sales. That night her parents were holding a New Year's Eve party, and he and Liz were off to Johnsonville to buy her a new dress.

He was in love with the car, the luxurious sweep of the seats sheathed in tan leather, the easy tug of power as he touched the gas. It was his first time behind the wheel and he was driving almost gingerly, wary of what the car might do. It floated so smoothly, almost without a sound, and yet under the wide, placid hood he sensed the reserves of power, something alive, even conscious, as if it were *asking* to be unleashed.

On the Bridge Street bridge, he laughed out loud.

"You like it?" Liz asked, with suggestive coyness.

She swung one leg over the other, with a whisking sound of material rubbing, a stretch of tweed skirt emerging from the soft, falling weight of her fur coat. In her violet, too-bright eyes was a triumphant knowing. She might have just presented him with wings.

He glanced at her legs, shapely and exposed nearly to the thigh in rose stockings. And her legs, too, became part of his excitement, as if her body and the luxury and power of the car were one. They passed onto the Flats. He was starting to accelerate, when suddenly Vern Melling's garbage truck was in front of them, stopped by the curb as Vern and his son loaded up an old couch. The opposite lane was blocked with oncoming cars. Joe hit the brakes and the Lincoln lurched to a stop. On the sidewalks, Bannerman's employees were streaming home for lunch. As he waited for the lane to clear, Joe saw his father appear past the end of the truck. He was walking by himself, wrapped in his thoughts, it seemed, his coat flapping open, his green workshirt partly untucked, and his hair, which was long overdue for a cut at Benny's, blowing wildly. Just then Alf looked up and saw him. His face registered recognition, but Joe, hardly knowing why, looked away. A moment later, Joe wheeled the Lincoln around the truck. In the rear-view, he saw his father stalking off down Bridge.

Joe turned past the mills and accelerated down Willard, scarcely aware of Liz talking beside him. She leaned forward to turn up the radio, and the Beach Boys swept up to wrap them in their frantic falsettos.

On the Johnsonville Highway, he opened it up a little. Effortlessly, the Lincoln took the long hill and fled down the winding road that people said had once been an Indian trail: past farmhouses and grey, leaning barns and low modern bungalows and Kanter's

Miniature Golf and Driving Range and the skeletal towers of hydro lines, stalking away over the snowbound fields like giants, arms outstretched under a lowering sky. Nudging the gas, Joe kept glancing into the rear-view at the salt-stained asphalt unrolling behind them. He was sorry they were only going to Johnsonville. He would liked to have kept heading south indefinitely, swept along on the keen-throated voices of the Beach Boys, calling from their land where everyone was young and without regrets.

From narrow windows, the Victorian mansions along Johnson Avenue surveyed the changes that had engulfed them: their lawns paved, their facades littered with signs and advertisements. Downtown, many of the old stores with their decorative brickwork and huge show windows were boarded up, their life sucked away by the malls on the city's edge. But a few of the city's old businesses persisted. Out of loyalty, and a kind of conservative good taste, the McVeys continued to shop at Cardy Brothers, a large, high-class establishment on Russell Street. Joe found a parking spot and they entered the vast, dull, tasteful store, with its ash-coloured counters and beige carpeting. The place was nearly deserted.

Joe sat on a low hassock while Liz tried on dresses. She would disappear for minutes at a time into the change room, leaving Joe and the saleslady to share an awkward silence while the tepid music played so faintly it might have come from a sunken ship. Then Liz would burst from cover, striding out decisively in a new outfit, her eyes meeting his with blazing directness, as if to say, Well? He liked this moment, the energy she brought back to the room, and the authority she placed in him, the freedom to scan her body. They had slept together only once, but now everything they did, he felt, was leading them again to sex. His anticipation lent an excitement to every new dress, and kept his interest flowing as she stood in front of the triple mirror, turning studiously this way and that, cocking her head or twisting to glance at her reflected back, while the saleslady murmured comments, or leaned in discreetly to flick at a hem.

Unable to decide, Liz took two dresses. The saleslady folded them into low boxes, whose lids bore the slashing, stylized signature *Cardy Brothers*, tied them smartly with string, and handed the boxes to Joe. "The man's job," she said, turning up the corners of her small mouth and all of them laughed, though the remark had not been funny. Liz thanked the woman effusively and turned away.

"Aren't you going to pay?" Joe said. He had remained beside the cash register.

"Daddy pays," Liz sang to him over her shoulder.

Joe was mortified, hoping no one had heard; he despised her for these airs. And yet, there was something about her that held him, something more, even, than sex. She had a power that drew him in her wake and when she stopped by the perfume counter he stopped too.

"I've just had an idea," she said, touching him on the arm. Her eyes were on his, huge and direct, filled with an exaggerated show of inspiration. He had a distinct sense she had planned this moment. "Why don't we take a look in the men's department?"

"I don't think –"

"Please? For me? Just a look?" Her gaze dropped to his mouth.

The men's department was even emptier than the women's. A few solitary people – half of them clerks – wandered about looking lost in the maze of counters and racks. Liz guided him to a place where shirts were arranged in armless rows, under glass. She asked a clerk to measure him. The clerk was a slim little man of about thirty, with an eager-to-please expression that Joe found oppressive. The world would *never* appreciate the service this man seemed so ready to lay at its feet. But he managed the tape with an expert gentleness, and it wasn't long before Joe felt a kind of collusion with him: they both had to endure the brisk, confident stream of Liz's instructions. She draped ties across folded shirts. She called for sweaters. She cajoled Joe into trying them on. The clerk and he exchanged looks, ironic and tolerant. *Women.*

Yet the clothes were so fine, he half-enjoyed the process – the make-believe. For that was what it had become for him, a kind of theatre. He was pleasing her, by doing this, and pleasing himself, by pretending that he could afford to shop here. Yet the whole time he was aware that he had only ten dollars in his wallet and this knowledge began to bother him: he felt he was getting into a situation that must leave him uncomfortably exposed, in the end. When she'd sent the clerk off on another errand, he told her he'd had enough.

"Couldn't we look at some trousers? I'd like to see you *complete*."

Her eyes filled with pleading sincerity.

He frowned.

"Look, I don't have any money."

Immediately he felt heat sear his face.

"We don't need money," she said, drawing her finger over his chest.

When he understood what she meant, his face burned hotter.

"No –"

"But it's *Christmas*," she said, her baby mouth pouting.

"It's after Christmas."

"You won't let me buy you a Christmas present?" She was still picking at his chest.

"No. I mean, I don't have anything for you."

He had just thought of this defence.

"I don't care. I just want –"

The clerk had come back and was hovering discreetly.

"We'd like to see some trousers," Liz told him.

Joe couldn't find the escalator, which made his escape rather awkward. He blundered around Overcoats and finally had to ask another clerk. Outside, the cold, damp air sharp with exhaust fumes hit him like a blast of sanity.

It was nearly ten minutes before she appeared. Under one arm were the two dress boxes. Hanging from the opposite hand was a large bag, also bearing the store's logo. She marched grimly past him and when she got to the car she waited for him to open the door for her, on the driver's side. She flung the packages onto the back seat, slid in behind the wheel, and pushed a key into the ignition. The Lincoln roared. He half-expected it to take off without him.

But she waited. He got in and slammed the door shut. Neither of them spoke.

She drove too fast, with a fierce competence. He was the first to break the silence.

"Did you buy those things anyway?"

She was steering almost carelessly, the fingers of one hand at the bottom of the wheel, chin lifted. The car took on momentum.

He stretched over the back of the seat for the bag, but it was just out of reach and he gave up.

"You did, didn't you?"

"I'll buy what I like," she said.

"Sure. But I won't wear them."

They were at a standoff. They sped past the School for the Blind, past the vast, rolling lawns covered with snow, the great maples and spruce. As a child, he had wondered how the blind children managed to avoid running into the trees. He had practised being blind, by closing his eyes and feeling his way around the backyard. He remembered this now: the lost feeling at the core of darkness.

They were in the outskirts, with the open fields ahead. The speedometer touched seventy-five.

"Slow down," he told her. She ignored him.

He settled into a stoic silence, hating her. Mercifully, the road was bare, though banks of frozen snow often obscured the view on both sides: the shoulders had all but disappeared. He glimpsed fields, stubbled with last year's corn, a swaybacked cow, standing in miserable immobility beside a steaming manure pile. He decided they were finished, he and Liz. He would tell her when they got home.

She was doing eighty now.

"C'mon, slow down," he told her, with a show of carelessness. "It's not worth this."

She glanced at him, her eyes empty of their usual drama and wilfulness and small lies. Now they were cold and appraising and absolutely without fear. He felt as if she had reached across the seat and casually stuck a knife in his arm.

The high rear end of a dump truck was coming up fast. She had no choice, he felt, but to slow. He could make out the bulge of the truck's axle, a gourd caked in salt. And the crudely painted letters on a flapping board: G. MARONI. PRESTON, ONT.

"Liz, for God's sake!"

She braked, and simultaneously flung the wheel over, pulling the car onto the narrow, icy shoulder where it scraped a snowbank and lurched back onto the road. He was yelling at her now, ordering her to stop. A few hundred yards farther on, she turned the Lincoln into the parking lot of a garage where a line of new cars sat blanketed in snow. When she finally stopped, he tore the key from the ignition. They sat in silence behind a snowbank.

He realized she was weeping: a thread of eyeliner on her cheek, she kept on staring out the windshield, in apparent defiance.

"Why did you do that?" he said. "I mean, for a few shirts."

"I knew what I was doing." All her patina of sophistication had crumbled.

"You could have rolled us back there."

"Well, I didn't," she said. Like a little girl, winning a point in some schoolyard argument.

"That's pathetic," he said, after a moment. "*You're* pathetic."

He had come up against her will – something childish and stubborn and dark. It was still in the car, frightening him and fascinating him and holding him in fury and wonder, as if some spell had caught them there, in the shrouded white parking lot. His throat was sore; a deep weariness had seeped into his limbs. "What were you trying to prove?" he said, rousing himself. "What would crashing us prove?"

"I didn't crash us," she said.

She glanced at him: a little girl, wary and beaten.

"All right," he said, gently enough. "Maybe I should drive."

He got out and circled to the driver's side, while she moved over. Before he could start the car she slid over to him with abrupt violence and burrowed into his shoulder.

She sought out his mouth with her own. At first he resisted but she caught his wrist and drew his hand between her legs. He worked aside her soaked panties, while she moaned extravagantly and tore at his hair. In the end, she huddled against him with her ruined face, sniffing and saying she was sorry.

That night, his parents drove to a Couples' Club party at the church. Joe walked up the hill to Liz's house, where he was soon put to work behind the bar, near the French doors overlooking the snowbound patio. In the opposite corner towered a decorated fir tree, a fairy-tale mountain of white lights and golden orbs topped by a golden angel with open wings of fretted gold, its mild face lifted as if towards a greater though invisible glory. The room was crowded, voices bubbling everywhere, and he was kept busy pouring wine and rye, or scrambling to concoct fancier drinks, Manhattans and Brown Cows, one eye on the chart pinned behind the bar.

He was drinking steadily himself – beer – and soon felt buoyed by a pleasant tide of sociability. Familiar melodies from decades past rose from the hi-fi, soaring on the blended voices of the Ray Conniff Singers. Through the raised doorway to the kitchen, he could see Liz, in her new dress of off-white silky stuff, talking to an older woman who kept touching her arm. Just by raising the fingers of his left hand to his nose, he could smell her: an earthy tang soap had not erased.

"Oh Joe!" Liz's mother, Mary, was approaching the bar, her brown eyes fixed on his with their habitual look of fractured, still-game hope. In the bottom of her glass a lemon rind lay like a wasted flower. Already that evening he had made her three gin and tonics; she'd been behaving noticeably less matronly with him, less correct, and oddly younger. He thought of Doc McVey's girlfriend, Babs Wilcocks. In town people said that she and Mary McVey had found a way to live with each other, and he wondered if Babs Wilcocks would turn up at the party. Something in this possibility, something in the mere *existence* of Babs Wilcocks excited him. Anything seemed possible this evening. Below the steady hubbub of the party, a kind of subterranean energy was roiling.

Mary was towing an old woman with a shallow cap of thin, bluish hair. "Marjorie, this is Joe, Liz's new beau." Mary seemed to love the word "beau," with its hint of a life more gallant and risqué. All evening she'd been introducing him this way, as if the engagement ring were already on Liz's finger.

"So this is the young man."

"I've been thinking of running off with him myself," Mary said. Joe dropped his gaze – there was some limit she was transgressing, just a little – and Marjorie Ford laughed with exaggerated glee, showing the gum-ridge on her false teeth. "Maybe you'll have to compete with me," she said.

The women left. Joe wiped down the bar. He didn't feel he was Liz's beau (whatever that meant), but at least being presented that way made it impossible for him to be mistaken as *only* the bartender, a point he was sensitive on. He hadn't come up the hill as a servant but as practically a family member. He was enjoying himself, enjoying with an almost proprietorial ease the spreading, merry rooms of this house, owned by the town's richest man, enjoying the friendliness of the town's best people – doctors and lawyers and businessmen and Bannerman's executives and of course their wives, done up to the nines in silky sheath dresses, their hair shaped in wavy bobs and other styles from the Thirties and Forties. He was enjoying being spoken to so familiarly by all of them, as if it were the most natural thing in the world to find him here. Even when someone said, "Oh you're Alf Walker's son," the little tremor of misgiving he felt was answered by no hint of condescension or disapproval. His presence as Liz's boyfriend spoke for itself.

Liz came down from the kitchen.

"Darling, I'm sorry about this –"

Tonight, he didn't even mind her theatrical "darling." The party was all a drama, in a way; they were all on the big stage.

"Sorry about what –"

"Having to meet all these people."

"I like it. I like your mother," he said, spying her across the room. Mary McVey had a large, low-set bosom, nested under dark-blue silk; he watched it as she put back her head to laugh.

"I think I'm jealous."

"You should be!" And for a split second he intuited a place – exciting and ill-defined – where both her mother and she were his. He looked pointedly at the deep slit in the bodice of her dress.

"Why don't we lie down behind the bar," he said, deadpan.

He sensed that she, too, was inflamed, feeling his eyes on her.

Then her mother was there again.

"I'm going to take him from you," Mary announced. She reached out and took Joe's hand into hers.

"Oh, Mother."

Mary squeezed Joe's hand and held it tight. Hers was surprisingly soft, but cold too, as if she'd been keeping it in a snowbank. "Don't listen to her," Mary told him. "Seriously now, Joe. Do you like older women? I think you do."

"*Mother*," Liz said in a fierce undertone.

"Sure," Joe said. But this was too much, even for him. He managed to extract his hand.

Mary wandered off, strangely out of place at her own party. She bumped into a man in a garish orange sports jacket and veered away. Bing Crosby was skating effortlessly through "White Christmas."

Liz said, "I think you better cut back on her gin."

Since their drive back from Johnsonville, Liz had been unusually attentive to him. Perhaps she was beginning to fall in love with him.

He felt a little remorseful about this, a bit of a fraud, and yet he felt so good being there, he felt flooded with goodwill. Leaning forward impulsively, he kissed her on the mouth and told her she looked beautiful. And she did: looking up at him, testing his words, her beauty struck through to him and he remembered how the small globes of her breasts had brushed his chest in the motel. There was a hunger in Liz McVey's wiry body, as genuine and convincing as her social manner was false – a frank hunger that suggested danger and aroused him.

Her sister, Sally, called her away just then, to see about the food, and he looked over the crowded room with a fresh surge of excitement, thinking about the next time he and Liz might be alone together. A few minutes later Mary came back, drawing behind her a man with a bald, darkly tanned head and a look in his eyes of sharp, confident inquiry. Joe had noticed the man earlier, as Mary introduced him to her husband. His name, she told Joe, was Bob Prince. She had known him at school, in Toronto, and now by coincidence he was working in Attawan.

Joe took the man's hand and felt the shock of a hard, wilful strength. As the pale-blue eyes met his, Joe thought of his father and looked away.

"He's going to university next year," Mary said of Joe. "And when he graduates, we're going to run away together."

"Oh-ho!" Bob Prince said in his effortless voice. He asked Joe what university he was headed for. Mary, who had been beaming at Joe like a prize child, was called away to the kitchen.

"Are you doing a general B.A. or –"

"I'll be majoring in history."

"Good. Good. Great preparation."

"Preparation –"

"For going on. Business. Law. What are you planning to do?" Bob Prince said genially.

"Just study history," Joe said, wiping at the bar. "Maybe teach, teach university. I don't really care for business."

This just came out, a flash of sullenness, of defiance. He sensed he was attacking the other man and that this showed him up as gauche. But he had taken an instant dislike to him: it was his polish, his smoothness, his smooth, irresistible voice, which under the velvet carried a suggestion of plate metal. He made Joe feel insecure.

Bob Prince darted Joe a glance from his superior height – he must have stood about six-four – apparently amused. "And what's wrong with business?"

Joe shook his head. His contact with business was pretty limited, he wasn't quite sure how he'd come to think it was a second-rate activity, not really a profession at all. He'd worked in business, of course, and the men he thought of as businessmen – the manager of the A&P, Scott Dowd, or the various bosses he'd observed at Bannerman's, seemed perpetually consumed by trivialities – by lost orders and deadlines, tearing their hair out over matters that didn't seem worth it. And then there were the owners of stores on the main street, or the men who came door to door, selling brushes and whatnot: what struck him most about them was their false friendliness. Yes, business meant selling things, and selling things meant turning yourself, he thought, into a glad-handing phoney.

"Just not attracted to it," Joe said, with another shrug. " 'Fumbling in the greasy till –' "

"Those are interesting words."

"They're from a poem," Joe said. Anna Macrimmon had showed it to him one day in the library.

"I take it you're a socialist then."

Joe shrugged, allowing as he was.

"Tax the rich, and give it to the poor, like Robin Hood."

"Something like that."

"The rich who've taken all the risks."

"You think poor people don't take risks?" Joe had heard his history teacher, Archie Mann, make this argument, and had adopted it as his own. He went on. "A poor man puts his health, his body on the line, every time he goes to work. That's his capital, and he's risking it. If he loses it, then he loses a lot more than some rich guy who drops ten thousand bucks he can afford to play around with."

Bob Prince laughed, a little too tolerantly, Joe thought. Joe's face was flushed. He was astonished at himself, his vehemence. He was not quite sure the other man was taking him seriously.

Bob Prince said, "But you're willing to enjoy the fruits of a businessman's labours." And he gestured in a general way with his Scotch glass: he was indicating the room, with its deep white couches and chairs, the splendid tree, the fire licking happily behind glass. He was indicating the whole house, and somehow, deep in the house, Liz McVey. Or at least Joe thought he was. He felt the contradiction at the core of his argument and he disliked Bob Prince for putting his finger on it with such casual accuracy.

He said, "I don't know. Is making money on the stock market labour?"

Bob Prince was shaking his head and grinning.

"I think we should all share, more fairly," Joe said stubbornly.

"So you'd like to live like they live in Russia?"

"No," Joe said. "They're not free in Russia. But at least they've grasped a certain principle."

They sparred like this while Joe wiped at the counter with a rag, like a real bartender, though without the neutral equanimity. He was convinced that the other man was just humouring him and this made him even angrier. After a while Doc McVey drifted over to refresh his Scotch. Behind his glasses, his babyish face seemed always on the verge of laughter, as if the world were a source of perpetual amusement: only a fool would take it *entirely* seriously.

"So, Bob, is our bartender giving you a hard time?"

"First communist bartender I ever met, Jack," Bob Prince said.

Doc McVey's loose mouth opened wider, happily.

"I'm not a communist," Joe said sullenly. He felt he was becoming an object of fun. The way they called each other Bob and

Jack, with a pointed, country-club familiarity, as if they had known each other for years, annoyed him.

"Communist, socialist," Bob Prince said, waving his glass. "Same thing."

Joe remained silent, refusing to be baited. He was convinced that Bob Prince, whatever his cleverness at making money, was essentially stupid. There was something thick about him that made subtlety impossible.

"So when does the revolution start?" Doc McVey said.

Joe wiped at the bar. "In ten minutes," he said. "You're all being taken to the basement and shot. Then your bodies will be dragged outside and burned."

Of course it was a joke, but there was a savagery in his remark that he instantly regretted. The difficult moment was quickly covered by the older men, who laughed indulgently and drifted away, but Joe was mortified, feeling he'd been hopelessly crude.

He stayed to the end, though: stayed through the uproar at midnight when everyone blew horns and kissed and on the TV Guy Lombardo and his Royal Canadians played "Auld Lang Syne" over the throngs packing Times Square. Just as the melee was subsiding, Mary found him and, pressing her body against his, kissed him hard. The quick darting of her tongue alarmed him and he gently extracted himself, but a minute later, remembering her soft mouth – the hint of experience beyond anything he had known – he became so excited he had to sit down, to hide the swelling in his pants.

Later, when the last guest had left, Liz asked him to come back to the family room, where her mother and father already were. Liz retrieved two packages from under the tree and held them out for him. "Your payment for tending bar so well. And because I like you."

"We *all* like you," Mary said, slurring a little. She was slumped beside the fireplace, in a deep armchair, and was staring at his chest. Doc McVey stood at the window with his back to them, gazing towards the yard where a black, solitary tree leaned into the floodlit space above the patio, releasing a few clots of windblown snow.

Joe took the packages, beautifully wrapped in gold paper. He could feel the flat softness of the sweater, the stiff horseshoes of shirt collars.

For a second he hesitated: something passed through him, leaving only a metallic taste, an emptiness.

Liz was beaming, a bit frantically, while Mary smiled sleepily to herself in her chair. Beyond Liz's shoulder, her father continued to stare into the floodlit yard.

"For you, darling," Liz said.

In her chair, Mary clapped her hands rapidly, like a child.

26

IT WAS AFTER TWO when he returned to the Island. He found his father in the kitchen, his plaid dressing gown sagging open to reveal the unbuttoned top of his pyjamas, a scrawl of hair on his pale chest. He was drinking a bottle of beer. Something about the man – his sunken eyes, with their aggressive glint, watching him sourly – put Joe's back up. He brushed past with his bag of presents.

"So how's life in the palace?" his father said.

"Better than here," Joe said. Why couldn't the man just leave him alone?

"What did you say?"

Joe didn't bother responding. He had almost reached the door to the hall.

"Hey, you!"

He kept going.

"Stop!"

He stopped, let out an exaggerated sigh – what nonsense this all was – and turned to meet the man shuffling across the floor towards him. He knew he'd gone too far, knew it by the old, familiar fear slipping through his chest like cold water.

He stared back, lifting his face as his father loomed in at him.

"What did you say?" his father asked again.

"I think you heard me."

"So you think you're too good for us now? Is that it?"

"Oh God," Joe said, starting to turn away.

As his father gripped his arm, Joe shoved him. They were at it in a second, slapping and pushing almost awkwardly, scuffling around the floor. Often, over the years, they had fought for the pleasure of it: wrestled or boxed on the living-room rug or in the backyard. But they had never fought in anger before, never set out seriously to hurt each other. Even now they seemed held back by old constraints, not quite sure what to do with the energy surging into their arms. But the fury was real enough. It had come up so fast it seemed to have always been there, in some deep well where all the resentments and rivalries and sheer hellbent love of chaos had been put away over the years. Finally immobilizing each other in a tangle of arms – in some part of their brains they knew it was less dangerous to wrestle than to box – they crashed to the floor. The table went skidding. The butter dish landed on a chair. They rolled together in a wave of tartan bathrobe and Joe felt the soft flop of his father's genitals against his leg. He shoved his father's head against the fridge and outside, Red, waking in his den under the back porch, put back his big head and howled into the wraiths of snow drifting from Lookout Hill.

Then Joe's mother was there, hitting them with a broom as she shrieked for them to stop. "Is this who we are?" she kept crying. She was almost singing in a wild, new voice, tremulous and high. "Is this who we are?"

Looking beyond his father's head, Joe saw her shins, nicked by the razor.

"All right, fella," his father said hoarsely. They were lying locked on their sides, in grim equilibrium, their faces inches apart. He could smell the beer on his father's breath, the stink of his father's unhappiness. "Let's get up," his father said.

Joe extracted himself, avoiding his father's eyes. As far as he was concerned, the other man no longer existed. This house no longer existed. He was through.

A couple of days later, Joe found his mother vacuuming in his room. "There's a letter for you," she told him, nodding at his desk where she'd propped up a small envelope with unfamiliar black-and-orange stamps. Joe carried it down the hall to the bathroom, where he locked the door and sat on the shut toilet seat to open it, in the steamy aftermath of someone's shower. It contained two sheets of airmail paper, covered on both sides in Anna's scrawling hand.

Dear Joe,

I'm sitting on the deck of the SS Independence. We're sailing east, towards Italy. Yesterday we had a day in Cannes, the best so far. We had lunch in a little place called Pont-du-Loup, just outside town – red-tiled roofs and white facades and long green shutters, under bushy hills rising to cliffs. The country is so rough but also beautiful. You wouldn't think people could live in it, I mean, as well as they do. The towns are wonderful, so many hills, so many views of the sea taking you by surprise, a smear of light in the distance. I'm looking at it now (the sea) where it hazes off towards Corsica (which I can't see) and Africa somewhere beyond that. I've always loved the idea of the Mediterranean and now that I'm here again, it's wonderful.

Mom and Dad rented a car, and we went exploring in the hills. Father Campion came with us. He's American, a priest

we met on the ship, and the best company – a great story-
teller. He doesn't wear his priest's uniform on holiday, looks
more like a retired businessman. He's plump, with a twinkle
in his eyes that when you look closer is as sharp as knives. He
enjoys his food more than anybody I've ever met, and loves
to talk about it. When he picks up his wineglass he's likely to
take ten minutes telling you where the wine comes from (he
seems to have visited a million vineyards) right down to the
exact hill. He says he's in love with me, and he's very gallant,
but since he's sixty-something it's really just a game. I tease
him and tell him he's not really a priest and he laughs till his
eyes disappear. Dad says he's probably having such a good
time because we aren't Catholic.

While he and Mom and Dad were visiting a winery, I went
for a walk. I climbed a hill and went along through some
fields. I met a shepherd. My first shepherd! He had a dog,
and his sheep were milling around at the edge of a field where
he sat eating his lunch on an old stone. (I guess all stones are
old, but this one looked older.) Actually, the dog saw me first,
and came barking, till the shepherd called him off. We had
quite a conversation, at least what I understood of it. The old
kind of French they speak here is pretty strange. The sheep
kept putting in their two cents. He might have been fifty, or
younger, with an unbelievably leathery face, and shy brown
eyes that seemed to belong to a much younger man. He told
me he'd been a shepherd all his life, ever since he was twelve,
when his father took him out of school. I asked him if he'd
wanted to leave school, and he looked away at the hills, and
then at the dog. I felt no one had ever asked him this before,
and he didn't know what to do with it. We were both embarrassed. But of course, being me, I didn't let him off the hook
– I mean, I didn't say anything to help him out. There's a part
of me that would be cool in a train crash, I think, just coolly

watching to see what happens. I felt the sadness of his life, and something more than that: his fate, maybe. The shape his life had taken.

I wonder if people have fates any more, or do they just have careers? Is everyone's life now so much like everyone else's, so bland and predictable, that a real fate can't happen? Or do we just pretend we don't have fates – but they happen anyway, in a dishonest, backdoor sort of way. No two fates are alike, and I think that's why we're afraid of our own. It means we have to embrace our own aloneness, our own uniqueness, and as much as we might say we want to do that, really, we're scared. Better to be like everybody else – and not stick out too much. So life misses us.

In the end, he just shrugged. It was like he'd said, "This is how things are. No use regretting." He gave me some wine, in a thick little tumbler.

I saw three dolphins this morning.

Tomorrow, Italy: Livorno, Rome, Naples. Thinking of you warmly, Anna.

He read it three times. The thin paper seemed fabulous in its blueness, as if at any moment dolphins might rise from its depths.

27

LIKE A SUDDEN INFLUX of fresh air after weeks indoors, her letter intoxicated him, as if she had held out to him the promise of a finer life; as if the landscape she had described – the blue Mediterranean glimmering at every turn – had sent its ranges and peninsulas into his own existence and he was already wandering with her there, in a partnership he could not clearly fantasize, for he had known nothing like it in his life. He stared at the edge of the bathroom sink, where a single plastered hair appeared like a crack in the porcelain, and wondered if the letter didn't mark a sea change in her attitude to him (wasn't there some hint of it in that phrase "thinking of you warmly"?) and at the same time, applying the lash of common sense, he told himself there was nothing in it but friendship.

But just that she had thought of him, over there, that she had sat on the deck of a great ship and aimed these words at *him*! It seemed she had reached across the world to create this space inhabited by only the two of them. And at the same time, her letter reminded him by contrast of his relationship with Liz, which every day seemed more false. He was spending a lot of time at her house, or driving around in her father's Lincoln, and yet he knew there was something temporary and, yes, dishonest, about his link with her, because the truth was, as much as he enjoyed her physically – and really, he couldn't get enough of her in that regard – he had to admit to himself (and he saw this clearly, in the sudden shift of atmosphere – the widening access of clarity – that Anna's letter brought) that he didn't like Liz McVey very much. The thought that Anna would come home and find him with her ignited an obscure shame.

The next Saturday he and Liz drove over to Johnsonville in the Lincoln to see a movie. All evening he kept meaning to tell her they were finished, and all evening he kept postponing the confrontation, though he managed to hold himself a little aloof. She must have sensed something was wrong, because she was even more attentive than usual, constantly touching his arm in the dark theatre, keying her laughter to his. Afterwards, in the car, she asked if he wanted to go to the motel. He'd been planning to deny himself that pleasure, but found himself helpless when she started to kiss him. Later, in bed, his excitement was extreme. But immediately afterwards, he regretted the tawdry room, the vapid sailboats on the wall, her pathetic, crouching nakedness as she washed herself in the long tub. They drove back to Attawan in silence.

One Sunday afternoon in early January, Smiley dropped by the house with his skates and stick. Joe was taken by surprise, he hadn't seen Smiley for some weeks, not since he'd dropped out of school and gone to work in Bannerman's dyehouse. But here he was, just like old times, planted on the kitchen doormat in his rolled-down rubber boots and bright blue-and-white hockey jacket, announcing that the Atta was frozen solid right up to the first rapids. Such perfect skating conditions hadn't been seen in years. There was no snow to shovel off, and the ice, Smiley said, making Jamie laugh with pleasure, was as smooth as a baby's bottom.

Joe leapt at the chance. He felt as if his old life – his life before the arrival of Anna Macrimmon and the complication of Liz McVey – had made a return, was offering the chance of a forgotten, uncomplicated happiness. Penny and Jamie wanted to go too, so there was a general rush to dig out skates and toques and hockey sticks. They were nearly ready to leave when Joe's father appeared from the cellar, carrying his ancient stick and the long, battered skates with thin blades that Joe hadn't seen him wear for years. Penny and Jamie danced around him: Daddy was going skating! But Joe, standing by the door with Smiley, felt that the day had been stolen from him. In the days since their fight, his relations with his father had existed in a state of suspension. They were friendly enough, in a formal, superficial way, but Joe sensed that each of them was waiting for the other to make the next move, but whether it would be towards reconciliation or fresh hostilities, he couldn't say. Just now, his father's gloomy face – smiling wanly at the young ones – seemed like the spectre at the feast. There could be no joy around *him*. At that moment, his father looked over at him and – to Joe's complete surprise – winked. Instantly, something in him started, gladdened.

They set off in a noisy gang. Margaret, who had never learned to skate, watched them go out the door. "Don't fall in," she said dryly. Smiley promised her he'd keep an eye on everybody.

Behind Bannerman's old hosiery mill on West Street, they descended to the millpond. Out on the wide ice, a dozen men and boys were playing shinny, gusting here and there like a flock of wind-blown starlings, under the cloudless sky. They sat on logs to put on their skates. Joe and his father helped Jamie and Penny. Then the two of them sat side by side, lacing up with numb fingers.

"So you think you've forgotten how?" Joe teased his father.

His father did not respond. His fingers were attacking his laces fiercely, with what might have been anger. Joe felt the shadow of their antagonism.

Then Alf finished and picked up his stick. As he skated away, he tossed back, "No one catches the old man," and the day was made whole again. Joe watched him skate towards the other players with slow, lazy strokes, accelerating suddenly for a step or two, his head down, then stroking easily again, rocking slightly as he sped along. He looked as natural, even more natural, than he did walking down the street, as if all his life had been an exile from the easy freedom of ice.

Joe followed a minute later. Smiley had dropped a puck, and he and Jamie and Joe's father were passing it back and forth. Joe streaked upriver. "Hey, Walker!" he shouted, and his father looked up and saw him. Joe took his pass close to his feet, lost it for a moment, then circled back with the puck, floating an easy pass to his brother. Jamie fanned on it and promptly landed on his back.

Joe was exhilarated by the huge expanse of ice. He felt he could do anything out here – wheel, fly, brake on a dime – under a sky that seemed to smile on every improvisation. He forgot about Liz McVey and Anna Macrimmon, that whole impossible tangle. What else mattered but to chase a puck across the wide, dark river? After a while Smiley and the Walkers joined the game of shinny. There was only one rule: whoever got the puck hung onto it as long as he could. It was fox and hounds, with nearly everyone playing the fox at some point. Joe laughed as his father took the puck and started to dipsy-doodle through the crowd like a madman, with his hair sticking out from under his too-small toque. Joe managed to poke the puck away from him, but it went straight onto the stick of Larry Langlois, easily the best player there. Larry was seventeen, tall and loose-jointed – it was said he'd been scouted by the Leafs – and he ragged the puck as if it were wired to his stick, covering the ice in effortless sweeps, his eyes laughing. He'd tempt you with the puck, throw in a body feint, and leave you crashing into air.

They started a proper game. Larry's team got only six players, to eight on the other side. The goalposts at one end were rocks and, at the other, a hundred yards away, someone's cowboy boots. The boots looked forlorn and absurd standing there, six feet apart, their toes pointed towards the distant shores with their low clouds of winter trees. Smiley's father, who despite being bald was playing without a hat, got the first goal with an explosion of reckless, windmilling speed that left the others whooping and laughing. As he coasted away from the goal, bent over his stick and gasping for breath, Smiley whacked him affectionately on the bottom.

After a while, Joe noticed that his father had left the game. Jamie hadn't been able to keep up with the older boys and men, so Alf had taken him off to the side and was laying soft passes on his stick. Jamie was working hard at it, digging along for the puck on ankles that barely seemed able to support him, falling down and bouncing up again with wild determination. Watching his brother, Joe felt a poignant stab of recognition. His father had once fed him passes in just the same way, and now, seeing Jamie, he was seeing himself, so eager to please the man, to best the man, who was both his god and his nemesis. But where was Penny? On the other side of the river, where some alders showed red against the grey of willows, he saw her, in her pink hat and mitts, pushing herself along with abrupt, erect strokes among her friends. Dipping, she opened her arms, extended a leg behind her, and became a gliding swan.

Later, tired of the game, Joe gave his spot to a new arrival and skated upstream. It seemed less cold under the high cliffs, out of the wind, and he pushed steadily along, gripping his stick in one hand at his side as he passed islands and the great, leaning trunks of the willows, all floating past with a dreamlike smoothness, to the rhythmic swish of his blades. The bottom grew more shallow and he began to glimpse weeds and rocks under the glass of the ice. It was a bit spooky, to be gliding above the water, the fish, and he was soon out of sight and hearing of the players. At a bend where he had once caught a half-dozen bass, he met Penny and her friends, returning from upstream. They were laughing and gossiping – skating with the short, quick strokes demanded by their burred blades. Penny, he noticed, was eating snow out of her mitt, though when she saw him she tossed it down. A few seconds later, as the girls fell away behind him, he heard them burst into giggles that finally died out around the bend.

He heard the rapids before he saw them. A soft, rushing sound that touched him with a faint fear. It was a reminder that the river was still alive beneath him, that this afternoon of skating was only a temporary gift, a kind of illusion.

Most of the rapids had frozen over. But the biggest wave was still visible, flowing like the smooth, darkly glinting body of a serpent amid jumbled crusts of ice. Water had spilled over the ice below, where it had hardened in a yellowish mantle, like wax. He stood at the rapid's edge, looking up to the swift coursing of black water, wondering if he dared bypass it by climbing up one side. At that moment, he saw the fox.

It was watching him from the smooth ice above the rapid. He was *sure* it had not been there a few moments ago, and yet he had not seen it appear. It was standing almost broadside to him, head turned inquisitively, the fantastic orange plume of its tail tipped with white, stretching straight out, nearly as long as its body, and, except for a stir of breeze in the thick fur, motionless. The fox lifted its muzzle, trying to scent him; it turned its head a little more, and for a second Joe's heart leapt as he met the fox's unblinking stare.

Then the fox trotted off, without haste, followed by the great, level plume. Something in the fox's movement seemed unusual. Joe saw that half of its right hind leg was missing: the thigh tapered into a dark stump. He just glimpsed the end of it, swinging uselessly below the fox's belly.

That night he fell ill with a high fever. He lay shivering and sweating while a small, cold moon moved over the house. Shining between the curtains, it seemed to be seeking him out, like a flashlight whose glare hides whoever is holding it. Twice he threw up. The first time he didn't quite make it to the toilet, and his vomit hit the hall floor with a sound like a mess of chains spilling. Then his mother appeared, and it seemed he was about four years old again, helpless before her tender scolding. She put him back to bed with extra blankets and a hot water bottle that in his delirium seemed to be a part of himself he couldn't quite incorporate into his body. He dreamed he was in a bare white room that had no door. He had climbed up to a ledge, and was balancing there, precariously, while the fox with three legs kept jumping up at him from the floor below, showing its sharp teeth in a kind of smile.

The next day, a Monday, he was still running a fever and vomiting, so there was no question of school. But he was conscious it was the day Anna Macrimmon was scheduled to come back. What he feared – what he was powerless to do anything about – was the reception he knew she would get from Liz. He could imagine Liz telling her, with an air of coy triumph, that she and Joe were steadies. Yes, she would somehow let Anna know that they were sleeping together, and this prospect seemed to expose him to the worst injustice of all – the injustice of being misunderstood, though exactly *what* would be misunderstood he did not let himself think too clearly about. Groaning, he turned violently in the bed and struck his fist into the wall.

By Thursday, his sickness had turned into a cold, and he was able to go back up the hill to school. In Miss Todd's homeroom, Anna

Macrimmon's desk, a sheen of birch veneer under a tall window framing a snowy sky, was empty. And it remained empty, in its various incarnations in various rooms, all morning. Her absence touched a note of hope – perhaps she hadn't come back yet, and so had not yet been informed by Liz. He still had time to tell Liz they were through, but there was one problem with this: Liz, too, was absent, her empty desk echoing Anna's in every room. Sometimes the two desks were far apart, but in French they were side by side, a constant reminder of the strange partnership he had made with them and, which in some obscure way, they had made with each other. In the hall after French, he fell in beside Brad Long, drawing him into a conversation about the schoolwork he'd missed. He asked casually if Anna was back yet.

"Got back Monday."

Excitement and despair rose in him at once. She was here again, but on the other hand, Liz had undoubtedly told her everything. Yet he had to be sure.

"Back here? At school?"

Brad looked amused: "Where else?"

"She sick or –"

"Some bug she caught over there. Some *foreign* bug."

Brad's eyes stayed trained on him, lit with mockery, and Joe had the feeling that his whole dilemma was common knowledge, as if Anna and Brad and God only knew who else had sat around a table discussing – having a good laugh over – the lovesick Walker.

As soon as school had finished for the day, he hurried downtown to the florist and chose a small bouquet of dried heather, which he tucked inside his coat in its paper wrapper. Then up the hill again, walking so fast he was soon out of breath and had to stop to spit thick phlegm into the snow. Behind the houses on Banting, the sun sent low beams across the ploughed street.

He mounted the front steps, under the little portico with its white pillars, in a straightjacket of self-consciousness, aware she might be watching. The house itself seemed alive. No light showed in the windows, yet each object he glimpsed inside – the top of an armchair, a lampshade withdrawing into dimness – seemed to take note of him.

He pressed the bell button. There was no sound from inside the house. An Irish setter trotted alone down the street, its long, matted fur carrying little balls of ice that clicked together. Joe fumbled open his coat and retrieved the small bouquet. The house went on considering him.

Then the door opened, and he saw a woman in a full-length white apron, her hair swept back from her face into an untidy bun. She was middle-aged and rather short, but there was something about the eyes – a distant glint of humour – that was familiar.

"I'm Joe Walker. I'm a friend of Anna's."

"Oh, Joe, yes, she's spoken about you. I'm Estelle Macrimmon. Why don't you come in –"

Her French accent made "in" sound like "een." Her warmth gave him courage. He found himself in a small entrance hall, aware of a staircase in dark wood, the smell of cooking.

She shut the door and again stood before him, regarding him in an open, pleased way. There was a pride in her carriage that created an almost aristocratic effect, despite her plump figure. He explained that he'd just dropped by to wish Anna well and give her the bouquet: he held it up almost apologetically.

"Well why don't you give it yourself? I'll go up and get her."

He waited in the hall. The house was much smaller than the McVeys and more sombre, with its dark woodwork and faded Indian carpets. In the living room to his right books were piled loosely on the floor. The walls were green with white trim (oddly, very like the walls in his own house) and hung with numerous framed photos and paintings. Propped on the mantel was a large oil painting of a seated woman with silver hair wearing a dress. Its pale-green folds, beautifully evoked, filled much of the old-fashioned-looking frame. Her lips held a vague smile, but her eyes conveyed a certain wistfulness.

Anna's mother reappeared on the landing above.

"She wants to see you up here. Come up, Joe."

He shed his boots and climbed the stairs. Her mother gestured towards an open door.

"Just *entrez*."

Anna was sitting in bed with her knees up, under a quilted spread. In the window to the left, the molten orange globe of the sun was settling into woods. Books were stacked on the rug beside her bed. A crumpled Kleenex lay nearby, like the head of a ghostly chrysanthemum.

She unwrapped the bouquet. He noticed that her upper lip was chafed.

"Heather! How did you know?"

Her voice had thickened, with her cold.

"Well, with a name like Macrimmon –"

"The hills go purple with it," she said, trying to smell the little dry flowers. "Have you ever seen it?"

He said nothing. He was standing beside the bed, feeling a bit like a servant who's delivered a message and will soon be asked to go. He could hardly believe he was here, in her room. Happy that he had pleased her, he stood secretly drinking her in, her pillow-flattened hair, the smocking of her flannel nightgown over her small breasts, her red nose. He could scarcely believe that *she* was here. She had been over there, and now she was here. She had been sailing on the Mediterranean, the actual blue, wet Mediterranean. Yes, just a few days ago, she had been in Europe – fabulous, distant Europe that he knew only from books. And now she was sitting in a bed in front of him, with a cold.

Her illness seemed part of her trip and its aftermath, as if going to that other place and back again, as if breaching the mysterious boundary between these two different worlds (for where did one end and the other begin?) was a stressful thing. It had worn at her health. Her illness was the cost she paid for accomplishing the miracle of existing in two places.

She told him to bring the chair from the desk. Picking it up, he glimpsed something of her private life. On a sheet of paper, half-covered by a book, he saw what seemed to be a poem – a ragged, narrow column of language in her familiar, jabbing hand. In the two seconds his attention lingered there, he saw the phrase "a mask of bees," and in the same glance he scanned the framed photo standing by itself to one side. Anna, her hair bound under a kerchief, was seated in some kind of boat – he could see water in the background, the arch of a bridge – beside a handsome man with blond, slick-backed hair and intense, serious eyes; his arm circled her shoulders with a confident possessiveness. Joe saw this in a flash, with a sense of excitement and grief, as if he had at once embraced her life and lost it.

He sat beside the bed while they talked. It was all he could do to contain himself, to make his limbs behave and not go jumping around the room in a mad dance. He kept shifting positions in the hard-backed chair.

"Your letter was terrific," he said. This seemed lame, a cliché – sometimes he felt he offered her nothing but. "I mean, I could almost smell those hills –"

"It's funny, I felt more like writing to you than to anyone. I have this feeling that you hear me better than other people."

"I do," he said.

"I'm serious. You seem to make the thoughts come. To draw them out somehow. You're a good listener."

"Well that's something."

"It's a lot," she said. The fading sunlight now left the room entirely. They sat in the dusk, not speaking. On her bureau, a clock ticked slowly. He felt as if his life were yearning towards its fulfillment. Everything he had ever wanted was here, so close at hand that all he had to do was – what? If he went to the bed and kissed her, he would spoil everything. She had made it clear they were to be friends only.

She blew her nose.

"Listen to me, a regular duck!"

She sniffed and said, "Liz tells me you've been seeing a lot of each other."

He had no doubt she knew everything and was being tactful. He felt fixed in his chair.

"We've gone out a few times."

"I'm glad you asked her to the dance."

"Well, I did it for you."

"And are you still taking her out for me?"

There was laughter in her voice. She blew her nose again. He said nothing.

"Sorry, that wasn't fair."

"I don't know why I'm taking her out," he said. "I'm not sure I like her very much."

She was silent, but he could feel her attentiveness, holding him, holding the entire room with its books and ticking clock, in the mild grey light. His confession, its edge of bitterness, seemed to float between them, not fading at all, something they had no choice but to consider. He felt a sad falling away, as if he had come to sobriety. A clarity. She was with Brad, and he was with Liz. And this was the basic architecture: his fate. Out the window, he could see the white fields of Wiley's farm, the thickets that bordered the Atta. "Sunday I went skating on the river. Just down there," he said. "It was incredible. Everything was frozen solid. There wasn't any snow so you could skate for miles. At the first rapids, I saw a fox."

He told her, as best as he could, about his strange sense of the animal as it looked back at him, the way their eyes had met and he had felt as if he were being given a privileged glimpse of life in its depths.

He told her how the fox had appeared in his dream. How it had seemed the same and not the same, with its stump of a leg, its menacing grin. "I was afraid of it, and yet I knew it wasn't going to bite me. It just wanted to come closer."

"And you wouldn't let it."

"No."

He felt a sense of failure. It seemed she was aware of it.

"You see," he said, "I couldn't tell Liz any of this – I wouldn't even think to tell her."

On the bed, Anna had let her knees drop.

28

PENNY WORKED AT HER BAR of laundry soap, carving carefully with her paring knife, trying to bring out the fish's gills. The overheated classroom was filled with the clank of radiators and the smell of wool drying and the slow clomping of Miss Hobsbawn's Oxfords as she strolled up and down the aisles with her hands behind her back, like Prince Philip.

Penny's fish was giving her trouble. Gouged from the hard, yellow soap, its head, she thought, looked an awful lot like a sheep's. She gazed out a tall window, where a flock of pigeons wheeled through a chalky sky, trying to remember the fish her dad and Uncle Pete had caught on Lake Erie. And suddenly she saw Uncle Pete coming up the trail to the cottage with a bucket of bass. He had cleaned them on a board nailed between two cedar trees, a cigarette hanging from his lips, squinting through the smoke while he worked with his special knife. She saw the narrow-bladed knife run along the fishes' bellies and cut behind their heads, saw it travelling flat through their sides, feeling its way, Uncle Pete said, along the ribs, as if the knife had a mind of its own; and then Uncle Pete lifting off the white fillets and putting them carefully on waxed paper. No one could cut a fillet like Pete, her dad said, the man could have been a surgeon! And she heard Uncle Pete talking, while the cigarette bobbled in his lips and seemed about to fall, talking about fish and what they could smell and what they liked to eat and where you could find them. He had picked up the waxed paper with the fillets and put it in her hands, letting her heft its weight while he grinned at her through the smoke of his cigarette, in the sunlight under the cedar trees: her Uncle Pete!

"Penny, are you all right?"

Wiping one eye with her wrist, Penny looked up. Miss Hobsbawn wore a grey skirt and a white blouse with a frill down the front. The story was that the teacher had had one breast removed. Penny couldn't see her without wondering which bump was the fake.

"Do you need your snack?"

The teacher was peering through her little glasses, fierce-friendly.

"No, Miss Hobsbawn."

Out of the corner of her eye, she sensed Bobby Tuckett twisting in his desk to look at her. Sometimes he just stared at her, with a teasing look, and sometimes, running past, he'd whisper, Diabetic! She wished Miss Hobsbawn hadn't mentioned her snack (the three Arrowroots wrapped in wax paper, tucked in her coat hanging in the cloakroom). She was supposed to eat them at recess, to keep from going into a reaction.

"Penny, that is wonderful! Absolutely wonderful!" Miss Hobsbawn boomed in her man's voice. "Class, look at this!"

And she scooped up Penny's fish and turned with it for all to see. "See what care she's put into the details," Miss Hobsbawn said, holding the fish between thumb and forefinger. "The head – look at that, class! The head! Penny, I'm afraid they can't see. Why don't you take it around and show everyone."

Penny went up and down the aisles, with the yellow fish in her open palm, trying to keep it balanced on its tummy. Some of the students hardly glanced at it, which was fine with her – she was embarrassed at having to show it – but a few studied it closely and murmured, "Huh" or "Good" and Ginny Lamport smiled at her as if she was pleased not just with the fish but with Penny too. She tried to slip by Bobby Tuckett's desk, but he cried, "Wait!" and plucked the fish right out of her hand and looked up at her, smirking under his long eyelashes.

At recess, she went off into a corner of the Girls' Yard to eat her Arrowroots. The whole yard, overlooking Shade Street and the river, was a trampled mess of slush. A black dog with a white streak down its nose was barking shrilly, while two girls picked their way between the puddles, trying to catch it.

"Still eating baby cookies, are we?"

Brenda Stubbs. Unlike her last name, Brenda was tall and skinny, with lank hair and red-rimmed eyes that were always getting infections. Ginny Lamport was with her, Penny saw, Ginny with her fair hair as smooth as silk, cut in a pageboy. How often Penny had stood in front of the bathroom mirror, wishing she had Ginny's hair, wishing she was Ginny!

Penny fumbled her last cookie into her pocket.

"Now be nice," Ginny told Brenda. "She *has* to eat them."

Penny heard the click of candy in their mouths.

She stood uncertainly, eager for them to like her. In her pocket, her hand abandoned the Arrowroot. She'd eat it later, in a washroom stall.

"I really liked your fish," Ginny said. Her eyes sparkled with amusement, as though Penny had done something cleverer than she knew. "We were doing soap carvings," she explained to Brenda. "Penny's was the best in the class."

Brenda held out a crumpled paper bag. "Want a black-ball?"

"I can't," Penny said.

"Licorice?"

"I'm not allowed." Her eyes followed the bag as Brenda drew it back. For a few seconds, no one said anything and Penny felt she was letting the other girls down.

"Shall we ask her?" Ginny said to Brenda.

"I don't care," Brenda said, screwing up her mouth as she looked away.

"We want you to join our club," Ginny said.

"Okay," Penny said. She'd never heard of their club before.

Ginny and Brenda looked at each other.

"It's a secret club," Ginny said. "You can't tell the name."

"I won't," Penny said.

Brenda turned and put her forehead into the chainlink fence, letting out a muffled laugh. Penny wondered if this was a trick.

Ginny led her off, one arm draped over Penny's shoulders.

"You can't tell the name," Ginny said. "Not to anyone."

Penny promised again that she wouldn't.

Ginny put her pale, freckled face to Penny's ear. Penny could smell the black-ball on her breath. "It's called The Bare-Naked Club," she whispered. This was so unexpected that Penny thought she'd heard wrong.

"The what?"

"The Bare-Naked Club."

Penny looked at Ginny, whose eyes were dancing now. Penny's body was hot, under her coat, under her clothes, burning with a heat that came all the way up to her face. Ginny was colouring too, her mouth open in a kind of frozen laugh, her tongue black as tar.

29

IT SEEMED TO ALF that the only clean thing in sight was the beer. The yellow beer floating in cylinders on Sid Walter's tray, the spots of yellow rising and falling around the crowded Men's Beverage Room of the Vimy House, the yellow pooling at the bottom of his own drained glass. Everything else seemed dim, squalid, dirtied by the light that fell from wall-brackets and reflected dully off the dusty Venetian blinds. The room had a kind of womblike privacy – if you didn't count the ten or so other patrons, who for reasons best known to themselves favoured the town's grimmest hotel. He signalled Sid for two more.

On the screen above the bar, players swarmed up the ice like insects. Leafs versus Red Wings. I never did get those tickets, he thought, lifting his glass an inch or two off the table and swirling the contents. He set the glass down. The thought had drifted to him out of nowhere, a fragment of normal life where fathers promised to take their sons to hockey games and sometimes forgot. But who was he fooling? He wasn't going to take Joe to Maple Leaf Gardens. Such things seemed as far from possibility now as the moon. Yet he kept on talking and acting as if nothing were wrong. *Do you want anything from the store? I'm just going out for a walk. Hand me that wrench, will you?* Normal life took place in him like something glimpsed in a fever. He watched himself go through the motions, but the motions seemed to have very little to do with what was actually happening to him. And what was happening to him lay beyond his understanding or his ability to express though it carried him like a current might, a cold current that swept him on, oddly fascinated.

At the small table opposite, Freddie Stone had been watching him since he'd come in: little Freddie Stone with his dishevelled face and watery eyes above the flagrant red of his bunched scarf, watching and smiling and nodding as if he and Alf shared some understanding that was a source of great pleasure to them both. He'd known Freddie all his life, retarded Freddie, who'd spent fifty years at least as an errand boy at Bannerman's. Now that he was retired he lived in a room at the Vimy House, supported by a couple of small pensions and a monthly stipend paid, people said, by Doc McVey.

Sid arrived with the beer, two tall, tapered glasses of golden light through which strings of bubbles drifted. Sid expertly corralled the empties with the fingers of one hand and swept them up with a clatter. When he was gone, Alf raised a glass and the cold, bitter beer slid under its own foam into his mouth. He wasn't drunk, not yet, but he had reached that state of clairvoyant wakefulness where it seemed he was on the brink of understanding more than he usually did, and this produced a feeling of imminent danger in him, as if he were venturing out onto thin ice. On the far shore he glimpsed a deeper drunkenness, where the danger would be past because there he would feel nothing: it was what he was aiming for.

Across the way, Freddie smiled with his wet, shapeless mouth and nodded and seemed to be saying, That's right, just keep it up and you'll get somewhere nice.

Alf raised his glass to him and drank again. Behind Freddie, Ron Carson moaned an obscenity and let his balding, scabbed head nod forward. The television over the bar bayed its crowd sounds and in the dim room a few men shouted. Alf had told Margaret he was going to the Legion. In the past he'd often dropped in there, of a Saturday night, for a bit of pool or to watch the hockey game. But he no longer had the heart for the Legion, with its noisy, forced camaraderie, as if the lot of them had only just got back from overseas.

He lit a cigarette and took its mild fire on the back of his throat. At least Margaret had stopped asking him what was wrong. Is it Pete? she'd said once, prodding. And he'd said, Yes it was Pete, of course it was Pete, what in the hell else could it be but Pete, and she'd responded by embracing him. He'd gone stiff and wanted to cry. In fact, he'd been on the verge of telling her everything, telling her that he'd betrayed his best friend and a lot of other people too, and now his best friend was dead because of it. But he'd stopped himself. Did his shame run so deep? Was he afraid she'd stop loving him? Each time he contemplated putting his crime into words, he felt he was approaching the edge of disintegration. He felt he could not survive confession. It had been the same, twenty years ago, after the war. It was when he had tried to tell Margaret what he had gone through – the tension and killing and sleepless nights, the German boy lying at his feet in the wine cellar – that he had broken down. He had hardly told her anything. But the mere approach to telling her had unleashed terrors he'd somehow kept at bay for his two years in France. That's when the tremors had started, the nightmares, the fear of the streets. Better silence, he felt, than disintegration. Better to grimly endure than to go to pieces and be of no use to anybody. Or so he told himself. But he kept wondering, Was he just making excuses?

Was he just trying to be safe? He didn't know, but in the course of his doubts he gravitated instinctively to silence, his old ally and fortress. It had been silence, finally, that had allowed him to bury the demons of the war. Perhaps he hadn't killed them. Perhaps they were alive (he knew they were alive) in some red-line crisis zone from which they made brief raids into his dreams, his life. But he had largely banished them from the light. And couldn't he do the same with this?

Freddie picked up his glass and shuffled across the narrow gap between their tables.

"Can I sit down, Alf?"

"Sure, Freddie. Make yourself comfortable."

Freddie sat with an odd formality, looking as pleased as if he'd just been invited into Buckingham Palace. His canny little eyes shone and his big lips hung open in a silent laugh.

"So how you keeping, Freddie?"

"Can't complain."

He had a rasping, fractured voice, as if each word was coated in phlegm.

Freddie said nothing more, but sat smiling at Alf as if this were all the conversation he needed – as if the most pleasant thing two people could do was sit at a little table and look at each other.

"Doing any work these days?"

"Oh yes."

"Over at Kellys'?"

"That's right."

Alf looked down at his beer. It was hard to bear the relentless focus of those watery eyes, that smile with its unguarded friendliness and innocence.

For some time they drank in silence. The Leafs got a goal and a few men roared while others looked up indifferently. A snowplough rumbled in the street, bone on bone. Freddie said, "You found your brother."

He was grinning his crumpled grin at Alf, as if Alf would know exactly what he was talking about.

"My brother?" Alf said, wondering. Surely Freddie must mean Jamie, the night they'd found him up the river, with Lucille Boileau's boy. But how did Freddie know about that?

"You dove down and got him," Freddie said, beaming.

"I dove," Alf said, wondering. Then he remembered. One summer afternoon in the early Thirties, he and his brother had gone swimming at Bannerman's Number One dam. And Joe had disappeared below the apron. Alf hadn't been worried, not at first. There was a place below the apron where you could slip between the timbers and come up in a sort of leaky cave, behind the damface – he had shown it to Joe himself. But after a few minutes, Joe hadn't reappeared so Alf dove to find him. And yes, his brother was there, in the dim cold cave streaked with the brown light of the Atta. He was sitting hugging his knees and he was crying in a muffled way, his mouth on his knee. Had he panicked? Alf didn't know. It had taken him a long time to calm Joe down. Finally, their heads had broken the surface together.

Freddie must have been there, standing on the apron, or on the stepped cement wall to the west: a thirty-year-old man-boy in his old-fashioned striped bathing suit that covered most of his body, gaping at them as they swam to shore. Perhaps Freddie hadn't known about the cave behind the damface, perhaps he thought Alf had rescued Joe from the bottom.

And Freddie had kept the memory fresh. Kept his admiration fresh. *You found your brother.* As if their slick heads had only just now burst from the icy, spring-fed hole below the dam.

"You remember that?" Alf said.

"Oh yes! You went far down."

"Not so far," Alf said. "He was all right, really." He did not have the energy to explain.

They drank for a while without speaking. Why had Joe been crying? Some hurt, some slight he would never understand. Alf felt he had spent most of his youth looking after his younger brother. *Make sure nothing happens to Joe*: his mother's battle cry. He had pulled Joe out of fights, he had fought fights for him, he had taken him everywhere, up the river with his friends when he didn't really want Joe tagging along with his manic gaze that was always broadcasting the announcement that he was twice as ready as anybody for whatever adventure they had planned. At times Alf had hated him, his mother's favourite. Once, he had pushed him out of a tree and, once, he had jammed a pea-shooter down his throat out of sheer spite. Mostly, though, he had done the job assigned him. He could never remember having an ordinary, relaxed time with his brother, because he was always looking out for him.

Yet he had loved Joe too, as he discovered one rainy night in the summer of 1944, when his sergeant had taken him aside in the barn where they were camped near the Dutch border to tell him his brother, who was serving in a different unit, had been killed. It had seemed impossible. Joe had had so many near-misses over the years, in cars, on the river, in hockey games, and barroom fights, that Alf had begun to think his brother was untouchable, a miracle-kid. Once – Joe couldn't have been more than fifteen – he'd climbed across the Shade on the underside of the CN trestle, manoeuvring among the black girders far above the water. Alf hadn't been there, but he'd heard. Why did you do it? he had asked. And Joe had said (Alf had never forgotten this), "When I think of something, I have to do it. Even if it's crazy. I can't sleep unless I do it . . ."

Alf's sergeant, his dirty face shining in the light of the hurricane lamp, told him that Joe had been napping in a ditch when a landmine had gone off beneath him. Apparently, he'd rolled over on it in his sleep. Alf left the barn and stood in the rain. Some time later, his sergeant found him and led him back to shelter.

"I wasn't always able to bring him back," Alf said.

"No," Freddie said.

"There are people you can't bring back. When you murder them, they stay dead."

Freddie shook his head: it was the sad truth.

Alf drank. He felt they understood each other perfectly.

Freddie finished his glass and stood up.

"Time for me to go upstairs, Alf."

He watched Freddie move off among the tables with his shuffling steps, nodding here and there in his courtly way. Across the room, a bottle broke with a pop and someone shouted, "Attaboy, Coach." When Alf looked again at the table where Freddie had sat before joining him, he saw that someone else had taken it. The man was wearing an old-fashioned tweed cap with a flat top and stubby visor. He had twisted in his chair to signal the waiter, so that Alf could not see his face, but Alf instantly experienced a terrified elation, as if he were about to fly off a cliff.

The man turned in his chair and Alf saw the scrawny-handsome features, the girlishly fine skin, the nose bent from a fight, the blue eyes fixed on his with a wild, familiar merriment, as if he were enjoying his little surprise. He was wearing the heavy tweed suit he had bought in Johnsonville for the victory banquet, after the Stingers had won the provincial championship in 1938. As Alf watched transfixed, the man touched one hand to the knot of his maroon tie with a curious, suggestive delicacy.

Alf had stopped breathing. His brother had not aged a day in the twenty-one years since he'd last seen him. And it seemed to Alf that since then he'd only been hiding. Joe had found some secret place where no one would ever think of looking, where even time, somehow, had been fooled into passing him by. He looked no more than twenty, with his smooth skin flushed with rose. And there was mischief in his smile as if he were more than pleased with himself, and happy too. Happiness spread from him like the power and hope of youth itself, as if it were coming not just from him, but from all the young men who had ever lived. And this power flooded to Alf, engulfing him in a warm, calming tide. He started to rise from his chair – he wanted to go to Joe, to embrace him – and in that instant Joe was gone.

But the feeling remained, a sense of well-being that penetrated his whole body. He wanted to call out, Hey, it's my brother! But he sat in a stupor, looking around the dim room where everything now seemed to glow – men's faces, and the flickering moon of the television, and the glasses in front of him, which seemed to contain a miraculous liquid, a distillation of yellow blossoms.

He had a craving for the depth and quiet of the night. At the door of the Men's Beverage Room he looked back in wonder at the table where his brother had sat. Two other men occupied it now, two men in colourless jackets, talking to Sid Walters as he put down their beer. And with a new shock of wonder, Alf remembered that it had been in this very room where the victory banquet had been held, in the days when the Vimy House still clung to a kind of propriety. He tried to recall the room as it had been that night: the long tables covered with white cloths, the draped flags and picture of the new King, the championship cup displayed proudly at the head table. He remembered roast beef, a tedious speech by the mayor, but he couldn't establish where Joe or he had been sitting.

Alf went on down the hall, conscious that his happiness was already fading. From the open door to Ladies and Escorts came a wave of laughter. It seemed to wrap his body, to pull him towards the room. "You don't!" a woman cried. She was answered by another woman's scandalized bray. The hotel cat lay curled on the desk. Its green eyes noted his passage indifferently, as if his body were of no more account than a movement in the air.

Realizing he needed to pee, he turned and went back down the hall. The stairs to the cellar washrooms were steep, and as he descended he experienced a moment of vertigo, as if the floor below him were exerting a magnetic pull. In the washroom he fell: landed on his back, on the floor of tiny white-and-black tiles in a puddle of what might have been urine. He scrambled to his feet immediately and for a moment stood gripping the edge of a sink. There was a mirror to his left, but he avoided looking at it.

He did his business in the ancient, foul-smelling urinal, where the porcelain was webbed with tiny cracks, and stood for some time afterwards, leaning his forehead on a cold, sweating pipe, aware of the soaked seat of his trousers, of the ruins of his life. "You're a fool," he said, and with this pronouncement felt a little relief. "Just a bloody fool." He wept a little, laughing at himself through his tears. In front of his face, the tan wall scribbled with graffiti somehow looked different than it had a moment before, the letters clearer. He supposed he'd been a fool all along, only like most fools, he hadn't noticed.

In the hall outside, he saw a pair of woman's legs in jeans coming down the stairs. She wore low black boots with silver studs and a blouse of grey, metallic-looking material. At her throat was a black choker with a cameo. Lucille Boileau. When she saw him, she broke into a grin. But it fell away as he went up to her and took her by the shoulders. When he bent to kiss her, he half-expected her to draw back or even to strike him, but in the last second before he closed his eyes he saw her own eyes narrow and darken, as she lifted her mouth to his.

30

SNOWFLAKES, ENDLESS SNOWFLAKES came glittering into the light Margaret had left on over the back porch, burning with a steady faithfulness that reproached him. He washed his face at the kitchen sink, scrubbed at it with a dishtowel, then saw he'd put the stain of Lucille's pink lipstick on the towel. He took the damp towel to the cellar and hid it under his workbench.

Climbing back up to the kitchen, he met Margaret in her dressing gown.

"Oh, it's you."

"Sorry. I didn't mean to wake you."

"I wasn't asleep. I'm worried about Joe. This snow."

"Where is he?"

"He told you," she said critically, studying him for a moment before she crossed to the window. Since he'd fought with Joe on New Year's Eve, she'd seemed more distant, just like Joe himself: the civilized side of the family, the Selwoods, closing ranks against the barbarian Walkers. "He and Liz McVey were driving to Toronto. Some kind of concert."

He watched her cup her hands on the glass and peer out, then turn to him.

"Are you all right?"

"I was just taking a towel downstairs. I got some grease on me, I was sponging it off –" He felt a need to explain everything, everything *but*.

There was an awkwardness between them, a mismatch of rhythms. He was standing at the top of the stairs, and felt frozen there as if he no longer had volition or reason to move. As if movement might betray him.

"Are the roads bad?"

"No, no. He'll be fine."

He bestirred himself, moving to the sink and taking down a glass, glad of the distraction. Yet again he had the feeling of being frozen in place, as if he had never been anywhere but here, watching the white rush of water from the tap, watching it splash and overflow his glass, sensing her gaze across the room.

The world seemed unreal, the glass in his hand both heavier and lighter than it really was. He felt he might drop it. As it touched his lips, he thought of Lucille Boileau, the dark mass of her hair spilling over his groin.

"He seems awfully serious about her," she was saying. "I don't know why he doesn't bring her by. I wonder if he isn't ashamed of us."

"Ashamed?" he said, turning. He had hardly been listening.

She left the room. For a long time he remained motionless. Behind him, the tap dripped: he'd been meaning to fix it for weeks. The wind shrieked briefly under the door. He went back to the cellar and took out the towel. It was dark with wetness, impossible to tell if the lipstick was gone. He hung it from a nail. Thoughts of Lucille Boileau kept coming back to him – the way she had undone her bra, her eyes fixed with mischievous triumph on his, as she knelt before him on her creaking rick of a bed. The memory of pleasure was in him, a pleasure of its own.

He bent to the space under his workbench and found the old metal tackle box that had belonged to his father. It opened easily, the tiered drawers revealing themselves like the terraces of a miniature garden. Each little compartment held lures: silver spoons with hooks and tiny beads; hand-carved wooden fish, their backs striped or spotted with yellow and brown paint, their clustered hooks tangled and rusting. One compartment was filled with various weights of sinkers, like little grey bombs, and with various sizes of hooks. There was a float, cleverly fashioned from a gull's quill, its tip painted red. When his father slipped off Bannerman's dam, the tackle box had remained on the cement ledge by the shore. Alf had left the contents just as they were.

In the bottom of the box were larger objects: pliers, a scaling knife, an old reel with black line, a gill-chain, a book with a tattered jacket, all smelling a little musty. He took out the book, *The Thirty-Nine Steps* by John Buchan. His father hadn't been much of a reader, and he'd been surprised to find the novel, though Alf hadn't actually opened it until several years after the drowning. The photographs were just where Alf had first found them, in an envelope tucked in the centre of the book. He took them out and laid them on the bench.

The pictures had been taken on one of the fishing trips his father had gone on with his old pal Shorty Bigwood. There was Shorty, with a beer bottle in one hand and a fishing pole in the other, mugging like an escaped schoolboy. And there was his father, standing near the stern of a beached rowboat, his slim face as brown as an Indian's, glowing with health and high spirits under his white hair. Alf guessed the photos had been taken some time after the war, perhaps only a year or two before he'd drowned. He picked out two photos and set the rest aside. In the first, his father was standing beside on open rail car in whose shadowy interior a few people were sitting on benches. His father had a suitcase in one hand, and had turned towards the car to help a woman negotiate the rather long step down from the car to the platform. This woman was tall, with cropped hair and round, dark glasses she might have worn to ward off the sun, though Alf couldn't shake the notion she was blind; it had something to do with the uncertainty of her smile, as if she were eager not to give offence by the burden she had placed on others. In the second picture, his father was sitting up to his bare chest in water, directing a wincing smile at the camera, while the woman in dark glasses sat on the steep, stony beach behind him, near the wild, white roots of a fallen tree. She wore a bathing suit; her folded legs looked pale and shapely, and above the bodice of her bathing suit the tops of her breasts were just visible. Alf had no idea who this woman was. When he'd first discovered the photos he'd been intrigued, and a little shocked, but he had still reserved judgment. He'd never had an inkling that his father had been involved with any woman save his mother. But now, studying the pictures, he felt sure: his father, in his early sixties, had had an affair with a woman at least a decade younger than himself, a woman who might have been blind. He found a magnifying glass and examined the woman's face. She had a strong chin and a small mouth. She was handsome rather than pretty, and in her posture – it had something to do with her straight back and the lift of her face – was a bemused pride. Alf moved the glass over his father's face, which was slightly averted from the sunlight. There was a smile in his father's face – a kind of smirk – that suggested the two of them, his father and the woman, were united in a common knowledge. *They were together.* It was as clear as if they'd been holding hands.

You devil, Alf thought. He felt as if he had understood nothing about his father until this minute, and even now his father seemed to retreat further into strangeness. What other secrets had he kept? He examined his father's face, at once so familiar and so distant. No son ever sees his father clearly. There is always a distorting glare that exaggerates or diminishes what is there, that leaves areas hidden that might not be hidden to anyone else, and reveals secrets warped in the deep eddies of old emotions. *His father had done what he, Alf, had done.* This realization charged Alf with a roguish excitement. After a fashion, his father's sin justified his own, for it was simply what men did. "You old devil," he said out loud.

At the same time, as if he were a boy opening a door he would later wish he had never touched, he heard the long echo of betrayal.

31

"YOU WANTA GO SEE RON?"

"Who?"

"You know, Ron," Billy said. His eyes had grown sleepy-sly, looking at Jamie sideways. "The Candy Man."

They were walking up Shade between the stores. At the mention of the Candy Man, the whole street suddenly became dangerous, the sunshine brighter, the salt stains on the sidewalk whiter. He'd seen the old man once, in the A&P, when he was with his mother. Jamie had hid behind her coat as she pushed their cart past the end of the aisle where the old man stood squinting at the shelves in a way that showed his teeth.

"I don't wanta go there," he said in a muffled voice.

"He said I should ask you."

Jamie said nothing, though he was shocked at the idea that the old man was thinking about him. It was like God thinking about you – "We're always in God's thoughts," his mother said – but it was like God upside down, a *bad* thinking. The old man might be thinking about him right now, he might be sitting in his old brown kitchen looking at his candies and thinking about Jamie. It put an icy feeling in his stomach. They crossed Bridge to Jarrod's Shoes. Outside the store, a line of boots was arranged on a table, one of each kind. Instantly excited, Billy picked up a boy's black rubber boot. At the heel was a little red rubber spur. Jamie, too, was intrigued – boots with spurs! – and as they examined the boot, passing it back and forth, they didn't notice that Mr. Jarrod had come out, not until a voice roared. Looking up, Jamie saw Mr. Jarrod's round face with its little moustache just like the cork smudge Jamie's mother had marked under his nose at Halloween. "You bloody Indian," he yelled, tearing the boot out of Billy's hands. He looked only at Billy, yelled only at Billy, as if Jamie wasn't there. "If I catch you around here again I'll call the police."

They ran up the street and around the corner of the last store, where the road fell to a flat place by the river. Billy stomped up and down with gritted teeth, his eyes crazy-blind. Jamie stayed away from him.

"I'll kill him," Billy said in a strangled voice. He stomped off to the river and spat at it. After a while they went along the river. They heaved in chunks of frozen snow, and watched them darken and bob away like little icebergs.

It seemed cold and unhappy by the Shade, the current hurrying by with a faint licking sound. Jamie looked upstream, past the dam where his grandfather had drowned, past the rail trestle to the edge of the pine forest where he and Billy had tried to cut the Christmas tree. The old man's house was that way, hidden from him now by the trees, but he could sense it there, waiting for him. "I gotta go home," he said.

As they came back, they saw a black dog having a crap. It had all four feet bunched together and was straining away with a funny look on its face, while a reddish turd hung down behind. When the dog was finished, they went over and had a look. Then Billy went off and picked up an empty cigarette packet that had blown into a bush. He went over to the poo and, using the packet like a little shovel, cut away a portion of the poo, scooped it up, and started back towards the stores. Following behind, Jamie kept asking what he was doing, but he was afraid he knew what Billy was doing, he was going after Mr. Jarrod with a piece of dog poo. But Billy didn't do that. He walked past the door of the store, right up to the line of boots on the table, and dumped the poo into the biggest boot. They ran like hell, around the corner, across the bridge, down the bank to a place underneath the bridge. And there, on the bare, frozen earth, safe from all big people, they stomped back and forth, whooping their heads off.

32

PENNY, GINNY, AND BRENDA were in Ginny's big bedroom, with its framed pictures of ballerinas in pink-and-lime tutus, and a pink frill – like a giant's tutu – around the dressing table. They were having a sleepover. Ginny's mother and father had gone out for an hour. "We have to be quick," Ginny said. It was Penny's first time with the Bare-Naked Club. Ginny looked at Penny with that secretly amused smile, as if she found her a bit backward, but nice just the same. Brenda was sitting on the bed, unbuckling her shoes.

Watching herself in the mirror, Ginny unbuttoned her blouse. An excitement was in the air. Penny wasn't sure she liked it, this feeling she was on the verge of things she didn't know about, wasn't supposed to do.

"C'mon, don't be shy."

Sitting on the edge of a chair, Penny bent to her shoes. She *was* shy. She took baths by herself now, not with Jamie like she had when she was little. She didn't even like her mother to see her now, with no clothes on. Sometimes, when she got undressed in her room, she could hardly stand having no clothes on. The air on her – all over her

– seemed to be gently touching her, *there* and *there*, where she hardly dared touch herself.

She was breathing a bit harder now. The other girls were down to their underwear. Under her white cotton undershirt, Ginny had bumps where her breasts had started to grow. Penny couldn't keep her eyes off them.

"C'mon, you're getting behind," Ginny said. She slid her underpants down her long legs and stepped out of them with a little laugh.

Penny took off her undershirt. On the bed behind Ginny, Brenda was already bare-naked. She was running strands of her hair through her fingers and staring absently at Penny. When she discovered Penny looking back, her face went blank.

"Take off your panties," Ginny said.

Penny did as she was told and sat with her shoulders scrunched up and her hands between her legs. A shivering was going up and down her legs and through her shoulders and she couldn't take her eyes off Ginny's bare chest.

"Come look at yourself in the mirror," Ginny said.

They were all at the mirror now. Ginny and Brenda were laughing and hardly able to stand straight: feeling each other's smoothness against their skins. Penny looked at herself in the glass, at her non-existent breasts puckering in her thin chest, and at her straggly brown hair that was neither straight nor curly, and at her face with its wide blue eyes, looking back at her as if she – that bare-naked girl in the mirror – were looking at Penny and wondering what she was doing out there, not joining in the fun.

Later, after Mr. and Mrs. Lamport came home, they made popcorn – Penny had a special, measured amount in her own bowl, no butter – and ate it up in Ginny's room while they leafed through old magazines. Later, in the dark, Penny lay on her side in the little bed that had been Ginny's when Ginny's sister Ella was at home, listening to the other girls talk in the big bed. They were chatting about boys, and it was all a bit alien to her. They seemed to have noticed and thought about so much that she hadn't – who liked whom, who was good-looking – though when Ginny said she was pretty sure Bobby Tuckett "had a crush" on Penny, Penny went hot under the sheets. "No," she cried, really outraged. "I *hate* Bobby Tuckett! "Why?" Ginny said. "He's so cute!" Penny fell silent, stunned by the idea Bobby Tuckett liked her. Stunned by the idea that he was *cute*.

After some time there was silence, the scraping of a snowplough. Penny had started to drift off when she heard an eruption of giggling and scuffling from the other bed. Then Ginny said in a loudish whisper, "Oh darling!" which set the two of them, Ginny and Brenda, snickering into their pillows. Then there was silence again, and more scuffling, and Penny heard Brenda say, "I don't like tongues."

"Shhh . . . ," Ginny said.

And Brenda said, "She's asleep."

"Is she?"

"I don't think Bobby Tuckett likes her."

"Sure he does," Ginny said.

"No, he doesn't. Who's gonna like someone with diabetes?"

There was silence for a while. Then Penny heard Ginny say, "My mother says diabetics can't have babies."

In the morning, the other girls pressed close as Penny gave herself her needle. She felt odd at having to do it in front of them – her mother usually left her alone with her syringe – but they had asked if they could watch. Mrs. Lamport watched too, hovering nearby and saying, "Girls, pay attention now, she has to do this *every* morning" – the three of them peering as Penny stuck her needle into the little bottle of insulin, plunged it right through the rubber top, and drew back the plunger of the syringe to the right amount, thirty-four units, and pulled the needle out and brought its tip to the outside of her upper arm.

"I can't watch," Brenda said.

They were all spellbound: Mrs. Lamport with her big front teeth, and Ginny, her pretty face drained of colour, and Brenda, her red-rimmed eyes looking from the hovering needle to Penny's eyes and back again.

Sometimes, at home, she hesitated for a long time before pushing the needle in. She was afraid of the pain – the thin, slicing pain that sang through her arm or leg. She tried not to believe in this pain. She told herself, she told her mother, she told her brother Jamie, "I *like* needles." But as often as she said this, she knew she did not like needles, she hated them.

Now, seeing their fearful, fascinated faces, she experienced a rush of triumph.

"I like needles," she said calmly, and pushed it in.

33

THE RAPID PIPING of the organ climbed above the church, into the February sky. Bach, Margaret thought, pausing on the sidewalk, and it was as if an old, dear friend she had not seen for years had surprised her. The lower notes were muffled by the thick cobblestone walls, but the clear treble ran on and on, a joy that never exhausted or repeated itself.

She entered the church as quietly as she could, so as not to disturb Helen. Near a brass railing she paused again to listen. Now the bass was clearly audible, running on its own merry way, tossing themes back and forth with the treble. It seemed a wintry music, sunlight glancing off icicles, that also contained by some mysterious alchemy the depths of summer.

Helen botched a run, started over, botched it again.

"Damn!"

Margaret laughed and moved forward to the steps.

"Oh you're here!"

"I've been listening. It was absolutely –"

"A mess!"

"No, no. It was lovely," Margaret said with feeling. She slipped off her coat and laid it on a choir bench. "Are you playing it for the wedding?" Her friend turned to her in the pool of light at the console.

"No, lucky for all concerned. Anyway, I don't suppose the Clarkes or the Williamses have ever heard of J.S. Bach." Helen screwed up her thin mouth abruptly, as though suppressing some more sarcastic comment, and held out some sheet music for Margaret. She was Margaret's age exactly, forty-two: a prematurely grey-haired woman with skimpy bangs and a slight stoop. Her husband was the editor of the *Attawan Star*. Often she and Margaret went off to Kitchener or Hamilton or Toronto in Helen's Buick, to operas and concerts. They had adopted a jolly, bantering, slightly superior tone, two women who shared a love of music and had little tolerance for humbug.

Margaret looked at the music Helen had given her: "Seven Wishes for You" by Anne-Marie Fletcher-Valois.

"Never heard of her. Are we going to do all seven?"

"If we want to get paid."

Helen picked out the melody with her right hand while Margaret read it over her shoulder. Finally she took her copy and stepped away from the organ. The empty pews seemed ready to listen. In a stained-glass window, a book carried by a bearded apostle shone like a ruby. She lifted her face a little as she sang and her body swayed slightly. Her family often teased her about "wriggling around" and she tried not to. But it was the effect of singing itself, the pleasure she felt as she became an instrument for the music, even the unexceptional music of Anne-Marie Fletcher-Valois.

"Seven Wishes for You" listed, as promised, seven wishes the newly married couple made for each other. It was a sluggish, sentimental piece, but there was a run of notes in the refrain she liked immensely, which gave a haunting lilt to the word "you." Each time she sang the word, shivers ran over her face and chest.

On the sixth wish, she ran into a problem. The verse ran: "I'll listen to you, I'll hear your troubles/ Even when you're far away." It was innocuous enough, but on the first syllable of "Even," her voice broke and she stopped.

The organ died out behind her.

"Sorry," Margaret said. Unaccountably, her face was burning. She made a point of not turning to Helen. "Just give me a little introduction."

It was worse the second time. As she broached the word "Even," a shudder went through her and she only stopped it from turning into a wail by clamping her mouth shut. She sat down.

"Are you all right?"

"It's the oddest – I'm sorry." She could hardly talk yet, but leaned over in the stall. Helen came and sat beside her.

"I just felt faint," Margaret managed. "The oddest –"

"Would you like some water?"

As Helen hurried to the parish kitchen, Margaret bent over, pressing her forehead on the hard, cool back of the next bench, struggling to fight down the impulse to weep. Tears wouldn't do, and especially they wouldn't do in front of Helen, any more than a true confession would do. She considered Helen her closest friend, but still, theirs was not that kind of friendship, she felt.

They decided to stop for the morning. Walking home, Margaret turned aside to the rail of the Shade Street bridge. Below, the Atta steamed from a narrow fissure in the ice, as it made its peaty way towards its meeting with the Shade. For some reason, the water drew her thoughts to England – gave her a sharp intuition of the English spring, with its distinctive smell of earth and damp woods and petrol fumes – and for a few minutes she was swept along by a deep nostalgia for her girlhood – for her mother and father, both dead now, for the green of a certain field, for the high, chalk-veined downs behind her house with their glimpses of the distant channel, that grey, strangely heartening infinity. As she wept, she dug frantically through her purse for a handkerchief, thinking, This won't do, This won't do. All she could find was a paper napkin.

By eleven-thirty she was busy in her kitchen, getting the children's lunch. Penny's took a special effort – everything had to be weighed on the spring scale, whose round, numbered face dominated the counter – and dessert was always a problem, since Jamie still clamoured for sweets. The dietician at the hospital had told her that the rest of the family should go on eating as usual, but when Margaret had set a lemon meringue pie on the table, Penny's face had fallen. Margaret had sworn never to torture her again.

Noon came with the plunging howl of Bannerman's whistle. A few minutes later Alf called to say he had to work through the lunch hour. She leapt at his voice, but though he was cheerful and warm enough, she felt he was impatient to hang up.

Then Penny came through the door, pigtails bouncing. The eleven-year-old launched into a story about a schoolyard quarrel and a moment later Joe and Jamie came in pink-faced, having raced each other from the edge of the Island. Margaret watched herself go into gear – the cheerful mother setting out bowls of tomato soup and plates of baloney-and-cheese sandwiches, listening and commenting on the stories they had brought. Then her children were gone, in a gust, and she was alone. Life itself seemed emptied away. A dozen jobs called to her, but she sat at the kitchen table in a trance, the sadness that had threatened her almost violently all morning a calm pool now, a pool that seemed to hold everything, the white daylight at the window, the crumbs strewn around the oilcloth like bits of sand or dirt that had blown in.

She had an urge to call Alf. "Don't be daft," she scolded herself, in her brisk English way. "Don't behave like some daft girl!" She never phoned the mill, except in emergencies. Two minutes later, she picked up the phone.

Matt Honnegger, the knitting-room foreman, told her Alf had left an hour before. "Funny," Matt said, "I thought he'd gone home."

She didn't see him until he showed up at five-thirty. He was in a good mood, almost too good, and he'd brought her a bar of Cadbury's milk chocolate in its dark-blue and silver wrapper, just like the old days. Margaret couldn't resist the tide of his good spirits. At the supper table, while Jamie was telling them about every turn and twist of some TV show, Alf looked at her and winked in happy complicity. Suddenly she felt insulted, patronized. It was the sort of wink you might give a child.

The next morning after the children had left for school, she walked over to the Flats. Passing the arena – its whitewash walls blinding in the sun – she turned down the lane that led to the mills. No one was in sight, though she could hear the thrashing of machines from open windows. Furtive now, almost dizzy with tension, she pushed through a heavy door into the vestibule of the sweater mill. The wooden rack of time cards hung beside the clock. She searched the array of yellow cards until she found her husband's: *Walker A. #117.* Pulling it out, she swiftly put it back again – someone was on the stairs above – but the footsteps faded and again she retrieved the card and found the day she was looking for: yesterday. The unevenly inked numbers printed by the clock showed that Alf had left the mill at one-forty, and not returned until five after three. She put the card back in its slot and pushed outside, blinking in the sun reflected from the snowbanks.

She had a hundred questions for him, seething inside her, but dared not ask them until they were safely alone together. And even then – it was ten o'clock that night and she was creaming her face at the dresser while Alf read a paperback in bed behind her – she hesitated, sensing a danger, as if a wrong word might plunge her into a situation she would regret.

She watched him in the mirror. He lay on his back with one knee up under the quilt, idly massaging the top of his head with one hand. His eyelids had sunk as he read, giving him a vaguely drunken look that irritated her.

She heard her voice say, cheerfully disinterested, to the deep glass, "So, did you ever get lunch yesterday?"

He grunted, scarcely hearing, apparently.

"Alf –," more sharply.

For a moment, the blue of his eyes shocked her in the mirror. Such eyes that husband of yours has, Helen had said to her once. Faraway-looking eyes, of a pale, electric blue. She knew other women found him attractive, more attractive perhaps than she did herself. And now those eyes were suddenly fresh to her, a shock and a rebuke.

"Yesterday, when you had to work through the noon hour, did you ever get lunch?"

He lowered the book. She knew her question must sound queer, caring about so trivial a thing a day later.

He was watching her over the fallen book. In his hesitation she sensed calculation. She turned on the bench to face him, in her flannelette gown. In the street a dog barked.

"I went out to the Rendezvous," he said at last. "Had a yen for a burger." He cleared his throat. "Why?"

She hesitated at his challenge. Of course she couldn't say, You were away for an hour and a half. Does it really take you that long to eat a burger? She would have to admit she'd read his timecard, and she didn't know enough to risk that. Maybe he'd gone for a drive. She could see him sitting in the car above the river somewhere, eating as he stared at the ice. But she couldn't ask.

"Nothing – I just wondered how you got on. I worry you're not getting nourished."

Immediately, "nourished" seemed false on her tongue, a too-elaborate word, hiding her own duplicity. He gazed at her for a long moment, then raised the book. Instantly, she was piqued.

She said, "Are we all right?"

"Hmm," he said.

"Alf!"

The book came down.

"Are we all right? Are things all right between us?"

She supposed she was making a scene, maybe unnecessarily. But there was something desperate in her, kneading with tiny fists in her chest and throat.

"Sometimes I think – we seem to be drifting away from each other."

"I'm not going anywhere," he said, warmly enough, and her spirit leapt at that, eager to believe.

"You still like me, then?" She lifted her face to him, defiantly, flirtatiously, feeling the remains of the cold cream like a mild burn.

"Hey-hey," he said, cajoling. He got off the bed and came towards her while she watched him with black, sober concentration, not sure whether he was approaching out of duty or desire. When he kissed her on the mouth, she strained to read him, his mind, through the pressure of his lips.

For the first time in weeks they made love. He was attentive and slow, just as she liked. She held him at the small of the back and focused with shut eyes on travelling to that place that was so elusive: that little patch of light that might, just might, expand suddenly into a meadow of pleasure. It seemed critical that she get there tonight, as if to seal a new pact with him. And suddenly – she had never done this before – she thought of him being with another woman. And for a moment *she* was that other woman, unknown to herself, holding on to Alf Walker's back, the back of a man who belonged to another woman. And pleasure rolled through her in a smoothly swelling wave.

But just as she seemed about to slip into a deeper pleasure, he pinched her nipple so hard she cried out in pain. Everything came apart for her then: the road to heaven filled with stones and briars. Alf was flustered and apologetic. Sorry, sorry, he told her, I just forgot. In the end she was left feeling raw and used. She lay in the dark as he slept, wondering what it was he had forgotten.

The next morning, alone in the house, she searched his clothes. In the pockets of his dirty factory greens she found a screw, a broken latch needle, a note that read *Eaton's, fifty-two pairs #367*, written in an unfamiliar hand, a half-used book of matches, bits of tobacco. Was he smoking again? She'd smelled smoke on his shirts and now the golden shreds of tobacco hinted at a life of illicit pleasures. She went into the cellar, to his workbench. It had an almost shrinelike neatness: the tools hung in ranks, the little jars of screws and nails graded according to size. She usually felt a tenderness on seeing his workbench. He had bought these tools for his carpentry business, back in 1949. They were all that was left of his plans, plans he'd once wooed her with, in England. But this morning she rummaged irreverently through his drawers. She peered into cans and boxes. In a deep drawer, under a bundle of electrical wire, she found an envelope containing half a dozen old-fashioned tinted postcards. Two were of French scenes: the Eiffel tower, the Place Pigalle. But the other four were of naked women. They posed in boots and berets: young, big-bottomed women with short, curly hair and heavily madeup eyes.

Their rising swaths of pubic hair shocked her. The young women looked stagily surprised, holding up their hands, palms out. On the final card, a blonde in a sailor cap was tweaking her own nipples. Her eyes with their huge false lashes conveyed a look of amazed innocence, as if she'd never thought of doing *this* before – tuning herself like a radio. Margaret remembered how Alf had hurt her nipple in the night. Was *this* his inspiration then? Was this her rival? Impossible, surely. Now she was indignant, scarcely able to believe he had kept the pictures. How could there be any pleasure in such little-boy stuff? She flung the envelope back in the drawer, not caring that the photos spilled out across the bottom.

The towel hung from a peg at the bottom of the board, nearly hidden between the bench and a sheaf of quarter-round. A blue-and-white-checked dishtowel: she'd *wondered* where that had got to. In a moment, she found the stain. It was lipstick, there could be no mistake: a pink halfway to cherry.

Margaret turned in the dim cellar and thought, Carrie Crean.

After lunch she changed into the rust-red corduroy dress she kept for parties, pulled on her Sunday coat and boots, and marched across town to Kellys' Irish Linens. Carrie Crean worked there as a clerk. At the New Year's party in the Parish Hall, at midnight, Carrie Crean had wrapped herself around Alf and planted a kiss on his lips that Margaret herself would have been embarrassed to give him, at least in public. She had seen the same colour lipstick then, on both their mouths.

Margaret pushed through the door into the fresh-linen and wool fragrance of the old store. Tablecloths, handkerchiefs, bed linens, and blankets hung from the pressed-tin ceiling: the place was a veritable forest of suspended textiles, and Carrie Crean was in it somewhere. Margaret went up the aisle, alert. She felt that all she needed to do was look into Carrie's face, and she would know.

Then Evelyn Brockhurst was there, turning from a display of fancy handkerchiefs. Her face was as wrinkled as a peach pit, her head shook continually with some kind of nervous disorder. She sang alongside Margaret in the Anglican choir, where her presence was a source of embarrassment. She whooped on the high notes, but no one had the courage to tell her she should quit.

"I hear you're singing for the Clarke wedding."

"Yes. Saturday."

Evelyn stared at her, while her head wagged back and forth. It was as if she was continually saying, Well who can believe *that*?

Margaret smiled thinly. She was aware of movement – of life – in other parts of the store, somewhere in that thicket of hanging cloths, that deep scent of fresh wools and linens. Perhaps Carrie Crean was eavesdropping.

"What are you singing, dear?"

"I'm sorry –?"

"For the wedding."

"Oh, just a little thing. It's called 'Seven Wishes for You.'"

"I've never heard of that! Is it nice?"

"Yes, lovely."

No, no, it's not, Evelyn's head said. Deep in the store, someone dropped a pair of scissors.

"And how's that boy of yours?"

"Joe?"

"Such a nice-looking lad. I'll bet he has to shoo off the girls. I think he takes after his father."

"Sorry?"

"So good-looking!" Evelyn cried.

It was a harmless, ordinary conversation, except that Margaret felt that Carrie Crean might be listening and this made every word both trivial – almost meaningless – and portentous, like a trolling drum. Finally she escaped. She moved on down the aisle and back up again, glancing into the bays, priming herself to meet Carrie Crean. But apparently she was not in the store.

In a few days, Carrie Crean's presence filled the town, to the point where the rivers and the very shape of the hills suggested her: suggested her blonde curls, her small, shallow, twinkling eyes, her strange, wide, thin-lipped mouth: like a frog's, Margaret thought, with fascination and loathing. She couldn't visit the stores now without thinking she might run into Carrie Crean, without a sense of dread that quickened her pulse and left her as alert as a soldier.

She watched Alf, dissecting his every comment and gesture, while pretending that nothing was wrong. He seemed in a much better mood than he had been around the time of Pete's funeral, and in fact he was quite affectionate with her. But she no longer trusted this affection, even when he suddenly hugged her or kissed her with real exuberance, for she suspected she was not the cause of his outburst, she was only catching the overflow. When he announced on a Saturday night that he was going to the Legion, she invented an excuse to phone him there. And he was there, a familiar voice like an island in the babble of background voices. She experienced a huge relief that died within seconds of hanging up: he might be there, but what was to prevent Carrie Crean from being there too? She supposed the whole town knew about Alf and Carrie Crean. Yes, they were probably laughing at her, or pitying her, and from then on she saw secret laughter or pity playing in the eyes of nearly everyone.

She told herself it was all nonsense, she hadn't a shred of proof. And for a few minutes, or an hour or two, she would keep busy enough to forget. But then she would remember, with a sickening plunge that seemed to prove by its very violence the truth of what she suspected. How could such strong feelings be caused by nothing?

She felt on Sunday she would know. She would see Carrie Crean on Sunday, since Carrie also sang in the church choir. Margaret did not usually wear makeup, but on Sunday morning she applied lipstick and rouge and a touch of eyeliner, then cleaned it all off in a fury of dissatisfaction. Carrie Crean was what, fifteen years younger than she? There was nothing in Margaret's bottles to compete with *that*. In the end, she used lipstick and rouge only, and felt as if she were wearing a mask, ungainly and comical.

Even before Margaret saw Carrie, the church seemed alive with her anticipation. The old doors to the Parish Hall with their chevron pattern, the brazierlike lamps hanging from the high ceiling, the crowd of choir members in their dark-red gowns, the familiar neat figure of Jack Ramsay, so brightly welcoming in his robes – all these things were as vivid to Margaret as if she had never seen them before. She pressed into the passageway where the choir gowns were hung. Beyond a half-open door, the piping, wintery notes of Helen's organ were filling the main body of the church. People were sliding into their pews. And there she was, Carrie Crean, standing right in front of her, between the gowns and the wall, talking to Brian Stokes, a gangly tenor who leaned grinning over the young woman.

Margaret's gown hung just behind Brian. She advanced towards it, smiling through her makeup mask.

Carrie Crean's mouth moved. Those thin, strange, froglike lips with their coating of pink lipstick shaped the words "Hi, Margaret!" and the tiny eyes brightened. Brian Stokes turned to Margaret. Greetings fluttered in the close air.

"I've decided to get that organ," Brian told Margaret. His long face loomed over her with a grin at once boyish and sepulchral.

"Oh yes?" Margaret drawled. But she understood nothing.

"I was just saying to Carrie, we might as well have it now, while Mom's around to enjoy it."

"Enjoy it while you can," Carrie Crean sang, with a coy, knowing glance at Margaret. And Margaret, blushing, managed to remember that for weeks Brian had been ruminating publicly about buying a Hammond organ. He'd been in quite a turmoil about it, but then, other than his sickly mother with whom he lived in a bleakly tidy house on John Street, he didn't have much to be in a turmoil about.

His breath smelled as if he'd been drinking turpentine.

"I don't play that well," Brian said, "but Carrie was just suggesting that Helen might give me lessons –"

"I daresay she would," Margaret said, casting a quick glance at Carrie Crean. The young woman gave her another complicit smile, though exactly what it knew or what it was trying to tell her, Margaret could not have said. For a moment she felt faint, and as she turned away to grope for her gown she nearly dropped it on the floor. She was in utter confusion. She'd been certain that when she saw Carrie Crean she'd know in a twinkling whether Carrie had betrayed her. But she found that she couldn't tell, one way or the other. Either the woman standing an arm's-length away was the destroyer of her life, or she was just blonde, innocent, indifferently pretty Carrie, chattering in a rather mindless way to someone about organ lessons.

They went together into the Parish Hall. Walking behind Carrie Crean, Margaret was struck by how small and slight she was: *petite* was the word. At her back, the border of her gown was turned under against her blouse.

"Here," Margaret said, suddenly commanding. "You're rumpled at the back. Let me fix you."

So Carrie Crean stood while Margaret smoothed her gown and passed her trembling hands over Carrie's shoulders for good measure. She was treating her kindly, and controlling her too, treating her like a schoolgirl. If she *was* guilty, then her kindness could only make Carrie feel guiltier, perhaps guilty enough to stop whatever it was she was doing with Alf, if they were doing anything.

Carrie's torso was extraordinarily slim – she was built like a boy – and Margaret felt an odd thrill of excitement as she touched her, for she was imagining how Carrie would feel to Alf.

"There," she said, her voice tightening. "All done."

Turning to her with a smile, Carrie did an extraordinary thing, so extraordinary that Margaret would think about it for days afterwards. The young woman pushed out that wide, pinkish mouth until there was just a little black hole shaped like a diamond in the centre of it and blew Margaret a kiss.

Margaret was left in a state of outrage. It seemed that Carrie had flung her an insult, a taunt. That kiss was too much! Ten minutes later, she could still see those lips sticking out at her.

All through the service, Margaret kept her eye on Carrie, who was seated just ahead of her and a little to the left, her cap of curls nodding now over her purse as she extracted a candy, unwrapped it with a rustle of cellophane, and popped it into her mouth. Margaret caught every twitch of her cheek. By moving her head a little, she could make out Alf, where he sat with the children, but it was difficult, at that distance, to see whether those pale-blue eyes were contacting Carrie. She was certain, though, that there was something between them. The more she thought about that kiss, the more it seemed proof – terrible, mocking proof – of everything she suspected.

On the drive home, she was short with Alf and the children, and while making their Sunday dinner (she had put a roast in the oven before church), she managed to break a bowl and burn the scalloped potatoes. The curious thing was she was no longer thinking of Alf and Carrie Crean. They had sunk into the blackness of a more general fury, for it seemed as she laid out her good plates – they were chipped and old-fashioned-looking and not nearly good enough – that her whole life was a mistake and an injustice.

That night, creaming her face as usual at her dresser, she nearly confronted him. She nearly asked (he was standing in his underwear as he hung up his trousers), Are you having an affair with Carrie Crean? But in the end she said nothing, and came to bed feeling armed by her silence. There was something about knowing his secret that gave her an advantage over him. And too, she was afraid of the truth, of the edge it might drop her over.

Then, lying on her back in the dark, all her cold, furious strength was gone in an instant. Tears slid down her cheeks and tickled her neck. Beside her, Alf seemed to be asleep. Moving very slowly, she touched the back of her wrist to his buttocks. She wanted to reassure herself of his reality. She felt the curve of his warm buttock on the back of her wrist and she remembered their first night together, in a small hotel in London. Twenty-four years ago. He had been so excited by her nakedness: he had wanted her to just stand there, in the light of the lamp, while he marvelled over her – worshipped her, really. She had felt awkward and ashamed and entirely oblivious to *his* nakedness, though she made a half-hearted attempt to touch his erection. He had hurt her, and ever since she had felt sex was something she did more for his sake than for hers. She had pleasure with him, of course – you couldn't help but have pleasure if someone was touching you the way you liked, in certain places. But she'd never felt excited by him, not the way he seemed excited by her, with a fever of anticipation. In certain moods (she hadn't seen him in one for some time, mind you), he could fairly prance with excitement, he couldn't keep his hands off her. It was all a bit of a mystery. She wondered if there wasn't something wrong with her when it came to sex. It just didn't seem to matter so much to her. It all struck her as faintly silly, even childish. She glanced down the room, where the mirror of her dresser shone like ice, and heard a cat howl in the street.

Perhaps she hadn't done her job, as a woman. Perhaps she hadn't worked hard enough at pleasing Alf, or at pleasing herself. She felt she had let her husband slip away through a net she might have mended. She pressed a little harder, with the back of her wrist. He smacked his lips and wiggled away.

The thought had occurred to her that if she confronted him – if there was a blow-up – he might move out. And where would that leave her? There was a woman, Edna Carnegie, who lived in the North End – who *had* lived in the North End, in a lovely old house with blue shutters, until her husband ran off with a hairdresser from Johnsonville. And now Edna Carnegie and her two children lived in a small house on Willard, beside the mills. Margaret saw her often, a tall, handsome figure buoyed by a desolate pride. Apparently she was working in a factory in Johnsonville.

She had always thought of Edna Carnegie with a kind of indulgent pity, but here she was, only a whisker away, perhaps, from the same fate. What could she do if she was left on her own – give music lessons? That would scarcely bring in tuppence! She lay looking up at the ceiling, where a thin spoke of light from the street had fallen. Life was so precarious: you thought you were as safe as houses, you had your family, your friends, your routines, they surrounded you like the walls of a fortress, but the whole time you and everyone else was hanging by a thread. "Oh God," she whispered. "Bless Alf and me. Help us –" Breaking off, she turned on her side. Her tears were coming freely now, a wild unhappiness. "Bless Edna Carnegie," she murmured. Suddenly, she was aware of the wide frog mouth of Carrie Crean. It seemed to be in the room with her, only inches away. Startled, she lifted her head and stared into the dark.

34

WALKING HOME FROM SKATING, Penny, Ginny, and Brenda stopped outside the Oasis, under the broken neon sign with its buzzing palm tree. A warm afternoon light flooded beneath the striped awning and caught the display of old-fashioned ice-cream-making equipment in the show window.

"So I guess you can't come in," Brenda said to Penny. She sounded stern, like somebody's mother.

"I can come in," Penny said, pushing past her.

Inside, she peered with the others into the long glass counter at the jujubes and sea-foam and licorice straps and candy pipes and candy cigarettes in little packages that said Camels and Lucky Strike. Putting her hand in her pocket, she touched her packet of cookies. She knew she should eat them, she could feel an insulin reaction coming on, but she was sick of Arrowroots. Besides, the cookies weren't in any shape to be eaten. Penny had left the packet in her boot while she was skating. When she'd come back, she'd forgotten it was there, and put her foot into her boot and mashed it.

Outside, they ran into Ginny's aunt, Karen Jones, who was pushing her baby, Jennifer, in a pram. While Brenda and Ginny leaned over and made a fuss over Jennifer, trying to get her to react, Penny hung back. The baby watched them all solemnly, her huge, grave eyes looking out from her bonnet. She seemed uncertain about all the commotion. It seemed so sad to be a baby, Penny thought, to be so helpless, while people came and stuck things in your face. When the baby looked at her, Penny smiled, and Jennifer, her toothless mouth opening and her eyes rolling up, laughed a silent laugh.

They walked down Water Street. Brenda and Ginny took bites out of their Choco Rolls, which looked like little round slices of chocolate cake with a swirl of white icing through them. Penny kept looking at the other girls' mouths: their voices had started to sound far away, as if coming down a pipe. And she was having trouble lifting her legs. On the bridge to the Island she stumbled.

"Clumsy-boots," Ginny said. She held out her Choco Roll. "Want some?"

"She's not supposed to have candy," Brenda said.

"I'm having a reaction," Penny said. She meant she *should* have a bite of Choco Roll. She needed sugar, fast, so her insulin would have something to work on. But Ginny had already gone on eating; Penny couldn't find the words to stop her.

They reached Brenda's house with its high porch and windows where the beige curtains were always shut tight. Ginny and Brenda started up the walk. Penny kept on down the street. Getting home was the most important thing now. "Where are you going?" she heard Ginny's voice calling after her.

Penny turned and saw her friends standing behind a snowbank. They appeared strange to her, with their white skates hanging like chunks of snow over their chests and their faces punctured with eye-holes and mouth-holes and nose-holes. She turned away.

"I know who your father's girlfriend is!" Brenda sang.

Penny heard the taunt as something small and bright and distant – nothing to do with her. She kept going. There was something she was supposed to eat. She thought of a cookie: the sort of soft yellow cookie babies ate, with scalloped edges. And this cookie existed somewhere, she was sure of it. The cookie was out there somewhere ahead of her, the cookie was *home*, and home was out there in the sun that had turned Water Street to a white blaze.

She thought, Girlfriend? Who your father's girlfriend is? Sometimes her father called her his girlfriend. He said he'd take her out on a date, and Penny would say, No, you can't! Daddys can't do that! But she liked being teased.

Her legs were getting heavier with each step, like trying to run in Lake Erie when the water was up to her waist. She could see her house now, a shadow in the dazzling heaps of snow. Then she fell down – the curb had caught her toe – fell to her hands and knees. She stared at the white, nicked-up toe of her skate that had fallen to the sidewalk: where had *that* come from? She was so heavy and sleepy now that she got right down on the sidewalk and curled up. But no – she couldn't sleep – she had to keep going. She rolled on her back and looked up into the blue, cloudless sky. It went on and on, as big as Lake Erie, and it seemed there was nothing to do now but sink into it. The sky got closer. At the same time, it got farther away, like Lake Erie when they drove away from it after a holiday, its light growing more distant out the back window of the car and a lump rising in her throat to think their holiday was over and it would be a year, a whole year of school and winter until they could come here again, to the blue lake where the waves danced and sparkled in, her dad had once said, from America.

A kick of panic – she had remembered the cookie. She struggled to her feet and started up the sidewalk to her house.

She saw a squat, pimply nose with big nose-holes. She saw a small eye-hole and a red scarf. It took her a moment to realize that these details added up to Mrs. Horsfall, their neighbour. Mrs. Horsfall was blocking the narrow passage between their houses.

"Oooooo. Gah ooh!" Mrs. Horsfall said in her deaf-and-dumb person's voice.

"I have to go, Mrs. Horsfall," Penny shouted. She started forward and fell into Mrs. Horsfall. She could smell her, like a wave coming up to smother her, a wave of sick-making perfume exactly like the smell of the flowers at Uncle Pete's funeral. Her face pressed into Mrs. Horsfall's bosom, but what she saw was Uncle Pete's sharp, waxy face in his coffin.

Half an hour later, Penny was sitting at the kitchen table, feeling almost normal. She had a headache, but she knew what was going on, clear as a bell. Her mother stood with her hands on her hips looking at her. Penny took another sip of orange juice. "You didn't *touch* your cookies," her mother said, pointing to the crushed packet on the table. "Penny – you let yourself go into a reaction. What were you doing – what happened to your Arrowroots?"

"I forgot," Penny said. This was half-true. Below the table, she had crossed her fingers.

"You could have –" Her mother broke off in frustration. But Penny knew what she'd meant to say, You could have died.

She felt ashamed for having a reaction, ashamed of frightening her mother, ashamed, even, of having diabetes: all of it was her fault. She moved her empty glass on the table, in a prickly misery of shame, and looked at the window where the wall of the Horsfalls' house loomed close, with its frosted-up window. With a lurch – she almost felt sick – Brenda's words came back to her.

"Does Daddy have a girlfriend?" she said.

At the stove, her mother stopped stirring a pot.

"What a ridiculous idea," her mother said. But her voice sounded high and hard. "Whoever told you that?" Penny put her head down. "Penny, who told you that?"

"Nobody."

"Somebody must have." Her mother turned to her. "Penny, who was it?"

"Brenda Stubbs," she said, barely audible. "I think she was just teasing."

"Just the sort of thing you'd expect from Brenda Stubbs," her mother said.

Her mother went suddenly to a cupboard. After rummaging for a few seconds she slammed the cupboard shut, walked to the cellar door, and disappeared. Penny could hear the washing machine churning away down there, *glug-glug, glug-glug*, like some bored, unhappy person who hated her work.

She went up to her room, which she saw her mother had tidied. She'd told Penny to tidy it, and Penny had, but her tidying was never good enough. Her mother had put everything away on shelves, her books, her dolls, even her skipping rope had been wound in a neat coil and tied up with string. The neatness of the room oppressed her, it was like nobody lived here, like her mother was acting as if she, Penny, had moved away. She felt so unhappy she flung herself on the bed.

After a while, she rolled to her back and raised her foot in the air. There was a hole in her red leotard where her big toe showed, and as she wiggled this toe, which seemed to have a life of its own – a funny little toe-person waving around up there, hello – she remembered the soap. Jumping off the bed, she tugged open the drawer of her table and there it was: her bar of laundry soap.

One day at the stores, when she and her dad were shopping, they had run into Miss Hobsbawn, and Miss Hobsbawn had told her father about Penny's fish, told him in her shouting man's voice about how fine a carver Penny was and looked at Penny with her eyes gleaming ferociously, pleased as punch. And afterwards, Penny's dad had taken her to the A&P and bought her this big bar of soap. "Don't carve it right away," he told her. "Think about it a bit."

Penny put the bar on her table. She took out her small jackknife and picked out its blade. She was excited now, as excited as at Christmas when she was the first downstairs into the living room where the presents waited in the dimness under the tree. She looked at the soap. Everything else was gone. Brenda Stubbs and Ginny Lamport were gone, and her diabetes was gone and her mother was gone. She was alone in her room, with her feet twined around the legs of her chair, staring in the stillness of happiness at a bar of yellow laundry soap.

35

THE WINDOWS in Matt Honnegger's office gave onto the flat, gravelled roof of the dyehouse, where pigeons waddled in the late-winter sun. Alf watched them absently.

"I'm afraid I'm stuck here again," he told Margaret into the phone. A new bird, white as chalk, sailed with breathtaking grace to a landing. It watched the others skeptically, head bobbing like a boxer's. He had stood just here, watching these same birds, when Margaret had phoned with the news that Pete was dead. Time had stalled. He had always stood just here, watching these birds at their puzzling rituals.

She said, "Well if you get free later, come home, will you?"

Her voice young, plaintive. He closed his eyes.

"Sure I will."

Each time he lied to her, he felt he was driving a small, sharp blade into her flesh. It was so sharp she could not feel it, and yet she was aware of it, he suspected, as if the sensation came to her from a long way off. At these moments, oddly, he knew he loved her.

He worked until nearly two, then punched out and drove off in the Biscayne, along Willard. The sun beat off the wilting snow, off abandoned porches: the Tuesday afternoon had filled with a Sunday languor, as if the purpose of life had failed. As he always did, he passed Lucille's street, Pine, finally turning up a stony lane that rose along the rail embankment towards the old pioneer cemetery. He turned into the dilapidated garage behind Lucille's house and sat for a while in the dimness, looking at the horned beast in the corner: the canvas-shrouded motorbike Lucille's brother, Frank, had ridden until a couple of years ago, when he'd died in a hunting accident up north. It was two minutes after two. Billy would be at school, while Lucille – who was now working part-time at Don's Variety – would be waiting for him. Advancing across her small backyard, past Fuzz's empty doghouse, he found the kitchen door locked: unusual. Light smeared the linoleum in the empty hall. For a moment she seemed not only not at home but gone in some more permanent way, dead or injured, and in his head a voice offered alibis to some faceless prosecutor. *I only arrived at two; they saw me at the mill at ten to two. You can check the time card.*

Then Lucille came down the hall. Her tight grey T-shirt had moulded to the abrupt mound of her breasts, showing the wrinkles in her bra. With a lightness like happiness, the arrow of desire fled through his chest.

She twisted open the lock.

"Trying to keep me out?"

She cast him a hard glance and began to clear the kitchen table. Plates and glasses crashed into the sink. She turned on a tap.

"You okay?"

She did not answer. He found a towel and dried for her. He had no idea what he'd done, but his guilt was on a hair-trigger these days. Penitent, cagey, he put up a glass.

"What is it?" he said, smiling.

She set a plate in the rack and stared straight ahead of her.

"I want to go out."

"Out –"

"You know, like people do. I'd like to get in that car of yours and go –" She waved her hand airily. Soapy water flew onto his cheek. "Out for a drive."

"We'd be seen," he said gently.

"Maybe we should be," she said, attacking a pan. "I think I'd *like* to be seen."

"But there's Margaret," he said. He spoke his wife's name warily, hating to bring her into it. He never talked about Margaret with Lucille. It had seemed a way of protecting them both.

Lucille shrugged.

He did not love Lucille Boileau. At that moment, watching her shrug off Margaret, he half-hated her. But he wanted her – with a fury of disappointment that made his mouth dry.

"We can talk about it," he said.

"What's to talk about? I get my coat, we go out."

Her eyes burned on his now, furiously challenging though at the same time there was something misfocused in them, something that missed him, by a hair.

"But if Margaret finds out –" He smiled again, placating. Why should he ruin his marriage for the sake of their pleasant afternoons? He was pained that she couldn't see this.

"Queen Margaret," she said, mocking. She studied him a moment. "You know, if all it is is sex, maybe you should pay me. You sneak over here, we go bang-bang, you pay me. A lot more honest, eh?"

"Lucille –" He felt she was tearing something valuable, in her anger.

"I've done it, you know. Out West there: Winnipeg, Edmonton. The good Johns of Winnipeg!"

Those black eyes held his.

"You're shocked," she said, with satisfaction.

"No," he said. "Yes." His face had gone hot.

She was still staring at him, darkly triumphant, as if she'd cut herself on purpose. "I started when I was thirteen. I can always start again."

"Don't," he said.

"Don't what?"

"Hurt yourself."

The look in her eyes changed slowly from triumph to mockery. She began to laugh, hoarsely and without joy. Then stopped.

"You kill me," she said. She tossed a sponge into the sink. "You don't want me to hurt myself. I wonder why that is. Do you love me?"

Helpless, he met her eyes shining with sarcasm. All her life, its desperation and defiant survival, seemed revealed in her face, daring him to gainsay it. Below her lower lip was a small scar in the shape of the letter C. She had told him it was from a skating accident. Now he doubted it. He doubted everything he knew about her.

And she knew he didn't love her: it was her trump card.

"I care for you," he said.

She snorted in disgust and walked away from him, towards the bare beige wall mapped with cracks. On a calendar he saw a photo of a jet fighter, silver on blue, like a holy medal.

She turned back to him, "You see, I've been here before. Except most of the others – I don't mean out West – I mean here in town –" She stopped and looked at him again. He felt he was being reconsidered, judged. She said, "I came back here to start over, you know. No more Johns, just good honest boys. That's what I was going to have – good honest boys." A cold hostility lit her eyes. He felt neither good nor honest. "They at least *thought* they loved me," she said. "At least they said they did. And who knows, maybe they did. I'm really not so bad, you know."

"No," he managed. Gazing for a moment out the window, a smile of pain twisting her face, she seemed not to hear him. An icicle fell, passing her head like a dagger.

"Then do you know what happens?" she said, turning back to him. "Do you know what *always* happens? They leave me!" Grinning, she flung out her hand; it fell and struck her thigh. "They up and leave me, all of them. Do you know why that is?"

He shook his head and stood waiting. Everything he thought of saying seemed trivial.

And besides, he knew that he, too, would leave her. He felt there was something missing in her: an absence where, for a man, there could be no rest.

"If I can do anything," he said finally. This seemed so pathetic he dared not meet her eyes.

"I told you," she said. "You can take me for a ride."

He thought he would take her straight into the country, where they were less likely to be seen. But she insisted on a town route, she needed cigarettes from a particular store that "gave her a deal," she said. Glumly obedient, wondering what this "deal" was, he took the Biscayne across the Bridge Street bridge and up Shade, then over to Station. She raised her broad face to the windshield, in a show of defiance. She was *going* to have a good time, a pleasant, normal time, or at least look like she was. Her eyes like black glass.

An old man was shuffling up Station Hill. Bent at the waist, so that his face peered straight down at the sidewalk, he planted his cane in front of him, then caught up to it with shuffling baby steps. He travelled miles this way, like a snail: Ralph O'Grady.

"Give him a ride," Lucille demanded.

"He's all right."

"No, stop!"

He stopped. He'd always felt it was only a matter of time until his secret came out, though he never imagined it coming out on an afternoon spin with Ralph O'Grady. But he felt helpless to resist. He knew he was going to leave her, was already guilty about *that*. Guilty, too, about getting her fired. He thought about the revelation she'd once worked the streets. He felt he owed her something, for the life she had had. But all these reasons were pathetic, weren't they? Put into the scales against even a featherweight of love, they were nothing.

And too, he had not yet given up on his afternoon. In half an hour, in an hour, they might be back at her house, in her swaying bed. All he needed was fifteen minutes with her, even five. Just looking at her in her packed jeans, as she went over to talk to Ralph, made him want her. Maybe he did love her. In bed, she had met him as no woman ever had, with an appetite equal to his, even greater than his. At certain moments they seemed to burn the world up, to replace it with something entirely their own. He was grateful to her for that, grateful to her for the pleasure of knowing her naked: her strong, thick body beautiful to him, as if life itself had taken her form and offered itself to him – those pooled, darkly budded breasts – in her swaying bed, each Tuesday afternoon.

He watched as she brought Ralph to the car. The old man was so bent she had to turn him around and ease him, bum first, into the back seat. Ralph cracked his head on the top of the door but hardly seemed to notice. "Oopsies," Lucille said.

They continued up Station Hill. In the rear-view, Alf saw the old man's twisted head and red eyes leering from under his cap. He wondered if Ralph knew where he was.

Lucille asked Ralph how he was doing.

"Oh, can't complain."

"At least the weather's warm, anyways."

"Is it?"

"We take you to your place then?"

"Who's this?" Ralph said. In the mirror, Alf saw the old man squinting at him.

"This is Alf Walker. You know him!"

"Oh sure, I know him!"

The caved-in mouth grinned.

The Biscayne passed the railway station, where pigeons dotted the tiled roof like stones, and crossed the humpbacked bridge into the North End. Lucille had turned sideways, her arm crooked over the back of the seat as she chatted with Ralph. Alf saw how one breast climbed higher than the other, under her wrinkled T-shirt. He was stalking her, he couldn't help it, even here where every window seemed to watch, where his reputation and even his marriage had perhaps already begun to unravel, all he could think about, really, was getting his hands on her. You pathetic bugger, he thought. He remembered sharks he'd seen once in a photo, swirling ecstatically in water reddened with their own blood.

After they'd dropped Ralph off in front of his little bungalow, they drove to the Junction, to Hank Hays' Lunch and Gas. Lucille strode briskly in front of the car, her head up like royalty, and disappeared in the door with its slanting Orange Crush sign. When a grey station wagon pulled into the pumps, Alf averted his face, praying that Lucille would stay inside until John Henson drove away. But in a few moments the stooped, grinning figure of the Anglican sexton leaned over to wave at him through the windshield. Alf had no choice but to roll down the window.

"Can you believe this weather?"

"Not really."

John Henson smiled his fixed, wincing smile. He always looked as if something sharp were poking him from inside.

The door with its Orange Crush handle opened and Lucille emerged behind John.

"I'm just giving Lucille Boileau a ride," Alf explained too soon. John went on grinning, clearly not understanding. Lucille passed in front of the hood and John glanced at her. But he didn't really take note until she climbed in beside Alf. Then the sexton's head came down and he peered at the woman in the black leather motorcycle jacket.

"I don't believe we've met," Lucille said.

"Hah! Well!"

John was grinning at full wattage now, showing tortured gums. He was never at ease around women, except perhaps very old ones, where he got to play the gentleman with a gallant hint of all the risqué things he would do if they were younger.

"Alfie, introduce us."

Alf had no choice. Lucille and John's clasped hands shook in front of his face. He didn't doubt that John knew who Lucille was, even if he'd never spoken to her. Every man in town knew who Lucille was.

"I'm just giving her a lift," Alf said, trying again.

"We're going for a little spin," Lucille said brightly, ruffling Alf's hair.

"Right," John said, his eyes bulging. He jerked up his thumb like an umpire calling *out* at home plate: "I'm just filling up!"

They drove away. A slow freight was drawing through the level crossing, each boxcar floating with majestic, drumming grace behind the barrier. Far up the tracks, the invisible engine wailed. Alf asked for a cigarette and she lit it for him in her mouth before passing it over. He considered: there was no predicting what John Henson would make of seeing him with Lucille. It would be a test of his Christianity at the very least.

They followed Danson's Lane to the old one-room schoolhouse, now a residence, and swung north among thawing fields streaked with black earth, low ranges of dirty snow, rivers of glittering ice-water. High behind them, the sun of early March poured its steep brightness onto the land. Smoking, Alf began to relax. Light flickered through the woodlots, and in a muddy paddock a black horse broke suddenly into a trot, throwing its head as if tossing invisible reins.

He thought again of what she had told him earlier. In his mind's eye, he saw an Indian girl in a skimpy dress, or maybe stovepipe jeans, grinning from the curb while men like him looked her over. The thought put a cutting loneliness through him, and yet he was fascinated. He glanced at Lucille. Her face tilted back a little, her eyes gazed almost dreamily up the road as it unfurled beyond the smoke from her filtered Caporal.

On a post, a sparrow hawk watched the Biscayne speed past, a momentary irrelevance. A high mountain of cumulus, nearly invisible in the north, slowing changed shape.

By the time they reached the village of Cairn, her silence had turned gloomy. Nothing he said could rouse her. She smoked fiercely, looking straight ahead, ignoring his remarks. He drove through the back streets to a place where a pond spread towards a cedar bush. The pond was still covered with ice and snow, perforated by a few dead trees. He stopped and rolled down the window. A woodpecker was tapping somewhere, with an irregular, bright exactness. The bird was in its own world, with something to do, work that wholly occupied it. But they were in the smoke-filled car, trapped in a kind of vacuum.

"What's the matter?" he said. He reached along the back of the seat to touch her hair. A quarter to three: he felt their afternoon might be salvaged yet. "You're so beautiful," he said. He meant it.

She gave him a sideways glance and a chill went through him. There was such hostility in her look that he felt instantly attacked. At the same time, she did not seem to really see him. Her look was blind, as if he might have been any man sitting there. As if he was merely a body.

They drove back to town by the Galt Highway. The sense of oppression in the car had deepened. It was as if some terrible thing had happened between them, and now it was impossible to speak without calling up the terrible thing itself. But what had happened? A look, a few words. No, the atmosphere of doom could not be explained by that look or those words, and yet somehow the look and the words had released it, like a spell.

She smoked steadily, with an impatience that verged on fury. She had to get back to the house, she said, Billy would be home soon. He suggested they still had time to go to her place, but even he could see the afternoon had all but slipped away. At the corner of Bridge and Willard she suddenly demanded to be let out. But when he stopped the car, she went on sitting, staring straight ahead of her, and it seemed to him that she was waiting for something from him: waiting with a stubborn, defiant anger to receive from him something he could not imagine, but which she seemed to believe she was owed.

36

WHEN LUCILLE SLAMMED THE DOOR of the Biscayne and walked away down Willard, Alf felt they were through. In a way, he was relieved – relieved she'd taken the initiative, which saved him the trouble of playing the bastard's role, or at least of playing it to the hilt. And anyway, the stress of lying to Margaret, of always worrying they'd be caught, had often seemed greater than the pleasure. He had promised himself a hundred times he would give her up. But when the pleasure came, and even more, the anticipation of pleasure, it obliterated everything, like a drug. By the end of the week he was having withdrawal symptoms. His hands seemed heavier, with the blood in them, lonely for Lucille Boileau.

Friday night, in a windless silence, it began to snow. On Saturday morning the large flakes – eyelid-catching flakes of indeterminate shape – were still floating down from an invisible sky, settling a pure whiteness over the yard. Alf and Margaret sat in the kitchen in their dressing gowns, over a late breakfast. From two rooms away came the squawk of the Saturday-morning cartoons. The renewal of winter had cast a feeling of snug isolation over the house and it seemed to Alf that he had returned home, to the simple pleasures of normality – a second cup of coffee, the scrape of a knife on toast, the Saturday paper – after a time of insanity that in retrospect half-perplexed him. When the phone rang, it startled them both. Margaret answered.

"It's for you." His wife held the receiver as if it were slightly repugnant.

"Alfie," the voice said. Lucille.

It was if she had erupted inside him, out of a still pool. Her familiar voice, raw with cigarette smoke, seemed in danger of spilling from the receiver.

"I've got a broken pipe," she said. "There's water everywhere."

"In the cellar?" he said, conscious of Margaret moving at the counter.

"It's an emergency," Lucille said.

"I'm not really a plumber," he said sternly. "I'm not sure I have the right tools."

"Oh you've got the right tools, Alfie."

He turned to the wall.

"Look, have you tried a plumber?"

"I don't have the money, Alf. There's a foot of water down there now. If you can't come –"

"I'll see what I can do," he said. "I've got to get dressed."

"Who was that?" Margaret said, when he'd hung up.

"Lucille Boileau. Her cellar's flooded. I *told* her – well, you heard me. I guess she doesn't have much money."

"I wonder why she'd call here?" Margaret said in a muffled voice to the coffee pot.

He shrugged, doing his best to look puzzled, innocent. But a wild, youthful happiness had invaded him: he felt like seizing his wife and dancing.

Alf had never been in Lucille's cellar, with its rough stone walls and low ceiling. Against one wall, a broken pipe spewed a ragged plume of water that crashed noisily into the flood that lapped at the bottom stair. Lucille watched as he sloshed around in his rubber boots, searching with a hoe for the main valve.

"Alf –"

Feeling under the icy water he found the tap. In a few seconds, the stream had petered to a dribble.

"Don wants me to work at the store. One of the girls phoned in sick. I wonder if you could keep an eye on Billy."

He looked at her on the stairs, stooping there in the weak light, her breasts free (he guessed) under her untucked plaid shirt. He was going to be here anyway – for hours, maybe. And besides, he'd do anything now to be back in her good books. It was a kind of madness, he saw: he was the drowning man who watches with curious equanimity the diminishing spot of light above his sinking head.

"He hasn't been well," she said, with a simpering smile that surprised him.

"All right."

She let him kiss her, briefly, on the mouth. "I'm sorry," he said, meaning he was sorry for their last date together – for whatever he'd done or hadn't done that ruined their afternoon. She tousled his head, like a boy's, and a few minutes later he heard the front door slam as she went out. As he was poking about with the hoe, trying to find the floor drain (wherever it was, it was plugged), Billy materialized on the stairs. He was sitting in stocking feet and jeans and a red T-shirt with ATTAWAN FALL FAIR printed on it. In his hand was a large toy soldier clad in army khakis and a G.I. helmet.

"You could float a boat down here," Alf said, trying to be friendly. He was in a good mood, feeling that he and Lucille were back on track.

The boy said nothing.

"I remember a flood when I was a boy. They had to come and take us out in boats. The whole Island was flooded. That was before they raised the dykes." And again he saw the ghostly ice-cakes creeping through the misted streets, the rowboats nudging up to isolated houses – the swift, mysterious rippling of waters.

Billy looked at his toy soldier, making him jump – or fall – down a couple of stairs, making sure it landed on its head. He might as well have been deaf for all the attention he paid to Alf. Yet when Alf turned away, he felt the boy was watching. He was like a wild animal with his dark eyes that darted into hiding at the suggestion of a look from someone else.

Alf found the drain. There was a rock in it, apparently. It was as smooth as the top of a skull, wedged solid. He tried to pry it out with his fingers, with the edge of the hoe, with a screwdriver.

"Somebody's put a rock in here," he said. There was no response from the stairs. Looking around, he saw the boy was gone.

He got the rock out, but there was still a lot of muck clogging the drain. As he dug it out, he could hear Billy moving upstairs. After a while, he went up to look.

He found him in his narrow room, sitting on his bed – which was just a mattress on the floor – with a mess of comic books littering the dishevelled blankets. There was a smell of stale urine, and in the uncurtained window, a ferny garden of frost did not quite obscure the clapboard wall of the house next door. Billy's gaze darted to Alf's knees, fled back to his comic.

"Your mom tells me you've been sick –"

"Yup." Billy's answer came from far back in his throat. It was like a little man talking, a tough little gangster, almost comical.

"Feelin' better now?"

"Yup."

"Good."

Billy was turning the pages of the comic book, too fast to be really seeing anything. Alf felt he wasn't just shy. The boy seemed frightened of him. He had an impulse to go away – to stop torturing him with his presence – but he was held by the boy's isolation. He wondered what his life had been, who his father was. Lucille had been with a lot of men. At that moment, Billy seemed to be the child of them all, abandoned and strange.

He said, "I'm Jamie's father, you know."

"Yup."

"I'm a friend of your mother's. We used to work at the same place."

"Yup."

"Are you hungry? Can I get you something to eat?"

"Nope."

Alf hesitated, at a loss. He had never met a boy like this. He remembered his silence, that night he'd driven him home. He watched as Billy twisted his comic book into a roll and bit his upper lip. He seemed independent of the adult world somehow, of all worlds, locked in a world of his own. He seemed to Alf to have a secret, as if he were guarding a secret, and at the same time waiting for someone to come and guess what it was. *He* couldn't tell.

"My grandfather drowned in Lake Erie," Billy said, tightening the roll. The statement seemed to come out of nowhere.

"I knew your grandfather," Alf said, squatting down, hoping to find his way into Billy's gaze. "One winter – it was a long time ago – we cut ice together, on the Atta."

The boy went on fooling with the tube of paper. But Alf felt he was listening.

"That was before people had refrigerators. They kept all their food in iceboxes. The iceman used to come around in the summer. He'd give us pieces of ice to suck. Sort of like Popsicles."

The boy's black eyes briefly met his, with a flash of amusement. And a stab of excitement – of life in the quick – leapt in Alf's gut.

"Sure," Alf said, warming. "Actually, he didn't give them to us. We'd steal them, when he was away from his truck."

Billy's throat emitted a little laugh: *Heh!* He understood *that*.

"We'd go down by the river and suck them. Or if it was hot, we'd rub them all over our faces and chests."

The boy was grinning at him now, his round face and black eyes and little teeth with their traces of rot shining up at him, happy and appeased. Yet even now, Alf suspected the boy had eluded him. His smile was like a mask, offered to a greater power – a smiling power who demanded a smile in return. But something else was going on behind it, in those evasive eyes, something he could not read, which moved him and held him there, in the little room.

37

THE TELEVISION FLOODED the McVeys' den with fake, flickering moonlight. Lying on the couch, his head in Liz's lap, Joe watched an old Fred Astaire and Ginger Rogers movie – that spry and dapper man moving like an elf down a broad staircase, taking his platinum-headed love in his arms. They wheeled around the floor with such exquisite synchronization there seemed to be no time at all between gesture and response.

Turning his head, Joe began to pick at the buttons of Liz's blouse, exposing her peach satin bra with its frilly edges. Without taking her eyes off the screen, she helped him slide the bra up. Her breasts came free. Absently, Liz smoothed his hair. They could not make love tonight because her father was out with the car and her mother and sister were up on the second floor. Her father, he supposed, was with Babs Wilcocks. Joe had seen the two of them a few nights ago, walking into the Vimy House's Ladies and Escorts, the tall man with the stocky, plain, fur-coated Babs on his arm, the two of them looking almost formal in an old-fashioned way and – casting greetings right and left – clearly making no effort to hide their relationship. Joe had never understood it – Doc McVey, the richest man in town, drinking in the Vimy House. But he was a regular there and had once, the story ran, got into a shoving match with Bud Reed over some insult Bud had sent his way.

Joe nuzzled a breast, licked it, looked at it. Above, Liz's blank face continued to watch the screen. Through the ceiling came a thump. He wondered if Liz's mother had fallen down. Two weeks before, he'd watched her – she'd consumed one too many gin and tonics – lean slowly sideways, like the Tower of Pisa, with a bemused *here-we-go* smile in her sad eyes. He'd just managed to catch her.

"You never tell me you love me," Liz said.

Joe looked up at the violet, too-bright eyes, watching him up there, beyond her pulled-up bra. She had told him she loved *him* once, whimpering it in a little-girl voice as he lay in her arms at the Executive.

"You know I care for you." Her face flickered in the lunar light, impassive.

"I don't want my mother's life," she said, tugging sharply at his hair.

"No, well, why should you?"

"The way he treats her," she said, her gaze sweeping his forehead, as though evidence of her father's sins lay there.

"Hey now, I don't treat you like that."

Once – this was driving up to Galt in the Lincoln – she had talked with remarkable candour about her father's affair with Babs Wilcocks. "He thinks it should be nothing, we should take it as nothing – after all, he's still here, or he is most of the time, he still loves us. He can't see the unhappiness he causes. I mean, he thinks it's unreasonable for us to be upset. He can't see why we can't all be in a good mood, and nice to everybody, like he is. Why do we have to *spoil* things – *us*, spoiling things! The crazy thing is, most of the time we play it his way. We pretend nothing's wrong. And then something snaps: Mom gets drunk or – Mom gets drunk." It was the most frank she'd ever been with him. He had liked her the better for it, had felt closer to her, once she dropped her theatrical airs. But at the same time, she had set a level of openness he couldn't match. She was asking for that now, he felt, her stare full of demands he couldn't meet.

Abruptly, he sat up. Hand in hand, Fred and Ginger were strolling happily through a crowd of partygoers. Neither was out of breath.

"Do you love me a little?" said Liz, ghostly behind him. Joe went still. Everything in the room seemed to demand his answer: the deep couch, the fine desk with its brass-handled drawers, the gilt-framed pictures, even Fred and Ginger, pausing now in an embrace to look at each other in suspended bliss: waiting for Joe's response to come winging to them from thirty years into the future and make all exactly right.

The thought of Anna came to him with such force he caught his breath. Earlier that day she had come into the A&P. She had seemed delighted to find him sweeping the floor in his apron, and stood chatting with him for a good five minutes. Since that time they'd talked in her bedroom, something seemed to have opened between them. But what? He felt held in suspense around her, as if a happiness he could not quite believe in was hovering nearby.

"Joe?" Liz said. "Do you –"

"Sure I do," he said. He was staring at nothing, scarcely hearing. But he managed to reach out and squeeze her knee in its patterned stocking.

It was just after midnight when he got home to find his mother in the kitchen. She was worried about his father. Apparently Alf had left to go for a walk at eight, saying he'd be back in an hour or two. She wanted Joe to drive over to the Legion and look for him. "Why don't we just phone," he said. "Joe," she urged, "please do this for me." There was a fierce, loaded concentration in her eyes. The pressure of unspoken things was in the room, and rather than broach them, he took the Biscayne and drove over to the Flats. It was snowing again, large flakes drifting out of the dark to settle an airy fleece on windshields and tree branches. He parked by the curb and approached the old brick house with its drawn curtains. He had never been in the Legion before – it was licensed, you had to be twenty-one to go in – and it had become a place of mystery to him. If the war was still alive anywhere in Attawan, it was alive here, and as he pushed through the heavy doors into the dimly lit entrance hall, he sensed the mood of the Thirties and Forties, preserved in these rooms like clothes in an old trunk. From around a corner came the roar of voices and music – "The White Cliffs of Dover" was flowing in its slow, nostalgic wave from the jukebox, a few people were singing drunkenly along. He was about to go on when he noticed the display cases on either side of the hall. They were full of flags and old photographs and newspaper clippings: "GERMANY SURRENDERS!" But what held him was the file of army rifles going right back to the Boer War. The nicked, polished wood and oiled metal of the Lee-Enfields spoke to him of the battles he had read about: Passchendaele, Vimy, Dieppe, Juno Beach, the Scheldt Estuary. There was a Mauser too, which seemed to contain the very essence of the legendary enemy. Beside it sat a German helmet – that mythic shape, like a pageboy haircut forged in steel.

Inside, he asked the barman, Nick Maroni, if he'd seen his father. Nick hadn't, but he tapped his head – a signal for Joe to remove his hat – and said it was okay for him to have a look, so he went gingerly through the rooms, his toque crushed in his hand, past the large framed picture of the Queen in her blue sash, saying hello to people who greeted him. Coming back he stopped at a large photo that showed a brigade of soldiers sitting around a square of improvised board tables, eating Christmas dinner from their mess tins. He scanned the scene intently, moved by the merriment of the young men in khaki, envying them the adventure of their lives.

Outside in the snowy silence, he looked at a small fruit tree, its branches loaded with white, and was overcome with a sense of having missed his father's life. His father had lived, and he, Joe, had understood nothing about it – nothing about a life that suddenly seemed laden with rich, unheralded meaning. For a moment, looking away down the poorly lit street over the snow-muffled cars, he felt bereft.

He drove around the Flats for a while, past the mills that seemed, just now, as desolate as prisons, then started towards home. On Bridge Street he saw his father tramping towards the centre of town. Snow had collected on the shoulders of his grey overcoat and in his dishevelled hair. As Joe drew up, his father stopped, and seemed to hesitate before coming to the car – seemed, almost, not to recognize the Biscayne – but then he moved quickly and got in, with a gust of cold air. There was a drop of moisture on his nose.

"Hey fella, what are you doing out here?"

"Oh Mom – you know how she is. Worried you'd got lost or something."

He was relieved and immensely glad to have found his father.

"I stayed longer than I meant to," his father said.

"At the Legion?" Joe said. His father glanced over at him. "You were at the Legion?"

His father looked away.

"I was just there," Joe said, a bit off balance. Since they'd played hockey on the river, that time with Smiley, they'd been getting along pretty well, as they usually did if they trod lightly. But now, he sensed an uneasiness in his father, which made him uneasy too. He drove forward, the tires spinning a little on the ramp to the bridge.

"I must have missed you," Joe said, eager to save his father any discomfort over the discrepancy. Perhaps he'd been in the washroom when Joe went through. "It's a great place," he said. "That collection of rifles –"

His father said nothing. Joe might have taken that as a warning, but he couldn't stop himself. Driving around the Flats, he'd remembered what his mother had told him, that before the war his father had been a different man. And now – the idea came with the swiftness of instinct – he wanted to make contact with that other man, that younger, happier man who could talk at his ease and enjoy himself. "I saw this picture, 'Christmas dinner 1944'? I wondered if you knew anyone in it. It was obviously taken in Europe. They seemed to be in a ruined church. They were having a great time. You remember any Christmases there?"

His father did not respond: he had sunk into one those baffling silences that made Joe feel he'd done something wrong, made him feel he'd been cast out, into a silence of his own. Waiting at Shade for the light to change, he saw another car draw up beside them. Doc McVey – his wide, bespectacled face emanating its usual arrogance – glanced past their hood to check for traffic. For a moment, his gaze lit on Joe and his father without apparent recognition, before he wheeled the Lincoln away up Shade.

"Coming home from his girlfriend's, I guess," Joe said, trying to bridge the gap with a joke.

"Just drive," his father said. Feeling suddenly chilled, Joe put the Biscayne in gear and they went on, between the darkened stores.

38

STANDING WITH BILLY below Rat's Hill, Jamie was shivering, his mittens and the seat of his pants soaked from repeated trips down the hill on the piece of ruined cardboard that lay at his feet. He wanted to go home, but there was a problem. Billy wanted to come with him.

"We could play with your soldiers –," Billy said, his mouth hardly moving. His eyes travelled cagily from the zipper in Jamie's coat to Jamie's nose to some spot in the air between them. Far above them, at the top of the hill, Wayne Cox stood with one foot on his toboggan, eyeing the ice-chute that gleamed like a long stream of saliva in the hillside. In a nearby house, lights had come on, with their look of snugness and safety. Jamie said, "It's time for supper. My Dad'll be home."

"We could go up to your room."

"I don't think so."

"I could wait in your room while you eat."

"I dunno. I don't think so –"

Billy went on grinning, refusing defeat. He wasn't wearing mittens and his coat didn't cover his brown, skinny wrists: he was shivering, and there was a drugged, sleepy cast about his eyes.

"I guess I better go," Jamie said.

As he walked away, Billy spat and fell in beside him, his rubber boots squelching in the wet snow.

"Anyways," Billy said, "your dad's gonna come and live in my house."

Jamie stopped and looked at Billy, who was grinning at Jamie's chest. And suddenly his body felt wrapped in hotness.

"That's stupid. He's not gonna –"

"Yeah, he is."

"That's stupid."

"Wanta fight about it?" This emerged so quickly Jamie knew Billy'd been planning to say it all along. When Billy had a problem, he would fight. If something wasn't true, he would make it be true, with his fists.

"No, it's stupid."

"I'm not stupid!"

"I know. But my dad's not gonna live with you. That's – silly."

"He came to our house."

"No he didn't."

"Yeah, he did. He kissed my mom. I saw him do it in the cellar. That means he's gonna live with us."

"No he didn't," Jamie said. But his face burned at the mention of the kiss. It didn't sound like Billy had made *that* up. The kiss made everything look different: the purple sky, the stain of the ice-chute in the hill, all had the cruel, bright look of something true.

Billy's shove sent him staggering sideways.

"Hey!" Jamie said, but Billy had that look he had seen so many times in the schoolyard when he was getting ready to fight, his eyes fixed almost sleepily on his, Jamie's, mouth as if his mouth alone had made Billy mad. As if Billy no longer saw him, but only a mouth, a chin, a chest: places to be hit. He thought that being friends with Billy had made him safe from Billy. But here it was, like something he'd always known: that gaze from which he, Jamie, had somehow disappeared.

He was walking rapidly away when he heard the churn of Billy's boots. Billy was on him before he could turn. They both went down, punching and wrestling in the slush. At the crack of Billy's fist a numbness spread up Jamie's nose and into his forehead. A few seconds later, Billy had straddled him. Jamie bucked and twisted, struggling to free his wrists from Billy's grip, looking up into Billy's face, which was all fury now, the bad teeth clenched in a sneer. And he knew that Billy had more fierceness in him than he did. He was going to lose.

Finally, he lay still. Billy's face was close to his, under the thatch of black hair. He saw the brown spots on Billy's teeth.

"All right," Jamie said. "You win."

Billy's twisted his wrists.

"Say it's true," Billy said.

"What –"

"Say it's true your dad's comin' to live at my house."

He looked past Billy's head into the murk of the sky. He could not say it. It was not true, it *could not* be true, and yet – some strange intuition drifting through his body – he sensed that to admit to it made it more likely. Words made things true, they made them *be*.

"*Say it!*" Billy twisted his wrists again.

He heard a car pass, on the road by the hosiery mill, a sound that might mean rescue, growing weaker. Distantly, across the fields behind the mill, a chainsaw stuttered and growled and he was filled with self-pity.

He thought of his house on the Island: the lit kitchen where even now his mother would be starting to make supper. It occurred to him that she did not know what was happening to him. The thought filled him with sadness. He saw the top of the kitchen table and the little glass dish that held the butter, the perfect square of yellow butter. "That was my mother's," his mother had told him.

"*Say it.*"

He was filled with longing for his own life. And yet despite this, he felt he had come down to something he had always known, though he usually managed to forget it, he'd come down to the fact of the cold, slushy ground and him lying on it, beaten. This was something true, and it was underneath all the other things he knew were true too – school, summer holidays, his father, underneath all those things there was this cold, wet place that made him want to cry.

"Say it or I'll punch your face in."

"All right."

"Say it."

"My dad's comin' –"

But he couldn't speak the words. His throat had swelled and he felt the first tear spill from the corner of his eye.

"Say it, crybaby."

He fought back, twisting and struggling. He got one hand free, but of course that meant Billy had *his* hand free: it made a fist and the fist struck him in the eye like a stone.

"*Say it!*"

Again they lay still, locked. Another car went past. It seemed much darker suddenly, though the wet, dirty snow gleamed from the hillside. He strained to see if Wayne Cox was still on the hill. But the brow was empty against the stark, high wall of a house.

His coat was soaked now. He was shivering harder than Billy.

"You can come to my house," he said. "We can play with my soldiers."

He knew his mother would never let Billy in.

Billy gave his wrists another twist and sat back, letting them go. But he went on sitting on Jamie's stomach, deciding something.

"You can borrow my tank," Jamie said. His best Dinky Toy. "You can take it home."

Billy let him up and they walked in silence down West Street, their arms brushing as if they were friends. They passed Donnie Whittaker's dog. In its mouth was a bloody bone. The dog slunk into the road, watching them with sneaky eyes.

Then a car drew up, and it was Truck Cassidy's taxi, its sides feathered with slush, and Billy's mother was inside. She told Billy to get in, time for supper she said, and when Billy wouldn't get in, she got out and grabbed him by the ear and marched him into the back seat. "We'll see you later, honey," she said to Jamie with a big smile. He looked at her huge, pink mouth.

The lights were on in Jamie's house, but the car was gone. He told himself Joe might have the car, but a moment later he saw Joe in the window, looking into the pages of a newspaper. For a few minutes he stood shivering in his soaked pants, wanting to go in but wanting even more to know where his father was. He was out with the car somewhere, but *where*? If he was just driving around, that was all right, but if he had gone over to Billy's . . . He ran back to the corner, but there was no sign of the car, not down Water Street, where the distant stores nested in the glow of the street lights, nor up West, where the road was disappearing in thick dusk. He turned and looked left, where the butt end of Water Street climbed the ramp to the footbridge. Beyond lay the dissolving whiteness of the hill clouded darkly with trees. When he saw the car, its headlights streaking among pines, he felt immediately it had to be his father, going to Uncle Pete and Aunt May's house maybe, or just going, as big people always were, on errands and trips that seemed to have no end. He ran up the ramp and onto the bridge. The car was visible now, it tires rumbling on the snow-packed road as it hurtled down through the dusk, but it was not his father's, he saw, not the brown Biscayne, but a low black car he did not recognize, speeding along the dead-end road as if it actually led somewhere.

At that moment he heard a sound like the report of a gun. He staggered sideways, and when he recovered, not knowing what it was, he froze in a state of hyper-alertness. His heart seemed to be beating in his whole body. Peering through the chainlink mesh of the safety fence, he saw the river moving under him, a huge white snake moving its rough back slowly through the land. Now repeated gun-shots came, and a rumbling like a train on the Shade Street overpass. Climbing up the mesh, he looked down and saw great blocks of ice shifting and climbing over each other's backs. Underneath him, the bridge banged and hummed as the cakes of ice struck the abutments.

As he watched, one particularly large cake climbed into the air. It reared straight up in front of him, taller than he was, taller than the bridge, and it was coming on slowly, towards the rail. He gazed up at it, unable to move.

In its underside, many stones and bits of weed were imbedded like eyes. It advanced within a silence of its own, bobbing slightly. It was like a creature he'd seen in the Christmas Parade, a giant leaning its huge, grotesque head over the crowd.

"Mommy," he whispered. It was almost on top of him. And still he couldn't run.

It's all right, the voice said.

"All right?" he echoed, mesmerized. He watched as the creature sank. Just before it reached the bridge, it bowed its great, dripping head, sweeping so close to him he felt the chill of its icy body as it slipped beneath the bridge. He climbed down from the mesh and hurried to the opposite rail and watched it re-emerge, a giant spear-head of white ice, descending among its smaller brothers under the ghostly mass of Lookout Hill.

39

PENNY CAME DOWNSTAIRS with her soap carving. She felt elated, yet nervous, the carving – which she had been working on for weeks and shown to no one – cupped carefully in her right hand. When she saw her father in his chair in the living room, gazing into space as if into another world, she caught her breath. But she had come down *hoping* to find him: he was her favourite for showing her artwork to. Discovering her, his eyes blued.

He held the little soap dog in his fingertips.

Penny writhed with suspense at his knee. "It was supposed to be Red, but I think it's – it's just a dog," she said, her heart falling. The yellow soap dog was too thin for Red, the legs too short: it seemed a mess now, no good at all.

"It's terrific," her father said.

He turned in his chair and put her carving on a book lying on the windowsill. Beyond, boys were playing road-hockey in the cul-de-sac. It was still light outside, but in the room the weak, silvery daylight had been hollowed by shadow.

Penny climbed into her father's lap. "Aren't you getting too big for this?" he said, and she said, "Nope" and settled in with her head against his shoulder while he swivelled the chair a little, back and forth. They both looked at the dog. She had made its ears prick, like little tents, like the skunk-cabbage sticking above the mud in Wiley's swamp.

"Reminds me of Queenie," her dad said, his dog when he was a boy. Immediately she felt hopeful. "Sure, that tail. That's Queenie to a T. And he's almost the same colour!"

They were quiet for a while longer, looking at the dog, which was looking out the window at the boys running up and down.

"Am I your girlfriend?" she said.

Her father said nothing.

"Hey you," she said, panicking a little. She poked him in the chest. She had felt so funny saying Am I your girlfriend, as if she'd dressed up in her mother's shoes and jewellery, something she did do sometimes, but only in secret. She didn't want to say it again.

"What's up?"

"Am I your girlfriend?" She was blushing now, with a sense of touching on forbidden matters.

"Darn right," he said, giving her knee a squeeze.

They were silent a while longer. She was not appeased, not quite. She waited, hoping he would say more.

"Absolutely," he said, bouncing her a little.

"Am I your *only* one," she said. Her face hot now.

She felt him pause, in a little shock of surprise, and in that moment, her own heart seemed to fail, on the edge of things she did not want to know. But he said, "Well, there's your mother. She's really girlfriend number one."

Penny let that sink in, and it seemed all right. Or almost all right. Looking at her yellow dog, against the moving heads of the boys outside, she sensed that there was something, still, that did not quite fit. But it was so small, smaller than a speck of dust, that she was able to brush it aside.

"Tell me a story," she said. Her father seemed not to hear. She nudged him with her elbow. "Hey you! Tell me a story!"

"Oh I don't know –"

"Tell me about Johnny North."

"I think you've heard all my Johnny North stories."

"Tell me the old ones then. Tell me *all* the stories." Yes, she wanted them all, a flood of stories to carry them both away.

For a long time her father looked towards the street. Penny glanced up at him, and when he began, she snuggled back in, idly watching her yellow dog, with its pricked ears, that was watching the street. The dog was all right now, it had found a home. Her father's hand gently gripped her leg.

Her father had known Johnny North when he – her father – was a boy. Johnny North was a man but in some ways, her father said, he had stayed a boy. He lived in a shack on the banks of the Attawan River. He had worked for a few years as a mechanic in the mill, but one day, her father said, using the words he always used, "He just walked away from all that." Johnny made a paddlewheel boat powered by a bicycle, and he would sit up on his bicycle seat, pedalling his passengers along, passengers who paid a nickel for a tour to the rapids. Sometimes he'd recite his poetry to these people. He wrote long poems about fires and train crashes and recited them dramatically, waving his arms as he guided the boat among the islands. In the newspaper he was known as "Johnny North, Bard of the Attawan."

Johnny North was quite a character, her father said, chuckling a bit as he remembered. "I don't think he ever took a bath, unless you count swimming in the river. The fellow stank – well, Pete used to say you could smell him coming around the corner."

"Around *five* corners," Penny corrected.

"As bad as that," her father said. And he recalled how Johnny would dress up in funny costumes – women's dresses, or a Japanese kimono, with driving goggles to keep the dust out of his eyes – and go around town pulling a little wagon with a phonograph on it and a sign that read JOHNNY NORTH, ENTERTAINER. A few people hired him to perform at birthday parties, where he'd sing or do magic tricks. Not everybody wanted to hire him, though, because of his smell, and because you could never tell what he was going to do. "I remember this once," her father said – and this was a story she'd never heard – "when Bob Drummond was killed in a fire, Johnny turned up at the front of the funeral procession. He was wearing a black dress and he did this strange, shuffly dance. Some people were pretty upset and wanted to get him out of there. But Lila Drummond – that was Bob's mother – she told them to leave him alone. She told them, 'Johnny's just showing how he feels.'"

"That was good," Penny said.

"Yup, that was good."

Another time Johnny had saved a boy from drowning – this was one of Penny's favourite stories. Johnny'd seen the lad struggling, from his shack on the bank, and had rowed out to him. The town had given Johnny a medal and held a party, where he recited all fifty-seven verses of "The Wreck of Ninety-Eight." The mayor's wife had fallen asleep in her chair.

In the winter, when people went skating above the dam, Johnny would keep a fire going on shore. He'd lace up the skates of the ladies and girls, always doffing his cap and calling each one Miss – "even if they were eighty-two," her father said. In the summer Johnny rented out rowboats he had built himself. "He only charged a penny, and if you didn't have that he'd let you have it for free. They leaked like the dickens, usually."

Penny loved the Johnny North stories: the stories were always there, they were always happening, it seemed, in a sunny corner just out of sight. Hearing them, she felt happy, being transported to a time when her father was young. *She* wasn't born yet, but this didn't matter: she felt safe, not being born, knowing that in the happiness of her father's life she was still to come.

When Johnny North got old, things were not so good, her father said. Penny went very still – she hadn't heard *this* story. Johnny had arthritis, and in winter, he stuffed his clothes with newspapers that made a rustling sound when he walked. He blacked his white hair with shoe polish. He still wrote poems, though. "I remember this one bit – he must have written it for the town's New Year's party. They printed it in the *Star*:

Onward nineteen-hundred and thirty-seven!
I am out of my mammy's home:
To wander in dark woodlands
Alone, all, all, alone."

"So sad!" Penny said, on the edge of tears. In the window, her yellow dog was walking with Johnny in his dark woodlands.

"Well," her father said, jouncing her a bit on his leg. "Some rich people in town took up a collection. They paid for Johnny to go to an old-age home, over in Johnsonville. He wasn't very happy there, though – didn't last more than a few months."

"You mean he died?" Penny said, sitting up. She had never thought of Johnny dying: *that* wasn't part of his story. It wasn't part of who Johnny was.

She looked at her father, who seemed startled. He started to smile.

"Well sure, eventually. We all –"

"No!" Penny cried fiercely. She threw herself back down against him. In the street, the boys continued to yell at their game. She clung to her father's chest while he squeezed and rubbed her shoulder. She didn't want to hear about Johnny North or about anybody else dying. She wanted Johnny at his fire in the snow, tying the skates of ladies. She wanted him peddling his boat upstream, proclaiming "The Wreck of Ninety-Eight." And she wanted her father to be with him, a boy still, and safe.

40

THE SNOW FINALLY LEFT for good, swallowed by the slowly thawing earth. On the northward-facing slope of Lookout Hill, only a few patches glowed among the bare trees. But the season that arrived was no spring: it was an in-between season of black branches and soaked, dead-looking lawns littered with paper and dog shit. Time had run backwards, it seemed, as though November had begun again.

One day, lying beside Lucille in her unsteady bed, Alf knew it was over. "Maybe we should lay off for a while," he said, touching her on the cheek. His tenderness was real enough. He felt sorry for her, and guilty, for he knew he was no better than her other lovers, all of whom had left her. Reaching for her clothes, she avoided his gaze. In her eyes was a stoic darkness – a despair that could not or would not rouse itself to anger or condemnation. He would have felt better if she had upbraided him. This way, he felt hopeless himself.

He drove up to the cemetery. The Biscayne passed through the wrought-iron gates that were always propped open, past the red stone where his mother and father lay, following the narrow road into its final loop, where the crop of gravestones petered out in a few acres of yellow lawn. Pete's grave was here, isolated from the others under the tall gloom of a spruce, as if his death were somehow different from the rest. May had erected a small grey stone with a polished front, where the word "Moon" had been carved, and under it, slightly to the left, "Peter Watson Moon, 1918–1965."

Alf stood under the spruce in whose branches the faintest wind could just be heard, like the distant hush of water over a low barrier. It was far from the first time he had stood here, looking at the wicker basket filled with plastic flowers May had set before the stone. But this time seemed more vivid, as if it were the first. He felt he had come back to something. What had his fling with Lucille Boileau been really but an attempt to escape this place? An attempt to burn up his guilt in her bed? He plucked a pebble from the half-frozen mud and cleaned it with his fingers. He had never realized, until his friend had gone, how much he had loved him. In fact, he hadn't really known he'd loved him at all – "love" was not a term he had ever used in connection with his male friends. But now it was a torture to think that as he picked his way into the fields of death, Pete might have believed that Alf had abandoned him.

"You dumb bugger," he whispered. Tears had come to his eyes, in a rage against his friend. "You should have fought it. You should have told *me*. Hell, I should have told *you*." Yes, if only he'd confessed to Pete, begged his forgiveness. But now the possibility of confession and forgiveness – with Pete, with Margaret, with anyone – seemed as remote as the dim grey line of bush crayoning the far edge of the field beyond the cemetery. He was in a place where no one else was, or seemed capable of approaching, a place bound in iron-clad distances. Overhead, the tree had filled with the cheerful rant of small birds.

Each morning, hearing the cry of Bannerman's whistle, it seemed that only moments had passed since it had released him from work the previous day. He trudged numbly up the stairs of the mill with the trudging incommunicado crowd, arriving in the room of tall machines that seemed to have been waiting for him all his life. He no longer had even a minimal pleasure in his work. He'd told Prince what he could do with the foreman's job; his ambition had become an offering (an inadequate one, he felt) laid on the altar of Pete's death. And yet, several times, he was appalled to discover himself staring at the fading notice on the knitting room bulletin board, as though some small, craven part of him hoped to be made foreman yet. Matt Honnegger was staying on, temporarily. Alf was still doing most of his work for him. It seemed that the foreman's job – its burdens if not its title – had come to him by default.

He did his work swiftly and automatically, with a curious sense that he was alone. Sometimes, though, he was wakened by a chance event that broke through his isolation. He might drop a wrench and, bending to retrieve it, be struck by the oddity of its existence: as if he had never seen a wrench before, or felt its cool heft in his hand, or looked at its square, silently howling jaws. And another time, one damp, cloudy evening, he had gone out for a walk and was just

passing along the rail platform by the station, on his way to the old
concrete steps that led to the Shade, when it seemed that someone
had spoken to him. *Alf*, a voice said, a voice both familiar and not.
Not seeing anyone, he stopped and looked around. Above him a
Manitoba maple made a rushing sound as its dry seed pods –
hundreds and thousands of pale-brown tags hanging in clusters in
the bare tree – stirred in a faint breeze. It was odd, but he felt as if the
tree had spoken, as if it had said, Look, and looking up through its
branches he glimpsed the moon in a blue tunnel of cloud: a little,
gibbous moon like a battered stone sailing along up there, and a
shiver of excitement – of life – ran through him, though it was gone
in a moment.

That night, he dreamed he stood before a knitting machine, taller
than any he had ever seen. It seemed somehow human to him
– human and fatherlike and commanding in its sense of quiet power –
and although it was not knitting anything (the threads were still, the
whole atmosphere was one of lonely stillness), it seemed about to
speak. However, it could not make a sound, and there was something
both painful and suspenseful in this failure. On the machine's great
head, where it wore a rack of white bobbins like a vast crown, each
bobbin was stained with a trickle of dark blood.

One day, soon after the midmorning break, all the knitters and fixers
were told to shut down their machines and come to a meeting in
front of Matt Honnegger's office. The last to arrive, Alf peered over
a mass of heads and shoulders at three men who stood waiting with
their backs to the washing-up sink. Matt was part of this triumvirate,
but the foreman had remained a little aloof, cradling his empty pipe
against his plaid shirt while casting a bland smile at the floor, as if
distancing himself from the proceedings. Beside him stood Wilf
Thomas, the manager of the sweater mill: a solid-looking fellow
whose Roman nose with its thick bridge lent him the gladiatorial air
of an old football guard or hockey defenceman. Wilf was talking in

low tones, his head down, to a man Alf had never seen before, a young man of thirty or so, with a taut, bony face and a brush cut so short it seemed his head had been shaved. He wore jeans, and a tight black T-shirt, and stood with his well-muscled arms folded, revealing on his left biceps a fading, bluish tattoo in which the hooked head of a hawk or eagle was just visible. He was chewing gum – so rapidly that it looked as if the lower half of his face were afflicted by a nervous disorder – and darting the gaze of his large eyes between the floor and the knees of the men and women who stood a few feet away, watching.

"All right," Wilf Thomas said at last in his gruff voice, turning to the crowd. Wilf gave off a sense of blunt integrity that inspired trust. Many of the workers had known him all their lives, as he had grown up on the Flats, the son of a spinner. "I won't take too much of your time, folks. But as you know, we've been looking for a new foreman for this floor, and though we've had lots of good applications, we felt we needed a specialist."

Alf's heart pounded: in a flash he understood that he wasn't going to be made foreman. He had tried to convince himself he no longer wanted the job. But all the same, the tenacious weed of his hope – now crushed – filled his chest with the hot acid of disappointment.

He heard Wilf out in a kind of dream, the manager's words coming with a sense that was also non-sense, as if he were speaking of some other, distant place that Alf new little of, not the mill where they now stood, surrounded by the great crowd of motionless machines. "The reason we need a specialist," Wilf went on, "is that Intertex is going to be putting a number of new machines in here that none of us know how to run, so we thought we should have someone who does. And I'm happy to say that in Kit Ford here, we've got one of the best. Kit comes to us from one of the most advanced mills in North America, and I know we're going to appreciate his expertise. He's already been telling me things I don't know –" Here Wilf grinned, showing a gold tooth, but the crowd in front of him did not respond. "Kit's staying in a motel in Johnsonville, but he's going to be moving into town, and I know you'll make him welcome. Oh yes, and I should mention that Kit was once in the Marines, so I know he'll waste no time getting us in fighting trim. Kit –"

Kit Ford said, "Yeah," with a slight drawl. He licked his lips and looked at them with a bright, earnest gaze and thin smile. He spoke in rapid bursts, almost too fast to be understood, in an accent that seemed southern – from the Carolinas, maybe, or Georgia – and in his eyes was a straining, plaintive quality, which gave the impression he was laying too much stress on his own sincerity. "Yeah, been knittin' most of my life," he told them. "Fact I see some machines in here haven't seen since I was a kid. The old Jacquards there – should be fun. Sure you've got a lot to show me. Look forward to that. Good to be in Attawan." (Somehow he made the name of the town foreign, as if they'd never heard it before.) "Used to come up to these parts as a kid, to fish, in Quebec there. Good to be back. Look forward to knowin' ya and workin' with ya."

When the meeting was over, Wilf Thomas called to Alf, who turned back through the dissolving crowd. As he passed Dick Kenshole, the knitter leaned in close. "That job was yours," Dick seethed in a demanding undertone: what was Alf going to do about it? Without responding, Alf went on to the place where the three men waited for him. He did not look at Kit Ford until Wilf introduced him, and then he calmly took his hard, damp hand and met the reaching, anxious sincerity of his gaze. In those wide-staring eyes he caught an insistent claim of innocence. I didn't do it, Kit Ford's eyes said. And though there was no indication of what "it" was, Alf felt a tremor of misgiving.

"Alf's our best man here," Wilf was telling Kit. "Really knows the place like the back of his hand." He turned to Alf, speaking in a slightly overloud voice that betrayed a certain nervousness. "Matt was going to take Kit on a tour, but I wonder if you wouldn't mind going along with them."

Alf glared at Wilf – he couldn't help it – and was rewarded by a slight, evasive ducking of the manager's head. He felt the least Bannerman's might have done was warn him this was coming: hadn't he earned *that* much in his years of virtually running the place? Behind Wilf, Matt was smiling nervously into his pipe.

Alf, Matt, and Kit Ford went down the aisles. Alf was in a state of turmoil. A sense of betrayal kept rising, bitter in his mouth. It made it hard to speak calmly about the machines and the routines of the knitting room.

And Kit Ford didn't help. No matter what Alf told him, he chewed his gum and nodded and said, Yep, yep, yep so rapidly and continuously that he gave the impression that he already knew *everything* Alf could possibly tell him: it was all old hat. Put off balance, Alf forgot names he normally knew, and several times had to be helped out by Matt while Ford looked at them both in that sincere, slightly pained way that suggested none of this incompetence was a surprise in the least.

Finally, to give himself a break, Alf asked Ford about the new machines Intertex was buying.

"A lot faster than these old junkers," Kitt said, somehow managing to keep chewing and talking at once. Alf did not like to hear the machines of Number Six called "old junkers." He had worked on all of them and kept them going for years beyond their expected lifespan, often by improvising spare parts: he had a certain pride in them.

He listened as Ford described the new knitting machines. They looked a bit like a jet engine, Ford said, a curious description Alf could not quite picture. They were computerized. They would take fewer workers to run. "Fewer hands, fewer mistakes," Ford said with his reflexive grin.

"My, my," Matt Honnegger commented mildly, shaking his head.

Kit looked at Matt, and seemed startled to find his predecessor there, smiling weakly over his empty pipe.

"Nothin' 'gainst the old ways," he said. "Good in their time. But you don't keep up with the competition, you die." He looked meaningfully at Alf and Matt as he said, "you die," and there was something overdone and faintly comical about this – after all they were talking about knitting, not cancer or war. And yet at the same time Alf caught a glimpse of a no-holds-barred tenacity and, behind this, a positive delight in the extreme vision he had just expressed. Kit Ford was telling them, in his melodramatic way, that in the game of survival they were all playing, he knew the real conditions, and was willing to abide by them, as a man should.

Over the following days, Kit Ford moved up and down the aisles so quickly – his rubber-soled shoes squeaking on the hardwood – that the workers in Number Six knitting soon dubbed him "the Roadrunner." Despite his claim that he was looking forward to knowing them, he went on confusing "Alf" with "Art" and "Mary" with "Eileen," and he never stopped for even a few seconds to shoot the breeze, as Matt had done to a fault, or joined them on the fire escape for their breaks. Worst of all, he spread a spirit of resentment by letting them know somehow that they were not working hard enough. It wasn't that he accused them of sloth in so many words, it was the atmosphere of haste and disapproval that emanated from him: the gaze of those wounded eyes that seemed to be suffering their poor performance in outraged silence.

On the fire escape, they made jokes about him. "I don't think he ever goes to the bathroom," Dick Kenshole said one day; and quick-as-a-whip Boomer Tomlinson answered in his droll bass, "I guess that's why he's so full of shit."

They laughed ruefully, weighed by a sense that their jokes were ultimately futile, and that an old world, more friendly to them, was passing away. They did not know what was coming, but with the glum fatalism of those who must await change passively, many of them suspected they were not going to like the new order. The machines Wilf Thomas had said Intertex was bringing in worried them because they were sure some workers would probably be made redundant. In their minds, Kit Ford and these new machines were already inextricably bound – the exhausting haste he had brought to the mill seemed just a foretaste of an even faster regime to come. In some way, they were *already* living with the new machines, which even before they arrived promised a world in which workers were going to have to become creatures of another kind, creatures like Kit Ford, as fast and efficient as the machines they served.

Alf, too, disliked Ford and his ways, but tried to suppress his bitterness. After all, it wasn't Ford's fault he'd been overlooked for the job. He did his best to sympathize with the foreman, telling himself that the new man, for all his experience, was nervous in the job, and deserved a chance to settle in. When the complaints on the fire escape escalated, he decided to offer Ford some advice. One evening after the mill had emptied, he dropped by Kit's office. The young man was sitting behind Matt's desk (Alf still thought of it that way), which he kept completely clear save for an order spike holding a mess of impaled papers, a clipboard, and a single orange pencil, sharpened to a clean point. There was something forlorn about all this. Alf was suddenly aware that Kit Ford was young, younger in some ways than his actual age. Sitting there with his large fingers hooked over the edge of his desk, motionless but for that perpetually working jaw, he seemed like a student awaiting some as yet undisclosed after-school punishment.

Alf started off gently. The workers were feeling a bit edgy, he explained, sitting forward in his chair and gesturing with open hands. They sensed there were big changes coming and were nervous. It might help if he, Kit, made an effort to warm up to them a bit. If he talked to them casually from time to time, even if he only talked about the weather.

Kit Ford looked back at him without comment, and it occurred to Alf that for Kit Ford chatting idly about the weather might be impossible. There was something overwound in the fellow, as if he had never been taught – never had the freedom – to relax.

"So they sent you to tell me this –"

"No, no," Alf said, smiling amicably, his face heating. "It's my own idea. I just think if you made a few gestures, you'd have a happier gang out there."

Ford looked from Alf to the pencil on his desktop. He was chewing more slowly than usual, and Alf sensed he'd confronted the foreman with a problem he did not know how to meet.

"So they're not happy –"

"Well, nothing too serious. I'm just suggesting, you know, make an effort to get their names right. It's a little thing, but –"

"So they sent you in here to agitate –"

"I'm not agitating," Alf said, trying to make light of the idea. "No one sent me here. I'm just saying –"

"You were an agitator in '49, isn't that right?"

Taken aback, Alf could only stare at the other man. All vestiges of the boy had vanished. Ford was the ex-Marine now, hard, perfunctory. He seemed to be looking right through Alf to the chair he sat in.

"I wasn't an agitator," Alf said softly. A weariness was enveloping him, a sense he had started up a hill he could never reach the top of. "I went out on strike."

"An illegal strike –"

"Well, that's debatable."

"Thank you very much for your advice," Ford said sharply. "'Preciate it." It was clear the interview was over. The foreman pulled the clipboard towards him and made a show of studying it. For a few seconds Alf did not move. He watched Ford – that angular face knotting and unknotting in its perpetual flow of tensions – and he looked out the window behind the foreman's close-cropped head, where the evening sky had grown luminous – a mirror in which he could not find his own face.

In late April, there was a spell of unusually warm weather, and the workers on the sixth floor were able to take nearly every break outside. In the morning, before the sun reached the west wall of the mill, it was still cool enough for sweaters, and the hot Thermoses of coffee and tea they unscrewed and poured into plastic cups were deeply enjoyed. But in the afternoon, when the sun beat into the bricks of the wall behind them, and threw the striped shadows of the fire-escape railing over their knees, they doffed their sweaters and opened shirts and drank the warmth they had so long missed. These ten minutes were precious: a time unclaimed by not just the tall machines fallen silent in the room behind them but also by the duties they owed their families. These little islands of time contained as much undiluted freedom as most people there enjoyed in a day, and they used them well: they talked, or ate, or read, or smoked, or looked out through the railings of the fire escape through the deep cube of the millyard, where sharp geometries of light and shadow shifted back and forth all day. And when the buzzer finally sounded with a subtle but penetrating violence, there was always a double sense that the minutes that had just passed had been deeper and slower and more important than other minutes, and also, that they had fled with the swiftness of a glance.

In the days when he had helped Matt, Alf was so busy that he often skipped break. But after just a week on the job, Kit Ford made it clear he didn't need him, so he increasingly took up his old seat just outside the door, on an upturned wooden box topped with a scrap of foam rubber that had turned a rich, golden colour. He didn't join in the conversation of the others, sitting on their long, makeshift benches that stretched along the wall to his left, but he listened with a secret pleasure, drawn by an instinctive need. Not so long ago, he'd felt he was a man with a purpose, a man with important things to do, and he'd forgotten this: how good it was to just sit with these men and women, many of whom he'd known all his life. So he smoked and drank his coffee and – wondering if the others knew of his role in the breaking of the union and were cold-shouldering him as a result – gazed through the bars, across the millyard to the gap between buildings, fixing almost unconsciously on the place where all their eyes tended, the little ribbon of river-water, visible between the dyke and the cement wall of the opposite bank, gleaming and flowing there like a banner.

Often at these times he thought of Lucille with a longing that surprised him. She had started to appear in his dreams (he saw her, once, driving away in a red car, from which she had looked back at him with a curious, watchful indifference). He worried that he had used her, though he had never intended to. He felt badly about this, and the worst of it was his sense that he had overlooked something when he was with her. When he glimpsed her from the mill, passing in the street, she – her beauty – seemed to promise an experience he could not name, but which he had missed.

One day, a windy Thursday under scudding clouds that seemed about to catch on the high, soot-stained lip of Bannerman's stack, someone on the fire escape said, "I guess they found another cat." Alf, sitting on his box, looked up. He'd been aware that for several months someone in town had been killing cats. The plague of small corpses seemed to have petered out for a while, but now, apparently, the skinned body of a tom had been found hanging on a wire from the Shade Street rail overpass. Down the balcony, Mary Carr cried out in dismay – she kept cats herself, and didn't want to hear anything about it – but some of the others got into an animated discussion of the killer's possible motives. ("He's just some poor sicko trying to prove he's a big shot," Dick Kenshole said with angry revulsion, summing up the general attitude.) Alf listened as the conversation drifted into humorous speculation about who the killer might be. A few tossed out the names of the town's most important citizens. The knitters howled expansively, then fell silent, sensing they had gone too far.

It was then that Book Cummings, sitting about halfway down the row, turned his big, pimply face towards Alf and said, "I think Alf did it."

Alf was shocked: his entire body seemed to wake from its torpor. It was not just the stab of Book's accusation, which was obviously meant in fun; it was the sudden exploding of his isolation. He had begun to feel invisible, sitting there in silence day after day on his foam pad. Now he realized that several faces had leaned out to catch a glimpse of him.

Struggling to keep his composure, he blew out smoke and said, deadpan, meeting Book's eyes, "That's right, Book." Still holding Book's gaze, he let a beat go by before adding, "You're next, cool cat."

They roared at that, since the overweight, bookish Book was anything but cool; they were relieved Alf had taken the jibe so well. The only person who didn't laugh was Woody Marr. Sitting with his pugface lifted sourly, he was habitually ignored by the other knitters, who believed he had ratted on the people who had been laid off in the fall.

After the cat incident, Alf took a more active part in life on the fire escape, though he supposed he was never what anyone would call talkative. What surprised him most was that when he did speak, the others stopped talking to listen. He felt he must surely disappoint them, for he never thought that what he was saying was witty or important or interesting enough to warrant the staring, expectant faces ranged along the balcony.

One morning all talk on the fire escape was of the big news that had broken over the town the previous evening: Bannerman's was closing its hosiery division. For almost a hundred years John Bannerman's original building on West Street (the tall mill with its tiers of white-trimmed windows and handsome mansard roof and bell tower) had churned out hosiery renowned across the country – fancy dress socks, women's silk hose (the silk supplied by special trains racing with their bales from the West Coast), work socks, children's socks, sport socks – but now the whole enterprise would be shut down by August. Almost two hundred people would lose their jobs.

The earthquake might have struck another mill, on the other side of town, but the tremors reached right to the iron perch above the millyard, reminding the workers of their vulnerability. They could do everything that was asked of them, and do it well, but this would never be a guarantee that their jobs would not disappear from beneath them. Many of them had friends or family members working in the hosiery mill. For them, its closure was not a distant or abstract event but one that cast a chilly shadow of deprivation, and behind it they glimpsed the behemoth, Intertex. It was not lost on them that in almost a century, Bannerman's had never closed a mill in town and, that within a year of acquiring Bannerman's, Intertex was now shutting down a fixture that had seemed as permanent as the hills that faced it across the Atta.

"I heard the place was makin' money," Steve Johnson said, in a high, complaining voice. He was leaning out from his seat, as if beseeching the rest of them for an answer.

"How could it have been," Mary Carr said tartly to the railing in front of her. She was from Newfoundland, a stringy, scoop-faced woman with strong opinions. "They wouldn't close it if it was making a profit. That's what these guys are in it for."

"That's right," someone else said, and that seemed to settle the matter. For a few moments there was silence.

Looking at his own hands, which suddenly seemed strange, animal-like – Alf said, "Actually, they were making a profit."

He could sense the stir, the awakening power of attention, his words evoked, and looking to his left he saw the mild, anxious face of Steve Johnson staring back, where he leaned with his elbows on his knees. Other faces had turned his way too, blank and expectant, half-hidden behind other faces and bodies. In the yard below them, an iron-wheeled cart rumbled over the rough asphalt.

"How's that, Alf?" Mary said.

"Well, I guess there's profit, and then there's profit. They were making only about two per cent over there, and well, I guess Intertex felt they could do better with their money elsewhere." Grant George, the assistant manager of the hosiery mill, had told Alf this a couple of days before the closure had been made public. Alf had run into his old boyhood acquaintance in the post office, and Grant, looking harassed and sounding grim, had barely been able to contain his disgust at the whole business. "No flies on these boys," he'd said sarcastically of Intertex. "They'd sell their grandmothers if they could get their price."

Silence greeted Alf's news. Below, the cart of bobbins rumbled out of hearing and a pigeon floated from darkness into light, while a second bird disappeared simultaneously into shadow.

"They were making a *profit*?" Boomer Tomlinson said, incredulously. "How could that be?"

"He told ya," Mary said. "They're not makin' *enough* profit."

"But what about all those people who lose their jobs?"

"They're not in business to make jobs," Mary said. "If they could run the whole thing off a control panel, like Harry Lumley and his boilers there, they'd be rid of us in a flash."

"You got it there," someone said.

But Boomer, rubbing his hands and screwing up his face into a rumpled mask of disgruntlement that showed his gums, was not satisfied.

"Alf," he said, still peering down the row. Alf looked at him. "How much profit are they makin' here? In the sweater mill, like?"

All faces turned to him, intensely interested in his answer. Feeling his mouth go dry, Alf shook his head. "I don't know," he told them. "Enough, I guess." They remained fixed on him a few moments longer, sensing or hoping he had more to say, but he could only repeat his gesture of disavowal and stare through the railing into the millyard, unhappy at his failure to satisfy them, wary of the hunger he had glimpsed in their eyes.

The following day it rained, and they spent their breaks inside, in the noisy third-floor lunchroom with its bare, beige walls and unpainted wooden floor, where people from so many departments were mixed together that discussion of any sensitive issue was impossible in the general din. But the next day, Wednesday, was fine again, and the workers from the sixth floor returned gladly to the fire escape. No more mention was made of the closing of the hosiery mill or, for a few minutes, of anything else. It was as if Alf's answer two days earlier, and the intervening rain, had swept their minds with silence. But then Boomer Tomlinson and Eddie Ray began to talk about where they might take their holidays that summer. Boomer told a story about a bear that had lumbered into a campground where he and his wife were staying, near Wawa, and created such havoc he doubted he would ever get his wife camping again. While he and Stella were huddled in terror in their little tent, the bear had pried out a window of their Plymouth. "He just slipped his claws in and peeled the whole thing out like the lid off your Tupperware," Boomer said. And that set others off with *their* bear stories, the best of which was Mary Carr's tale of how, as a girl, she had been trapped in her grandmother's outhouse by a bear that sat down outside the front door. "That door was so flimsy," Mary said, "a skunk could have pushed it over," and there was something so absurd in the notion of a skunk pushing open an outhouse door that they all laughed. "He looked like he was just waitin' for his turn in the loo," Mary said. "I was so scared I was ready to jump in the hole." In the end, though, her grandmother had saved her. "She come yellin' out of the house with her broom. Drove him right off. Really she did, cross my heart. She was a bear herself, my grannie. There wasn't no one in the whole of Wrong Harbour who wasn't scared of her. She was as big as an outhouse herself."

The nasal bleating of the buzzer sounded oddly distant and irrelevant, like a parental command the children do not yet take seriously. Other, sterner warnings might come later, but for now, there seemed no harm in sitting on in the sun. Someone started another yarn, and Alf, flicking the butt of his cigarette over the rail, thought suddenly of a bear story Pete had once told. There had been a campfire, and a bear lurking at the edge of the light. He couldn't remember the rest, but the image of Pete's knowing-unknowing face with its eyebrows raised in innocent surprise plunged a sickle of grief though him. A little cry broke from him, like the small, muffled cries people give in their sleep. His neighbour, Eddie Ray, turned to him and at that moment a high, tense, familiar voice scolded above Alf's head, "People, people, this isn't the way."

Along the balcony, the talk and laughter broke off. His face heating, Alf glanced covertly to his right and saw Kit Ford's blue-jeaned leg and black running shoe swinging inches from his shoulder. The foreman was leaning from the open door, like a conductor from a train. Some of the knitters stared up at him, with blank faces. Some glanced once and turned away to look impassively into space. There was a sense in the air of obstinate denial. They were used to obeying the buzzer, to obeying every order that came from above, but today, in the light and intoxication of their laughter, they seemed to have taken a communal decision to ignore the foreman.

Ford stepped down to stand on the board that served as a step. He clapped his hands. He might have been trying to raise a flock of geese. "Come on, people! Let's go!"

Still they sat on, in silence. Alf could feel the tension, feel it in the back of his neck, as if at any minute the man standing above him might strike him. He could hear Ford breathing, in a labour of controlled fury. Bending his head and shoulders forward, Alf slowly rose. As he climbed into the mill, he ignored the murderous gaze of the foreman, who stood by the door with crossed arms. From behind Alf came the sounds of cups being screwed on Thermoses, of lunch boxes being shut, of bodies shifting, as taking their time, the workers prepared to follow him in.

41

"SO WHAT WAS THAT?"

Alf stood before Kit Ford's desk. On its surface lay a scrap of paper, on which a twist of gum had been deposited like a pink grub. Ford's eyes, bright with sarcasm and pent rage, had locked on Alf's.

"What was what?"

"That!"

Ford jabbed two fingers towards the door.

"Shut the door," the foreman ordered.

Alf hesitated for a moment, then turned and slowly closed the door. The hum of the knitting machines subsided a little.

He turned back to the foreman.

"Sittin' there five minutes after the buzzer went –"

"I don't know," Alf said. "We weren't paying attention –"

"The damn thing is *deafenin'*!"

They had heard the buzzer – at least Alf had – but it had seemed to sound distantly, from another life. He was a bit mystified by what had happened. But he would not be spoken to like this, as if he was fourteen. His defiance had taken the form of an exaggerated calm.

He stood with his hands in the pockets of his factory greens, looking steadily at the foreman, motionless.

"It's a beautiful day," he said, with a shrug. "We forgot."

"*Forgot!*" Ford's eyes grew larger, filled with outraged sarcastic glee, as if he'd just caught Alf in a whopper. "Even after I told you to get in you still sat there."

"Yes, I guess we did."

"And why *was* that?"

Alf let a sigh escape him and looked down at Ford's desk, at the curl of pink gum. He agreed with Ford that things had gone off track. But to pursue it this way – there was something so wrong-headed about it.

"I'm asking you!" Ford demanded.

"I don't know," Alf said. "You took us by surprise."

"You bet I did." The foreman's gaze roved in angry frustration, from the desk to Alf's belt, from the belt to his chest. His jaw worked, as if in need of gum.

"I've never seen it happen before," Alf offered. He doubted Ford would get his hint that it hadn't *needed* to happen before, but he had to try. "I doubt very much it'll happen again."

"I guess you can see to that, can't you?"

Alf met Ford's hard gaze, suddenly wary.

"You're the ringleader."

Alf felt himself colour. "There was no ringleader."

"What was it then, spontaneous rebellion of the working class? C'mon, man, I got eyes. They didn't move out of there till you moved!"

"That's crazy," Alf managed. But he felt guilty, as if the foreman was speaking the truth. "It could have been anybody."

"Be that as it may," Ford said, glancing at a clipboard, "I'm holdin' you responsible. They do it again, I know who to look for."

The foreman picked up the clipboard and made a show of looking at it. Was the interview over? Alf went on standing, his calm in tatters. Slowly, he took his hands from his pockets: they felt weighted, as if all the blood in his body had poured into his fists.

At ten the next morning, the workers paraded onto the fire escape as usual. Near the end of the break, when everyone had fallen silent and a cool breeze from across the yard was lifting a page of Book Cummings's paperback, Steve Johnson glanced at his watch and spoke the thought that was on every mind. "So I wonder if the Roadrunner'll be out today." Someone chortled darkly, and Alf felt the backs of his arms tingle. I should go in, he thought, before the bastard comes out, but he sat on, ignoring his own better wisdom. Kit Ford had taken up residence in his thoughts like a conqueror from a foreign country. He couldn't stop thinking of their meeting, thinking of what he *might* have said, thinking of the injustice of the whole damn business. He blew smoke, and watched it pass, a shape-shifting genie, through the railings over the sunlit yard.

Just as the buzzer went, a motion to his right made him turn his head. Ford had stepped swiftly from the mill and positioned himself at the end of the fire escape. The foreman stood facing his workers, his fingertips wedged in the pockets of his jeans.

Silence ran along the balcony. No one moved. Then Boomer

Tomlinson leaned forward as if to bang his head on the rails, and let out a low groan.

"You have a problem, Mr. Tomlinson?" Ford said.

"Just a headache," Boomer said, without looking at him.

One or two knitters rumbled their amusement – Ford was the obvious source of Boomer's "headache" – and still they kept their seats, not so much, as on the previous day, out of defiance but because they were confused and, in a sense, disciplined into immobility by the foreman's presence.

Alf sighed, flicked away his butt, and prepared to get up. He was dreading the result, figuring the rest would follow suit; then Ford would have more "proof" that he was their ringleader. But he figured he was doomed as well, if he went on sitting, especially if the others also kept their places. He put his hands on his knees and leaned forward, but before he could rise, Mary Carr leapt up. "So let the fun begin," she cried out, with black irony. They stirred as one then, and shuffled into the mill after Mary. Alf was one of the first to pass Ford; he pointedly ignored the foreman, who stood with his arms crossed, watching them all with thin disapproval, as if they had only barely passed muster.

By the time the afternoon break arrived, most of the workers were anxiously anticipating Ford's reappearance. They had talked enough about his behaviour in the meantime to work up a good head of opposition: who knew what would happen if he tried his funny business again? But Ford was wiser than Alf dared hope. The foreman didn't reappear at the end of the break, even though a few of the workers waited a half-minute extra for him. In fact, he didn't reappear again on any day, and the incident, with its two chapters, passed into the general fund of factory lore, a story to be retold over beer, and embellished with witty comebacks that hadn't actually been spoken, celebrations of courageous determination "to not let him get away with it" that had been tentative at best.

The workers' actual behaviour on the fire escape told a different tale. Alf noticed that now, as the end of a break approached, the workers grew restless. They furtively consulted their watches, and put away their lunches and books a little earlier than before. And though they still sat on after the buzzer, this traditional period of defiance had grown shorter – to the point where it hardly existed at all.

Several weeks after the fire-escape incident, Ford again called Alf into his office. On his desk lay a strip of patterned sweater cloth, loosely folded. Alf looked at the deep-blue cloth warily: he had made it himself.

"Alf," Ford began. The foreman was putting on his most sincere, concerned face. "I'm worried you're doin' too much there – workin' the Richardsons and fixin' too. It's a lot for any man."

Alf sensed where this was heading. Pushing his hand over hair, he said, "Well to tell the truth, since you've come I've had a lot less to do. As far as I can see, you're doing about three times as much work as Matt ever did. I had to spend a lot of my time helping him out."

"'Preciate that," Ford said, with a twitch of a gaunt cheek. "But 'fraid we got a problem here." He deftly flipped open the top fold of cloth. It was a rich, subtle blending of dark-blue yarns, with just a touch of red running through it. Alf had made it on one of the Richardsons, the only machines on the floor sophisticated enough to turn out such a pattern. "You see what I'm talkin' about?"

"Not sure I do." But his face was heating. He watched the foreman's blunt fingers shove the cloth forward.

"You used the wrong red."

Alf picked up the soft length of cloth. The red surfacing in random streaks, glimpses of fire.

"It's supposed to be Persian red. You used barn red – too bright."

Carrying the cloth past Ford's desk to the tall, unshaded window behind it, Alf held the cloth up and saw that Ford was right.

Ford's high voice jabbed at his back. "There's fifty yards of it spoiled, Alf."

Alf looked out the window and saw the gravelled roof of the dye-house: the pulsing necks and breasts of the pigeons gathered there. An irony he did not fully grasp tugged deep in him, the shape of an obscure joke.

He returned to his place – how quickly and completely it had become his – in front of Ford's desk, tossing down the cloth with a gentleness that belied the tension setting in his face and chest. It seemed pointless to say sorry, to say anything. In nearly twenty years of knitting he had never made a mistake of this order, a mistake that would cost the company dearly.

He could not understand it.

"What I've decided to do," Ford said, frowning with great seriousness at his desktop, "is take you off the Richardsons. If you're workin' on some of the easier machines, then you'll be able to con-centrate better, on knitting and fixing both."

The foreman looked at him. Behind his look of concern, triumph glinted.

Alf said nothing. He felt oddly neutral, almost untouched by Ford's announcement.

"I want you to switch with Marr," Ford told him. "He knows how to run the Richardsons – ain't that right?"

Alf grinned bleakly.

"What's so funny?"

"Nothing," Alf said. Beyond the window, pigeons were ascend-ing, a storm of grey wings.

He left the office and walked by the motionless Richardsons, refusing to look at them, but sensing their tall mass as if they were watching him pass their ranks like a disgraced soldier.

Woody Marr's stand was at the back of the room: four old underwear machines now used to make cloth for T-shirts. Alf reached them just as Woody emerged into the aisle, a bobbin of white cotton in one hand. The knitter barely glanced at Alf as he went about his business. Since the previous fall, they had done their best to avoid each other.

"Now?" he barked, incredulous, as Alf told him what Ford wanted.

"Seems so."

Woody shot him a look of pure malevolence. Alf felt jolted awake, as their mutual history rose into fleeting acknowledgment. He turned away without expression, pretending to interest himself in the state of Woody's machines.

It is one thing to accept your fate; it is another to go on accepting it, as if there was no argument to be made for an alternative. Within half an hour Alf was scouring his brain to understand how he could have mistaken barn red for Persian red. They were as unalike as red wine and a Coca-Cola sign. Had he been operating in *that* much of a fog? After a few minutes he marched off to the yarn room, where he flipped a switch and sent a pale, shuddering fluorescence over the rows of deep wooden bins, scarred by generations of use. The bins of barn red and Persian red stood side by side, heaped nearly to overflowing with the huge, head-sized bobbins. He looked from one bin to the other, in a state of self-lacerating wonder. A child could tell the colours apart. He couldn't shake the sense that he'd been tricked – most likely, by himself.

But still his sense of injustice – that something had been done *to* him – went on raising its complaint. Moving to one of the long windows set in the thick brick wall he looked down across Willard to the old house that held General Office. Bob Prince's dark-blue Fleetwood was parked in its usual place, under the willow whose massive crown showed a faint blush of green. At the sight of the wide, polished car with its low fins, a current of anger surged through him, and for another few seconds he raged silently.

After the Richardsons, running Woody's old machines was a breeze. Alf had more time on his hands than ever before: time to be bored and look at his hands, time to hope for a breakdown somewhere so he could fix it (though he hated meeting the looks and, worse, the condolences of the other workers, who felt his demotion was unfair), time to look bitterly up the aisle where Woody hurried around the Richardsons, time to chat with Coreen Appleton.

She ran the stand across the aisle, a young woman in her twenties with two young kids at home, pretty, with an open face and brown, eager eyes that smiled at him with no hint of flirtatiousness or guile. She usually wore a plaid shirt tucked into jeans, which fit her in a way Alf found quite pleasant to look at, a way that emphasized the fullness of her pear-bottom, the sudden narrowness of her high waist, cinched with a white plastic belt on which a red heart design had been printed. She sang sometimes as she worked, in a childish soprano, old Teresa Brewer songs from the Fifties. She gave his days a lighter touch, and though he enjoyed her fresh looks, he wasn't drawn to her physically. She was so bright and cheery there seemed to be no mystery in her, nothing hidden that called to his own hiddenness – not the way Lucille had called and still called, sometimes. He saw Lucille in vivid, isolated fragments. Bending to roll up some cloth, he'd flash on her eyes, searching his without expression, or on the black cloud of her pubic hair as she slid down her jeans.

One morning he was tending his machines when he heard Kit Ford's high-pitched voice across the aisle. The foreman and Coreen stood shoulder to shoulder with their backs to Alf, talking. Alf watched as the foreman's square hand rose across Coreen's blouse and lit for a second on her far shoulder. Then the hand dropped, brushing the hollow of her back and lighting, palm open, fingers spread, on the fullness of her bottom, squeezing as Coreen tried to twist away. In three strides, Alf was across the aisle. He was acting so quickly, so impulsively – powered by a rage against Ford that had never really gone away – that his action seemed almost rehearsed, he accomplished it with such efficiency. Careful not to touch Coreen herself, he took the foreman's wrist and flung away his arm, flung it like something rotten he scarcely wanted to touch himself.

"Hey!" Ford said, turning. In those wide eyes, where innocence and outrage usually held sway, Alf saw a stab of fear, a hint of the boy again. But it was gone in a second, buried under a smirk of patronizing satisfaction, as he recognized Alf.

"Keep your hands off her," Alf said in a dry voice. The words seemed unreal to him, as if he'd taken up a role in a play.

"Back to work, fella –"

"Please," Coreen said, pleading with both of them. "Alf, there's no need –" But neither man was aware of her now.

Alf had stationed himself inside Ford's space, and loomed there, a little taller than the other man. Ford pushed at his chest.

"Go back to your squaw," he said.

It was as if the foreman had touched a red-hot brand to Alf's face. Alf pushed him and felt the plated muscle of Ford's chest, saw him briefly stagger. Then Ford advanced with a gloating smile, and in a matter of a second or two, Alf had absorbed two quick punches to the head. Instantly drunk, he was aware only of Coreen crying out, and of Ford stepping closer to him, with his fists up on either side of his chest, like a boxer in an old photograph. Alf let his head drop. His own punch came almost lazily, as if out of a stupor, taking Ford unawares on the side of his mouth, sending him backwards with a surprised grunt. His head roaring, Alf made a terrific effort to crawl up the slope of his own fatigue, and in a moment he had closed with the foreman. They punched with staccato fierceness, bent on maximum damage, blundering between the tall machines that went on churning out cloth with a stately imperturbability, as if nothing else could ever matter.

42

TURNING OFF THE ENGINE, Alf examined his face in the rear-view of the Biscayne: the slitted right eye, embedded in swollen flesh like a turtle's; the scraped, purpling cheek; the bloodstain, like a little brown goatee set crookedly under his cut lip.

His untouched eye looked back, expressionless.

As he let himself into the kitchen, he heard someone drop the lid of the piano bench in the dining room.

"Hello?" Margaret.

They listened to each other's silence.

"Just me," he said, stooping stiffly to untie his shoes. As she entered the kitchen, he straightened, showing his face.

Her cry gratified him. In an odd way, he was proud of his damaged face. There was something honest about a fight, and besides, he had not been beaten, no, he had not been beaten, though he had not won, either. At the moment this seemed important.

She came over to him and stopped, her hands half-raised, not daring to touch him. For a moment he felt as if he had done something extraordinary: crossed a desert no one had ever crossed, or come back from the dead. He met her gaze frankly, with a sharp, threatening pride. He had not felt so alive for weeks.

"I was in a fight," he said. He was daring her to counter him – to breathe one word of criticism. This was what she had married, this. He would not hide it. He would not feel ashamed.

She looked down at his ruined shirt.

"Gave as good as I got," he said tersely. "Maybe better –" He was fudging a little. After a couple of minutes, the knitters had separated him and Ford, and just in time: the younger man's strength was beginning to tell.

"Who did you –"

"The foreman," he said.

"Matt?"

He grunted sardonically. "A new guy." And when she furrowed her brow: "I didn't get the job, Margaret. They gave it to somebody else."

She stared at him in confusion. He had told her nothing about Kit Ford, and now it irked him that he had to explain. It seemed as if *she* had brought it up, to torture him.

"Somebody –"

"*I didn't get the job! Is it so difficult?*"

He glared at her, as if to punish her for her very existence. She looked down with reddening face. He crossed to the sink, reaching into the cupboard for a glass. Water ran from the tap in a silver rope, twisting and splashing as he stared blindly, struggling to subdue his reawakening fury. He kept seeing Ford's pale, grinning face, feeling, again, the ridge of the foreman's cheekbone as it met his fist. His hand trembled with the effort not to crush the glass. Finally he drank, and the cold water travelling across his parched mouth and plunging down his throat gave him his first relief.

"I've been fired," he said quietly.

"Oh Alf," she said. "What happened? Who fired –"

"Ford!" he cried. Did he have to explain *everything*? "The foreman. The guy I fought."

She said nothing more. He looked around and saw that she was staring into the space between them, as if seeing other realities entirely. Her reverie – how could she go away at this critical moment – enraged him further.

"Well?" he demanded, almost shouting.

"Alf, I'm sorry!" There were tears in her eyes. But he did not want tears, or the threat of tears, and he turned away, leaning on the counter with both arms. She crossed the space between them and tentatively touched his upper arm. "Tell me what happened."

"The bastard's ruined the place," he said. "He's alienated everybody."

"The new foreman," she said.

"Yes goddammit, the new foreman!" he yelled to the back of the sink. Spittle swung from his mouth in a bloody thread. He had only begun to understand his defeat, and was wild at his impotence.

Afterwards, his wounds treated with iodine and bandages, he stood at the bedroom window and watched Penny coming along the road, on her way home for lunch. She was wearing her winter coat, and was carrying pussy willows, like a sheaf of knobbed whips. Her skinny legs in their red tights skipped up the curb. Suddenly she stopped and looked up at the house, wary.

He shrank back from the window.

Moments later he was hovering at the top of the stairs, listening as she entered the kitchen. First came her chiming voice, innocent and cheerful. Then Margaret's lower murmur. "Just tell them I've had an accident with a knitting machine," he'd instructed his wife. He was determined to stop the damage from spreading. He would keep everyone safe, yes, everyone would be all right if they just believed what he told them. "Say I look banged up, but I'm all right. Don't mention about the job. We'll tell them later. It'll be all right."

As he came down the hall, Penny ran to meet him and, as if she were suddenly younger and smaller, launched herself with a cry into his arms. He carried her awkwardly to the kitchen, her face buried in his neck, though as they passed into the brighter room, she reared back to have a better look. "Oh Daddy!"

His face felt stiff, false.

Jamie arrived breathless, bursting with pride. "I ran all the way from the –" Stopping, he saw his father, and his sister crying in his father's arms. Turning from the sink with the pussy willows in a vase, Margaret tried to explain. But Jamie's face had gone ashen. "Are you going away?" he said to Alf, almost whispering. His eyes sprouted fat tears. "Is he going away!" he cried to Margaret as she bent to him.

"No, no," Margaret said, trying to inject a lighter note. "How many times do I have to tell you, silly goose, he isn't going anywhere."

Soon they were all eating in relative calm at the kitchen table – all but Joe, who phoned to say he was staying at school for a floor-hockey game. When the phone rang a second time, the sound startled everyone, but especially Penny and Jamie, who looked up as if the knitting machine that had hurt their father were about to come lumbering into the room. It was Boomer Tomlinson. The whole of

Number Six was in an uproar, he said. "They're on the verge of sit-down or somethin'."

"Sit-down," Alf said sharply, not quite understanding. At the table Jamie froze: wasn't he already sitting?

"We're gonna get you your job back, eh? I'm gonna speak to Wilf Thomas."

Alf returned to the table in a state of astonishment. In his mind, he and Kit Ford had been alone in their battle, and the battle was over. But now, the workers were going to risk their necks for him?

The phone rang again: Coreen Appleton, weeping and scarcely understandable. He'd been so good, sticking up for her like that, and now – it was so unfair! She, too, said she was phoning Wilf Thomas, the sweater-mill manager.

Everyone looked at him as he came back to the table.

"Just asking how I am," he said, scarcely daring to look back. He picked up his spoon and contemplated his mound of ice cream. He wasn't sure if all this was good news or not. There was something almost disappointing about the idea of getting his job back. In a way, he liked the extreme place he'd got himself into. There was something honest about it, about his fight with Ford, as if he'd come back to ground after years of floating about. And there was a sense of freedom. He didn't have to go to the mill tomorrow.

Again the phone rang.

"Aren't *we* popular," Margaret said, getting up. The children watched her make the trek to the shrilling phone. She spoke briefly and hung up. "Wrong number," she announced. In his chair, Jamie pulled a face and began to laugh – hah, hah, hah – with grating, theatrical harshness.

"That's enough," Alf told him sharply. Jamie stuck out his jaw and glared at the butter dish.

Later that afternoon Alf was alone at the kitchen table, nursing a cup of cold tea and leafing without much heart through the help-wanted pages of the *Johnsonville Gleaner* when the phone rang again. It was Wilf Thomas. He came straight to the point.

"Alf, I've heard what happened. Listen, if you can guarantee that kind of thing won't happen again, I can offer you your job back."

Alf bridled at the implication (as he saw it) that he was at fault.

"And Kit Ford, what does he have to guarantee –"

"Alf, he is the foreman here. I'm going over his head to make you this offer –"

It came out of him without warning, on a tide of sudden defiance and clarity: "I won't come back unless you get rid of Ford. He's destroying that place –"

"Alf, be reasonable –"

He wasn't reasonable. After he'd hung up, he turned and stared at the kitchen table, stunned at what he'd just done. And yet he knew he'd spoken the truth. He couldn't, wouldn't, work for Ford again, any more than he could drink the man's spit. But he was shocked all the same, to realize he'd cast his life adrift. In the blue vase, the paws of the pussy willows were furred with sun.

Over the next few weeks, he made the rounds familiar to the unemployed. He filled out forms and waited in company waiting rooms, where stacks of ancient magazines spilled onto rugs the colour of mud, where photos of company officers and sports teams stared from the walls with the confident serenity of those who know they have a place. Once, on a loading dock he was interviewed by a foreman twenty years younger than himself, a stocky, harassed-looking fellow who scarcely glanced up from his clipboard and spoke to him in a coarse, offhand way Alf found so insulting he refused to move when the man dismissed him. A moment later the foreman went inside and Alf heard him say to someone, "If that asshole out there doesn't leave, call the cops."

He had become *that asshole out there*. It was how he sometimes felt. It was his face, maybe, his ruffian's face still blotched with yellow and purple bruises that put people off. Or perhaps (as he sometimes suspected) it was Kit Ford, reaching out to block his chances. Or perhaps it was his lack of real interest. Somehow his focus was still on Bannerman's, as if he were only waiting to come out for a second round and fight again under the tall machines. There were times when to be looking for work anywhere else seemed an abandonment of his principles. Of his *rights*.

It didn't take long before he was sick of the whole business – sick, too, of knocking around at home on those days he didn't look for work. Margaret seemed increasingly impatient, snapping at him for trivialities. He could hardly blame her. They were having to make do on his unemployment cheque, less than half of what he'd made before. They were buying the cheapest grade of stewing beef, bread from the day-old bin. He tried to be helpful by doing long-postponed jobs around the house, but increasingly he felt underfoot. One warm grey day in early May, he stuffed a peanut-butter sandwich and an orange into the pockets of his windbreaker and, taking Red with him, crossed the footbridge to the park, heading for the woods and river-flats northwest of town. The big dog kept stopping to lift his leg against various trees and pieces of playground equipment. Alf chose the path along the top of the dyke, aware as he walked of Pete's bungalow perched in the wooded hillside above the park. Its closed garage door (hiding the Saratoga, which May had insisted on keeping) and curtained windows seemed to be watching him. He glanced at the house, and struggled not to glance at it again. But he couldn't help it. He looked across the park to the slope of yellow lawn cut by the gravel drive that led to the garage. It was almost as if Pete himself were hiding up there, watching him. Yes, Pete seemed very close: he was in his house, or behind the next tree, or waiting for Alf on the wet path meandering above the hurrying river. And he was smiling, in revenge perhaps, now that Alf knew what losing his job felt like, or in simple merriment, preparing one of his stories. But it was all crap, wasn't it? Alf was alone, more alone than he'd ever been in his life. "You stupid bugger," he said to the house. His face had turned feverish. "You should have fought harder."

He reached the end of the park and entered a grove of cedars, following the flinty main trail that kept closest to the Atta. Ahead, Bannerman's Number One dam made its hushing sound as the river thinned across its wide apron. He was directly across from the hosiery mill. With its mansard roof, the tall building had a graceful presence above the dark river, and for a few moments he stopped to look at it. Several windows had been propped open, and he could see people working inside – people who had jobs now, but who in a few months, he remembered, would be unemployed, when Intertex shut the mill. Soon you'll be footloose and fancy-free, he thought bitterly, just like Pete and me.

Red had reappeared beside him. He sat down and his ears pricked as he watched something across the river. Following his gaze, Alf saw a heron, standing motionless in the shallows. Very slowly, the tall, grey bird lifted one leg and planted it forward. Then its entire body flashed out on the horizontal and crashed in a belly flop among the stones. But it had caught a little fish, a wriggling flash of silver across its rapier beak. Alf watched, transfixed. He'd never seen a heron fall before, never imagined one *could* fall. Standing upright again, the bird put back its long throat and, with a couple of tosses, the fish was gone.

Beside him, his tongue hanging out, Red seemed to be laughing.

He went on, a little more enlivened, past the dam and into the woods that bordered the millpond. The dog trotted ahead of him now, his curled tail bobbing above the trail. Occasionally he paused to look around at Alf. The trail had been hardened by generations of use, and nothing would grow on it, though in the empty woods to his left and right the first green flames were licking among the tree trunks. He caught the chirpings and wheedlings of invisible warblers and, from a distance, the tongueless cry of a crow forever saying what could not be understood. He knew exactly the grove of pines it was probably sheltering in, crows had sheltered there when he was a boy.

By two that afternoon he and Red had walked to Devil's Cave by the high woods trail. Alf had always loved the place where the deepening Atta flooded the basin below the cave. As he stood looking at the river, Red disappeared. For a moment, Alf felt a stab of panic, as if he'd been abandoned by some loyal guide, though he knew the dog would eventually turn up at the house. He returned across the river-flats dotted with wild fruit trees just starting into blossom. In the woods beyond he found the white, shy stars of trilliums, motionless among their leaves. The woods were still and warm. The sand-coloured duff, soon to be smothered with new green, crackled under his feet as he left the trail.

He sat in the empty woods, with his back to a large beech, listening to the birds. There was one song in particular – he had never known what bird made it, though he had heard it all his life – that had a curious spiral quality, as though the notes came curling down a long pipe. The song was fascinating, too strange to be called simply pretty, and somehow it gave a greater depth to the woods. But at the same time it left him feeling far away from everything. There was a melancholy in the close air now, a threat of rain. His limbs seemed weighted. He felt he never wanted to move again: to remain under the tree as the woods sank into dusk.

He might have been sitting there for an hour when he heard a new sound, far to his left. At first he thought it was an owl, hooting in its sleep. Or a duck or a goose, blundering inland from the river. It faded, then came on again, growing stronger with each minute. Then he glimpsed a black coat moving among the tree trunks. A man was walking along the trail, weeping. Weeping openly and unselfconsciously, as though it were the most natural thing in the world to be shuddering and sobbing and howling as he plodded through the trees. Alf froze against the beech in a kind of horror. He didn't want to be seen, didn't want to interrupt or embarrass the man, and though the man's way lay not sixty feet in front of him, Alf guessed his best chance of remaining invisible was to stay where he was.

And so the man passed him, on the slightly elevated trail, appearing and disappearing among the trunks of the beeches and maples. Alf did not recognize him, though he seemed familiar. He was in his sixties or seventies – wiry and stooped, with a deeply tanned face and a shock of white, unruly hair that for a moment put Alf in mind of his own father – except that this man's hair was patched with black, as if he had been painting a ceiling black (this thought actually occurred to Alf) and spilled some. He was wearing a bright-red tie that stood out sharply, like a long wound that had opened inside his coat. Just as he came opposite Alf, he stopped. Afraid he'd be discovered, Alf lowered his eyes, and at that moment the man blew his nose with a terrific honk, followed by several minor honkings and snifflings. Then he continued on his way, weeping.

Alf listened to the sound growing distant in the trees. All the birds had fallen silent, as if listening too. A light rain pattered on the duff, among the great trunks. Again came the sound of the man honking. Then the woods were silent.

43

"I'M NOT SAYING IT'S BAD," Mann said with a sigh. "It's just not up to your usual standards."

Joe was glad the lights had not been turned on in the deserted classroom. His face, his traitor face, was heating. He and the teacher were sitting side by side, in two student desks. Before Joe lay the twenty foolscap pages of his essay, "Hobos and Handouts, A Study of Charity in the Great Depression." Mann had filled its margins with blocks of criticism, in his tiny, sawtoothed script. He'd given Joe a B, the worst mark he'd ever had for a history project.

"Sorry," Joe managed, not looking at the teacher.

Mann waved his hand.

"Don't apologize. It's nothing personal. It's just something, well – when you're writing papers in university, you'll have to use better sources than just your required reading. You didn't use any of the books I recommended. Couldn't you find them?"

"No," he lied, feeling his embarrassment increase.

"I asked Miss Keynes to put a number of books aside."

"I guess I didn't look hard enough."

Beyond Mann's severely angled face, through the window, the narrow thicket of a Lombardy poplar burned orange. In the hall outside the classroom, the janitor's broom hissed.

"What happened? Didn't you leave yourself enough time? It felt hurried."

"I guess it was."

Mann waited. He gazed at Joe with unreadable calm. The teacher had said this matter wasn't personal, yet Joe knew he was disappointed. And now his silence, a silence Joe felt Mann was perfectly comfortable with, had filled the room. In the corridor, the janitor's wide broom hissed by again. A locker slammed. But here, the silence waited. Joe felt he owed this silence something: another apology, maybe, or some kind of explanation. He frowned, and pushed his essay around a little. As Mann had guessed, he'd written his whole essay the night before. He hadn't thought it was so bad at the time. In fact, he'd congratulated himself on how smoothly and quickly it had gone. He'd made some clever points, he thought. But Mann had told him that "Hobos and Handouts" (how proud he'd been of that title, and Mann hadn't even mentioned it!) contained far too few useful facts. As a result, he'd had to depend on speculative arguments that chased their own tails.

And the thing was, he'd *known* this at the time. In his rush to finish the paper, and even in the midst of his self-congratulation, he'd had an uneasy perception, he now recalled, that "Hobos and Handouts" was a bit of a con job. But he'd crashed on, drunk on his own forced optimism, ignoring the knowledge standing just outside his vision. He knew the truth was there, all he needed to do was turn his head and look at it. But he wouldn't turn: he had fallen into the habit of living dishonestly.

He was still with Liz McVey. In spite of having promised himself, scores of times, that he would break up with her, he had drifted on as her "steady." "Joe and Liz" had become one of the ongoing features of the school's social life. They were coupled in the same breath by their friends in the North End gang. Even the teachers had grown used to seeing them come down the halls together, Liz with her head back, and Joe at her elbow, playing his role, but so much of the time secretly critical of her. He couldn't stand the way she called him "darling" in her fake accent, or looked into people's eyes as if they were more important to her than anything. She pretended an interest in history, or in poetry, but her opinions always sounded cobbled together, he thought, as if she had lifted them from a bin of approved opinions. She only grew truly impassioned when she was talking about herself.

So why was he still with her? Was it sex? There *was* something in her slim, round-shouldered body, and yes, in the searching of her babyish lips that he couldn't get enough of. Sex with Liz always felt slightly off-colour and somehow desperate and illicit. But it was never satisfying. It only *promised* to be satisfying, endlessly. Whenever they finished one of their trysts, it seemed to him that the world had drained of meaning. He barely had the energy to put on his clothes – and at the same time, he couldn't leave her fast enough. It was then that he felt most like telling her they were through: but he could never summon the nerve. It would have been unconscionably cruel, he thought, to make love to her and then announce he was going for good. So he postponed the moment for another time – and when the time came, his desire to make love to her superseded his desire to leave. And so he went in circles, like a goldfish in a bowl. He hated himself, for his weakness, for his inability to spare her from himself.

So he went on being cheerful and helpful, to all appearances a contented young man. People remarked on his thoughtfulness to Liz

McVey. What other boyfriend touched his girl's hair so thoughtfully as they went down the hall together, or reached up to pick a bit of lint from her sweater. He had the reputation, even among the teachers (though he wasn't sure about Mann), of being a real gentleman.

He went on enjoying the privileges Liz's company brought: driving the Lincoln, lounging about her fine house, being one of the "in" crowd, the North End gang. There were solaces, after all, for being with Liz McVey, and not the least of them was seeing a great deal of Anna. He and Liz went out frequently on double dates with Anna and Brad. They travelled in the Linc, or in Brad's Oldsmobile, to movies in Johnsonville, or to concerts in Hamilton or Kitchener. Every hour of those outings was sacred to him, because he was close to Anna. He felt they had entered an understanding. They were closer to each other, friends and perhaps more than friends, with a secret communication that cut below their loyalties to their respective partners. When they were out with Brad and Liz, he felt his actual pairing was with Anna. And perhaps she shared this view. "Oh, Joe and I are leaving," she'd said once, in disgust at something Brad had said and Liz had seconded. And she'd put her arm through Joe's and drawn him off a few steps, laughing, while Joe's heart pounded. It was as if she was letting him know that she was waiving her old requirement that he keep a certain distance. Often he felt on the verge of asking her where he stood. But he was afraid of another rebuff.

His dishonesty with Liz had infected him. He could sense it, just below the surface of his life. He had caught himself adopting some of the same airs he disliked in her: calling her "darling," and referring in bored, familiar terms to "the Linc" or to "J-ville," her family's name for Johnsonville. Increasingly he lacked patience, and rushed from one thing to another without finishing anything, almost angrily. He had developed a mania for speed. On the nights when he *should* have been working on "Hobos and Handouts," he was driving the Lincoln down the highway, pushing the needle of the speedometer into the nineties, while Liz nuzzled beside him, saying languidly, "Be careful, Joe. You'll kill us both," and stroking his thigh as if she were half-attracted to the idea.

And now he saw the reflection of his entrapment in Mann's gaze. Yes, the teacher knew. He had caught Mann watching him and Liz intently – disapprovingly – in the hall. And he was ashamed before his gaze, as he was ashamed before his own weakness. Now the teacher seemed to be waiting for him to confess all.

Mann broke the tension by looking away. "The important thing now is getting ready for the finals," he said, frowning. "You're going to have to prepare a lot more material than what's covered in your history text. They'll be looking for some kind of depth. I was thinking, if you wanted to brush up on the Depression, or any other topic – the two wars maybe – I've got some books I could lend you."

"That'd be great."

"Why don't you come home with me now?" Mann said, bestirring himself. "I'll see what I can root up."

They went together down the hall, past the ranks of massed dull-green lockers. Exiting at the rear of the school, they found several students unloading cartons from a van. "Hot off the press," said a boy with a high forehead and premature widow's peak: John Butler. He had ripped open a carton and was holding out a folded copy of *The Poet's Quill*, the school literary paper. While Mann examined the gift, John handed another copy to Joe. Anna had told him she had a poem in this issue. He was more eager to read it than if he'd written it himself. He tucked the paper among the books under his arm and strode off with Mann, momentarily lifted by the thought of her.

In Mann's upstairs study, under a slanted ceiling, several windows gave a view of the distant Shade. A scarred wooden table ran beneath the sills. There was a casual, slightly dishevelled look about the place, created by the stacks of books on the floor, the old *New Yorkers* scattered around the jute rug. Joe loved the room – its light, its books, its feeling of important work being done. Mann, he knew, was writing a history of Attawan. Parts of it had appeared in the *Attawan Star*.

He felt privileged to be here: privileged, and almost forgiven for his poor performance in his essay. He wanted to be an historian himself, and to come here was like being admitted to some secret, initiatory stage of the long process that would lead him forward. He was alert to everything, keen to make a good impression. He sat between the high arms of a low chair – the pink duster covering it seemed a bit incongruous, even shocking – sipping his tea and looking at the books the teacher took from the shelves and rubbed with a cloth, before handing them to Joe.

"You won't want all of these," Mann said with a grin. Inexplicably, the teacher was blushing. "At least I'm getting my books dusted."

Mann handed him a large format book with a dark board cover, and knelt with cracking knees beside the chair as Joe opened it. The book was full of black-and-white photographs from the First World War: wagon wheels fattened with mud, ragged files of grinning soldiers, the lifeless common of no-man's land. Reaching over into Joe's lap, the teacher leafed through the pages until he found a picture of several soldiers in a trench. They all had dirty faces, and had paused in various activities – eating out of mess tins, cleaning their rifles – to smile at the camera.

"That fellow there," Mann said, tapping on the page to indicate a figure sitting on a crate, his soup-plate helmet pushed straight back from his blackened forehead. "My brother, Gordon."

Joe looked at the figure and caught a hint of Mann's own square face and dark eyes, circled with dirt or fatigue. "Vimy Ridge," Joe read.

"Not long after they'd captured it."

"He was at Vimy?" Joe said with excitement. The name of the great German strong point successfully stormed by the Canadians – after British and French forces had failed for years to take it – was a mythic name to him, and as with all such names, it came as a surprise to discover that someone he knew, or at least a relative of someone he knew – an actual human being – had been there. It was like finding a ladder into a world that was bigger, brighter – infused, somehow, with immortality.

Again Mann tapped the page. "Look at those grins. They're always grinning in these pictures. It shows their youth – what *good boys* they were. They were living in hell, but they still couldn't help going on their best behaviour when a camera appeared. It tells you a lot, I think, about how well disciplined they were – I don't just mean as soldiers, but as social creatures. They were so eager to please. I always find it sad."

Joe studied the picture, and was moved by a curious sense that he knew what it was like to sit there, in the cold mud in France, eighteen years old, with his friends.

"Maybe they're just happy to be alive," he said quietly.

Mann studied him for a moment. In his brown eyes was something moist, searching – entirely too intense. Joe had to look away.

Mann went on kneeling beside Joe as they examined the photographs. The teacher's left hand hung on his shoulder. Joe shifted away, a little uncomfortable. He could sit in a crowded church pew beside his own father and hardly notice that their legs were touching. But with Mann he became increasingly self-conscious. He became aware of the chapped back of the teacher's free hand, which was trembling a little, and the white flecks in his nails, and always the man's unpleasant breath, like the smell of a machine. Mann, he remembered, was retiring at the end of the year; he was old.

When he left, Joe felt immediate relief at being outside, in the mild bright evening. From a lawn a robin sent out its shivering cry. He hurried to Shade Street, and along to the corner of Banting, where he sat on a low wall of cut limestone and took out his copy of *The Poet's Quill*, hunting through its newsprint pages until he found her poem.

WHIRLPOOL

Eyes
in the green whirlpool
looking up at me,
blinking and darkening and letting go.
Eyes of water
emerging, submerging –
the eyes of some vast green beast
who knows it must only lazily
circle
until I fall –
devoured by my hunger for looking.

Then you
standing by the grey rock,
a land-man, not of the river
with your startled love-look
beyond mere looking.
I was more afraid of you than the river,
more afraid of you than death.
Your eyes offered something more complicated than water,
wilder than the turquoise river.
Let me go
back to the pleasures of looking.
Let me drown on the bottom with my words.

– Anna Macrimmon

He read it several times. Was he the "land-man"? Yes, surely he
was the "land-man"! And he remembered the day he had driven with
Anna, Liz, and Brad to the whirlpool: saw again the wild water,
surging past the rock where Anna had stood.

What was she telling him? "Let me go/back to the pleasures of looking." Was she telling him to leave her alone? He looked up, scarcely aware of the cars streaming past, or of the Bannerman mansion across the road, its grey stone warming in the late sun. She was telling him to let her go. But she wouldn't tell him that, would she, unless he had a power over her – more, maybe, than he had guessed?

44

A WEEK LATER Joe and Brad drew up Anna's sloping drive. It was the evening of the Spring Frolic – a clear, fragrant evening, unseasonably warm. With a slight stiffness, ever the wounded athlete fresh from hockey or basketball wars, Brad, resplendent in his tux, left the Olds and took a jogging step or two as he crossed the lawn to her house. Joe got out and climbed into the back seat with the tiny carton that contained Liz's corsage. He couldn't stop thinking about the over-sized black shoes he had borrowed from his father – clown shoes, surely, their toes stuffed with newspaper – shoes that seemed to broadcast his father's current difficulties, as if their shine betrayed the loss of his job, his unhappiness deepening through the house like an unpleasant odour. Joe had not wanted to wear them, but he owned only brown shoes himself. Staring at Anna's front door, he was aware his hands were shaking. Then the door opened and he saw Anna in a coat he hadn't seen before, a beltless white coat that came to her knees but did not entirely cover the long, pale skirt flexing below it as she picked her way across the lawn. "Joe," she said, smiling at him as she got in. He had to remind himself that she didn't know he'd read her poem – the new issue of The Poet's Quill wouldn't be distributed until next week – and this helped him subdue his nervousness.

A few minutes later, the Olds swung into the McVeys' drive, stopping with a lurch behind the sky-blue Lincoln. As he plodded to the door, Joe could hear Brad's laughter in the car behind him. He felt barely composed, a just object of mockery, the evening already fraying beyond control.

And yet, and yet: *she* was here. On the short drive to the school, the world seemed to survive only by grace of the sleek head in front of him. Inside, gusts of music swept through the dimly lit corridors. Couples in fancy dresses and suits, in tuxedos and evening gowns, with hair creamed and combed, bouffanted and permed, paraded towards the gym with a sound of whisking cloth and tapping shoes. Joe glimpsed Sandy, looking entirely different from the person he still went out of his way to avoid. She was wearing what looked like false eyelashes and a puffy, Popsicle-green dress, and she was clinging to the arm of Sid Miller, a North End boy with a reputation. There was an excitement in the warm air, almost an anarchy, as though some long repressed power was nearing its point of release. Two teacher-chaperones, watching from the shadows, seemed out of place.

They climbed the stairs to the classroom serving as a cloakroom. Fluorescent light fell harshly over the desks heaped with coats. Helping Liz off with her wrap, Joe stared past her at Anna. She, too, had just shed her coat, and he was mesmerized by her appearance in her simple, white, form-fitting dress with its square neckline that mirrored the cut of her bangs and left her arms completely bare. He was made breathless: by her naked arms, by her rebirth, once again, to newness, by the beauty of her face, smiling across the desks as she discovered him. She wore no jewellery.

They went down to the gym and sat at the little table reserved for them. A candle fluttered in its bottle, signalling to the dozens of other flames winking around the perimeter of the vast room. The floor was crowded with dancers, their heads and shoulders touched with the racing moths of light reflected from the multifaceted globe turning overhead, above a ten-foot high model of the Eiffel Tower, its girders wrapped in aluminum foil. On stage, the Morganaires had stood up in their pale-blue, silver-trimmed blazers, leaning forward to release the deep voices of their horns. The outside doors were open and the mild night air stole in and mixed with the warmer, perfumed air inside, making the candles flicker.

Liz drew Joe onto the floor. She hooked her bare arm over his shoulders and drew in close, possessively. Her body seemed un-cannily thin to him, and hungry, pressing at him as if to staunch a wound in her midriff. They turned among the other couples in a slow, shuffling drift. Her hair smelled of a new perfume, a flowery scent he found too sweet. He pushed her away a little, and tried to dance more energetically, aware that Anna might be watching: wanting her to know he was ready to break with Liz.

"Anna looks nice," Liz said, closing with him again. He grunted something noncommittal and twirled Liz. She came back to him, her face with its gash of red lipstick expressionless in the blizzard of light.

Half an hour later all four of them were at the table, arguing in a slightly forced way about the Beatles. Only Brad seemed to be enjoy-ing himself. With one elbow propped on the back of his chair, his open jacket revealing a frilled shirt and cherry cummerbund, he grinned in his amiable way and announced that the Beatles were for thirteen-year-olds. Joe glanced at Anna. She was twisting her paper napkin – they had been eating cake – and sticking out her jaw in an odd scowl.

"Would you like to dance?"

He was surprised by how collected he felt. He could sense Liz and Brad's sudden stillness, on either side of him. But Anna had not heard: her reverie had taken her entirely away.

"Hey," Brad said to Anna. He seemed hugely amused. "You've got an admirer."

The Morganaires had started into "Twilight Time."

He felt he had never touched Anna Macrimmon, not really, though sometimes their hands had brushed as a book or paper passed between them. Now, out on the floor, she turned to him with a half-smile, her face both revealed and hidden by the flakes of light that streamed over her head and shoulders. Her hand in his was cold and dry: was she merely tolerating him? He placed his right hand on her back – his fingers touching ever so gently into the firm groove there, under the soft, rucked material of the dress. As they moved off, she miscued a little and trod on his shoes.

"Sorry."

"It's all right. My shoes, they're my dad's, actually. They stick out too much."

He could not believe he had admitted this. But he scarcely felt in control of himself.

They danced a little awkwardly, unable to find each other's rhythm. His hands were sweating, and he lightened his touch on her back, not wanting to stain her dress.

Her face was close to his, a little below. He drank in the perfume she wore, which had almost a non-smell: a cleanness, like vanilla. A wisp of her hair brushed his cheek. Between them was the orchid Brad had pinned to her bodice, a senseless mouth gaping upwards.

They grew a little more competent, and she settled in closer. The singer wailed his anticipation of the coming night.

Her breast touched his bottom rib. The entire front of his body felt as if it had opened, like a door. He closed his eyes.

And then it was over. They parted, standing at a loss among the chatting couples. He thought to move back to the table. But she was looking at him blankly, her head raised, a little to one side. He returned her look, held it for a breathless moment, until her eyes darted away. Flecks of light swam over her face and shoulders. There was something primitive in the way the light masked her: an ancient, living camouflage, like light penetrating a woods. Terror was in him, and at the same time he felt remarkably calm, remote. He had read somewhere that animals went calm, knowing they are about to be killed by a larger beast: he thought of this now. He looked around, pretending to be interested in what the emcee was saying, up there in the spotlight. But he was only impersonating normality. He put his hand in his trouser pocket and felt the handkerchief folded there: it, too, was his father's.

"Hey, I read your poem," he said, turning back to her with a grin, as if his news was a little joke, nothing important.

He thought she flushed. In the speckling light it was hard to tell.

"'The Whirlpool,'" he said. "I got an early copy of the *Quill*."

She looked at him.

"And what did you think?" Her voice hard.

"I love it," he said. He could no longer be casual. His whole body had become a drum, pounding. "I memorized it. Actually–" He realized, too late, that "actually" was a word Liz used, ad nauseam. "I didn't set out to memorize it. I just read it so many times it stuck. It's a great poem. It's –"

He was smiling helplessly. Why wouldn't she help him? She was looking at him without expression, her head a little tilted in that way she had, skeptical and distant and penetrating. "I was wondering if it had anything to do with me. I know you often make things up, or people do, when they write a poem. But I couldn't help thinking – that day we went to the whirlpool. There was a moment – well."

"Thank you," she said finally, softly. He could not read her expression, but something had crossed her face.

The Morganaires started into another piece. It was a mercy: he was sure he was drowning in his own incompetence. He felt his face must be the colour of Brad's cummerbund. The loud music made more conversation impossible. It was a fast tune this time: an orchestrally jazzed-up version of an old Presley song. All around, couples flung themselves into the music. Joe thought Anna looked reluctant – in fact, he wasn't very good at fast dancing himself – and they turned as if by agreement, walking back to the table. He was a failure. He had spoken his secret and nothing had changed. She was leading him away from the dance. The revelation that he thought had existed in "The Whirlpool" – that he was special to her – did not exist.

Liz and Brad weren't at the table. For a while Joe and Anna made themselves busy trying to pick them out in the crowd. *There* they were, dancing in the swarm of little lights as if born to it. Brad moved elegantly, Joe thought with envy, with a certain casual grace, like a tall black man he'd once seen on television: Cab Calloway, or Duke Ellington. Liz danced, as always, as if she were totally disinterested: but she, too, moved well, in her long dress in which her body bent in a willowy way.

"They look good together," Joe said. His voice had caught in his throat.

Anna Macrimmon said nothing. Though her silence had an oddly palpable quality, as if she had conjured up a large stone that now sat on the table between them. More than ever he felt she belonged to another world: a world with the blue gem of the Mediterranean in its centre, so far from this one, and so superior, that it must be a torture for her to sit here, at a dance called, of all things, Springtime in Paris. He felt as oafish as any boy from a farm, a hayseed wearing his father's shoes: perhaps someday she would tell the story of this night to friends he would never meet. For a laugh.

"There's Mr. Mann," Anna said, looking past Joe's head.

In the balcony at the west end of the gym a number of people had come to watch the dance. Craning around, Joe saw the shadowy groups sitting on the wooden benches. The teacher stood behind a railing, his white hair unmistakable. He was staring towards the orchestra, though Joe had an intuition that, only a moment ago, the teacher's gaze had been fixed on him.

45

THE FOUR OF THEM drove to Liz's house to change into more casual clothes, then went on to Laura Becker's place, the first stop in a series of all-night parties. Laura lived on the river side of the Shade Survey, in a big ranch-style house of yellow brick, with a run of picture windows looking east across the backyard and the distant river, towards chains of lights that marked a gravel pit. Joe left the others in the house and went into the yard, where a group of boys were smoking and drinking by the fence. Petie Brennan, a broad-chested farmboy in thick glasses and an oversized white dress shirt, open at the throat, held out a wine bottle. "Get loaded," he said thickly. It was not clear if this was a statement or an order.

Joe took a deep swig from the flattish bottle – the wine was fizzy and sweet, almost like pop – and stood looking over the wire fence, listening to the others talk. It was over, he felt, his long, solitary campaign to win Anna Macrimmon was over. Clumsily, he had made his move and nothing had come of it. He might as well get drunk.

After a while he turned, letting his weight sag back on the wire. Above the yard, the expanse of candle-lit living-room windows suggested a dark aquarium, swimming with the flailing forms of dancers. He couldn't see Anna, though he momentarily glimpsed Brad's tall form sliding through the light from a doorway. Liz came to the window and peered out, then her pale face retreated. Below, in the brightly lit rec room, a game of ping-pong was in progress. The wretched hopping of the ball seemed to be taking place inside his own head.

He turned again to the valley. Low in the east, an orange fire raged: the moon, edging slowly from shadow. Below, the Shade glinted like scrap metal. He drank again from the bottle and passed it back. "You can't say that," a nearby voice said. "Nobody says that."

"Anybody got a cigarette?"

At her voice – the familiar-unfamiliar light voice – he turned and saw Anna Macrimmon approach the crowd of boys. She did not look at him, though he sensed she knew he was there. Several of the boys began hunting for their packs, but Dick Christopolous beat them all to the punch, and in a moment had his lighter going too, shielding its flame under her dipping face. She blew out a plume of smoke with an experienced, blasé air, like a woman in an old movie.

"So is this a special club," she said, "or are girls allowed?"

Strangers to irony, they all hastened to assure her that girls were allowed.

Petie Brennan and Bob Black signalled each other with wide eyes.

Joe watched in amazement. She stood with her back partially turned to him – her back in its tight, short sweater, talking to Dick Christopolous and the others – but especially to Dick. Dick's usual type of girlfriend had teased hair, smoked as a matter of course, and had a reputation. His sharp-handsome Greek face, under the well-oiled droop of his forelock, leaned close to hers, his mouth twisted slightly in a wry smile.

Her smoking shocked him. It was if she'd revealed a coarser side than he'd suspected, though he wondered if it wasn't an act. Just her being out here shocked him, behaving like some ordinary girl happy with the kind of chatter Dick Christopolous specialized in. The other boys, too, hung on every word that was said, occasionally putting in their two cents' worth. She talked to them all, laughing every so often. Only once did she glance over at him, with a look that went straight to his eyes, a look without expression, yet which seemed to brim with meaning, angry meaning. Was she upset with what he'd asked her about her poem? Well, let her be.

After a few minutes she thanked Dick for the cigarette and ground it out under her shoe. "Think I'll have a look at the moon," she said. She went along the fence, away from Joe and the others, towards an old wooden gate held shut by a loop of wire. She unfastened the wire and let herself into the shadowy tangle of bushes and small trees. Joe watched her descend out of sight. A few seconds later, Dick Christopolous, gently touching the fingers of one hand to his forelock, walked out the gate. He, too, went down the hillside, with his hunched, high-shouldered walk, his cagey air, disappearing into the mass of bushes.

Joe watched in despair. He could hear voices: Anna Macrimmon laughing, and Dick Christopolous going on in a low monotone, making her laugh more. Then their voices were lost in the throb of music from the house.

"Fuck me," a boy said in a low voice, near Joe. Andy Schull flicked his butt over the fence.

"Fuck *her*," someone said.

"Don't you wish," someone answered.

The boys were all at the fence now, staring as one into the night. All of them, Joe suspected, were virgins. They were probably thinking that acts they could only dream of were about to take place, down there in the dark. He twisted the fence until it hurt his hands and turned around twice, in a spasm of indecision. He went back to the house. He looked in the window at the ping-pong players. He returned to the fence. The valley was dim, though as his eyes became accustomed, he was able to see more trees and bushes, picked out by the moon, and what looked like the tin roof of a shed. Farther away, the empty flats stretched towards the river. From the gravel pits across the river came a faint clanking sound; a truck grunted as it changed gears. Anna and Dick Christopolous had been swallowed by the night. He felt he knew nothing about love or sex at all. She had chosen *Dick Christopolous*! Dick the hard rock; Dick who was said to sleep in his car; Dick who spent half his life in the pool hall! She was down there with him now, doing God only knew what.

After a while the other boys heard a rumour of food and went back to the house. A few minutes later, Brad came out. He was eating a slice of pizza; a second slice drooped from his other hand.

"You seen Anna? She wanted some pizza."

"She's down there," Joe said, turning back to the fence.

Beside him, Brad peered into the darkness, his mouth open in a silent, disbelieving laugh. "She's with Dick Christopolous. She might not want you disturbing them."

He felt wonderful, saying this, and terrible. The gloss of happiness disappeared from Brad's face. He went out the gate and down the hill into the darkness, with his pizza.

Joe went back towards the house. In the light from the rec room, he examined his stinging hand. Blood had trickled onto his palm, from the cut the wire had made in his thumb. Upstairs, he stood by the huge fridge, pretending to nurse a glass of punch. The kitchen counters were loaded with food – several kinds of pizza and sandwiches with their crusts cut off and paper barrels of fried chicken and a chocolate cake dotted with jelly beans. Laura Becker's skinny, red-haired mother, a woman whose voice seemed pitched at near-hysteria, was walking around with a paper hat on and an empty glass, encouraging them to eat. Joe had no appetite. He considered going home. Liz came in and asked him to dance. "I dunno," he said with a brutal evasiveness and continued to stand there, ignoring her. She hung on beside him, talking with an inclusive air to people who came by, as if Joe were actually present. She made enough social noises for both of them, pretending to be enthusiastic about things he knew she didn't give a damn about. Of course, like everyone, he had done the same thing himself, but he didn't think of that now. Finally she went off with some other girls to dance. From time to time she danced near the light that fell from the kitchen, putting herself squarely in his sight, twisting her body in a way that was meant to attract him, while her face with its pinched-in lips remained cold. She was his fate, the best he could do, and he loathed her. He looked up at the clock, its face like a pizza with numbers on it. One-thirty-two.

Sixteen minutes later Anna came in, followed by Brad, her eyes preternaturally bright. Her upper lip was stained with pizza sauce. He supposed they'd been kissing. But where was Dick Christopolous? Had she been kissing him too? No, he no longer understood a thing. Maybe all you had to do, if you were a boy, was go over and kiss her. Maybe it was that simple. "Joe, you should see the moon!"

"He's *seen* the moon," Brad said sardonically. "We've *all* seen the moon."

Ignoring Brad, she took Joe by the hand – hers was as cold as ice – and began to draw him across the kitchen. "You have to see how it looks on the river."

He let himself be drawn to the stairs. So now, apparently, it was *his* turn. Maybe by the end of the evening she'd have them all down there, even Petie Brennan with his thick glasses. For a moment, in the rec room he drew back. He'd be damned if he went one step farther with her. She glanced around at him. He followed her out of the house.

Beyond the fence, the paths in the scrub were worn deep, like troughs. "I think they're goat paths," she told him. "At least it smells like goats." She was proceeding down a steep path ahead of him. Beyond the light from the house, the grey moonlight held sway, turning the trees and bushes to blotches of dull silver. He glanced back at the yard, half-expecting to see Brad coming after them. But no one was there and he experienced a flash of triumph. Maybe she was only being nice to him, one boy among many, but he was with her, and Brad wasn't. She had asked – *ordered* him to come with her and he stumbled along, following her down the hard-packed trails.

On the flats, under a grove of black willows that obscured the houses and lights above, she turned to him. The moon, a battered, ancient coin, hung over her shoulder.

"You were supposed to follow me the first time."

"What?"

"I look around and there's Dick Christopolous."

"You don't like Dick Christopolous?"

She laughed bleakly, pushing at his chest, and went on. Suddenly energized – the numbness and passivity of months seemed to be falling away, though he was still baffled by what was happening – he hurried after her.

They crossed the flats to the river, entering in a few steps its cold atmosphere, with its smell of decaying weed and slime. On the black water, a swath of moonlight glittered like a school of minnows.

"Very nice," he said.

"Look at me –"

He turned to her. His own face half-shadowed hers in the grey moonlight. The noise of the party drifted down the hill.

She put her hands on his chest and shoved him backwards, along the damp path.

"God, you make me mad," she said. And a moment later, a cry of dismay: "I can't believe I'm doing this!"

She strode away along the path that followed the river. He hurried after the white flicker of her running shoes.

"Anna. Anna, stop – can't believe you're doing what?"

She stalked on, nearly falling at one point when she stepped into a small hole. He sensed she was crying – why crying? what had he done? – but was unable to see her face clearly.

Then she stopped and faced him.

"This is crazy," she said. "We should go back."

"Okay." He started to turn.

"No, wait!"

He turned back. More used to the darkness now, he could make out her features, but could not quite read her expression. Her cheeks were definitely wet. And her voice, when it came again, seemed to be struggling for breath.

"You want me, don't you? I mean, you want to be with me?"

"Yes."

He did not move.

"If we do this," she said, "we're going to hurt people."

"Yes."

He hardly dared let himself understand her, and at the same time his understanding leapt forward, wildly.

"Anna," he said. They stood looking at each other, half-seeing each other, in the dim moonlight. His months of holding back held him back now. Everything he wanted was here, but he couldn't move.

Suddenly, with a small cry, she lunged forward, took his head between her hands, and kissed him awkwardly on the mouth. For a moment she pulled back to look at him. Then she put her arms around him. Holding her now, moaning her name, he drank in the smell that was almost a non-smell, which rose from her hair, scarcely believing he was feeling the press of her long body against his.

They went together up the river. They went silently, almost gravely, holding hands, conscious of a deed done. She kept sighing as if dismayed at herself. When he asked what was wrong she shook her head and said nothing. The path ran above the sharply edged, shallow bank, descended to cross the mouths of streams, ran on again. Neither of them had ever been here. From time to time they stopped: each time he kissed her he felt he had never kissed her before. He had to keep kissing her so that he could remind himself that what was happening was true. Between kisses he forgot what her mouth tasted like, forgot what her body with its small breasts felt like as it pressed against him. Then he remembered: *it was like this*.

Now they could hardly go twenty steps without embracing. They embraced and separated, embraced and fell down. She was laughing with him in the hollow place behind a fallen tree trunk, laughing and weeping both, with a fluidity of exchange that left him bewildered: she was balancing above him on the trunk like a ten-year-old who cares about nothing else. They went on. The ground sloped up to what looked like a flat platform. Climbing up its side they saw a long pond, with a little dam gurgling at one end. Under the dark surface fish were rising, breaking the velvet membrane of the water with delicate kissing sounds. The moon was in the pond now, wobbling and broken. "There are many moons," she said, leading him around the path. She had grown sombre, as if instructing him: a virginal priestess pointing out the mysteries of the place. "Every moon has a different name. They're sisters."

He had no idea if she was making this up on the spot, or reciting some old mythology. It didn't matter: everything she said was miraculous. He threw himself into the game. "Every kiss is a fish, and every fish – is delicious."

She contradicted him violently. Fish were sacred to Aphrodite, she told him. "We don't eat them."

"Never?" he said.

"Not unless we want to lose her favour. Which I don't think we do."

She kissed him with slow deliberation now and, before they could separate again, took his hand and placed it on her breast. The moment had the formal aura of an offering, as if Aphrodite were not some old name from the past but a power hovering over them even now, infusing every touch with divine meaning. She watched him in the moonlight. "Sooner or later, everybody loses her favour," she said. "She's easily bored."

"I'll never be bored with you," he said. "I couldn't be."

But already he feared she might be bored with him. It might happen tomorrow, it might happen in the next five minutes: he seemed held aloft by a kind of spell, not quite daring to believe in what was happening. If he had suddenly found himself alone by this pond, shivering in the damp like that guy in the Keats poem, he wouldn't have been entirely surprised. He wanted her to echo back to him: I won't be bored with you either. But she laughed and touched his mouth as if to stop his words and turned back to the pond. A frog splashed from the bank.

There was a second pond, higher than the first, behind another gurgling dam of iron and cement. In this second pond there were no fish, or at least none rising. The moon in this pond was clear, only wobbling a little with the slight movement of the water. They were near a barn, and could sense the slow presence of large animals – cows or horses – and smell the heavy sweetness of hay and manure. "You know I can't smell horse manure without thinking of vanilla ice cream," he told her. "It's the ice-cream man – his wagon was pulled by a horse. You could hear his bell, all up and down the streets." He was saying anything that came into his head, with no worry about its irrelevance, because tonight everything was connected. Moon, ice-cream man, horse manure, love, his soaking shoes: all part of the same thing, a thing that had no name but which contained them as the grey moonlight contained them in its silver bowl.

Laura Becker's house was quiet, the great windows blazed from empty rooms. Everyone had gone on to the next party. Not quite everyone. Turning a corner into the front yard, they saw the black Olds waiting by the curb. Behind the wide windshield sat the twinned, accusing shadows of their guilt.

They slipped into the back seat. It was Anna who spoke first, telling Brad she wasn't feeling well. (Was it a lie, Joe wondered, or had the events by the river made her ill?) She wanted to go home. No one spoke as the Olds cruised the moonlit streets. Brad dropped off Joe and Liz first. "We can take the Linc," Liz said as they climbed the steps to her house, as if they would simply continue to the next party.

She went up to the bathroom. He waited in the family room, looking out at the floodlit yard. He felt capable of anything – it was the promise of Anna's touch, given secretly across the back seat before he left the car – and now as he heard Liz come into the kitchen behind him, he turned to her. "Come here," he said softly, the executioner calling to his victim.

As he poured out his deadly mixture of truth and lies, she watched him without expression, her heart-shaped face pale in the dimly lit room, her beautiful eyes fixed on his with their look of startled candour, at once ferocious and cold and completely vulnerable. Her silence unnerved him. She was doing nothing to defend herself, only watching him with the calm air of someone who has expected such treatment all along. He was fumbling now, fumbling out his apologies like a fool. "I'm sorry," he said, for the third or fourth time. "I know it isn't fair –" Not knowing what else to do, he moved to embrace her. She was stiff in his arms. He let her go, looking around uncertainly. "I guess I better go."

"Anna won't have you," she said, her voice small.

Her eyes were still fixed on his.

"She was involved with someone else. She told me – she told me she can't love any more."

He stared at her.

"Someone else," he said numbly.

"A man," Liz said, and her gaze seemed to push his eyes back into his head. "Not a boy like you."

He moved off but, at the stairs to the kitchen, looked around again. She was gazing out at the starkly lit patio, at a glass-topped table where someone had left a pair of hedge clippers. He was chilled by her isolation, it gave her a strange authority, and for a moment he nearly went back to ask her what she meant. Finally he crossed the kitchen's glare and left the house.

The black Olds was coming along Robert. It pulled up to the curb beside him. "Hey, guy," Brad said, subdued. "Mind having a few words –"

Joe got into the front seat. The Olds swept under the shadows of trees and poles, through the Junction past the ghostly silver barns of the Fairgrounds and out of town.

He glanced at the speedometer: the green ribbon had crept to eighty, and was still extending itself. A thrill of fear went through him. Brad was leaning forward a little, over the wheel, as if wanting to embrace it.

"You wanted to talk."

Brad said nothing – no matter what Joe said, Brad met it with a hostile silence. He supposed Anna had told Brad it was over between them: at least he hoped she had. But as Brad's silence went on, it suggested there had been complications. Perhaps Anna had not freed herself. Perhaps – he knew this was a primitive idea, and hoped it was wrong – they were going to have to fight for her. They swept past the glittering deep lakes of the gravel pits, white as chalk in the moonlight, past sleeping farmhouses and mailboxes and ancient maples and fields darker than the night up the grey highway, its white centre line – now broken, now a single streaming thread – speeding under the wide hood of the Olds. At the tops of hills, they seemed about to leave the road and fly. At a rail crossing, Brad barely slowed: the Olds thudded on its springs as if it had been dropped from the sky. The speedometer read a hundred.

"Slow down," Joe shouted at him. "For God's sake, it isn't worth *this*."

"Nothing's worth this," Brad said with an irony Joe couldn't read.

"What did Anna tell you?" Joe said. He was desperate to know exactly how things stood, desperate to start a rational exchange that might sap Brad's focus on speed. But all his words were absorbed by the pact Brad had made with the open road. Every thought Brad had, every sorrow, was channelled away from speech and into this relentless pressure on the accelerator, this calm, expressionless focus on the highway revealing itself beyond the wheel. Brad was furious – that much seemed clear – but he was letting the engine of the Olds deliver his fury, in a storm of working pistons. He was furious, and grim, but the car seemed almost triumphantly happy, roaring out its hallelujah in the extremity of its power.

They were in the wrong lane now, approaching the crest of another hill. Joe swore at Brad while scanning the smooth horizon for the headlights of an oncoming car. He was on the verge of grabbing the wheel, or perhaps the gearshift – throwing it into neutral. But there were no headlights, there was no other car. They broached the crest, and again seemed about to fly over the expanse of moon-bleached countryside. A few lights burned at the ends of lanes: little beacons of sanity.

He buckled his seatbelt, ignoring Brad's snort of derision. They were approaching the village of Cairn. They would have to slow down, surely: there was often a police cruiser there, Joe remembered. But as the village's outskirts hove into view, Brad veered off in a skidding turn down a sideroad. The car fishtailed on gravel. A mailbox on a post reared in front of them, a square-headed victim frozen in the headlights, and went down with a thump and the sound of breaking glass. They sped on. Brad flicked on the high beams – the low on the right had been smashed – and then, with a sudden, jabbing movement of his left hand, turned off the lights altogether. Now their way was lit only by the moonlight pooling on the road, between the shadows of big trees, turning the fields on either side to seas of ghostly absence. Joe knew they were going to die. At any second Brad might turn the Olds into a tree. Or a culvert (there was one now, dangerously close) might catch the wheels and flip them. He sat in horror, unable to read Brad's mind, unable to gauge the edge over which he might or might not tip them. Everything he saw now seemed a clue to their fate: an open gate, a mailbox, a tractor parked by the road; all threatened, and all, as soon as they had swept past, became part of life's mercy. In the ditch an animal's yellow eyes glinted and went out.

Then Brad began to slow. At the next crossroads he brought the Olds to a stop. Breathing hard, trembling, Joe looked over at him.

"Maybe you should get out," Brad said to the windshield.

"Let me drive," Joe said. "We can talk."

"Get out." Brad said. He was still hunched forward, as if bound to the wheel.

"At least turn on the lights."

Brad looked at him.

"The lights –"

Brad obeyed. The powerful beams stabbed down the road, lighting trees, the corner of a shed.

"I'm sorry," Joe said. He knew, now, that he had won.

He started to walk towards Attawan. Behind him, he could hear the Olds rumbling over washboard, headed deeper into the country. Turning, he saw a cloud of dust rising beyond a field, a white spectre in the moonlight as it trailed towards him. He was five or six miles from town. It hardly mattered, he would have walked a hundred, gladly, through the earth-scented night, through the moonlit fields under the great rustling trees that lined the pale road and cast their living shadows ahead of him.

46

THE NIGHT WAS FULL of sounds that drifted through the open windows above the table where Archie Mann sat working – music, voices, the clanking of the conveyor belts across the river – all made small and enticing by distance.

Again he clinked the lip of the Glenfiddich bottle to the little earthenware cup. He was drunk, he realized, pleasantly and thoroughly drunk. *I could sneak up on them,* he thought with an amused grunt. He imagined his surprised students discovering him in the bushes, with his binoculars hanging from his neck. *They could hardly fire me at this stage in the game.*

He put down the cup, looked for a few moments at the small, age-browned snapshot lying on his desk blotter, and uncapped his fountain pen.

Dear Esther,

The photo you sent – well, to be frank, it was a shock. Only I think it was taken in Regent's Park, that time you and Walter came down for a play at the Old Vic – remember? I think you took it. The four of us had a picnic beforehand on the lawn, just to the east of the zoo. August 1935. Those are Nash's terraces in the distance. Jeremy and me still enjoying our golden age, all five or six months of it. But the photo's a revelation. I mean, every picture ever taken of us shows something new, don't you think? If you look closely enough? I think I look positively sheep-eyed, rather pathetically devoted, no wonder he left me! Jeremy looks rather more intense than usual, staring at the camera as if determined to impress it. He had more vanity than I was ever willing to give him credit for. Walter – that way he had of carrying himself – real noblesse in that man of yours, though here he looks a little weary, as if secretly fed up with the rest of us. Do you think he was ever fed up? Not with you, my dear, but with Jeremy and me. We were rather déclassé compared to him, I mean in every sense. But it's heartbreaking to see us on the very summit of our youth and happiness, don't you think? God, what life is!

Glenfiddich thoughts. I'm sitting at my long desk with the windows open, pleasantly sloshed and listening to a group of my students make merry at a house near here. I wish I was eighteen again. There's a boy here reminds me so much of Jeremy, not in looks so much (he's fairer, to Jeremy's dark, and not quite so handsome), but he has the same look of anticipation, eager for something the rest of us can't quite see. I'm a sucker for that, makes me want to protect him. He's a gifted student, maybe the best I've had, and with my encouragement is going on to university next year. His family's working class, one of the rising type. I think his mother is actually middle class (English, a war bride), while his father works as a mechanic of some sort in the mill. The whole family has this – bearing. There's something superior about them, not snobbish, but dignified and open. I had the boy here in my lair, just last week, showing him some books. My hands were shaking. I was that close to kissing him. One kiss – and there goes my pension, or at least a thirty-five-year reputation as an honourable man. I mean, I don't think he'd have welcomed it. Lately he's been snared by a poor little rich girl with vamp eyes. But then I'm jealous. And drinking good Scotch. Anyway, they're doing it, I'm sure. You see what a pathetic old lech I've become. Only I don't want her to sabotage him. His last essay not up to snuff – I worry she's undermining him.

But Jeremy. I remember you said, one time after he'd left me, that it was probably a good thing, for me if not for him: Jeremy too self-absorbed and, likely, you said, "to pull me down with him." But why couldn't I have pulled him up? People do pull other people up, don't they? Or do they get pulled down a little too, no matter what? Of course all this is irrelevant, really, because the fact is, in the end, he didn't want me. I still don't understand what happened, I mean what his real thoughts were. I don't know if there was someone else, I mean some special someone else. He was so damnably opaque, and I let him be, out of some misguided notion of kindness. I never pressed him. I wished I had, now. We talked so much, and in the end we talked about everything except why he was drawing away. That last summer in London, in the borrowed flat on St. Marks Crescent, we were getting along so beautifully. Then one day (I don't believe I've told you this, forgive me if I have) I was pulling on my clothes, hurrying to get to work, and I look up and see Jeremy looking at me from the bed. Jeremy of the wide shoulders and far-seeing eyes – and his face had gone cold. I went cold. It was as if he'd seen me, some fatal flaw of mine, for the first time. I'd always thought I was lucky beyond deserving to have him – he was better-looking, smarter, the target of a thousand other boys, etc., etc. But I'd almost got used to him being there. And then this look. I believe I lost him right then. In a look. And I still don't know what it was about. But I can tell you this, there are moods – Glenfiddich moods – when I feel that look was the central event of my life. That it's the biggest thing that's happened to me. In some way it's happening still.

Enough of this. Did I tell you I'm writing an essay about our founder, Abraham Shade? The man has got under my skin. I'm living in his house, of course, and maybe it's just old age, but I seem to feel him around here, more and more. A poet-farmer, a personality, but what moves me most about him was his affection for the valley. From his first arrival, he was struck by the beauty of the place – as I was, you know – and for the rest of his life he was concerned about it, wanting to make sure the public buildings were put in the right places, not wanting to obscure any views. I think there may have been some nostalgia in this – wanting to preserve something of his original, pristine discovery. From my yard I can see the hill, across the valley, where he sat on horseback one fine day *in 1822 and looked down on the forks for the first time. He knew in a flash (this isn't speculation, I have his diaries) he had to make a town here. To my mind (a most unhistorical notion) he's still there, on the crest of the hill, holding the town in his gaze; and it's this, somehow, that allows the town to go on existing.*

As I say, Glenfiddich moods. I feel sometimes as if thirty-five years have gone by in the time it takes me to put down one exam paper and take up another. But we make do, don't we? We rub on. I think your Walter was the best man I ever knew. He was older and wiser and funnier than the rest of us and I loved him as I love you. Forgive your old friend his rambling. I will definitely come to Cambridge this summer. Archie.

He left the house and moved behind it, out of the light. The party sounds had stopped. Distantly, across the river, the conveyor belts went on with their fretful clanking. The moon stood almost at the high midpoint of the sky. For a long minute he looked up at it. Then he drifted to the south side of the house, and gazed down the valley towards Lookout Hill, where it commanded the deep centre of town. On the hill's crest, not quite visible in the mass of trees and houses, the lone horseman waited. What was time? He was supposed to be an historian, but Archie Mann felt he had no idea what time was, really. It certainly wasn't what got measured by watches and clocks. *That* time was a tidy illusion, made for businessmen. Real time was something else, wild and unknowable. Just now it seemed that time had only been born that instant, everything was fresh with the impetus of new beginnings: the infant skull of the moon riding over his shoulder; the wild blue light in the valley; the dank earth-smell of the river; the lights twinkling downstream. He moved on a little farther, into a deeper darkness. Across the valley, the horseman watched, motionless above his dream.

47

THE DARK-GREEN EDSEL brought Alf to a halt. There was no mistaking those protruding, rust-eaten headlights, the drift of papers on the dash. The main street, split lengthwise by sun and shadow, had grown vivid.

"Alf!" That torn-cardboard voice. Doyle, dressed in a sports shirt flecked with tiny red dots and shapeless grey trousers, was coming down the post-office steps. One massive hand – a badger's paw – extended.

Alf, incongruously, felt he was being congratulated. He knows I've been fired, he thought.

"You got a few minutes?"

He felt he had nothing to lose. It was one of the advantages of being unemployed. At first you sensed everybody's eyes on you. Then you realized you were invisible.

He followed the organizer into the Vimy House, past the empty desk where the same asbestos-coloured cat slept, up three flights of stairs following a trail of filthy mismatched carpets to Doyle's room. Alf took the chair by the open window that looked down on the empty street. Somewhere nearby, pigeons cobbled the air with their watery murmurs. Wheezing from the climb, Doyle sat heavily on the edge of the bed and immediately began rolling a cigarette. His tongue swept the edge of the paper. "Trying to quit," he growled. "They say you smoke less if you have to make your own. Drink?" he said, nodding at a bottle of rye on the bedside table. The amber liquid contained a light of its own. Alf looked at it for a moment. His social reactions had slowed.

"No thanks. I wouldn't mind a fag though."

"I thought that was one fault you didn't have."

"I have them all now," Alf said.

Doyle chuckled darkly as he handed the cigarette across. He tossed Alf his lighter and silently rolled another cigarette for himself. Alf smoked and looked into the blaze of the street, worried. He knew he hadn't been brought here to make small talk, and he feared the exposure of even a small part of what he had kept to himself.

After a while, Doyle said, "I hear you had some bad luck."

Alf shrugged. "Nothing worth talking about." He could feel Doyle waiting, on the low bed across the room. He could feel the powerful draw of Doyle's silence, tugging on his secrets. He resisted, settling himself, a man in a hole. And still Doyle went on waiting, perfectly comfortable, it seemed.

Doyle said, "They treated you badly."

Again Alf shrugged, feigning nonchalance. But he saw in his mind's eye Kit Ford sitting smugly behind his desk, on the day the foreman had taken him off the Richardsons.

"Tell me."

Alf studied the glowing tip of his cigarette, reluctant to offer a single syllable. Silence was the one province he still ruled. And now another man was asking in.

But Doyle would not be put off. He sat on, like a statue, like a man whose chief occupation and talent is waiting. He could wait ten years, calmly smoking, his small eyes glinting in his rough face, his big hand going slowly up and down with his cigarette.

"Kit Ford," Alf said to the rug at his feet. "You might have heard of him."

"Oh yes," Doyle said, with a tone that suggested he had both heard and disapproved. Alf experienced a slight opening inside himself: an access of hope, like a glimpse of distant water. He licked his lips and began, very slowly, to tell Doyle about Ford's arrival in the mill, and the events that had followed. Occasionally he had to stop, to catch his breath, which curiously kept failing him.

Doyle's gaze stayed fixed on him, through a scrim of smoke. When Alf told the story of his fight with Ford, the organizer heaved with amusement. For the first time since the day of the fight, Alf experienced a certain pleasure and even pride in what he'd done. Margaret had made him feel ashamed of fighting Ford. But Doyle asked him questions about their scrap, clearly relishing it. And when Alf told Doyle about being fired, the organizer shook his head and muttered, "Bastard," and it was as if he was pouring water into the mouth of a thirst-stricken man.

When he finished, they were again silent. Alf looked into the street. Far below, several schoolgirls were walking along with skipping ropes bunched in their hands. Their chiming voices seemed far away, a dream in the bright sunlight. And in a few seconds all the relief he had felt in telling his story soured into remorse, a sense that he had given some critical part of himself away. He was exhausted. It had all meant nothing.

"So, you found anything else?"

Alf shook his head, reluctant to talk more. His failure over the weeks to find work was far worse than being fired. He had once thought that any fool could find work, but he seemed to have come up against something impenetrable. Perhaps it was some flaw in himself he'd never sensed until now, or perhaps fate dealt in conspiracies: he was caught in the crosshairs of events, unable to escape their deadly focus. The effect was to make him feel foolish, unnerved, and yes, inexplicably embarrassed. He had recently developed the habit of putting his hand over his mouth as he talked – as if he were casually scratching his upper lip. In fact, he was hiding the depths – the rotting, untrustworthy depths – his words came from. He was hiding from his own suspicion that he was lying, without quite knowing whether he was.

"How you'd like to work for me?"

A brief laugh rasped in his throat. Doyle's offer seemed a bitter joke.

"I could give you sixty a week. Not much, but better than you're getting on unemployment insurance."

"And what would I do?"

"You'd help me organize this place –"

Alf looked at him in disbelief.

Doyle nodded. "There's a lot of people on side already. It's the closing of the hosiery mill. They realize just how little they mean to these sons of bitches. There've been some changes with us too. We've got more money. I've got some girls to help me. There'll be four of us. We'll visit people at home – wherever we can find them. In the evenings, mostly. Put on a real blitz."

Alf said nothing. The last time Doyle had played this game, several people had lost their jobs. He felt he was being asked to live his worst mistakes over again. Yes, time had circled back on itself, and the evil was here again, in Doyle's dim room. It brought back memories of another room, the sailboats on the wall.

He went on smoking, staring at the labyrinth of pink roses in the filthy, wornout rug.

"You don't want me," he said at last.

"Why not?"

Again Alf shook his head. Given how he felt about himself these days, the answer seemed self-evident. But at the same time, he felt incapable of expressing it. Expressing it meant confession, and he could no more confess than fly. His guilt had become a dark weight his body had accustomed itself to, like a tree growing around a buried axe-head. He went on staring at the dilapidated rug, his cigarette growing a drooping worm of ash.

"You're worth fifty votes to me," Doyle said, butting his cigarette. "Maybe a hundred."

Alf looked up at him, hardly trusting his ears. But the organizer was studying him gravely.

"People will follow you," Doyle said. "They know you were treated unfairly."

"That's no reason to follow anybody."

"No, but they trust you. You're a sort of leader to them."

"Oh fucking hell," Alf said. "I wasn't born yesterday."

Doyle went on watching him, through smoke.

"You're out of date," Alf said bitterly, "if it was ever true. Which I doubt. I've fallen off the table."

Cigarette smoke drifted along the sloping walls and ceilings. In the street, a fire-truck's engine rattled. "So what do you think?" Doyle demanded, after a while.

Looking away to his left, Alf saw the sunlit asphalt far below, and remembered the old man he'd seen in the woods, the man who had come trudging along the trail that day, weeping. He saw again the black coat opened to reveal the red slit of the tie; heard again his sorrowful howling; saw him stop among the trees to blow his nose, then go on. It was as vivid to him as if it were all happening again, as if he were there in the grey mild air of the empty woods, with his back to the tree. Except that this time, grief – who knew where it had come from – welled up through *him*. He felt tears come, and turned his face aside.

After a few seconds, he composed himself and looked back to Doyle. The organizer had averted his eyes. In the smoke-layered dimness of the room, his pitted face gave the impression of great age, as though he had come through centuries of lifetimes. To Alf, Doyle seemed somehow connected to the old man in the woods, as if the organizer were thinking of him too. Alf felt a stab of affection for the other man; he hardly knew him, and yet – here they were in this strange knot of intimacy, more intimate, in a way, than anything he had shared for weeks with his own wife.

Late the next day, Alf stood across from Margaret as she sorted grimly through a heap of children's jeans. Through the vast barn of the Johnsonville discount store, tangled piles of clothes had been dumped out on long rows of trestle tables, under the arctic glare of fluorescent lights. There were suits and dresses as well, their hangers squeaking incessantly as people shoved them along the racks. He and Margaret had not come here in the old days when he'd had a wage, and he sensed it was a burden on her, to shop alongside the kind of people who frequented this wasteland of bargains. Not far away stood an Indian woman with long, greasy hair. Under her pink, slack-necked sweatshirt her vast breasts fell away to either side. She wore bedroom slippers, rimmed with fur, and brown slacks with a stain like dried mucilage down one thigh. Yet there was something proud in her carriage, frowning and royally disdainful, as she flicked through the mess of clothes.

He pawed through the trousers and from time to time held up a pair, which Margaret dismissed with a sharp glance and shake of her head. He felt, almost, as if she were dismissing him as well, for the pretty pass he'd brought them to. For a couple of weeks now, she had seemed short with him. He had tried to blame it on her time of month, but it had gone on too long for that. He worried that she'd found out about Lucille. It seemed possible: probably half the town knew about Lucille.

They paid for a pair of jeans and went out into the menthol brightness of the evening to the Biscayne. He asked Margaret if she'd like an ice cream. "We can't afford it, can we?" she said dryly, and this, too, was a jab at him. But this evening he would not take an insult. He drove to the Dairy Queen and bought two small vanillas. Heading home, he took a longer, more scenic route along unpaved backroads, past ditches where shoots of new green flamed among cans and papers. They were mostly silent, turning their ice creams under the steady lathing of their tongues, burrowing into the parallel solitudes that had become their habitual form of being together, comfortable after a fashion. On the horizon, the sun had begun to sink, filling the car with a blood-red light. Glancing over, it seemed to him that her face had grown younger. Suddenly he felt a tremendous hope – and in the same moment, launching himself into its wide air, he felt himself sinking – afraid of how she would react to his news.

But it was too late. He had already spoken, "I've got a job."

Looking over at her again he saw that her gaze had remained fixed on the road, as if in a trance. On her chin was a spot of ice cream, like a white mole.

"Margaret? I've got a –"

"I heard you."

She looked at him. The sun's red light burned over one eye. He saw he had kindled nothing in her, nothing like the wildfire of fear and hope he felt. It was as if she had lost the meaning of the word "job," its aura of safety. And yet there was something helpless about her too, as if she had been cut adrift. He saw she was alone as he was. Something in him reached out to her.

"Do you remember last summer – that Irish fellow who came around to organize a union?"

"No."

"Doyle. Malachi Doyle."

"When all the people were fired," she said.

He bit his lip. "He's actually not a bad fellow."

"You're working with a union," she said, her voice flat with disapproval. She was looking out the windshield again, into the thickening light. "After all unions have done for you." She had been irrational on the subject of unions since '49. Even more than he did, he knew, she blamed his involvement with the union for the failure, later on, of his housebuilding business.

"It's a *job*," he said. "I'll be making sixty a week."

She blew out dismissively.

"What's the matter with a union?" he said. "They're not perfect, but they've done a lot of good for people."

"Yes, like Pete."

"Goddamn you, woman!" he roared to the road. Ice cream was running over his hands, over the steering wheel. He managed to get the window down and fling out his cone. "Goddamn you," he said. This was more than a job to him. The last couple of days, knowing he would work with Doyle, he'd begun to feel like himself again. But this feeling was weak, and here she was killing it.

They were silent for a while. The sun had disappeared. In the darkening blue, intersecting jet contrails made a cross of St. Andrew's.

"I can help those people," he said, struggling for calm. "The people who were fired. If we can get the union in, we can negotiate their jobs back." Doyle had promised him this: it was one of the main reasons he'd taken up the organizer's offer. He felt it would be a way of making up, at least a little, for what he'd done. But she seemed unmoved. She went on staring out the windshield. "And anyway, it's not forever," he said. "If the union goes in, I'll get *my* job back."

"According to *Doyle*," she said, with infinite sarcasm.

"Margaret, you've got to trust me!"

"I've trusted you well enough," she said. She was sitting with the remains of her cone, like a miniature version of itself forgotten in her fingers, looking straight ahead. "I trusted you with Carrie Crean."

"What?"

"I think you heard me. Or are you going to pretend you don't know her name?"

She was looking at him now, her black eyes glazed with tears.

"I know about her, Alf. I know what you've been doing."

He steered blindly, hardly seeing the road. That she had come so near to the truth, without actually striking it, made him feel like a bullet had singed his hair. It was more shocking, in a way, than being hit. Somehow she had struck on the essential fact of his betrayal. He had not seen Lucille for months, but his sense of guilt was still raw, and she had put her finger right on it.

"Bastard," she said, "bastard."

He had never heard her use that word. The runt cone was melting over her fingers. A small muscle in her face twitched. He felt as if a craziness had broken out in the car and infected him. He was a hair's breadth from driving them into the ditch.

"Stop the car," she told him. "I want out."

He kept driving, in a kind of panic.

"I'm going to be sick," she said.

Even before he had completely stopped, she opened the door and climbed out, stumbling a little in her flats on the gravel. They were beside a kind of paddock. There was a metal gate, which she climbed awkwardly, her skirt riding up to expose the white straps of her garters. Beyond was a flat, green area spotted with cow dung, and the ruined foundations of a barn. She walked towards its caved-in doorway as if she lived there.

As he clambered over the gate, she went round the corner of the ruins, out of sight. When he finally caught up to her she was standing stock-still, looking at a mass of cattle in the corner of the compound, under the skeleton of a dead elm. They were looking at her from their furred, dirty-white faces, lowering their heads and backing against each other nervously.

"Come on," he said. He took her arm, but she shook him off and went on staring at the cattle, with her head down, almost like them, as if the key, the secret, of her life lay there, among their broad hooves squishing in the mud, their wild, pink-rimmed eyes.

"Margaret, there was never anything between me and Carrie Crean."

"You're lying," she said numbly to the cattle.

"I'm not lying."

In the corner, a few of the cattle were drifting from the herd, lowing and moving towards them. The second time he took her arm she allowed him to lead her off, in her mud-clogged pumps.

They climbed the gate. But when he opened the car door for her she turned to him, her huge eyes searching his. He told her he loved her. He did his best to look back at her candidly. But he felt she was reading his guilt in his face, and much, much more than his guilt: her own loss was there, it seemed, her own hapless wandering was there, as if she were no longer sure what his eyes meant, or his mouth. She no longer knew him.

LATE THE NEXT AFTERNOON he went back to Doyle's hotel room.
Doyle had been joined by two of his fellow workers, Shirley and
Deirdre, who were to help with the organizing. Mary Carr,
Alf's mate from the sweater mill was there too, as a volunteer. The
little Newfoundlander walked up and down the soiled carpet,
exultant at being the centre of attention, jabbing at the air with her
cigarette while she gave the names of possible supporters to Doyle.
The organizer sat on the edge of his bed, writing her suggestions
down while he squinted through the smoke from his own cigarette,
stuck like a white peg in the corner of his mouth. The air was
full of smoke, blue ranges and uplands of smoke, drifting and
slowly dissolving.

Alf had his old chair by the window. With each name Mary came
up with he grew more uncomfortable, taking hard drags on his own
cigarette and looking bleakly out into the sunlit street. On the sidewalk, two women had stopped to talk. The world outside seemed a
haven of sunshine and normality. But here, in this room, they seemed
to be up to something else: an activity of smoke and shadows, conspiratorial, illicit.

Mary stopped and looked at him. For this special occasion she
had rimmed her small eyes with liner and painted her lips bright red.
But there could be no disguising the oddness of her scooped-out face
with its pointed chin.

"Can you think of anybody else, Alf?"

He frowned a thoughtful frown.

"What about Matilda Barnes?" she said, wondering.

The name jolted him. Matilda had been a friend of his mother's,
a woman in her sixties now who worked in the cutting department
of the sweater mill. As a boy, he had often visited her house. Her

husband had kept pigeons. Alf had loved to feed them while the soft birds balanced on his shoulders and even his head, their little claws needling his scalp.

His whole instinct was to protect Matilda. He suspected that if he asked, she would sign a union card. But he didn't want to lead her into a situation where she might be fired.

"I wouldn't think she'd go for it," he said. "Too close to retirement. Not really the union type."

Across the room, Deirdre and Shirley were watching him. Deirdre Hoar was a stocky woman of perhaps thirty, with short black hair and beautiful fine eyebrows, a hooked nose, and a look of pent outrage, like a baby owl or hawk. Shirley Dearing was about the same age, tall with hunched shoulders and a long, attractive face within a thin fall of hair. Alf was aware of a certain shrewdness in the way she looked at him. Her presence intimidated him more than Deirdre's, because it made him want to perform well.

"I dunno," Mary said, demurring. "Matilda's a pretty independent type. Ain't her husband in a union, over in Johnsonville there?"

"Well, I could be wrong," Alf said.

"Anyways, you know her, don't you?"

"Years ago," Alf said evasively. He could feel his face heating, and was glad of the dimness of the room.

A silence descended. Alf did not know where to look, caught on the slippery slope of his own lie. He could almost hear the others thinking, incredulously, If you know her, why don't you approach her? His own subterfuge had shaken him. He had come to this room full of enthusiasm, wanting to help. But something about surrendering names had awakened an old reluctance. In a way, he had come full circle. He was back in Prince's motel room. Again, there was a man with a notebook, waiting for names.

"I'd give her a try," Mary said to Doyle.

Doyle looked at Alf, his thick eyebrows raised: it was Alf's call.

"I wouldn't," Alf said, as nonchalantly as he could.

"All right," Doyle said. He studied the tip of his ballpoint. Alf licked his lips. Across the room, Deirdre was motionless in her chair, her eyes fierce.

"Well?" Doyle said.

Alf realized that several seconds had passed. He had lapsed away.

"I'm sorry, I –"

"Mali just wondered if you knew any other names?" This from Shirley, with a note of gentleness, of provisional support.

"Right." Alf looked at the door. Its pale, scarred rectangle stood only a few feet away, just beyond the gauntlet of legs and feet and shoes. He could stand up and say, I'm sorry. I've made a mistake. Or he could simply walk away. But he sat on, not knowing what he was going to do, only knowing that he would do *something*. He was, almost, a fascinated spectator of himself, waiting in a clarity without foreknowledge or understanding. Was he simply afraid to leave? No, something else was keeping him here, the pull of something he did not understand.

He said, "I don't want to put these people at risk –"

Across the room, Deirdre swore.

Doyle frowned. "Alf, I think I told you we're not having any more meetings like the one at Pete's. At least not until there's so many of us they can't fire us."

"You said no meetings."

"What's going on, Mali," Deirdre said. There was something comical in her anger, it was so immediate and extreme. Doyle ignored her.

"If we can collect enough cards, there won't have to be any meetings – not before certification. After we're legal, it's a whole new ball game."

"Have you ever done this before?" Deirdre asked Alf, critically.

"Not for many years," Alf said.

"Because this is pretty basic –"

"All right," Doyle said, placating.

"So give us some names!" Deirdre cried, slapping her thigh.

"Not if you ask like that," Alf said, fixing her with hatred. There was a certain joy in looking at her like this: all his strong emotion finally finding a focus. For a few seconds they simply stared at each other through the smoke.

"All right, *brother*," Deirdre said finally. She sat back in her chair with her sinewy forearms crossed, scowling.

There was silence in the room. All were waiting for him now: the two women in their chairs, Doyle on the squeaky bedsprings, his carved, ancient face hovering in smoke like some tribal god. And Mary Carr with her back to the door, her bleak white face with its circles of eyeliner looking across to him without expression, the hardness of her life having purged her of any airs, any bother with false, encouraging smiles. All the people in the room were hard, he saw. There was something desperate and pinched about them, they had the air of underdogs. But at the same time they were true, as a chunk of rock or a good hammer is true. They had given their hardness as an instrument, to a cause.

He said, "Ellen Kelly."

"Good!" Mary said, stabbing her finger at him. Doyle printed the name while the others watched, like people who don't write themselves and have an immense, almost superstitious respect for the scribe in their midst. Alf was momentarily lost in the associations conjured by *Ellen Kelly*: the narrow house on the Flats, a bed of prize dahlias, Ellen's fleshy arms. Yes, a name was more than a name. It was a life. What business did people have even uttering other people's names – flinging them about like stones. There was no telling *what* might happen. He remembered reading about some Indian tribe where everyone had two names. One was for public use, the other was secret, and could not be uttered by others. How well he understood this. How he wished Ellen Kelly had another name, to make her safe.

"Any others?" Doyle said, glancing at him pointedly.

Alf looked up wondering, his brow sweating. Their faces hovered in smoke, like masks.

He saw faces but could remember no names. He saw eyes, and gardens, and front porches; he saw a rowboat, tethered under willows, and a green Plymouth with furry dice hanging from its rear-view; he saw faces in their crooked singularity. But he could think of no names.

The only name he could remember was his own. It had stuck in his head like some fragment of a song he couldn't shake. "Alfred William Walker Alfred William Walker." As if he were five years old, chanting it like a bit of magic.

Then another name occurred to him.

"Sidney Clarke," he said.

Sidney lived on West Street, about a hundred yards north of the Island. Alf and Doyle found him in his backyard, bent over his hoe on a strip of black earth. Below the sharp cut of the bank behind him, the Atta churned up pompoms of foam. Smoke poured from a pile of branches and leaves. Walking ahead of the organizer, Alf saw the stoop of Sidney's labouring shoulders and was filled with second thoughts. What business did he have walking in here, asking Sidney to risk his peace and quiet? He felt the warmth of pity, only a hair's breadth from self-pity.

As always, Sidney was glad to see Alf. He kept his eyes fixed brightly on Alf's, as Alf explained what he and Doyle were up to. From time to time, Sidney glanced at the organizer, and though his smile of boyish eagerness remained intact, it revealed a hint of something hard and suspicious. But when he turned back to Alf, his rapt expression returned. It reminded Alf of Pete, and he had to look away. Had he pulled Sidney's name out of the air because Sidney was so much like Pete? If so, this was the *last* place he should have brought Doyle. What in the hell was he trying to do?

To make matters worse, Sidney agreed almost at once to join, said, Yep, Yep I'm in, even as Alf, shifting his feet in the dirt, silently urged him to refuse. He felt Sidney was joining on his account only: the man didn't know what he was doing. As Pete, he felt, had not known.

"The deal is," Doyle told him, "you sign a card, pay us a dollar, and when we get fifty-five per cent, the union's in." He had taken a card from inside his jacket. The grin froze on Sidney's face as he eyed it with blank apprehension: a good patient watching the doctor load his hypodermic.

There was no flat surface to sign it on. So Alf bent over and Sidney signed the card on his back.

Sidney had left his wallet in the house. As he trekked away to fetch a dollar, Alf and Doyle turned to look at the river. It was beautiful just now, a hurrying ribbon of bronze lit with the elusive earth-tints of the spring evening. But Alf felt unconnected to the scene in front of him: he had stepped over a frontier, onto the questionable side of good. He turned, at a cry from the house, a woman's high-pitched voice leaping in anger. Doyle chortled and looked back at the river. Alf was appalled. A surging unhappiness had invaded his limbs: he must *do* something. He found a flat stone and whipped it sidearm over the river.

"Her father went out in '49," he told Doyle, accusingly. "Lost his job, in the end."

"Well maybe this time," Doyle said, "she'll learn who to blame."

"We're all part of it," Alf said, striking back at him. Doyle looked at him sharply, and for a moment, before Alf turned away to find another stone, their eyes met and their easy companionship was exposed as an illusion.

Sidney came back down the yard, pale and trembling but with a smile still struggling for prominence on his thin face. Protruding from his hand, the way a child might carry it, was a stiff new dollar bill. As he handed it over, no one spoke of what had just occurred, but Alf could see Jeanie Clarke's small face peering out a window: a vision of concentrated fury.

Fifteen minutes later, they were sitting in Ellen Kelly's front room, surrounded by wallpaper in a suffocating floral print like a dying jungle. Ellen worked in sewing: a heavy, grey-haired woman with doughy arms that wobbled underneath as she handed around a dish of peppermints. The scooped top of her flowered dress showed a sun-roughened chest, like so much pink crepe. Sitting back in her armchair she rolled a peppermint around her mouth with a clicking sound and looked sharply at Alf and Doyle and occasionally glanced at her husband, Jared, who had dragged a chair into the doorway to the dining room and sat bent over with his elbows on his thighs, staring at the floor as though his back and his patience had given out together. The house stank of Brussels sprouts.

"So you can't get enough trouble," Ellen said in a loud, demanding voice to Alf.

"Guess not," he said.

"It's all right for you boys," she said. "If this blows up, you still got your jobs. Not like us. They catch us signing one of your cards and we're gone."

"That's right," Jared said absently to the floor. The bald patch at the back of his thinning brush cut gave off a yellow shine in the lamplight. He had been a mechanic in the air force, and now worked in a garage in Johnsonville. There was a weariness about him, as though he had long ago given up his interest in life, and was only waiting, a little disgustedly, for it to end.

"I'm three years from retirement, I got my pension to think of," Ellen said, glancing angrily at her husband as if this were *his* fault. "Maybe if I was twenty –"

She looked at them with bulging eyes. Her big jaw worked on her candy and her eyes demanded, Well? Her refusal was enough for Alf:

he stirred in the couch to signal he was ready to go. But Doyle went on sitting with a faint smile as if he was settling in for the night, oblivious to the uncomfortable silences that fell. He said, "Think of it maybe as a legacy. Something for the younger ones who've got a lot more than three years to go."

"I got eleven grandchildren," Ellen barked at him. "That's legacy enough for me."

"Eleven!" Doyle said. "That beats me. I've only got nine."

Ellen went on rolling a peppermint around on her tongue, apparently unimpressed. She was dead set against them, Alf saw. Why was Doyle wasting everyone's time? Feeling embarrassed on behalf of them both, Alf cleared his throat and said, "Well" and looked towards the window where pots of African violets and baby's tears floated against the dimming street. He was beginning to believe that Doyle was more than insensitive: there was a kind of brutality in him, unsoftened by pity or remorse, like a salesman who means to exhaust his victim into submission.

Doyle said, "My daughter's husband, he's in this plant in Toronto – makes shock absorbers for trains. Good union – he's a steward – sits on the board alongside the bigwigs. They actually have a say in how the place is run."

Jared said, "Fat chance of that here."

"That's what they said there, apparently," Doyle said coolly. Jared snorted and went on staring at the floor. Ellen glared at her husband. Alf felt he had stumbled into their secret life: a life of humiliations and unsatisfied rage, contained in this orderly little house where everything was spotless and exactly in place.

Doyle went on for a time about unions he was familiar with, talking about how normal life got once they were established. Even the bigwigs ended up being happy with the situation, he said: a long contract let them predict their costs accurately, without surprises. Hell, he even knew one boss who bragged about what a good union he had – and this guy was one tough cookie. He'd fought the union like a Mafioso when it first went in. But he'd come around. He seemed almost proud of *his* union – as if he knew he was finally on the side of the angels.

As Doyle talked he took a union card out of his shirt pocket and toyed with it in his big hands. He bent it between thumb and forefinger, stropped it on his index finger like a blade, touched it to his red, pitted nose. Ellen scowled at the little white card.

Suddenly Doyle stopped talking. He looked at the card and seemed almost surprised to find it in his hand. He looked at Ellen, as if to say, What am I going to do with this? He raised his thick black eyebrows.

"All right," Ellen said. "Give me the damned thing." She shot another poisonous look at her husband, who was staring at her, apparently in shock.

Doyle gave her the card, and she signed it on the small table beside her chair. She sent Jared out of the room to find a dollar, which he brought to her with evident distaste, holding out the bill and averting his head as she took it. She extended one arm, and as Doyle took the dollar and the card from her, she looked over at Alf and, without changing her dour expression, slipped him a wink.

After, in the car, Alf said, "I was ready to walk out of there."

"Sometimes it's the right move," Doyle said. "You develop a feeling. That one was a believer, I knew it when I came in."

"A believer," Alf said, gently mocking. He was beginning to think that Doyle was a bit of a hot-air artist. They were driving down Shade, between the closed stores.

"She's mad," Doyle said. "You could see it in her face. She knows there's injustice in the way things work – knows it in her gut. The whole time she's saying, No, no, and doing the sensible thing. But inside there's a tough old gal standing with clenched fists saying, Just give me a shot at the buggers."

"You seem so sure," Alf said critically.

Doyle looked over at him.

"You must have sensed something yourself there."

"Not me," Alf said.

"Then why'd you give me her name?" Doyle said. Alf was startled. Why *had* he given Doyle Ellen's name? He looked out at a passing tree, its new leaves orange in the tide of light rolling in from the west.

They got five signatures that night, with four refusals. The last refusal came at a house in Erie, a village a few miles outside of town, where the door was slammed in their faces with a report that filled the silent, shadowy street. They drove slowly back towards Attawan. Through the open windows came the thick, drowning sweetness of lilacs, wafting from roadside groves as big as transport trucks.

"A good night's work," Doyle said. He was slouching back with one arm falling over the seat behind him, the other straight to the wheel, his big head on angle: the posture of a fulfilled man. Alf envied him his lazy pleasure in his achievement. Doyle seemed someone who believed, who had brought home the harvest of that belief. There was nothing sweeter in life, perhaps, but Alf could not share his sense of a job well done.

"I feel like you did it all."

"We wouldn't have got half those cards without you."

"So what am I – a pretty face?"

"That's right," Doyle said. Alf chortled and looked out the window where the fields revolved among the great, dark citadels of the bush-lots. He *had* felt moments of satisfaction in getting the cards – there was something about being with Doyle that normalized the whole enterprise and made it seem more possible than he'd imagined. He'd even experienced a sweet surge of vengefulness – against Bannerman's, against Prince, against Kit Ford. But revenge wasn't enough. To do this work properly, he sensed, you had to be a believer.

He *wanted* to believe, with the same kind of certainty Doyle had, or even with the inchoate angry belief of Ellen Kelly, but he kept coming up against a barrier in himself.

"How do you justify it to yourself," he said, "risking these people's jobs, in the chance you'll get a union in?" It was the question that troubled him most, just now. He hadn't worried about it when he'd worked for the union in 1949: he'd been so excited by the tactical, almost warlike side of the campaign, so caught up in the hope of making a better world, and yes, so mesmerized by the head organizer, Cary Winner, that he hadn't really taken in the risk to anyone else. He had now, though. He was older and, besides, what had happened to Pete and the others had left him wary of fooling around with people's lives.

"Hey, what we're doing is *legal*," Doyle said with gentle sarcasm. "And what *they* do, I mean firing people for organizing, that's *illegal*, brother." After a while, sounding a good deal more weary, the organizer added, "I worry about it, of course I do. I guess I believe in the big picture. To be frank, I don't believe in it the way I used to, when I was a tyro. But I believe – I guess I believe we can push this bloody society to a place where the values are a little different. Where an ordinary person's job, just a decent bloody wage for God's sake, is more important than the ability of some obscenely rich bastard to add a new wing to his house in Palm Springs."

"But if he's earned it," Alf said. It was the old independent businessman in him speaking, the guy who had once wanted to build houses, to someday build a fine house for himself.

"Has he earned it?" Doyle said, a new ferocity in his voice. "Or has the unfairness Ellen Kelly knows about just allowed him a god's leverage on things, a leverage no human being should have? I mean, I don't deny the punter his reward, but too much is too much. I know men who'd rather let a hundred or a thousand other men go to the dogs than give up a straw of their privileges. They haven't earned it any more than I've earned the air I breathe. They've just taken it away from the rest of us."

Alf knew Doyle had a point. A world where a few men had a hundred pairs of shoes and millions had none was not a just world. But hell, wasn't there room somewhere between those two extremes? What, after all, was the matter with wanting to have a nicer house, a better car? Yes, for all he'd been through, there was something in him that was still hopeful he might rise one day. And a union wasn't about rising – it wasn't about life lived on the vertical. It was about the horizontal life, it seemed to him, a life where you couldn't rise, unless everyone else rose with you, equally. The thought of a purely horizontal life depressed him.

He looked out the window. They were crossing a bridge; the murky water of the Attawan drifted in mist. He was caught, he realized. He was not a committed union man, he felt he was doing it to help those who had lost their jobs, and to make up something to Pete. And, yes, because he needed the money. At the same time, he was afraid that history might be repeating itself. If their campaign was discovered, there might be even more job losses than last time. There seemed to be no way out of this. He struck a match and lit two cigarettes. For the rest of the way home, he and Doyle smoked silently, turning their faces occasionally to the windows, to exhale into the rush of night air.

They paid their visits mostly in the evenings, and on weekends. That left the days free: long, rather tedious stretches of time in which Alf worked around the house. Sometimes Doyle came over and they sat outside, drinking juice or beer on the picnic table under the apple tree. They were becoming friends. Whatever the difference in their political beliefs, a deeper current was at work in them – a kind of sympathetic vibration. They liked each other, they shared a similar sense of humour, they had both fought in the war, Doyle as a member of a British regiment, an experience that had grated rather hard on his then Northern Irish, Catholic, nationalist sentiments. "I was just like Hitler," he liked to joke. "Fighting a war on two fronts."

For Alf, Doyle's presence was a kind of gift. After Pete, he hadn't expected to have a close friend again. In a way, he was already closer to Doyle than he had ever been to Pete. With Pete, he had always felt a bit superior, a big brother looking out for a younger. But he and Doyle seemed more like equals, mutually respecting. He had a sense he'd never had with Pete, a sense that Doyle understood him.

One afternoon he and Doyle climbed with their beer over the dyke and sat on a log near the deep bend of the Atta, where it swung below Lookout Hill. They were talking about the war, and Doyle told a story about falling asleep one night on sentry duty. That night, the Germans had attacked the camp he was helping guard, killing three men, one a friend of his. No one had known he'd dozed off, and in any case there had been several other sentries, so no one had blamed him – but he obviously blamed himself. "If I have one regret," he said, and broke off his sentence. In the silence that followed, Alf watched a gull that had settled on the river, like a small white boat adrift under the shadowy bank. His mind was full of Pete. Hadn't it been the same with Pete and him – his one slip-up leading to a result he'd never intended – to a regret that would never go away? He had thought it impossible he would ever tell anybody about what he'd done to Pete. But now, his heart surging, he felt he was about to.

Yet he shied away at the last moment, not at all certain his friendship with the organizer could bear it. Not sure *he* could bear it. Instead, he told Doyle about the German boy he'd shot in the wine cellar. Except for the death of his brother, it had been the worst moment of the war for him – when the cellar door was flung back and he saw the boy at his feet, the broken wine bottle in his hand. "I suppose he meant to kill me with it, but he couldn't have. I'd got him in the heart."

"Jesus," Doyle said.

Alf dug at the sand with the heel of his shoe. He hadn't told the story well, hadn't conveyed at all his shock at what he'd seen: the freshness and youth of that lifeless face.

And Pete was still alive in him, a pressure.

49

ONE SUNDAY EVENING when Doyle was out of town, Alf got a call from Mary Carr. She'd been fired. "Somebody must have squealed on me to the Roadrunner," she told him. "Can't figure who it is."

Joe had the car – he was off with some girl, a new one, Margaret said – so Alf walked over to Mary's house on the Flats. It was a tiny, stuccoed place – one end of a long, oddly curved building that had once been a rail station, in the days when a line fed into the valley. His father had left from this spot to go to France in 1915. Red roses bloomed against the brown stucco.

Mary lived here with her twin daughters. Her husband, Carter, had decamped years ago, for the West, a runty little guy with an aggressive manner who, as Alf remembered, had been in trouble as a boy for stealing a shotgun. When Alf knocked on the door, one of Mary's twins (was it Susie or Sharon?) looked out with wide-set, eleven-year-old eyes.

"Who's that!" he heard Mary bellow. From deeper in the house came a sound of childish sobbing. The girl with her prominent, curved chin, like Mary's, withdrew her head. The door swung open a little.

"Alf, come in! I'm on the phone. Deirdre."

He waited in the cramped living room. There was a couch, which looked as if it folded out into a bed, two armchairs, a couple of small tables, and an old-fashioned radio topped with a statue of our Our Lady, her robe painted a bright blue, her arms out in succour. One of the hands had broken off. Mary stood with the receiver in the kitchen doorway, saying, "Yeah, yeah, yeah" while looking blindly in Alf's direction. The twin who answered the door had disappeared. The sobbing had stopped, replaced by sounds of a TV pumping out the opening theme of *The Ed Sullivan Show*.

Mary hung up the phone and threw herself into a chair opposite Alf. Her shorts revealed slim, very pale legs.

"The fucker," she said angrily. "He had the nerve to take a cup of tea off me. He comes to fire me, and he sits right there where you're sittin' and takes tea!"

"Who?"

She looked at him as if not understanding, blinded by her anger.

"The Roadrunner! The son of a bitch smiled as he told me. 'We know you're with the union,' he says. Well I didn't deny it. I should've denied it, I guess. I mean, what proof did he have? But I couldn't – there was somethin' in his face, I just wanted to hit him with the truth. He's lucky I didn't hit him with a brick. I did it to myself, no less!"

And she held Alf's eyes in disbelief, as if *he* might tell her why she'd acted against herself – why she'd admitted to the Roadrunner that she was with the union when all she had to do was deny, deny. Of course, as she said, he *might* have laid her off anyway, but then at least she could have said she'd done everything she could to defend herself and her girls.

"The bastard wanted me to spy for them," she said, throwing one long leg over the other.

"Spy –," he said. He felt he had woken from a dream-state, in the deep chair.

"You know, I find out who's signed cards, I can keep my job. The swine."

"And you refused," he said.

"I guess I did," she said. She shook once, with a brief, silent laugh. Then tears glistened. "What am I gonna do with my girls! I can't keep this place on unemployment!."

"I'll talk to Doyle," he said, struggling to find his voice. "He'll put you on salary," he said, promising wildly. "At the least, when the union goes in, we'll get you your job back."

"That's what Deirdre says."

"Well there you go. We'll fix you up."

It was almost dark when he left her house. He walked down Willard to the corner of Bridge, and for a moment looked down the race-way, to the mills in their Sunday stillness. He had spent nearly twenty years in those buildings; his mother and father had spent most of their lives there. But now the mills seemed opaque, a mystery, with their countless windows reflected dully in the water below. In his chest, a little anger flickered and was gone.

He went on up Bridge past the mound of the arena and came to the bridge, where he stopped and leaned on the rail. A hundred yards away, Bannerman's dam made a thick, white, churning line, in a deep shush of falling water.

He felt tired, too tired to move. He thought of smoking a ciga-rette, but even this seemed too much effort, so he went on staring at the river, his forearms braced on the rail, in a kind of hopelessness. He spat, and watched the fleck fall in a long curve, under the bridge.

The car arrived soundlessly behind him. He heard only the hush – like a nearer emissary of the dam itself – of a window sliding down. The dark-blue Fleetwood seemed darker than black could be, in the feeble street light.

He stooped to the open window. Prince was leaning towards him across the seat, smiling affably as if whatever had passed between them in the past had left only a residue of casual goodwill. The exec-utive's handsome face, over the open collar of his shirt, shone a little in the glow from the instrument panel.

"I was wondering if we could talk?"

Alf experienced a moment of triumph, realizing he was beyond the man's power. *I was wondering if.*

"The union," Prince said. "I may have a deal."

Doyle had warned him this might happen, he recalled. If the company felt they were going to lose, they might offer to let the union in unopposed, for considerations.

"I'm not the boss," Alf said, not bothering to hide a note of hostility. "I don't have the authority."

"For this you do."

"What is 'this'?"

"Why don't you get in? Probably not too good for either of us if we're seen together."

Glancing up and down the street, Alf got in. He knew he shouldn't, but he was curious to see what Prince had up his sleeve, and at the same time, he hardly cared. Before him, the wide windshield framed the main intersection where a red light glowed. Just beyond, a man in a baseball cap, oddly familiar, ducked into the porch of the Vimy House. Prince swung to the right and they began to rise into the North End. "Got some kind of ping under the hood," Prince said, apropos of nothing. "The garage can't seem to find it." They swept past the grey bulk of the Bannerman mansion, like a grim fairy-tale castle set back on its sloping lawns, and so down the maple-shaded avenue.

Passing the high school and the hospital, Prince turned down Golf Links Road. He drove with his head up, with that sense of easy nobility that emanated from him so naturally, two fingers lightly touching the bottom of the wheel. He talked about sports – he had been to see a softball game behind the arena, and the quality of play had impressed him, he said. "I was shortstop myself. Loved not having a base to cover, you know? That sense of freedom." Alf said nothing. The air conditioning made him feel he was enclosed in a bubble, removed from the night. Even the road itself felt far away, its imperfections smoothed by the magnificent carriage of the Fleetwood. They floated past the high hills of the golf course, past a mink farm crowded with long pens, past old trees that for a moment grew huge in the sweeping scrutiny of the Fleetwood's headlights. Off to the right, a darkness watched by silent groups of cedars, the Shade ran towards town.

"So what's the deal?" Alf said, bestirring himself. Already he regretted coming.

"Well, Alf, I hope I'm not out of place here, but I want to make you an offer."

Alf let a beat pass, as he looked away at a paddock of churned mud, blazing under a floodlight. "I'm not too fond of your offers."

A few seconds passed. Objects materialized in the dream world outside. In a weedy field, a white horse bolted, its neck flattening. "We made a mess of that," Prince said at last. He sounded genuinely aggrieved, sorry. "You know, I really did want you for that foreman's job. But I was under pressure to bring new people in."

"I'm not interested."

"I can't blame you for being teed off, Alf. Seeing someone walk in and take the job that belonged to you. I'd like to make amends if I can." Prince paused, and seemed to be considering his next step. In the headlights the asphalt gave way to washboard, a distant rumble. "How would you like to be assistant manager of the sweater mill?"

To Alf, Prince's words seemed as unreal as the countryside startled by their lights.

"As you've probably heard, Gordie Henderson's left. You could start right away."

"You must think I'm one eager whore."

Alf was taut with anger. And yet there was a place in him, beyond defiance, beyond conscience, where he was still hungry for a different life, where Prince's words had raised a ripple of excitement. Disgusted by his own weakness, he added, "Or some kind of idiot. You're just worried we're getting close. You're trying to buy me off."

"Of course there's some truth in what you're saying," Prince said, after a while, "but the offer's real. I think you'd do a good job in that office."

"If you mean it, you'll offer it to me *after* the union goes in."

Prince fell silent. Alf chuckled bleakly to himself, thinking he'd scotched him.

"Take me back to town," Alf said. "This is pointless."

They were nearing the top of a long rise. The Fleetwood slowed as Prince guided it sharply to the left, the headlights revealing an unfenced earthen track, and a spot fringed with tall grasses where the car came to a halt. Prince turned out the headlights. They were looking over the edge of the Reid Hills, with woods at their back. Three or four miles distant, the glow of the town dusted the horizon.

The engine remained idling with a low, nearly imperceptible vibration. The air conditioner put out its steady exhalation. Alf shifted impatiently.

"If I can have a few minutes," Prince said, "I'd like you to hear my side of things."

Alf shrugged in the darkness, he had little choice. And besides, he was curious. It felt safe to give his curiosity play; he was impregnable in his refusal, protected by his hatred of Prince. Like the sailor in the old story, who had himself tied to the mast, he could listen to the sirens without harm.

He listened to Prince's voice as it went on: reasonable, humorous, intelligent, self-deprecating. But there was something else there, as well, under the surface, a hardness of will not quite disguised by these other qualities. Alf felt that Prince was, in some sense, acting. Because while he seemed relaxed sitting behind the wheel of the Fleetwood, turning over ideas at random, he was in fact pushing, pushing, with a directness of purpose that irritated Alf and kept him on his guard.

"You don't like me," Prince said. "I can hardly blame you, not after the way things turned out. But let's just say, for the sake of argument, that the circumstances were, in some way, beyond our control. I know that might be hard to believe, but I don't own this company, I'm only a vice-president – one among many." He chuckled before continuing, "But what I want to say is this: I have great respect for you. I respected you when I first met you – that day you showed us around the floor. Later, I asked for your help in putting down the union. You balked at that, because it would have meant betraying your friends. I respect that too. Of course, I was on the other side, I had to play for keeps, but I admired you for your decision. Really, Alf, I did – I still do."

Alf glanced at the other man. Above the vivid white of his shirt, Prince's head seemed as much shadow as flesh. He was smiling at Alf with a strange, youthful eagerness.

"The thing is, Alf, the story of what you did, or didn't do, is out there now. I blame myself for this. I'm afraid it's being given a dishonest slant."

"What are you talking about," Alf said, suddenly alert.

"I was talking with Kit Ford, trying to demonstrate the kind of fellow you were, to show what we were up against. So I told him the story of what happened between you and me, in the motel room. To me, it showed your integrity. But Ford, I'm afraid, well, he pounced on the fact that you gave away one name. He's spreading the story that you were a company plant. Or as you might say on your side of the line, a stooge. He's telling people that you helped us break the union in the fall. He's suggesting ah –" Prince paused, and went on only reluctantly, it seemed. "He's suggesting you're helping us break it this time too. He's just doing his job, of course, trying to undermine your side. But I'm afraid it may leave you caught in the middle."

Alf sat in shock. And yet he was not surprised, not entirely. This moment seemed to have been coming at him for months. He had hoped he had eluded it, but that was clearly foolish. Too many people – Woody, Prince, perhaps others – knew what he had done. He stared over the dashboard towards the distant town.

Prince went on. "So what I'm saying is, you may find – not to put too fine a point on it – that the union doesn't want you any more. I could be wrong, of course. Maybe this will all blow over. Speaking strictly on a personal level, I hope it does, for your sake. But if it doesn't – well, you could find yourself out on the street. And if that happens, the assistant manager's job is there for you, Alf. You might be glad of a place to jump to."

Alf was silent for a long time. He could not tell if Prince was being sincere – he sounded sincere, painfully so – but in a sense it didn't matter. What had caught him seemed more like fate than the machinations of an enemy.

Prince continued, "The thing is, the thing *you* have to remember, is that you're a management man at heart. You have the ability, the *authority*. It's something that can't be taught. You've got it, Alf. You're meant for better things than knocking on doors with Mr. Doyle."

Prince paused. Outside, the night seemed far away, a few isolated lights in darkness. A reddish star throbbed faintly. "You want me to hold that job open for you, until after the union goes in? Or until the union kicks you out? I'll do my best. But the thing is, right now I know we can bring you in. Later, who can say? But once you're in, you can prove yourself, and what came to you under, shall we say, special circumstances, will seem perfectly natural. It's certainly deserved."

Silence filled the car, tempered by the steady rush of the air conditioning. Outside was the night, but it felt distant, insubstantial. The real world was here, in the comfortable bubble of the car: yes, here in the quarter-light behind the complicated, glowing instrument panel of the Fleetwood was all the world, all the future a man needed. Everything a man could desire was here, or within reach of here. Alf thought of Margaret, and a wild sensation of regret pierced from far away. He went on sitting, feeling the wash of coolness from the dash. He licked his lips and was about to speak when suddenly – a rising panic in his chest – he felt he was suffocating. He needed a cigarette. He grappled for the handle and pushed open the door. Immediately he was met by a rush of scents, warm, earthy, sharp. Some cricket was picking an out-of-tune banjo. Behind him, Prince was saying, "People respect you, Alf. Whatever you decide –"

Alf shut the door and walked a few feet from the car, sucking in the night air. He lit a cigarette and stood smoking as he looked off at the burnished horizon where the town lay. For a few moments, all he was aware of was what touched him: the ground underfoot, the scents of the night, the faint howling of a dog, down on the plain, the burn of smoke in his lungs. He was this and only this – this tenuous infinite thing, the night, the glow of a cigarette in the night's dark.

He started walking. He passed the Fleetwood and re-entered the road, between its high, bushy banks, striding down the hill towards town. Behind him, the Cadillac's headlights struck out over the shadowy fields. Then the car crept up behind him, its tires crunching on gravel. A window hummed down. Prince spoke with humorous irony.

"Hey, buddy. Give you a lift?"

Alf gave no sign he was aware of Prince's existence, but went on walking, walking and smoking, down the shadowy road.

50

WHEN MARGARET HEARD JAMIE'S CRY, her heart slammed against her ribs, as if she, too, were struggling from nightmare. She raced to his room and gathered his wiry, trembling body in its soaked pyjamas, rocking him against her. "Was it the same dream?" she asked, and the damp, tousled head nodded fiercely. His father was driving away in the Biscayne, and Jamie, stuck in the cellar, could not run after him, because an old man with no teeth and fire in his eyes was hiding in a box by the cellar stairs, threatening to eat him. For several weeks he had been so frightened of this dream he had resisted going to bed. Margaret got him into fresh pyjamas and changed the sheets. Finally easing him to sleep – he lay as he had when he was much younger, with his knees up and his thumb in his mouth – she carried his damp things to the cellar and put them in the laundry tub to soak. Reaching for the box of Tide, she knocked over a jar of soapy water the children had used for blowing bubbles; it tumbled off the shelf, breaking with a loud pop on the cement floor. Margaret cried out, furious, and kicked at the shards among the spreading pool. By the time she'd cleaned it up she was weeping quietly to herself. Her period wouldn't come and she was feeling as if she'd gained twenty pounds; she was irritated with everything and everybody – especially with Alf, who had said he'd be back in time to help put the children to bed. She was set against him perpetually these days. Their fight by the roadside had changed nothing. What had happened, or not happened (or might be happening still) with Carrie Crean was still lodged in her stomach like a cold stone.

Returning to the kitchen, she had started to make tea for herself when she heard a knocking she at first thought was Penny, padding down the hall to the bathroom. Then she realized: someone was at the front door.

A very tall, strongly built bald man in a white shirt, open at the collar, was waiting with bowed head. Seeing her through the screen, he raised one hand, palm open, as though wanting to communicate that he was harmless.

"You're Margaret Walker," he said as she opened the door. He had beautiful teeth. And a low voice so marvellously at ease with itself she thought of a movie actor. For a moment, understanding nothing, she experienced a stab of fear. "Bob Prince," he said. "I'm an executive with Bannerman's."

"Is something wrong?"

"No, no, not at all. Sorry, I didn't mean to frighten you."

"Alf's not in right now."

"We had a talk a little while ago. I just wanted to add some things to what I was saying."

She looked behind him, at the expensive-looking car gleaming in the weak street light. Despite his reassurances and friendly manner, a sense of something critically important was in the air, ominous. She was wary.

"He should be back any minute."

"Ah," he said, and when he did not move, she added, "Would you like to wait?"

She had made the offer out of politeness, and was a bit disappointed when he took her up, but a few moments later, there he was, perched on the edge of her couch, in his faultless khakis and loafers, which showed a couple of inches of beige sock, pulled up tight. His legs were oddly short and spindly-looking, she thought, for such a big man. But what really struck her were his eyes: they were the same blue as her husband's.

He did not want coffee or tea. She made a few attempts at small talk, but Bob Prince seemed almost oblivious, sitting with his big shoulders hunched forwards, frowning at his own thoughts while he drummed his fingers on his knee. She felt a bit put out, having him on her hands, having him see the shabbiness of her house; and disloyal somehow, to Alf, though she could not quite say why. Of course, with Alf in the union now, this man was on the opposite side of the fence. But now the name came back to her. Wasn't it Bob Prince who had praised Alf last summer, when Alf had taken him on a tour of the mill? It was Bob Prince – wasn't it? – whom Alf had gone to see, that night he'd phoned during supper?

"I offered your husband a job tonight," he said abruptly. He had been staring at her rug – her old green rug with its streaks of burlap backing showing – but now he looked up at her. "He turned me down, as I feared he would. Or at least I *think* he turned me down. I just feel I didn't make all the arguments I could have."

"What kind of job?" she said, not quite trusting what she'd heard, wondering what kind of job it was, if arguments had to be made for it.

Again he seemed not to hear her. He was frowning and sighing and staring at the floor as if the weight of the world was on his shoulders. But suddenly he looked up and saw her – a flash of those eyes, as if he were surprised to discover her there. For a moment he stared at her. "Assistant manager of the sweater mill."

She seemed to come awake, into a clarity of disbelief. "Not foreman? You want him to help run the sweater mill?"

"That's right." He smiled his dazzling smile. "You seem surprised."

"Well you did fire him." Her cheeks burned, at the sharpness of her tone.

"Well, *I* didn't. That was some fool down the line. He's one of the best men we've got. Or had. We let him slip through our fingers, I'm afraid."

She had given up hope that Alf would ever rise. It was a dream of their youth, like wanting to be rich or famous or simply extraordinarily good at something. *That* fate only fell to a very few, and she was resigned that it would never fall to them. What she was intent on now was surviving – getting them all through this bad patch they were in.

Her visitor's news seemed incredible, yet there was some spark in her, never completely extinguished, that leapt to it. She sat watching Prince, those pale-blue eyes that seemed so familiar, scanning her poor rug, lighting on a sagging armchair. She felt a surge of affection for Alf. He *was* a good man, and finally others were realizing it too.

"I guess he's committed to what he's doing with the union," Bob Prince said. "I must say, though I disagree with him, I have to respect him for it. Your husband's a man of great integrity, Mrs. Walker."

She looked at him. He was a big, strong, bluff man with an important job. But there was a touch of helplessness about him, she thought. And he seemed overworked, judging by the shadows under his eyes.

"You know," he said, holding her with his gaze, "I feel he left the door open a little. He *did* say, that after the union went in, he'd be happy to take a look at our offer."

She watched him closely, alerted by something in his tone.

"The trouble is – and I've explained this to him – I don't know if we'll be *able* to make the offer then. I mean, if it was up to me alone, he could have that job any time he wanted. But some of *my* superiors –" Bob Prince hesitated. He ran his hand over his bald head.

Margaret looked out the window, where the slightly parted drapes gave a view of his car, glinting under the street light. A cat jumped to its hood just then, padding gingerly on the warm metal. It's me he came to talk to, she thought. Not Alf at all. She turned back to her visitor. "Perhaps the best thing is for you to go," she said. "I'll tell my husband you were here."

After the Fleetwood drove off, she spent a restless half-hour waiting for Alf. She swept the kitchen floor, washed a few dishes, put on coffee. Thinking she heard Jamie cry out, she went up to check, but the boy was asleep on his back, his mouth open, one arm flung out across the pillow. Downstairs, the screen door ajar, she found Alf in the kitchen.

Her husband was sitting at the edge of a chair, stripping off a sock. She cried out at the raw, round spot on his heel and brought him iodine and a bandage.

"How did you get that?"

"Walking," he said grimly.

"You must have walked some distance."

He went on tending his wound, intently, like a boy, with his foot up on the chair. From outside came the faint, stuttering cry of a nighthawk.

Shutting the screen door and the inner door, she sat down at the table.

"Alf, we had a visitor tonight."

He grunted, more interested in his doctoring. He tore off the flap of rucked skin.

"Alf –"

He looked up at her, his eyes hard.

"Oh Alf," she crooned, forcing her affection a little.

When he considered her – not quite sure, apparently, what she intended – she flushed. Then plunged into the heart of the matter. "Bob Prince was here tonight."

He stopped short, a bandage in his hand.

"He came to see you. He told me about the job offer. He said there were some things he neglected to tell you –"

"He came *here*?" he said. "When the hell was this?"

"Tonight."

"*When* tonight?"

"Please don't raise your voice," she said, struggling to smile. "He came about ten o'clock. He left half an hour ago. Alf, we have to talk –"

He smashed his fist onto the table, making the glass top of the butter dish jump, his expression fierce. She was startled, and put out by his outburst.

"You can't just throw this away so easily – for what? For the union?"

Again he struck the table, in real fury.

"Oh good," she said. She spoke sarcastically, powered by an anger she could no longer control. "Someone offers you something and you can't even bear to talk about it."

She watched him stand up and go to the sink. There was something animal-like, bullish, in his shoulders, she thought, as he filled a glass with water and drank. *This* is what she had been struggling with in him, all these years: this roughness. It enraged her, she had borne so much because of it.

"You've worked years to get ahead," she said, trying to remain calm. "For heaven's sake, at least *hear* what he has to say."

He went very still, stooped over the sink. Was he just going to slip away into another of his silences? She was at full throttle now, remembering all the silences she had endured from him. This was part of his roughness too, wasn't it? Her husband hardly spoke to her, not when it came to important things, not even when it came to the simple matter of keeping her company. He might as well have been deaf and dumb, like the Horsfalls.

"You once had a business of your own," she said. "Now you're knocking on doors for *signatures*."

He turned and looked at her. A bit of spit had bubbled at his lower lip.

"It's honest work," he said.

"Digging ditches is honest work! Why can't you see where your advantage lies?"

"Be quiet," he said.

"Tell me," she said, getting out of her chair and going to him. "Just tell me – since I apparently don't understand it – why knocking on doors with your Malachi Doyle is better than assistant manager. Assistant manager, Alf!" He turned to her, eyes flashing. Good, she thought, good, this is long overdue.

"The people who sign, they depend on me," he said in a rusty voice. His eyes seemed almost unfocused, lost in space, as if he was reciting some idea by rote.

"And what about *me*?" she cried. "What about your children? Aren't *we* depending on you? Your son's up there – did you know he has nightmares every night about your leaving? It's no wonder, is it? You're away every night. We hardly know you any more!"

"This is what I'm doing," he said, after a moment.

He was so *thick*, she thought: she wanted to pull his eyes out.

"You're ruining yourself. You're ruining this family."

"I have a job," he said flatly, watching her.

Her fury mounted at the dead end of her life.

"I think you're a coward," she said. "You're afraid of the responsibility, that's what I think. You *like* being mediocre. It suits you. It doesn't matter what happens to *us*, so long as you can go on digging your miserable little ditch with –"

The back of his hand caught her in the centre of her face. He had never struck her before, or even threatened to. There was the surprise – the sheer force of it – and then a numbness, almost an unreality, as she sensed the kitchen suddenly retreating. The pain had not started yet, though she wondered if her nose was broken. Her laugh came out of her in an odd cry, hysterical. She leaned over the table, nursing her face with one hand, half-expecting another blow. When it didn't come, she looked around. He was standing with his back to her, at the window. When he turned, she saw he was weeping.

51

ALF SPENT THE NIGHT tossing on the couch, pacing and smoking in the backyard. He had done it now, he felt. He had crossed the line beyond which there was no forgiveness, no return, he had done the unthinkable thing he had despised other men for doing, and now he was no better than the worst of them. In a sense, he did not understand what had happened. He had struck his wife, yes, but at the same time it was as if a wave had come up out of nowhere, a vast, powerful wave that had rolled them both about, and in the confusion and fury his arm had flung out and caught her, willy-nilly, on her nose. The next morning, Margaret, setting out the breakfast things, ignored his attempts at apology. Her lower lip was swollen – one section pale and inflated like the thick part of an earthworm; a bruise shadowed her cheek and nose. He hovered in remorse, trying to be helpful, then froze as Jamie and Penny tumbled in for breakfast. It didn't take them long to discover Margaret's face. "*What happened,*" Penny said in a hushed voice, her eyes moving from her mother to her father and back again. Alf couldn't speak, and was gratified when Margaret told them almost cheerfully that she'd run into a cupboard door – she was all right, she said, and would they please eat their Shredded Wheat, they were late for school.

At eleven, Doyle came by. Alf met him outside and took him to their usual place by the river. He seemed to be moving in a dream now, felt he understood nothing, but he clung to certain thoughts he knew he had to express. Doyle sat on the driftwood log, smoking as he looked down to the Atta, spreading calmly through its shadowed bend. Alf stood woodenly before him, speaking in a rasping voice of the things he'd kept hidden: Prince's offer the previous fall, his betrayal of Woody Marr. He did not mention Pete. But he told Doyle about his latest conversation with Prince, the news that Ford was spreading the story, the offer of the assistant managership. He spoke mechanically, without much emotion, knowing only that he owed this to Doyle. The shame that had attended his secrets scarcely affected him. Nor did he feel any relief.

When Alf had finished, Doyle stared at the ground for a long while, the smoke twisting above the forgotten stub of his cigarette. To Alf, his silence seemed to open a gulf between them, which deepened with each second: he was sure his friendship with the organizer had just ended.

"I wish you'd told me about this before," Doyle said finally. He squinted up at Alf, whose back was to the sun. "So what do you want to do?"

Alf looked towards his house. In Joe's bedroom window, he could see the small, pale moon of Margaret's face, the bruise barely visible at this distance, watching him. She still had not spoken to him, and yet there was some quality of expectation in her look.

"I'll quit if you want," he said. His voice a dry, foreign thing. He looked at his own shadow on the sand before him. "But what I want – is to go on with the union. If the union will still have me."

Doyle got up heavily, paced. Snapped away his butt. Swung his thick, scabbed arm at a scrub willow. He turned back to Alf.

"All right, mate," he said. "I think we'll be all right. Everybody knows you were fired unfairly. They won't believe Ford's stories – or very few of them will. We'll just keep on, steady as she goes –"

Alf nodded. The sun beat on the sand, on the stunted bushes, on Malachi Doyle's red face, on the back of his neck. He stood by the hushing river, his eyes half-closed, aware of nothing but its heat.

52

PENNY RODE HER BICYCLE up West. Near the bridge, several girls were skipping double dutch: the two long ropes turning against each other like the beaters in her mother's Mixmaster, slapping the road under Ginny Lamport, who in Penny's opinion was the best skipper on the Island, her ponytail bouncing, her white socks jogging up and down, faster and faster, as the ropes snicked under her. The other girls, the turners and the watchers, sang out in saucy voices:

> One Two Three A-Laura
> Four Five Six A-Laura
> Seven Eight Nine A-Laura
> Ten A-Laura Secord!

Ginny ran out through the speeding ropes and another girl ran in. Seeing Penny go by, Ginny, her face flushed, called out for her to join them.

"Can't," Penny said and kept riding. Pedalling off the Island and up West – it was pretty much on the level all the way to Bannerman's hosiery mill – she could hear the girls' voices crying out behind her: "First comes love, Then comes marriage, Then comes Linda with a baby carriage!" At the hill, she stood up in the heavy old bike with the balloon tires and wicker basket – it had once belonged to her babysitter, Joyce French – and managed to ride halfway up until she finally had to get off and push. Far below, to her left, the river glittered through the trees that crowded up the steep bank to the road. She was not quite sure where the path was – it had been at least a year since her father had showed it to her – and when she turned off the road, hiding her bike below the guardrail, and started down the narrow slot in the weeds, she still wasn't sure she had the right place. But she soon came to the clearing. It was shielded from the road above by trees, and looked out through a gap in the trees below to the water. Yes, there was the weedy hump, the sticking-out bits of old boards and a crooked window-frame with slivers of glass hanging in it – the remains of Johnny North's shack. She was here because of a dream. She had been lying somewhere, unable to get up, for the heaviness of her body, lying in misery, as if she had been abandoned by everyone, and cold, for she had no clothes on. But a man had rescued her – Johnny North. He was wearing a black coat and he was young. His hair was *really* black, not stained with shoe polish. He had smiled down at her with his broken teeth – she had not been frightened – then scooped her up, putting her right on his shoulders. Suddenly, Johnny North had got big, so big he had turned into a giant. And she was so high she had been able to see the whole world as he walked over it – the countries, the mountains, the islands dotting the silver oceans like stepping stones.

She looked around a bit nervously, then began to remove her clothes, putting them on a flat rock: her sleeveless T-shirt, her red leather sandals, her shorts with her package of Arrowroots in the pocket, her underpants with their blue Bannerman's label. When a car passed on the road above, she looked around wildly for a hiding place. But she knew she had to do this, the idea had been with her ever since she'd woken up. She *had* to do it, though she couldn't have said why. She stood straight and closed her eyes and felt the air on her bare body. When a fly landed on her arm, she brushed it off. "I'm here," she whispered. She wasn't sure whom she was talking to, the trees or Johnny North or the river rushing over its dam or the sloping fields of Wiley's farm or someone who was all of those things, and more. "It's me, Penny." She breathed in the presences. She could feel them drawing close, touching her with their fingers of air, drawing faint perfumes by her nose, opening the valley –

But there, that darned fly was back. She opened one eye and glared at it.

53

THEY LAY ON HER BED, kissing and talking. Slipping his hand under her blouse, Joe cupped her small breast, under the soft fabric of her bra. Hooking his thumb under the bra's edge, he began to peel it up.

He was acting with a playful casualness. But he was tense.

"I don't have much feeling in my breasts," Anna told him.

She was watching him a little distantly: those green eyes with their irrepressible spark of humour. On her cheek was the birthmark. Up close, it revealed its subtlety, like a burn of many colours: the white, the tinges of pink, blending into tan. He had caressed it and examined it and kissed it, this badge of her uniqueness.

As his hand closed on her breast, he was aware that her nipple was not standing up. He squeezed, stroked. Finally he lifted her blouse. Her nipples were extraordinarily pink, like a kitten's tongue. He licked, sucked. The little buttons of pink flesh remained flush with their aureoles.

She pushed at his head.

"I really don't enjoy that."

"I'm sorry, I just thought –"

"That you, my Prince Charming, would succeed where all others have failed." She touched his hair affectionately, but he was chagrined. He didn't like to be reminded there had been others. What had she done with these others, that was the question. He'd assumed they would sleep together, as he and Liz had slept together: had assumed that Anna Macrimmon was at least *that* experienced, but for two weeks now they had necked and petted only. He wondered if Brad had got any farther – Brad, who these days was acting as if he, Joe, didn't exist (except, that is, for a floor-hockey game when Brad had thrown a vicious elbow Joe had barely managed to slip). He wondered about the handsome man with the swept-back blond hair, so clearly older than she, whose arm cradled her possessively in the boat, in the gold-framed photo facing them even now on the back of her desk. "A friend," she had said, with a casualness that told him nothing.

She was fussing, almost maternally, at his hair. She had not said she loved him. Twice now he'd told her he loved her – and he did, with a feverish certainty unlike anything he'd experienced – but it seemed wrong to press her for the same avowal. There was something in her he was a little afraid of. More than anyone he'd known, she seemed provisional in her presence. I will stay here if, her presence seemed to say, but there was no telling what came after that "if."

"Are you a virgin?" he said. The light went out in her eyes and he feared he had just committed the act that would make her disappear. The atmosphere around her was charged with invisible sanctions.

"No," she said, looking at him frankly.

"Then why can't we –"

He burned red, not at the sexual innuendo, but that he was exposing his own eagerness, which seemed clumsy to him, a failure to appreciate some subtlety.

"What – *do it*?"

"Ya, why don't we do it?" he said, catching her tone of mock coarseness. "Don't you want to do it? I mean, what did those other guys have that I –"

She rolled swiftly from the bed, went to her dresser, picked up a brush, and stood dragging it fiercely through her hair at the window. The late-afternoon sun made the flying wisps shine.

"Anna?"

It was the first time she had reacted so sharply towards him.

She turned to him.

"Don't ever refer to *other guys*," she told him. "I'm not a highway!"

"I didn't mean that!"

"Then don't imply it!"

"Anna, I love you –"

"That's no excuse," she said, really angry now. He sat up in a kind of shock. "You can't just say 'I love you' every time you get yourself into trouble, like it was some kind of abracadabra to fly you out of there. I won't have it!"

"No," he said bleakly. He was still not sure what he'd done wrong.

"Love is the biggest alibi in the world," she said.

He stared at her and she sighed, letting the hand with the brush fall to her side. Her blouse hung out over her skirt.

"I don't understand you," he said.

"You weren't meant to."

She came to the bed and sat facing him.

"I just want to go slowly. Is that all right?"

"Sure it is. I'm sorry." He was thinking of what Liz had told him. *Anna can't love. It was a man.*

A man, not a boy like you.

"You told me once you'd had a bad time," he said. Her look darkened. "Does that have anything to do with wanting to go slowly?"

"I suppose."

"Maybe one day you'll be able to tell me," he said.

He was touching the back of her hand, with its two silver rings. Suddenly she leaned forward and kissed him, more openly, softly, than she had before. He resisted the desire to pull her down with him.

He was willing to be a patient suitor. Unlike Sandy or Liz, Anna Macrimmon inspired him with a hunger to be better than he was.

He ate supper with her family in the backyard, at a small table her mother had covered with a white cloth. They were under a large maple tree, where the bare earth was littered with the chains of greeny-yellow seeds that fell from the tree, almost caterpillarlike, sometimes into their plates of stew, even into the glasses of red wine Andrew Macrimmon kept refilling with a slightly wicked insistence as if determined to get them all drunk. Anna's father was a slim, fair-haired man with wire-rimmed glasses through which small, intelligent eyes the same colour as hers – though not the same feline shape – peered a little sadly. He was near-sighted and a bit stooped (his posture seemed to Joe to go with his position as senior accountant at Bannerman's; he imagined him slaving over a tall, old-fashioned desk like Bob Cratchit in *A Christmas Carol*), but he also had a robust laugh that subsided to a silent, up-and-down shaking of his body. Joe felt that Andrew Macrimmon had to know about his father's firing, his work with the union, and almost certainly disapproved. But if he did, thankfully he kept his opinions to himself.

Anna's mother, Estelle, sat very erect in her chair, her plump face held a little up in pride, as if conscious of some higher standard of behaviour, some Old World noblesse that was under constant siege. Joe was reminded of his mother, who carried her Englishness like a badge of honour. But there was something frantic about Estelle: he saw it in the way her hair strayed from her untidy bun, and in the restlessness of her square hands, which kept touching things on the table as if to reassure herself of their proper placement, or perhaps of their very reality. She spoke English with the same enthusiastic articulation as French, so that her conversation was rich and dramatic if sometimes incomprehensible.

Joe liked her and felt a gallant urge to support her; he imagined she must feel out of place in Canada. He tried out his poor French on her, which set her smiling with pleasure even as she winced at his pronunciation. He wanted desperately to be a success with her and her husband, not just for Anna's sake, but to make himself a place within the family, which seemed so much more desirable than his own. His father's attack on his mother had set a cold wind prowling through the house on the Island. He wanted to escape it, wanted to escape the tawdriness that always seeps in after violence: now, every imperfection of his home life – the worn kitchen linoleum, his father's guilty, dishevelled presence – seemed part of a morass that threatened to swallow him. Here, at the table under the tree, was another world.

But his escape was problematic. As he was trying to tell a story, in French, he watched Estelle's face grow hard. Thinking he'd made some terrible gaffe, he rushed his telling, then fell silent. A train was passing – the main line connecting Toronto and Windsor ran in the hillside, just below the back fences of the houses along the south side of Banting – and for a few minutes it became nearly impossible to hear anybody speak as the cars throbbed and clattered by, out of sight below the fenced edge of the yard. A stink of oil and heat crept under the maple tree. Estelle picked solemnly at her food. A deep unease had spread around the table. Joe felt he was glimpsing the outskirts of some ongoing family crisis. There was a tension, as if Anna and her father were half-expecting some outburst from Estelle. Her ears, below her untidy nest of hair, had grown bright pink.

When the clattering and rumbling finally grew distant, under the retreating wail of the diesel, Anna began to chat volubly about some restaurant in France. But Estelle kept under her cloud. She scowled and picked at her food and generally gave the impression, for all her dignity, of a sulking child.

Suddenly interrupting her daughter, she turned to Joe.

"This is your last year at the school?"

"Oui –"

"Et l'année prochaine? L'université?"

"Oui – l'université de Toronto. Je vais étudier l'histoire."

"Ah bon!" Estelle spoke rapidly in French, and a bit irritably, to Anna. Joe hardly caught a word. He did, however, recognize the word "Sorbonne." It was where Anna planned to go, in the fall. He had glimpsed a letter on her desk, bearing the rich purple of a French stamp, with the Sorbonne, Paris, as its return address. He'd tried to persuade her to go to Toronto with him, but without actually contradicting him, she had seemed amused, at best, by the very idea. She was planning to leave in August. Already – and it was only May – he was dreading the end of the summer.

Anna bowed her head, under her mother's scolding. She shook her head, and smiled with closed lips in a way that suggested she was making a familiar refusal, in a state of bland tolerance. But she was upset, he could see: her arms were moving, where they disappeared out of sight below the edge of the table. He supposed she was tearing at her hangnails.

Andrew was murmuring to his wife in French, placatingly.

Estelle looked haughtily around at their empty plates and asked Joe, with great formality, ignoring the others, if he would like dessert.

After supper they escaped for a walk. Down Banting, the rich, low light of the spring evening infiltrated the deep crevasses in the bark of ancient maples, making them glow like golden cork. She had shown him a special way of holding hands, two fingers interlocked in an unusual way, and they fell into this manner now. To him it was a secret language, the pledging of a pledge. It established a claim on the future.

Her hand was fine-boned and light in his. She seemed a creature of lightness. She walked with her mother's erectness, her head held up and a little back.

"Mama's not very happy. I guess you saw that."

"I thought she was ticked off at something I said."

"No, every time a train passes, she's reminded of where she is. She has no friends here. She doesn't understand the way of life. She thinks people here are crude, the life here is crude. It's all about hurry, and money, she says, and – a lack of pleasure in things. She'd go back to France tomorrow, if she could."

"Is that what she was saying to you?" He felt included in her mother's criticism.

Another train was rumbling behind the houses, sounding its blatant horn. Her hand slipped his.

"She likes *you*," she said. "She was telling me I should go to Toronto with you."

"A wise woman!"

"An angry woman," she said. "She talks against herself. It's like there's a splinter in her, she has to push it in deeper. I'm just glad it wasn't worse."

"You mean she doesn't really want you to go to Toronto?"

"I don't think she knows. But she likes you, she really does. It's wonderful the way you spoke French to her.

"Let's go down here," she said suddenly, pulling him to the right.

The sidewalk on Peter gave way to packed earth thick with spruce needles. They passed an old mansion, gloomy behind its wall of dark green, and came to the black iron rail bridge. It rose a little in the middle, and from this summit they looked to the west. The tracks gleamed in their great arc, rounding towards the Junction, where an old water tower, like a block on legs, stood silhouetted against the sunset. To the left, from the depth of the valley, thrust the mansard roof of Bannerman's hosiery mill, with its dormer windows. "Like a château," she said. That it reminded her of France both pleased and saddened him. Sometimes she seemed to be travelling away from him and coming closer, both at once.

Beyond lay the sloping fields of Wiley's farm, fringed with darkening woods that hid the bend of the Attawan as it made its way into town. A huge, molten sun had settled on the horizon.

"Sometimes I wish I was a painter," she said, leaning forward at the rail. "I'd paint this. Though I'd never get it. No artist ever gets anything, really. It kind of makes you ill – the failure to *get* anything."

"It's beautiful," he said.

" 'The edge of terror we're just able to bear.' "

"What?"

"It's from a poem."

"One of yours?"

She shook her head, apparently amused.

"What's so funny? You're laughing at me because I don't know the quote."

"No I'm not."

"You are. You think I'm a bit of a clodhopper."

She looked at him with great seriousness, alarmed.

"I don't," she said. "I don't at all."

He was only half-appeased, and embarrassed at exposing his own insecurity. He turned back to the rail. The sun was a thin, low hillock now, quivering as it sank.

"Anyway, I'll bet this is just as beautiful as anything in France."

She was still looking at him. When he turned back to her, the light in her eyes – wounded and fond – sparked a desperate desire in him. He kissed her gently, holding the back of her head with his hand. When he opened his eyes, to peek, she was looking at him. He wondered if his kiss had touched her at all.

"You didn't close your eyes," he said, piqued.

"I wanted to see you."

They looked back to the valley. A jet was tracking overhead, outracing its own vacant, drifting thunder. Its vapor trail shone and slowly separated. Down the sky, a few solitary clouds had turned sumac red. He drew his fingers across the small of her back, touched her hair, as he looked out at the flaming sky. He seemed to be touching the pulse of life itself. It would be impossible to get closer. Though he wanted to reach out and seize it all, he knew that only a delicate touch would do. There was a sadness in him, a faint, sad desperation, that he was so close, and yet could get no closer. Life could not be taken by force: life was elusive, this light brighter than noon was elusive, a thing to be briefly touched, not held.

They descended into the shadowy lower town. On Station Hill, near the house where the Catholic sisters lived, two birches glowed in the bluing dusk. She stopped to watch a cat hurry across a lawn. It was long and black with a look of slinking determination, a cat on its way to kill.

"Take me to your house," she said impulsively. "I want to meet your family."

"Now?" He had taken pains never to mention his family. He wanted to be born out of thin air to her, with no past.

"You've seen my family. I want to meet yours."

He told her she could meet them another time – perhaps she could come to dinner some Sunday – but she insisted with such tenacity he finally gave in.

Flush with her victory, she went along swinging his hand, excited by the idea of a neighbourhood called the Island. He knew she was bound to be disappointed – as he told her, in self-defence, it wasn't exactly Hawaii. At the low bridge over the race, she stopped and peered at the dark water littered with old boards and rubbish while he watched in a misery of apprehension. "You see what I mean," he said. "It's not much of an island." "Shut up," she told him. "It's an island to me." She looked down the little street crowded with houses. "Actually, I think I was here once, on one of my walks. I just didn't notice it was an island." Nearby loomed the metal sheds of the town yard, with its dimming piles of sand streaked with salt, a scarred yellow road-grader – signs, to him, of the decline in neighbourhood since they'd come off the Hill. But she spied an old snowplough, its curved, rusted blades rising like wings. "An iron angel," she declared, running her palm over the scabbing paint.

When they reached his house, she stopped and looked at it, while he fidgeted beside her. "We're planning to move," he told her, clutching at the family myth, which normally he despised. Before them, the whitewashed facade with its dark-green shutters (one had begun to sag badly!) looked out with a starkness that appalled him. "It's like another century," she declared. This was apparently a compliment, though with her he could never be sure, irony shadowed so many of her enthusiasms. A sprinkler was throwing twists of silver around the tiny front lawn.

His mother was in the back, working in her garden. She had seemed weary and remote of late, her eyes shadowed with a darkness he found painful to contemplate. But it was the yellow-purplish bruise staining much of her right cheek that he was acutely aware of now. She had told him the whole sordid tale – his father's refusal to take the job of assistant manager, his striking of her – with a tone of cheerless exhaustion he had never heard in her before, all the while watching him steadily, as if demanding to know what *he* was going to do about it. Not long afterwards, he had confronted his father in the backyard. Alf had born his (embarrassingly) tearful recriminations – *Hadn't he taught Joe never to strike a woman?* – in a silence that unsettled Joe because it made him wonder, later, if he had the whole story. In any case, his mother's revelation had gone on working inside him, like a chemical reaction producing anger and revulsion. He was set against his father, but really he was sick of both of them, of their standoff that had filled the house with a deepening tension.

To his relief, his mother roused to her old bright, English self. And in the dusk, the bruise on her face hardly showed. He was hoping they could have a few words in the garden and leave. But she insisted they have tea. Joe followed miserably into the kitchen, where Anna walked around the kitchen table, complimenting his mother on her decorating – that blue with that yellow – so cozy and bright! "It reminds me of farmhouses in France," she said. "That's what I was thinking of," Joe's mother said. "I used to holiday there when I was a girl." They talked cheerfully of Normandy while Margaret boiled water and put out a plate of Peak Freans at the kitchen table. "We don't keep much in the way of biscuits any more," she apologized. "Not since Joe's sister got diabetes." Joe sat beside Anna, smiling thinly, conscious of the bruise on his mother's face. It seemed to him that the good cheer that had filled the kitchen was a sham created by Anna's politeness. He was aware – surely Anna was aware too – of the nicks on the kitchen chairs, the cracks and worn spots in the linoleum, the sad, weak light from the overhead fixture.

A noise in the hall startled Joe, who feared his father was about to appear. But it was only his sister and brother. Introducing them, Joe watched Penny sneaking glances at Anna's birthmark. Jamie, dressed for bed in his yellow-and-brown polo pyjamas, was more straightforward: "What's that on your face?"

"Jamie," Joe's mother scolded.

"Did you hit it on a cupboard?"

Joe's mother turned away.

"No," Anna said, laughing. She explained to Jamie about birthmarks, while he stared like someone at a zoo. "You can touch it if you like," Anna said. As the boy tentatively put out his fingers, she slipped a smile to Joe.

A few minutes later, they were all sitting at the table when Joe's father came in, his face weary, his hair collapsing over his ears. Joe was instantly on guard: he felt he no longer had anything in common with the man. Yet he didn't want Anna to think ill of him, so he managed a warmer note than usual with his father as the two of them shook hands.

"You're even more handsome than your son," Anna told Alf.

"Well, I've tried to teach him as best I can," his father said. His pale-blue eyes, suddenly decades younger than his face, blazed happily at Joe. Joe looked away.

"She's got a birthmark!" Jamie cried.

"Yes, I can see that," Joe's father said, looking at it frankly. "I'd call it more of a beauty mark."

Anna laughed, charmed. To Joe's dismay, his father made himself comfortable at the table. Across the kitchen, his mother had retired into silence. Whatever was between his parents was in the room, he felt: a dark pool spreading beneath the merriment. "We've been talking about France," Anna told him. "Ah yes, France," Joe's father said, running his hand over his head in a contemplative way. "I once spent a good many months in France."

"On holiday?" Anna said.

"No, no," Joe's father said, blushing a little, with a glance at his wife. "The war –"

"I forgot!" she said. "You were in the war!" A new tone had come into her voice, at once excited and reverential, almost breathless. Joe waited in suspense: this mention of the war seemed bound to drive his father into an awkward silence. Around the table, Joe's brother and sister lowered their gazes to their half-finished glasses of milk. Like Joe, they'd been brought up not to ask about the war.

To Joe's astonishment, his father seemed not the least bothered by Anna's questions. Sitting back in his chair, he told a story Joe had never heard, about borrowing two bicycles with a soldier pal of his and heading off into the hills. They had stayed with a French family. He recalled their warmth, and the fine bread the woman had made in an outdoor oven. "It was the only time I actually felt like I was *in* France," he told them. "The rest of the time – you were just too – wrought up. You'd see some spot – some village or a grove of trees – and you'd *know* it was beautiful, you'd *know* you wanted to spend time there, but even if you did, you weren't really there, you know? You couldn't really get comfortable. France was, I don't know, sort of a dream. I kept thinking, Later, when the war's over, I'll come back, I'll really have a look at the place."

"And did you?" Anna said. Joe looked at his father, who was shaking his head. He could hardly believe his father was telling her, a stranger, details he had never told Joe; he almost resented it.

"Nope – never made it back," Alf said, colouring. He seemed embarrassed by his failure to return.

"Oh, you *have* to go," Anna cried. "It would be a pity if you didn't go. Mrs. Walker – you both love France – you have to go back!"

Joe shifted uneasily. Anna seemed unaware of the tension in the room, she seemed unaware that not everyone could just go off to France. His father looked over at his mother, his eyes bright. "Maybe we will one day," he said softly. Joe saw that his mother was staring at the floor, and missed his father's glance.

"Did you drive a tank?" Jamie said. Everyone looked at him. His voice had chimed into the silence like a small bell.

"I should have been so lucky," Alf laughed, tousling his head. "No, I'm afraid I walked the whole way."

Outside, in the dark, Anna took Joe's hand.

"I love your family," she said as they went along. "I think that's how a family should be – noisy and happy. Not gloomy like mine. We don't live in our house, we *haunt* it."

Joe said nothing. He wasn't about to tell her what she had missed: if she *had* really missed it. There was no point dwelling on unhappiness. It was like admitting failure – yes, unhappiness *was* failure – whenever he looked into her face, her beautiful face, he knew this.

54

ONE EVENING LATER that month they climbed the steep stairway between two short, fluted pillars, pushed open a heavy door, and climbed farther, into the high-ceilinged main hall of the library, with its deep rose walls and white trim, its polished, creaking hardwood that made every step significant. Anna stood before the unused fireplace, looking up at the twin portraits of Abraham Shade and his wife, Rebecca. Both were seated, both wore sombre clothes, their strong bloodless hands gripping the arms of their chairs, their pale faces, stark as axe-blazes against the paintings' shiny black backgrounds, looking out sternly. "A pretty gloomy couple," Joe said, moving in beside her. His arm tingled where it brushed against hers. "But look at his eyes," she said. "There's real life in them."

He did as commanded, and saw the dots of brightness in the founder's pupils. No matter what he showed her, she pointed out some detail he had not seen. He almost resented it, this constant revision of a world he thought he knew.

"He wrote poetry, you know."

He told her about Shade's diaries, the sonnets and other verses Archibald Mann had found in one of the volumes. Most of them were nature poems, Mann had told him, Shade's stolid attempts to evoke the beauties of the valley. Anna watched him closely as he spoke. Her green eyes roved over his hair, his mouth, as if she was not only listening but taking in all of him. It thrilled him like a stroking touch. Still, he couldn't help worrying that she already knew what he was telling her, or if he was making some mistake (he was talking about poetry after all).

"Have you read them?" Anna asked.

"No. But maybe Mann'd show them to us."

"Why don't we visit him? How about Saturday?"

She was squeezing his arm as she urged him. There was a force in her that was always saying Yes, yes, pulling him on to the next novelty. Her glad, hectic approach electrified him, it broke some barrier of caution in him, but at the same time he was suspicious of her recklessness, which seemed to leave some vital knowledge out of account. She did not seem to remember that the rose had thorns; or perhaps it was simply that she did not fear them. He did not know which.

At the counter, the librarian cleared her throat in a discreet warning.

"I have to work Saturday," he whispered, a bit put out that she never remembered this.

"Sunday then."

They studied at a table behind tall shelves crammed with nineteenth- and early-twentieth-century novels – three copies of *Lorna Doone*, complete sets of Dickens, Thackeray, Eliot, James. The worn covers smelled pleasantly of decay. They turned pages and made notes, her feet planted between his on the floor, held between his insteps with a snug rightness that kept distracting him. When he looked up, she was nearly always deep in concentration, pushing unconsciously at the birthmark with the rubber end of her pencil or picking at her cuticles as she stared at a page. He looked back to his book. He was studying a chapter in his Latin composition text entitled "Constructions with Verbs of Fearing, Preventing and Doubting." Looking up, he saw she had pushed her text aside and was busy devouring *Daniel Deronda*, fished down from a nearby shelf.

He scowled at his book, and tried to concentrate. He looked up again, watching her for a while before he spoke. She was slouched back in her chair now, one bare arm slung over its back, her mouth a little open as she read.

"You should be studying."

"I don't think I would have *liked* George Eliot," she announced without looking up.

He sighed and tried again.

"Study your Latin, girl! These are important exams!" Their finals, in fact: for all purposes their entrance exams to university. He tapped with exaggerated sternness on her Latin book, sheathing his command in a smile. She looked at the book, then up at him, with a sharp, penetrating candour, almost hostile. Her anger always seemed close at hand.

"Okay, *don't* study your Latin," he said with a shrug. She went back to her reading. He was acting indifferent, but her look had chilled him. Anna's independence was something, for all his desire to honour her freedom, that could gall him. She might have at least entered into the spirit of his reprimand, which rose out of concern for her, he felt. But she had looked at him so coolly she had made him feel like a stranger, a person of no account.

For the rest of the time in the library, he brooded. He was so on edge around her. He felt as if security lay with her, and if he could only draw close enough to her, he could have it too. But the way was fraught with traps, and a terrible provisionality. He could not forget for more than an hour that she was going away in August, everything they did lay in the shadow of that fact, and there seemed to be nothing he could do about it. This was bad enough, but what really unnerved him was that she was apparently not the least bit upset that she was leaving.

When the library closed, he walked her up the hill. *Daniel Deronda* rode with the other books, pressed to her chest by her folded arms.

They reached the edge of King's Park, stepping through its border of old trees. Up ahead, the little bandstand appeared like the point of a rocket emerging from the earth. The grass had been cut, leaving drifts of dead clippings here and there, a smell of hay.

"*Fieri non potest quin te amem*," he said.

He had memorized the sentence from his Latin text, and now waited with pounding heart for her response. His textbook had translated the sentence as *It is impossible for me not to love you*. He'd got the message that she didn't like to hear him say "I love you," at least not as often as he'd been saying it. But he couldn't help himself. He was fishing desperately for an answering "I love you."

"Is that you talking," she said after a moment, "or page 167?"

"I find I agree with it exactly," he said.

Again she was silent, stepping along over the grass. A slight rain had fallen earlier, dampening things, intensifying smells. A scent of blossoms drifted from somewhere, sickly sweet.

"How about you?" he said nervously. "Would you say the same holds true for you?"

"I'm suspicious of the word 'love,'" she said, a bit impatiently. "I mean, I always feel a bit queasy about putting it in a poem. I think that tells me something –"

"What does it tell you?" he said, reluctantly taking up her line of thought. He felt she was avoiding his challenge.

"I'm not sure," she said. "It's as if it means too much, so it ends up meaning nothing."

"Too vague?"

"Something like that. And maybe sentimental. And maybe a bit – easy, somehow. If you feel that way about someone, better to show it in your actions."

"So better that I jump off the railway bridge –"

"No," she said, looking up at him. "Definitely not that."

He walked along in silence, then said, "But it *is* a definite feeling – everybody knows what it is. Even you know what it is, I'm sure. But if we can't *say* it, then, I don't know, the whole world's going to be pretty frustrated."

"I'm just talking about me, not the whole world!"

"But if you think it's wrong for you – and for me – don't you think it's wrong for everybody?"

"I guess I do," she allowed.

"You'd like to do away with the word 'love' altogether then?"

"A ten-year moratorium," she said, "and then we'd see –"

"So even parents shouldn't say to their children, I love you –"

"Even that."

"That's *monstrous*," he said, stopping. She turned to face him, perfectly calm, it seemed. "Without love," he said, gesturing with his free arm, "there'd be, I don't know, no *glue* holding things together. It would be awful –"

"I'm just talking about the word," she said. He felt her smile was false, a placating of him, a bit patronizing. "I know there's something there the word refers to – I just think we should think about it a bit, before we throw it around."

"So what I just did was throwing it around, even in Latin –"

She looked at him. He was breathing hard, really upset. He felt his heart had been laid bare and, in some way he could not quite put his finger on, mocked. He kicked at a little pile of dry grass. "Now I feel you're trying to put *me* in a straitjacket, telling me what I can and can't say."

She came up behind him and leaned her head into his back. They stood like this for some time. He was sulking, really hurt. He could not understand why it wounded him so much, this refusal of hers to have him use the word "love." To her, it was just an intellectual matter; to him, it was as if she had rejected his deepest self.

He turned to her. In the weak light of the street light her face seemed misshapen, as if bent by the atmosphere. But there was concern for him there, real concern, though he saw, too, that spark of amusement in her eyes. Nothing, it seemed, could quench it.

"You say what you like," she said quietly.

"I will," he said. "You can just take your chances."

They looked at each other. She leaned up suddenly and kissed him on the mouth. He seized her by the shoulders, intending to plant a firmer kiss. His tongue sought hers. But she pushed him firmly back, with her free arm. They went along together, through the park. The sense of disjunction between them seemed stronger than ever to him, a sadness. It seemed to come out of the ground, out of the damp hay and blossom scents, out of the branches of new leaves: a sadness and, yes, a sense of deepening vulnerability. Like a trapeze artist, he had abandoned his swing to throw himself into the air towards her. He had to be sure her hands were there to catch him. Perhaps, he wondered with a kind of terror, she was warning him off love in an attempt to get him back to his perch. But it was already too late. He was tumbling through the air, his arms outstretched, his hands open.

55

ARCHIE MANN PULLED the plastic wrap from one of Shade's diaries, exposing the leather-bound volume to the air of his study. He opened the book carefully, turning its parched, crackling pages. At his elbow, Joe and Anna saw the brown loops of the founder's hand.

"I like this one best," Mann said, handing the book to Anna. "Be careful. The pages are halfway to dust."

Anna held the book at chest level, bowing her head to decipher the block of writing. As Mann stepped out of the way, Joe moved in beside her.

> The flowing streams of this enchanted place –
> Enchanted and enchanting both, a boon
> To whosoever haps upon its tune
> Of waters – trees, hills, Arcadian grace
> Bidding at every turn –

"Rather Wordsworthian," Mann said.

"Rather hackneyed," Anna said with a laugh. She went on reading. Joe felt the stab of her comment. He wanted her and Mann to get along; he wanted her to find some reason for pleasure in Shade's poems. Her brutal judgment seemed to put a chill in the room. He struggled with the dense tract of handwriting, but gave up before the end.

"I like it," he said. "It sounds like he meant it, anyway." He did not actually know if he liked the poem or not; he was trying to smooth relations between Anna and his teacher.

"*I* think he did," Mann said, a bit testily. He had moved down the long table, where he had picked up a magazine. Now he tossed it down again. Anna turned a page.

"Are there others?" she said.

"Two pages over," Mann said.

Again Joe read at her side. She had recently torn a hangnail from her thumb: a livid red strip ran beside the tan page.

" 'The robin tenders his note from the vale,' " Anna said, quoting. "That's a nice phrase."

Mann said, "I think it's rather wonderful that a man as busy as he – he was a very successful businessman – would write such a thing. I mean, it's rather graceful, even if the phrases, as you say, have been used before. I wonder how many businessmen would attempt such a thing today?"

"Not too many, I hope," Anna laughed.

Joe flushed at her lack of tact. He looked over at Mann and saw his face knotting, the dark, hooded eyes frowning into some lower region. Joe wanted to please the teacher, and to see him so obviously displeased unsettled him. It was a bit shocking: Anna wasn't speaking to Mann as one would to a teacher, with a note of deference, but candidly, as if he were just another person. To Joe, she was verging on disrespect.

She said, "But there – he fumbles the next stanza *entirely*."

"Well, I'm not making *literary* claims for him," Mann said, sounding really piqued now. His brown eyes flashed. "You see, to me the poems are evidence of a very interesting man. An unusual man. I mean, he had practical reasons for founding a town here. But he was much more than practical, in the narrow sense. He fell in love with the place, really. He never got over it. By the way, I think it would be a very good thing if our businessmen wrote poetry, or painted, or were at least interested in poetry and painting. They might come at things in a broader way. We'd all be better off."

"But if their poetry is bad," she said, lowering the book.

"It doesn't matter. The point is, by coming into contact with the complexities of poetry – by paying some sort of homage to it – they're going to enrich themselves." Mann smiled at his own choice of verb. "In more than the usual way, I mean. Shade was an enormously complex man. Just read his diaries . . ."

The teacher gave them dessert in the old belvedere. Sitting on its narrow, unpainted benches, facing each other a little awkwardly, they scooped at the little dishes of homemade chocolate mousse. "You wouldn't find better in France," Anna enthused, mollifying Mann a little. Far below, the Shade glinted under the rail trestle, as it spread towards the deep centre of town. The spring evening, a Sunday, was unusually warm. A bumblebee drifted through the belvedere, rising towards the green sky over the treetops. Mann took up his old theme again, talking about Shade. He seemed determined to make Anna understand his own fascination. "He was a more complete kind of man than is generally found now," he insisted, gesturing absently with his tiny spoon. "He was a woodsman, an entrepreneur, an alderman, and mayor for many years, a much-loved figure, really. Many's the needy family he helped out. He was a farmer –"

"A farmer-poet," Anna offered graciously. "Like Virgil."

Mann bowed his head in acknowledgment and went on: "And all this was part of the same ambition, somehow –"

"To serve God?" she suggested.

"Something like that. But here's the interesting thing. He wasn't formally religious, which was very unusual in a man of his position. He didn't go to church. Still – this is where the poetry comes in – he had this passion for place, if I can call it that. He loved what was here, it was in his care, somehow. In his latter years, he could get tremendously exercised if – well, if someone was going to change a view by chopping down a grove. And this was a man who'd chopped down thousands of trees, in his time.

"You see," Mann continued, leaning forward. His gaze swept between Joe and Anna. But mostly he spoke to Anna. Joe was still guarding the bulwarks of propriety (long after they'd been breached) while these two went on hammering each other as equals. It was thrilling, and a bit unsettling. "I think he was in love with beauty," Mann said. "He was in love with this place, with poetry, with – you know, the beauty of life that passes us by with hardly a glance. You're a poet, Anna – that was a wonderful poem you had in the *Quill* – so you know what I mean. It's the thing that should make us happy, and does, but also makes us melancholy, because we can't keep up with it – it's too quick for us, too eternally – young."

When the visit was over, they trooped down the hill. Joe was carrying a knapsack and the rolled blanket his father kept in the Biscayne: when it got dark enough, they planned to do some star-gazing. Mann had suggested they visit the old pioneer cemetery on the east side of town, where Shade and his family were buried. Joe had never been there and was as keen as Anna, so they crossed the

Bridge Street bridge to the Flats and found the stony, deeply rutted lane that climbed behind several houses to a locked iron gate. They climbed over, into the isolated scattering of small, pale tombstones, with the rail line and the gravel pits guarding its back and, to the west, the roofs of the town gleaming in the dusk. Joe had never seen the town from just this angle, and stood picking out familiar buildings. The dark pyramid of the Presbyterian church roof dominated all, but there were other spires to the south, and a rolling sense of buried life, under the dark canopy of trees.

The Shade monument was the largest in the graveyard: a tall plinth of white marble with a wider base on which the names of the founder and his family were carved. They prowled around it, reading the inscriptions out loud to each other, deciphering the Shade family tree, their scrutiny touched with a bittersweet sense of familiarity. They drifted among the other stones. Anna found notice of an eight-year-old boy, Julius Broad, who had drowned in the Attawan in 1896. The inscription read *The river took him. Now God has him.* "It must have been wonderful to be able to believe that," she said. "If they really did believe it." She sniffed, and he looked at her, realizing tears were running down her cheeks. "What Mann said was wonderful," she said. "The truth is we're just shades ourselves. We're only here for about two seconds. Then – well."

"Yes," he said, slipping his arm around her. Her bare shoulder was cool under his hand. He was not feeling what she was feeling, but he was grateful for the chance to comfort her. After a few seconds, she dug her little notebook out of the canvas knapsack and went off by herself. He continued his tour of the cemetery, reading the fading inscriptions on the white, leaning stones. From time to time he looked up and saw her legs, or her shoulder, sticking out from behind the Shade monument where she sat on the ground, writing in her book.

One time, he saw that the notebook now lay several feet away from her, open on the rough lawn. He crossed to her. She was sitting hugging her knees, staring blindly.

"Are you cold? Do you want your sweater?"

She shook her head, almost imperceptibly. He went and picked up her notebook, glancing at a page before he closed it. There was a scrawl of words and darker, crossed-out bits.

He held out the notebook for her. She glanced at it and looked away.

"I'm no good," she said, and a moment later: "That's not true. I'm very good. But very good in a poet – oh! It's no better than no good at all. The world doesn't need any more *very good* poems." She spoke angrily, with tearing sarcasm. "*Very good poems*. They're about as useful as a – a three-legged horse. If you're not a genius, you shouldn't even try."

"Maybe you are a genius," he offered with complete sincerity.

She snorted. "You don't know anything. Emily Dickinson was a genius. Sappho was a genius. I'm just a pretender. Well –"

She took the notebook from him and abruptly got up.

"So what do we do now?" she said.

"Well, the stars are almost out," he said hopefully. "We could put out the blanket."

But she was too restless to settle down. She walked around the cemetery and he spread the red tartan blanket. They had brought a bottle of wine and an opener she'd taken from a cupboard at home. Joe drew the cork and placed the bottle on a fallen stone. "Wine's ready!" he called out to her. When she made no response he looked around and saw her stooping in the tall grasses at the back of the plot. Finally she came back to him with a bouquet of wild grasses, which she presented to him rather formally, with a clumsy curtsey, apologizing for her outburst. "You must be getting heartily sick of me," she said.

"Well, luckily I'm a tolerant guy," he said.

"I know you are," she said. "And I thank you for it." He looked at the bouquet she had brought him: the stiff, whiskered grasses, trembling in his fist.

They lay on their backs, looking up at the stars. They picked out the Big Dipper – Ursa Major – aslant across the sky, and the North Star beaming feebly. Orion tilted in the south, with his sword-belt. She pointed out constellations he did not know, pressing close to him so he could sight along her arm. The Milky Way was a vast twinkling road – it passed, she said, not only across the dark fields of space, but through their bodies as well, entering just at the bottom of the breast bone and passing out their backs: could he feel it? He thought he could. Watching that great dusting of stars, that was beyond comprehension, it seemed he was drawn into it, and it into him, through some mutual gravity that bore them along together in the darkness among the stones.

After a while they changed positions, sitting up with their backs to the Shade monument, trading the bottle back and forth. When she laughed at some joke he made – laughed with an almost shocking abandon – he realized she was getting drunk. He felt tipsy himself, released to a giddy freedom beyond his usual restraint and deference. They drank toasts to the stars, and to individual constellations, and let their minds run wild in speculation. He told her his old childhood fantasy, that the night sky was really the roof of a great tent, and the stars were pinholes where the light from beyond got through. She was intrigued by the idea of a light from beyond: a light so bright it could not be borne by human eyes, she said. It was like the radiance people attributed to the naked presence of God. And that set her off wondering about the power of God, if there was a God, was He wholly benign, as people generally supposed, or a dangerous and even destructive force that might on a whim destroy people's happiness – hadn't he done that to Job, for the sake of a mere bet? – or burn the earth to cinders. Her imagination was apocalyptic. She began to talk about nuclear war, and how it was impossible to think about it – all those Russian and American missiles pointed at each other – the end of the world, at any given minute, was only a few minutes away. She was appalled by this, and yet there was something else in her that seemed to thrill to the idea of such power, as if the devastation sleeping in those warheads were simply another facet of nature, great and mysterious like the stars.

They lay down and kissed for a while. Suddenly she rolled away on her back. He made to roll on top of her, but she pushed him off, instructing him to lie beside her.

"On your back," she said. "Lie perfectly still. Your arms at your sides."

He lay still, looking up at the stars. One was blinking: a high jetliner, crossing among the constellations. Its roar sounded soft and far away.

"We're lying like *they're* lying," she said. "Only a few feet above them."

"I don't like pretending I'm dead," he said, after a while.

"We are dead," she said very quietly. He felt his breathing stop. The winking jetliner traversed the sky, in the remoteness of another life.

After a time they heard the blare of a train's horn, in the countryside to the east. Soon they saw its headlight, striking through the night, shining past the little cemetery towards the trestle that crossed the Shade. They were silent as it passed in a roar. They could make out a few passengers in the sad, isolated light of the nearly empty cars, reading newspapers, looking out into the dark.

The engine rumbled onto the trestle. There was a deeper thunder as hundreds of iron beams and wooden ties shook, and thousands of fittings rattled like crude tambourines above the sudden valley. Then the train was gone. They could hear its mournful bleat as it tore towards the Junction, straining for the fields beyond town.

Anna got up. "I hadn't realized we were so close to the bridge!" She began to walk rapidly through the cemetery, clambering a bit drunkenly over the grassy mound at its border, through the ditch and up the embankment to the tracks. Joe stumbled after her. Ahead, the surface of the trestle stretched away, with darkness on either side. The two sets of rails glinted placidly in the weak starlight, across the infinite articulation of the ties. There were no guardrails.

She was walking with some difficulty between the rails, where the gravel was not quite level with the ties.

"What are you doing?" he said as he strode along behind her.

"I'm going out on the bridge."

"You can't," he told her. "People get killed out there."

"You don't have to come," she said with disdain. Immediately, she stumbled on a tie. He seized her arm, but she pulled away. Again he grabbed her.

"Don't!" she cried.

"I'm telling you, it's dangerous –"

He went swiftly ahead of her, to the trestle, and saw the Shade in its calm lake behind Bannerman's dam, a hundred feet below. The lip of the dam glistened and put out a soft roar of falling water. He had crossed the bridge himself, with Smiley. But they'd checked the passenger schedules first, and put their ears to the tracks to listen for approaching freights. And they hadn't been drunk.

He turned to face her on the tracks.

"I won't let you," he said. "We're too drunk. We'll do it another time."

She tried to get by him, but he met her every dodge. She stamped her foot and made demon faces at him. He had become simply an object in her way. She flailed when he grabbed her and once scratched his face. In despair – he was convinced he was throwing away his chances with her – he was tempted to give in. But he clung to his sense he had to protect her.

Finally she gave up and walked quickly back to the cemetery. He followed, disconsolate. Off in the distance, a diesel horn sounded. He realized dully that another train was approaching, this time from the west. In a few seconds the freight roared onto the trestle. They had not been aware of it, assuming that the sound of its horn was coming from the first diesel. Anna seemed oblivious to the train, but went about folding the blanket and putting the bottle away, with a cold briskness that dismissed him utterly. He stood in amazement, watching the boxcars rumble and bang past. "You see," he said, turning to her. "If we'd gone out there, we would have had to dodge *that*." But she wasn't listening, and he felt like some old fuddy-duddy, a parent who can only say no, who must fence in life with common sense and fear. All he could do was limit her, it seemed. Even if he had saved her life – and who knew, perhaps he had – his role beside her was negative, secondary. They walked out of the cemetery, down the hill to the Flats. Under the branches of maples – their foliage bright green in the streetlights – a few silent cars gleamed by the curb.

He had to hurry to keep up with her. Perhaps she wanted him to simply vanish; perhaps the thing to do was just to let her go on, out of his life. But he stuck to her stubbornly, wild with a sense of unravelling love, angry that she couldn't see what he'd done for her. At the corner of Willard she stopped. She closed her eyes and put back her head, taking long breaths. He waited in trepidation beside her, thinking she was preparing some final speech. To his shock, she turned into him suddenly, pressing her forehead into the side of his neck. She said she was sorry: she'd been childish, an idiot. She said she didn't deserve his love. He had saved them, and she had been terrible. He circled her with his arms and felt her slim, trembling body, under her cotton dress.

She didn't want to go home, so for a while they wandered on the Flats. They walked slowly, with their arms around each other, up dim lanes past garages and gardens and silent porches. A black-and-white cat followed them for a while. They came back along Willard, under the vast east wall of the mills that rose sheer from the race.

They went along the fence together, looking down at the still, dark water, the cloudy, inverted reflection of the mills. A duck quacked sleepily and glided off, leaving its trembling wake to glitter in the street light. Above, the white-framed windows, many tiers high, gazed out from the dim brick. They came to the narrow metal footbridge, with its pipe railing, which crossed the race to the mill. At the other end, a windowless door had been left ajar. The door looked small and secretive, the one opening in the vast wall.

"Can we go in?" she said.

"I don't know." He knew the night watchman must be about. Perhaps he was just inside. He couldn't imagine the door had been left open by accident. But he let her draw him forward.

"Come on," she said, cajoling. "We can't be killed here, can we?"

Her ironic challenge piqued him: he didn't want to be always saying no. So he followed her across the bridge and in the little door. He shut it behind them, but did not draw the bolt. A single bulb lit a corridor. He smelled the piney fragrance of Dustbane. He picked his way along warily, hushing her at every turn and listening into the great stillness of the mills. To her, he sensed, this was an adventure, a glorious lark, as if these huge buildings, even the spectre of the watchman, had been put here for her amusement. But he took trespassing more seriously. He was the son and grandson of mill workers, he had worked here himself: to take the place casually was impossible.

They stole through corridors and up stairways, into vast rooms where long trestle tables shone dully, in a pleasant odour of new cloth. She put her face to a stack of finished garments and breathed in deeply. She touched her fingertips to the cool, oddly shaped metal of machines. "It's so strange," she whispered to him. "I never thought of cloth *coming* from anywhere. Cloth, our clothes, just *are*. But then there's all this – it's like looking underground and seeing the elves and dwarfs working away." At one point they saw the watchman crossing far below them, his light darting here and there through the millyard. He disappeared into the power plant, near the vast, round base of the stack. Joe was anxious to leave, but for her sake he pressed on with their tour, all the while watching and listening.

He showed her where his father had worked. The tall knitting machines stood silently in their rows, uncannily still under their wide crowns of bobbins. She had to know everything: how the yarn flew up through the loops of wire above, and down into the churning drum of needles. She stooped to look at a tube of cloth, hanging between a machine's legs. She could not get over how it seemed to appear out of nowhere. From just a few strands of yarn appeared this pale-blue cloth, as soft and fragrant, she said, as a baby's skin.

A sudden clattering startled them. Outside, pigeons – wakened perhaps by a collective nightmare – swarmed from a roof, their wings whirring past the windows.

They moved on, walking through a covered bridge, several stories above the millyard, to another building. In one hall, bales of raw wool were piled to the ceiling. The wool was rough to the touch and exuded a sharp smell of dried dung. They passed through further rooms, past great, shining vats and tubs, and came to a large bin. Inside was a mass of clean, whitish wool, smelling richly of lanolin. To his surprise, she climbed over the side of the bin and threw herself back in the wool, like a child playing on a mattress.

"Come here," she said, holding out her arms.

"I don't think – the watchman –"

"Come here."

The wool was too scratchy on their naked skin, so they spread the red tartan blanket. Even so, the wool curled over its edges, around them. As he moved on her, it tickled his sides, his forearms, and formed white balls, like snow, around her face.

ONE WARM JUNE NIGHT, several weeks after his fight with Margaret, Alf sat in the Biscayne, too tired to get out. Cooling metal popped. In the dim yard, the apple tree rustled at the edge of a square of light from the kitchen. The back of his shirt had stuck to the seat. For all the visiting he had done that night – he and Doyle had taken to working alone to double their effectiveness – he'd picked up only one card. The women hadn't done much better. The union was just fifteen or so cards from the total needed, but something in the atmosphere had changed. Many people didn't want even to open their doors. They spoke through screens, shadowy prisoners of their fear, or simply gestured through windows for the organizers to go away. Mary Carr, whom Doyle had hired several weeks before, blamed the change on Kit Ford, who was playing the heavy for the company. "I'm telling you, everywhere we go, seems like the Roadrunner's just leaving. Lila Soames didn't even wanta open her door to us. I don't know what the Roadrunner's been saying to people, but it's working."

It wasn't just the Roadrunner. Ford, Alf had heard, had taken to driving around with a bodyguard, a big fellow from Johnsonville whom Doyle usually referred to as "that goon." This development had occurred after several union supporters had threatened Ford in a restaurant. The goon accompanied Ford when he was visiting workers after hours. Ford hadn't unleashed his henchman yet, but he hovered in the background, a hint most people weren't slow to pick up. The atmosphere in town was getting more tense by the day, and Alf, who remembered the violent strike of 1949 all too well, was afraid they were slipping towards a repeat of that mayhem.

He got out of the car and trudged to the back door. Margaret had left the light on in the kitchen, it seemed a good sign. He was foraging in the fridge for something to eat when she came in, crossing in her dressing gown to the sink. He watched as she took down a glass. "Your tomatoes are coming along well," he said. "That was a good idea, getting the greenhouse starts." She said nothing but, filling the glass at the tap, turned to leave.

"Margaret, we can't keep this up!"

She sighed and looked at the glass. He heard Jamie call out, upstairs.

"Tell me what I can do, Margaret, and I'll do it."

She looked at him for a moment. "Jamie wants a drink." She moved towards the door. When he put out his hand to touch her shoulder, she twisted away. A bit of water slopped to the floor.

She was soon gone, her slippers scuffing quickly down the hall. Then Joe was there, pushing in from the night. Greeting Alf tersely, he went to the cupboard.

Alf watched him take down a glass. Everything he had wanted to say to Margaret was still burning in him. "Joe," he said, his voice parched. "What happened with your mother, Joe, I need to talk to you –"

Joe turned, his face impassive. Alf sensed the common front between mother and son. They had their reasons for punishing him, good reasons maybe, but in some obscure way he felt the entire story had not been told. That night in this room, just before he'd struck Margaret, it seemed that she had touched something in him that should never be touched – that she had reached inside him and cut his very soul. He felt she had meant to do this. He had reacted with the fury of someone who, in an instant, feels his life threatened. Yet this seemed absurd to him now. How had his life been threatened?

Standing before his son, he struggled to explain something of this. "I know there's no excuse, for a man striking a woman. But you see, I love your mother, and so when she says –"

His throat had constricted, and he stopped. They were both embarrassed.

"Okay," Joe said softly. His fingers brushed Alf's arm as he went out, leaving his empty glass on the counter.

The next evening, Alf left after supper to visit Carl Schmidt, a spinner who lived a couple of miles outside town. The man had already turned him down once. Alf drove down the back roads in a fatalistic mood, not hoping for much.

As he headed along the dead-end lane that lead past Carl's place, he glanced in the rear-view and saw a red Chevelle turn in behind him. If it was Ford – and the sudden leap in his gut told him it had to be – then the foreman was clearly following him.

Alf knew it was impossible to visit Carl now – it could get him fired. The Chevelle was keeping well back, hardly visible in the dust drifting behind the Biscayne. "Come on, it could be anybody," he told himself. "Get hold of yourself." But the blood was pounding in his chest and face. He passed through a grove of old maples, out into the sun in front of Carl's place. A movement of his eyes showed him Carl's dilapidated front porch, flickering behind the grey, decaying survivors of an orchard. Carl was nowhere in sight, though his Ford pickup was parked on the grass outside the kitchen door. Alf drove on.

A turn in the lane cut off the view behind. Dust hung, shining, under a pine. Alf eased the Biscayne over a rib of white bedrock, down through a pasture spotted with wild fruit trees.

And the river was there, swimming under the willows on the far bank. The road ended at a rotting wood barrier that blocked the ramp to a ruined bridge, and forced him to the left, along the sand-flats, where he finally stopped by a clump of scrub willow.

Feeling he needed room to manoeuvre, to confront the man following him, if it came to that, he got out and walked towards the river. A length of driftwood was lying at the water's edge. He picked it up and started to look around for stones. He could hear the other car in the pasture now, its engine growing louder as it descended towards the flats. Making a show of indifference, he found a stone and whacked it with his heavy stick, watching as it knifed across the river.

As the Chevelle crossed the flats behind him, he turned to look. In the passenger seat, gazing over at him, was a mop-haired, dark-skinned fellow in sunglasses. His massive forearm hung outside the door with a queer indolence, as if it were broken. Behind the wheel, erect as a soldier, was Ford.

Alf went back to his game. Rattled now, he swung at another stone, and another, missing both. Hearing footsteps on sand, he turned.

"Kit," he said. He had let the stick droop, at his side.

The foreman stood a few feet off. His eyes, shadowed with fatigue, took in Alf's weapon.

Ford's goon had stopped a couple of steps away from his boss. He was well over six feet, too heavy for his height, with a look in his eyes of lazy contempt. Held loosely in his left hand was a tire iron.

"You guys got a flat tire?" Alf said.

A strange coolness had invaded him. He was ready to fight, but at the same time, he almost didn't care what happened. There was something absurd about them all standing there like schoolboys getting ready to brawl. He wondered if this was Ford's idea of revenge. He'd considered his fight with the foreman to be pretty much of a saw-off, but maybe Ford himself didn't see it that way. Alf waited, with the river at his back, feeling no need to talk. But he did not take his gaze from Ford's staring eyes.

There was an evasion there, a refusal to see. Ford's shrunken pupils had found their focus somewhere just in front of his face. Alf was put out by this. For God's sake, he thought, at least look at me.

He sensed the goon shift his weight, getting ready.

"Alfie," Ford said, and his voice was more strangulated than usual, "I want you to stay away from our people. Anybody who works for Bannerman's, I don't want you near them. You got that? Or do we have to teach it to you?"

Alf chortled. Ford was sounding an awful lot like some movie cowboy.

"What's so funny, asshole? Stay away from our people."

"Is this how you want to spend your life?" Alf said quietly.

Ford's head jerked, almost imperceptibly, as if he'd been struck, and for a moment, a moment only, he looked directly at Alf. Alf saw, not for the first time, the boy in Ford, the lost, plaintive boy at the centre of all that hardness. Alf, too, was affected, at the unexpected contact. A kind of electric shock went through him.

Tossing down his weapon, he kept looking steadily at Ford.

"You just watch it," Ford said. But his voice was hoarse now, without authority; in his eyes was a watery sheen.

He walked quickly away, towards the Chevelle.

"Watchit," the goon told Alf, pointing at him with the iron. Scowling, he turned to trek away across the sand.

Alf watched the red car bump its way up the pasture road. Turning to the water, he found himself swept by unexpected emotion. It was as if some old grief had been exposed in him – a heaviness that verged on sorrow. It saturated everything around him – the warm air smelling of sand and willows, the implacably moving water, carrying along bits of grass and weed, funnelling under the ruined bridge. He had no idea of what had just happened between him and Ford, but the world had changed, he could feel it: the world had grown sadder and heavier and more itself. The very light seemed to lie on the land with a slow, viscous, golden weight. He watched two swallows skim the river, twisting and dodging with breath-taking alacrity, rising on wings so quick they seemed aflame.

57

THAT NIGHT, he made four visits and picked up as many cards, including one from Carl Schmidt. "I guess I'm just sick of being afraid," the spinner told him as he signed a card at his kitchen table.

When Alf got back to the Vimy House, he discovered that the other organizers had been successful too. In fact, they had put the union over the top, in fine style. They'd signed up almost fifty-seven per cent of the workforce, two per cent higher than was needed to achieve automatic certification. People who had held back for weeks had suddenly found reason or courage or weariness or anger enough to sign a card. It was as if there had been some change in the atmosphere that had tipped the mysterious mechanism that releases a decision. Doyle couldn't explain it, though he said he'd seen the phenomenon once or twice before. "An earthquake in China," he said, shrugging, "who the hell knows?" As the organizers celebrated in the Vimy House, Alf felt oddly distant, though he had a pleasant shock when Shirley, her head snaking forward almost apologetically, planted a long, dry kiss on his mouth.

The following week two union negotiators arrived from Toronto to hammer out a first contract. They asked Alf for the names of people who been laid off or fired over the past year as a punishment for supporting the union. The idea was to lever these people back into Bannerman's as part of the collective agreement. Alf put his own name on the list. He told the negotiators he didn't want to go back to knitting, he couldn't stomach the idea of working again under Ford, but anything else would be fine. A few days later, he was offered – and accepted – a job on Bannerman's maintenance crew.

He was soon spending his days patching and painting, often working alone, and often out of doors, which suited him well enough, though it all seemed a bit tame after the drama of organizing. One of his first tasks was on the roof of Number Six, his old mill, repairing some leaks around a ventilation shaft. He worked at his own pace – it was a relief not to be hurried along by machines – and from time to time, with a melancholy sense of freedom, paused to gaze across the roofs of the town towards the humped hills of Wiley's farm, cutting the fresh sky of early summer.

In late July, the workers approved their first contract, and the union held a victory party in Lions Park. All afternoon, tall clouds drifted from the west, casting a double mood of sun and shadow over the thousand or so people who spread their blankets on the parched grass, in the shade of maples and willows. Taking a chance, Alf asked Margaret to come with him. She was speaking to him again, but she said she had a choir rehearsal at the church. Jamie and Penny came gladly, though, excited by the promise of hot dogs and prizes.

Doyle had returned to town for the celebrations. Dressed in Bermuda shorts even redder than his face, he insisted on making the rounds with Alf. "It wouldn't have happened without this guy," the organizer told people in his gruff way, while planting his large, moist hand between Alf's shoulder blades. Alf was chagrined by the attention – Doyle's praise seemed exaggerated, to him – but, also, he was secretly pleased. Everywhere, he met approving faces: that look of admiration and hopefulness he'd first encountered on the fire escape. It had unsettled him then, and it unsettled him a little now, this discovery of something in himself people seemed drawn to. When the time came for speeches from the bandshell, Doyle barked into the microphone that Alf should stand. He got up warily from the picnic blanket he was sharing with Jamie and Penny to the largest ovation anyone got all afternoon. Then, sitting down, he found himself gazing at Pete's house, on its hillside above the park. The garage door was open. Pete's Sarasota was there, facing outwards, its windshield dark.

Later, he stood talking to Doyle by the river. Below them, the shallow current collared rocks with foam. Alf felt a certain poignancy. Something was coming to an end. After this picnic, Doyle would get in his dusty car, and he might never see him again, though they had promised to get together.

"So I can't persuade you to change your mind, you bastard," Doyle said. Despite Alf's lack of interest, the organizer had kept pestering him to join him as a staff organizer for the UKW.

Alf grinned at his friend's persistence.

"I don't think organizing's for me," he said. "I never got over the feeling I was just bothering people."

"Pah! People need to be bothered. *Someone* has to wake them up."

Linda Connaught, the new secretary of the local, called Doyle away. He was to be starter and general announcer for the races. Jamie ran up to Alf with Billy Boileau. Billy's dark eyes fixed on Alf's chest.

"There's a father-and-sons three-legged race!" Jamie said.

"You think we can win, eh?"

"Sure!"

Alf looked at Billy. "Shall we get you a partner then?"

Billy glared into the air, at nothing. "C'mon, I bet we could get Dick Harmer to run with you."

"Nope," Billy said in that trapped, hard voice of his. With his fists jammed and working in his pockets, he seemed to be expecting something that had not been offered, demanding it.

Over at the course, Alf tied Jamie's leg to his. There wasn't much time to practise. The mothers-and-daughters race was already being run. Penny had found a partner in Alf's old school chum Annie Stone, they stumbled their way along in the middle of the pack, and soon the fathers and sons were ready to start. Bellowing, "Go, Brothers!" Malachi Doyle dropped his big arm and the horde of men and boys hopped over the grass, towards the strand of red yarn held taut by Mary Carr's twin daughters. Alf and Jamie finished fourth or fifth, Alf laughing so hard he nearly fell over, while Jamie kept yelling at him, put out at his lack of seriousness. For prizes, all the children received mechanical crickets that soon filled the park with their clicking.

Afterwards, Jamie went off to the swings with a group of other boys. Alf noticed Billy sitting up on a picnic table by himself, intently watching the others. He brought him a cricket.

The boy looked at the toy in Alf's outstretched hand but did not take it. Alf set the cricket on the table and climbed up beside him.

"There's going to be regular races. You don't need a partner for them."

Billy made his trapped-in-the-throat sound: *Heh*.

"I'll bet you're pretty fast."

It was like talking to a post. But again Alf found himself drawn, almost painfully, to this skinny little boy with the mop of luxuriant hair, sitting hunched beside him with his hands on his knees, and a faraway, slit-eyed look in which Alf glimpsed just the trace of a smile. Alf began to talk about the different kinds of runners: the sprinters, and the long-distance runners, the ones who could keep going all day, like Tom Longboat. Tom Longboat was an Indian, Alf dared to say, and caught for his reward a slight turn of Billy's head. So he told him about the great Tom Longboat, how he was from a reserve not far from here, how he'd beaten all the great marathoners of the day, including the Englishman Alf Shrubb, flying along in the tradition of the great Indian runners who in the old days had carried messages long distances between villages without stopping to eat and only drinking what they could scoop from streams as they splashed through them.

Once, twice, Billy glanced up at him, suspicious interest in his narrowed eyes. But a deeper gleam was there too, perhaps it was delight. Alf reached out and touched him affectionately on the back. It was like making contact with a little dynamo. The tension there was palpable, in the hard flesh.

"So maybe you could give it a try," Alf said. "I think they're almost ready."

Doyle, holding up his clipboard, was calling out in his raw voice for runners. First, girls, eight to eleven. Then boys. Jamie and his friends were trooping back from the swings. Alf noticed his son eyeing him and Billy warily. Just then, Billy jumped off the table and walked rapidly towards the trees at the south end of the park. He was like a wild animal, bolting at God only knew what tremor of danger. In a few seconds he had disappeared into the trees that climbed the flank of Lookout Hill.

Jamie, who had turned nine that month, came second, despite being matched with older boys. The lad was obviously a sprinter, Alf thought, as his Uncle Joe had been. And for a moment, Alf saw his brother cross the finish line at the high-school track meet: his head tossed back, his mouth open in a crazy, tortured smile of triumph. Afterwards, he'd stuffed his red ribbons in a drawer as if they were nothing.

Jamie came over to the table, his face shining with pride.

"Ah, you'll do better next time," Alf told him, as if he'd failed by coming second – and felt his own heart sink as he saw the shadow cross his son's face. Why had he said that, when in fact he was proud of him? He tried to make it up, praising the boy, ruffling his hair. But the damage had been done. Alf watched him go off towards the crowd with his prize, a red balloon, bobbing behind him.

He sat on disconsolately. Why did he hurt people – his own family most of all? It was as if there was a blade in his hands that had a life of its own. He looked off towards the woods flowing up the side of Lookout Hill. He'd been kind to Billy Boileau, and cruel to his own son. What in hell was he trying to do? He thought of Billy in the woods – he imagined him walking hard up the narrow trails, or sulking on a rock. The image pierced him, but he suppressed it, feeling disloyal to Jamie.

Well, he would make it up to the boy. He looked around. The last race had just finished. The crowd was dissolving and Doyle was walking away in deep conversation with two other men, his voice growling under theirs. A cloud was just passing over the sun, the park had slipped into shadow. He was unable to pick out Jamie among all the people – it seemed as if he had made the boy vanish by his cruelty.

It was then he saw Lucille. He had not spoken to her for months, though in truth he'd never stopped thinking about her. And here she was, as if emerging from one of his own daydreams, striding towards him. He half-expected a rebuke. Unusually for her, she was wearing a dress: short, scoop-necked, her brown knees flashing as she walked.

He knew she was working again at Bannerman's, in her old job as a seam-stitcher. Alf himself had put her on the list the negotiators had asked for. Her smile shocked him. He wondered if she'd found out he'd helped her.

"Do you know where Billy's got to?"

He supposed she had noticed him with the boy. But he felt it was him, really, she had come to see.

"He went off to the woods."

"That kid – he's a regular escape artist!"

Her black eyes, suddenly empty of expression, searched his. He had left her without an explanation, simply walked away. He felt he deserved hostility from her, but there was something else here instead, girlish, wondering. Shame heated his face, but he was glad, very glad, to see her.

It was threatening rain. The air was soft, close; the park felt wrapped in sadness. His hands had grown heavy. He was aware of her bosom, rising below her smooth, exposed chest, and of a faint twist in the left side of her mouth.

"So I guess you're a hero now," she said.

Was she speaking ironically? He could not meet her eyes.

"I wouldn't say so," he said.

"Why did you leave me?" she said, looking straight at him.

"I'm sorry, Lucille. I –"

"Well, you're a busy man." She turned away and stared at the crowd for a moment while he watched her. He wanted her, and was appalled at himself that *this* should crop up again. "I really hated you for going," she said. "I sort of thought – well, stupid me, eh?"

"There's nothing stupid about you," he said.

"I just thought we might have, you know, talked about it."

"I was a bastard," he said.

The space between them filled with an awkward silence.

"Well," she said, "I guess I better find Billy."

"I'll help you," he said.

As they walked off together, he realized people must be watching. Before, he had taken great pains to hide his connection to her. Now he told himself they were only going into the woods to hunt for her boy: they were innocent entirely. Careful not to touch each other even accidentally, they walked across the dry grass, her sandals slapping at her heels. They did not speak, and again he felt that strange blankness, almost a deadness, that descended on his mind whenever he was with her. He wondered if she were only tolerating him now. Men stuck to her, clung to her like burrs: it was something she was used to. He didn't care. That was the main thing, he didn't care. At the woods they had to separate, to enter the mouth of the trail. He followed her down the dim path that smelled of mud in hidden springs, watching the white tag of her dress where it had stood up against her neck, white on brown.

58

JAMIE WATCHED THEM GO into the woods. His balloon tickled its string lightly through his hand and slipped away, unnoticed. By the time he reached the trees, it had sailed, a red dot, high over the river and the Island.

He climbed through the dim mass of trees. After a while he stopped, below a tall clump of cedars. Water slimed and rutted the trail. The fragile, tentative tap of a woodpecker came from space grown ominous.

Billy had said, *He's going to be my father now*. Now it had happened, he felt. He'd watched Billy go into the woods. Now his father and Billy's mother had gone after him. The three of them were together.

He heard a laugh. It came from just up ahead – his father's laugh! And for a second he felt everything was going to be all right – that's what his father's laugh meant to him – and he remembered a time when they had gone swimming at Devil's Cave. His father had stayed a long time underwater, then burst up, the water pouring off his head, laughing. He floated up the trail. A flicker in the leaves told him his father was close by. Stopping, he turned a little and saw his father and Billy's mother. They were standing right in front of him, facing each other, and his father's hand was on her face, touching her cheek.

"Dad," someone said.

For a minute he thought it was Billy who had spoken: that hard little voice. But it was himself, Jamie, his voice like a stone.

His father's hand dropped from her cheek. They looked at him.

"Jamie, hey! We're just looking for Billy."

Looking for Billy in Billy's mother's face. He stared at his father, who came forward with a grin. "Hey guy, *you* seen Billy?"

His father mussed his hair.

They went back down to the park together, the three of them. Billy could find his own way home, his mother said.

In the park, she went off. His father took him across the bridge and off the Island to the stores. He wondered, Were they still looking for Billy? His father took him into the Oasis and bought him a double-scoop chocolate – for doing so well in that race, he said. They walked back towards the Island. On the bridge, his father stopped and leaned on the rail. He lit a cigarette and tossed the flaming match towards the water. Jamie stood licking his cone and watching his father's face. Ice cream melted cold on his fingers, and somewhere down the shadowy race a mourning dove cooed three times.

"What you saw there," his father said, "that was just Billy's mother being sad about something. It's okay, really. We don't have to mention it to your mother. Okay?"

Jamie licked at his cone. "Are you still my dad?" he said, in his strange, new voice. It seemed, almost, to come from outside him. The mourning dove had stopped.

He was falling, falling through the mild air. His father laughed. A large hand caressed the back of his head. "What a crazy idea!"

59

THESE DAYS – the long summer holidays of sun and burnt lawns and the whining lathes of the cicadas in their high, secret workshops – Joe would have spent every hour he had with Anna, who was leaving in a month. But he had to work. He had to prowl the dim aisles of Bannerman's shipping department, invoices in sweaty hand, taking down sweaters and T-shirts from their shelves, fitting them into cardboard boxes stamped with the logo of the Boy Scout with the banner. The place was miserably hot under its flat roof and, despite the pine scent of Dustbane sprinkled liberally everywhere, stank of human waste. The toilet faced directly into the workplace, its saloon-style doors revealing the dropped trousers and shins of whoever was inside. The shins always looked vulnerable, pathetic, the source of endless jokes – *Show us your knees, Maggie* – which Joe quickly grew tired of.

One low, filthy window looked out on the straw-pale playing fields behind the arena. By putting his face close to the left side of the glass he could peer over the arena roof and just make out the cloud of trees obscuring the North End. They seemed alive with Anna's presence, like the blank sky above, and the steep roofs of the Bannerman mansion nestled in foliage. He was impatient to get up the hill again, to renew the spell at its source. He kept glancing above the shipping-room door, where the hands of a large clock jerked arthritically through the day, and was startled by a paradox: he was wishing the hours away, but every one of them, when it was past, was another sixty minutes deducted from her time in the town. She and her mother, who was going back to visit family, had already bought their tickets.

When the five o'clock whistle went, he was always first down the stairs, first across the playing fields. At home: a shower, fresh clothes, then a quick bite and out again. His mother kept asking if he didn't want to invite Anna home for supper. "Such a lovely girl" she said warmly, more than once, "clever too." But Joe resisted. "Love you," he'd tell her as he brushed past with a quick kiss. He *did* love her, it was easy these days, love seemed to spill from him without effort: he even loved the cozy, familiar kitchen with its banged-up furniture, he loved his brother's bicycle, abandoned on its side on the dry grass . . .

Something had shifted between him and Anna. It was their love-making in the mills that had done it, he felt – pitching them into a new level of intimacy. He had never forgotten Liz's words: *Anna can't love. It was a man, not a boy like you.* Well, he had proven her wrong, hadn't he? And now, surely something could be worked out about France. He told Anna he could visit her in Paris; maybe he could become a student there himself in a year or two, if he could find the money. Yet his enthusiasm never generated anything definite from her side. They made love a few times more, in her bedroom when her parents were out, and once, at his insistence, in the lowlands beside the Shade where they'd first got together on the night of the gradu-ation party. But even so, he began to fear that, for her, nothing essential had changed. She actually seemed to be looking forward to going away. He wondered if she felt any pangs at all. Couldn't she see, couldn't she guess, what he was going through? His desperation grew cagey, his desperation, and, yes, his jealousy. He wondered if her old boyfriend was still in the cards – the *man*-friend Liz had men-tioned. He wondered if it was the man in the picture on her desk.

One Sunday afternoon they were reading in her bedroom. Sitting at her desk, he could hear Anna flipping pages on the bed behind him. Unable to concentrate, he kept studying the photograph in its gold frame – the picture he'd first seen that winter afternoon he'd brought her the heather. He worried over the handsome face of her friend, the heavy eyebrows, the unreadable expression of the rather deep-set eyes, the sense of casual ownership implied by the loose draping of his hand over Anna's shoulder. In her head-scarf she had the air of a convalescent, bundled against the chill.

The man was movie-star handsome, Joe thought, but there was something vacant in his face, as though it had been hollowed out from within. It was a mask of handsomeness, from which unhappy eyes stared. He had constructed a theory. This man was the man Liz had referred to. Anna had fallen in love with this man, and he had abandoned her. She had had a terrible time. Here, in the photograph, her unhappiness was already coming upon her, because the man –

this man with his cold, careless face – was in the process of leaving her. She had been a long time recovering, and now she was wary of love, of love's abandon, because she could not allow herself to go through it again. Even if she loved Joe (and he was almost convinced she did), she could not let herself feel it. He needed to go slowly, to be patient. She needed patient, tender care and of course he was willing to give it to her, only there wasn't much time left to be patient in.

Twice he nearly spoke, to the rustling on the bed behind him. Each time he hesitated. Any attempt to enter her intimate space always seemed to embroil him in new sorrows. She was a nest of trip-wires. You never knew what anger or rebuke you might set off. But he had to know.

Offhandedly, he sang out, "Say, who's this handsome friend of yours?"

When she didn't answer, he turned in his chair. She was lying on her stomach, propped on her elbows over her book. She was wearing Bermudas and a sleeveless blouse. Those green eyes looked at him across the carved mahogany of her bed.

"In the photo," he said.

"Enrico," she said matter-of-factly. "He was my best friend in Europe."

She went on looking at him, while he conducted a rapid analysis of her words. She had spoken so casually of this Enrico that he wondered if he *had* been only a friend.

"Very good-looking," he said, struggling to maintain a disinterested note. "Were you in love with him?"

"In a way," she mused, still watching him.

He could no longer stop himself.

"Will you be seeing him – when you go back?"

"Yes," she said in a muffled tone, looking down at her book. Staring over the back of his chair, with the false smile dying on his face, he felt suddenly emptied. In two seconds, the happiness and confidence of the entire summer had evaporated.

"So this is my rival," he said. His voice came out as a croak.

She turned a page. Her bare feet were twining with each other, and this seemed to him the twining of naked bodies, of which his was not one.

"Anna," he said.

"I feel like you're picking me apart," she said to her book.

"It's a natural-enough question," he said. "I'm naturally curious, in a jealous sort of way, about my rivals."

"He's not your rival," she said in a flat voice.

"He's here on your desk. You don't have a picture of *me* on your desk. What happened to that little picture I gave you?"

She looked up at him again, without expression: she was displeased. But he brazened it out with her, making no attempt to hide the misery on his face.

"He's homosexual," she said finally, looking down again. She sighed and pressed two fingers into her closed right eye, as if to force back some incipient pain.

"Homo –"

"He sleeps with *men*," she said.

"I know what it means," he said, flushing. He stared at her. He might know the word, but he didn't know any homosexuals himself, though occasionally some boy at school would be denigrated with taunts of "homo!" or "faggot!" There was something other-worldly in the term, since no one really knew what a faggot was, in any experiential sense: the boy might as well have been called a centaur.

On the bed, Anna rolled to her back, holding her book with one hand above her face. After a moment she flung it aside, as if in impatience or disgust, while he watched intently from across the room.

The day before she was to leave, they walked up the Atta to Devil's Cave. In front of the cave was a sandy depression littered with the remains of old fires: charred logs, nuggets of wadded tin foil, cruel shards of brown glass. Clearing a place for their blanket with his feet, he watched as she stooped to peer into the deep recess between two enormous slabs of limestone. She was wearing white sneakers, jeans, and a white T-shirt that barely reached her belt. It had slid up, revealing the softly notched serpent of her spine. They had not made love for a week, not since his questions about the photograph, he noticed, though her own explanation was that she was having her period.

She came away from the cave without comment and stood near him, looking at the river where it slid into the pool. It was the deepest place he knew of on the Attawan: formed by the river as it rounded a sharp bend and met the sudden resistance of the limestone. The water here, opaque with its burden of soil, was in a constant state of agitation – its surface crossed with little whirlpools that popped up mysteriously and as mysteriously disappeared. Upstream, the bank ascended gradually to a cliff of grey clay, sharp-edged against the almost painful brightness of the sky. There was something oppressive in the look of this cliff – she was staring at it now, one hand shading her face – something rudely prehistoric, as if it had endured from the era before life, the slick, leaden clay falling almost sheer to the water.

"There's an odd feeling about this place," she said, coming back. "It's like there's somebody else here. I keep feeling I'm being watched."

"We could go somewhere else."

She trailed along the edge of the bank without answering. He went on putting out their picnic things. Every object he touched – the pink Tupperware container of sandwiches, the Thermos of coffee, the tinned cheese from France he'd bought in the A&P – seemed oddly insubstantial: cardboard fill-ins for the real thing.

They sat side by side, picking at the ham and cheese sandwiches his mother had made, looking over the coursing water. He had come here all his life, first with his father, then with friends: it was a favourite swimming hole, though at least two drownings had occurred here when weak swimmers had been trapped under the bank. He told her about these deaths now, with a secretly hostile eagerness, unable to stop himself. "One fellow – Graham Lessing – he used to be in my class – when they pulled him out and worked on him, he came to. He sat up and asked for a glass of water and then he lay back down and died."

"*He asked for a glass of water?*"

"I know. It's like he didn't appreciate them pumping his lungs out."

"How did he ask? I mean, was he conscious?" she said skeptically.

Joe admitted he hadn't been there; he'd only heard the story later.

"Aha," she said.

He was deflated, feeling he'd failed to communicate the strangeness of the drowning. Upstream, near the cliff, the river swished at a broken willow branch. He had always loved this place, but today it had a heartless quality, as though it cared nothing for human beings. "I have to ask you something," he said.

She glanced at him, a bit guardedly.

"What happened to you, before you came to Attawan? You said you had a bad time."

She was silent, working the remains of her sandwich between her fingers. Earlier, he would not have dared to ask such this question, wary of the limits she had imposed on him. But now he wanted facts, no matter how treacherous.

"Yes, well, it wasn't all bad," she said, tossing the little ball of bread towards the water. There was something new in her tone, a calm, simple sincerity. "I had an affair, this was in France, in Paris, and well – I sort of got in over my head."

She paused, looking at the sand in front of her. He was scarcely breathing. It was the word "affair" that had done it. It sounded so mature, and somehow dangerous.

"He was a painter," she said. "The previous fall, he'd taught a few classes at our school. All the girls were crazy for him. When he asked me if I'd model for him, at his studio, I sort of jumped at it."

So she told him about Guillaume. Guillaume in his paint-stained jeans and T-shirt. Guillaume, who had travelled the world, and kept in his studio a drum from Borneo he said was made from human skin. Chunks of temple carving from Thailand. A six-foot papier mâché dragon from Mexico, its fierce jaws clamped on the body of a hapless victim. He painted richly coloured oils of the human figure – nearly always a naked female extended diagonally across the canvas like some rough, tilting landscape. He was thirty-three. She had just turned seventeen.

She didn't describe how she came to sleep with Guillaume, she spared Joe that, though he gathered that she had been happy with him in the beginning. "My parents didn't know," she said. "At least at first." She broke off and stared bleakly in front of her, as if whatever came next in her story had somehow deprived her of speech.

"Things started to go wrong," Joe said, prompting. He wanted – needed – that part of the story now.

A bitterness entered her voice. "If you think someone doesn't like your body, there's really no place to hide. He'd tell me I was too heavy. Too slow. I was *stupide*. I was reading the wrong books. He didn't have much money, so I'd steal francs from my mother and give them to him. I even stole paint. I'd go into a store and come out with my pockets full of tubes. He used to call me his *petite voleuse*." She shook her head. She seemed baffled and dismayed by her own behaviour, and at the same time fascinated by it.

"I wasn't eating," she said. "I wasn't doing my homework. In school, all I could think about was getting out so I could go by his studio. Then he started making these little speeches – I needed to get out more in the world, I needed to have a boyfriend my own age. One afternoon he told me he had to go away for a few days. Stupid me, I started standing in the park across the street, watching his building. When I finally went in, the concierge told me he'd moved."

She raked at the sand with her fingers, once, twice, three times, gouging a small trench. She flung away a handful of sand.

"I saw him again, one day in the street," she said. "And it all started up again – at least for a couple of hours. Afterwards, he went completely cold. He was like that. He said he just didn't want to see me again. He meant it this time."

Joe tried to hug her, but she pushed him off. For a long while, she stared at the sand. When she began to speak again, her voice had flattened, gone almost dead. "Everything seemed raw, too bright. I began to get headaches all the time. I wouldn't leave the apartment. I refused to go to school." She glanced up at Joe, and he saw she was ashamed: ashamed she had gone to pieces over this, ashamed, now, that he was seeing what had happened. "It was weeks. My parents didn't know what to do." Finally, they had sent her to a psychiatrist, but after three sessions she quit. "He was an iceberg," she said. "I hated him." Her *real* doctor, she maintained, was Enrico, the man in the photograph on her desk. He was the son of friends of her parents. She had known him since she was a little girl. He spent hours visiting her, he coaxed her outside, on walks.

And then her father, who worked in Intertex's Paris office, was offered a chance to set up new accounting procedures at a mill in Canada, a job that would take one or two years. "Canada seemed safe somehow. I hadn't lived here since I was ten – my dad was from Montreal – but I had good memories. I had this idea I could start over again, you know, live a kind of normal life, a schoolgirl's life, nothing so – extreme."

She fell silent. Her story had come to an end, it seemed, and yet he still didn't know the most important part. She was dragging her fingers through the hole she'd made in the sand, with an awkward-ness that to Joe's eyes made her seem much younger. He wanted to comfort her, but wasn't sure she wanted him to. She seemed far away now, isolated in her unhappiness.

"And it worked," he said, "coming here?"

"We didn't come here right away. We went to visit my mother's family, in Brittany. That's where I started to get better."

"Ah," he said.

"It's been fine here," she said. "It's just that – well, I don't think I'm really a small-town person. I can't pretend I'm someone I'm not. It was foolish to think I could."

She spoke haughtily, almost angrily, as if lashing out at him, as if *he* were somehow to blame for her failure to belong in Attawan. He looked at her. "Liz says you can't love, because of what happened." He had thrown the accusation at her, sharply. He suspected now she never *had* loved him.

"What does Liz know?" she said, and got suddenly to her feet. She walked towards the river, where she stood watching the shifting currents.

"I love you," he breathed. The words – the tremendous emotion – had come swimming up from his desolation like a new discovery – the discovery he was fated to make over and over.

Turning back to him, she met his eyes. Then her gaze fled.

They stripped off their clothes and walked upstream, following a narrow path that ran along the base of the cliff to the fallen willow that lay aslant the current. He watched her intently as she moved ahead of him: her wide shoulders, her long legs, and her skin so smooth it seemed unnatural. In the shadow of the cliff, she hugged herself and complained of the cold. He showed her how to climb out on the trunk of the willow and drop into the current. She plunged in with a cry, and the river carried her off. He caught up to her downstream, in the pool by the cave, where they briefly kissed, her legs wrapping him in the coursing, tickling water.

Immediately she had to get out and do it again. He stayed in the pool, watching her hurry up the narrow path below the cliff. At the willow, she turned and waved to him. Her nakedness hurt him, yet he could not tear his eyes from her. Against the whiteness of her skin, her bush seemed like some small, dark animal that had clung there.

When she dropped into the water, he did a surface dive and swam for the bottom. It was dark almost immediately, the yellow-brown water of the surface layer turning to impenetrable purple. On the bottom was an old, waterlogged pine trunk, the stumps of its branches stippling it like the cruel knobs of some medieval club. He managed to grasp one of these, using it to keep himself down. Crouching on the cool ooze, he peered up into the haze above, hoping to get a glimpse of her. He stayed down as long as he could – he and Smiley used to play this game, their record for staying under was about a minute and a half – and finally, with burning lungs, he kicked towards the surface.

Broaching with a gasp, he could see no one. She was not in the river. She was not anywhere on shore. He called her name, turning and turning in the pool with a rising concern. His feet scraped bottom: the current had carried him towards the exit of the pool. Swimming back to its centre, he dove again, clawing his way down to where the current was weaker, making his way along the bottom while groping blindly with his hands in the dark. Finally he touched a limb. But it was only the end of the pine tree, slippery with algae. Again he rose to the surface. Again, there was no one there. Panic took him now, ice in the gut. Upstream, the sun was a blaze of thorns above the cliff. Then she was there: popping up not five feet from him, her head slick as an otter's. She had not seen him.

She was crying out his name, sending it out with thrilling desperation to the empty shore. When he spoke, she screamed and turned to him, her eyes filled with fear. "What *happened* to you? What *happened* to you, why did you do that!"

"I just dove," he said. "I must have missed you when I came up –" He was feigning innocence, secretly gratified at her alarm. He had meant to worry her, with his first dive, he had meant to make her afraid.

She swam to him. He realized she was weeping, her face rubbery like a little girl's, weeping and hanging on him – inwardly, he triumphed. On shore, he wrapped her in the red tartan blanket. Shivering, she huddled against him.

"You see," he said, hugging her protectively, "you do love me a little."

She shuddered and snuggled in closer, while he looked past her, to the dark, oppressive cliff that, like her, had not answered.

That evening, he ate with her family in the backyard, under the maple tree, on the old deal table with the gamey leg, which swayed a little under its white cloth. Her parents were mostly silent – there seemed to be some tension between them – but afterwards Joe and Anna were able to escape in her father's Bel Air. They drove north out of town, following the winding highway across a plain sectioned into farms. A ripe goldenness suffused the fields, the heightened life before dusk. At Anna's prompting he turned down a gravel sideroad that ran straight east. They came to a small pioneer church, sheltered in a grove of maples. The pointed doors were locked, but they walked in the churchyard, past the cobblestone walls with their even rows of smooth, egglike stones. The foliage lashed above them with a dry, wild sound like surf, in a wind that seemed to carry the orange light that washed everywhere. To the north, the wooded Reid Hills crept out, blue skirmishers at the edge of the plain.

Anna had more energy for exploring than he did, so he trailed around after her, faintly pleased when something pleased her – an old gravestone, the absorption of a wire fence by the bark of a tree – but also resentful that on their last night, she could bother with anything but him. He could not forget her story. It was obvious, that compared to her painter, he had hardly touched her.

He watched her as she stopped to scratch a bare leg, watched as the wind plastered her dress against her thighs, revealing their shape – that sudden suggestion of hidden nakedness. It seemed he was seeing her for the first time, everything about her seemed that novel, that fresh – though it also occurred to him that this might be the last time too. The last time and the first – the two times had become one, painful in its vividness. He turned away from her, to the field behind the church. Someone, he saw with a start, was walking there – a tousle-haired child of three or four, walking by himself through the wind-whipped grain. His heart leapt in recognition, though of what he couldn't have said. A moment later, he saw that the "child" was only the upright iron seat of an old mower, abandoned at the edge of the field. But the vision had moved him. He turned to Anna, thinking to tell her about it. But words seemed pointless now; words could do nothing.

Later, as they drove away through the light-swept fields, he looked over at her where she sat against the door, gazing at a line of tossing maples.

"I have to," he said, his voice breaking harshly. "I have to make love to you."

She did not even seem to have heard; he felt that, in some way, she had already left.

"I don't care about your period," he said. And a moment later, throwing away the last of his pride: "Anna!"

"All right," she said, looking over at him. He did not entirely believe her smile, but he was grateful for anything now. He swung the Bel Air up the river road, into the Reid Hills, sliding it into a narrow lane in the woods. When he began to kiss her, she stopped him. "Not here," she said, "outside." He led her down a trail, through poplars and spruce. They were sheltered from the wind now, in a kind of sandy bowl at the top of a cliff. They gazed east, over the Shade, the river descending through woods and fields. Far below, in the shadow of the cliff, the dim water whispered around a solitary rock.

They spread an old blanket and an afghan they had brought from the car, quickly stripped off their clothes, and slid into their makeshift bed. He wanted this lovemaking to be better than anything they'd had – it seemed a kind of last chance. She seemed determined too, but there was soon a problem. The mosquitoes were out. Even when he was moving in her, she seemed more aware of them than of him, continuously brushing the insects away from their faces, laughing at the discomfort they caused.

Afterwards, sulking, he pulled on his clothes in silence. He wanted her to speak first, he wanted her to ask him if he was all right – to show *that* much care for what he was going through – but with only her panties on, she gathered the rest of her clothes and hurried back to the Bel Air. When he got in a little later, he slammed the door and stared out the windshield towards the thicket of birches. "I felt you were hardly there," he said.

"I was there," she said. Her answer came so readily, with such hardness, he retreated again into silence. They drove towards town. They were separated by a gulf now; he was almost relieved, feeling they'd come to something more honest. At least, he felt less vulnerable in his anger. But after a while, she slid over to him and with a sigh put her head on his shoulder. He was desperate to experience every minute with her, as if something yet might be achieved that had not been achieved, or found, before. He put his arm around her and steered with his left hand, watching the headlights of the Bel Air pick out trees and mailboxes.

It was after eleven when they embraced at her kitchen door. He was planning to come back in the morning, to see her off but, still, he didn't want to let her go. They clung to each other in a kind of inert exhaustion, like those marathon dancers he'd seen in old newsreels. He was trying to convince himself she was holding on as tightly as he was. Finally, she broke away.

That night he woke at three. Unable to get back to sleep, he dressed and walked up West Street, past the old hosiery mill, its windows boarded now, and up the rail embankment to the Macrimmons'. The wind had subsided, under an obscure sky. In the yard, everything was still, ghostly: the table where they had eaten so many suppers, stripped of its cover; the dim mountain of the maple; their four chairs scattered forlornly on the packed dirt. He sat with his back against the maple watching her window. Some time later, the chaotic caroling of birds woke him, and he walked off his stiffness in the yard before resuming his vigil in a chair. He must have fallen asleep again, because the next thing he saw was Anna's face. She was kneeling before him in her dressing gown. For a blissful moment, he forgot she was leaving, and simply smiled at her.

"You should be in a novel," she scolded him delightedly as she led him into the kitchen, "waiting out there like that." He sat at the kitchen table while she made eggs, standing at the stove in her dark-green dressing gown. He had never seen her in it before. He kept staring at the overly long sleeves she kept pushing back, her slender wrists – there was so much about her he didn't know, might never know now. It seemed unfair that her novelty should go on unfolding so effortlessly before him, even on their last morning.

"What about Guillaume?" he said, and immediately felt sickened by his own need to know, in the face of what she'd been through. From upstairs came the sound of voices. Her parents would soon be down. "Do you think you might run into him again?"

At the stove, she went motionless. Then she turned, the spatula in her hand, and looked at him in what seemed incomprehension. For a moment, she fell into an abstraction, as if considering the idea further. Turning back to the stove, she shook her head a little – did it mean no, he wondered, did she mean she could hardly believe he'd ask such a thing?

"Anna," he said.

"If I do," she said, almost cheerfully, "I'm sure I can handle it."

"Good," he said. "That's good."

Everyone ate breakfast on the fly, while trying to do a dozen other things. Her father, who was driving Anna and her mother to the airport, acknowledged Joe gruffly and went off to call his office. Her mother hurried here and there as she kept changing her mind about the clothes she would take to France. He stood around, feeling he was in the way. He tried to make himself useful by cleaning up the kitchen. He helped Andrew Macrimmon carry Anna's trunk downstairs. Everything was remarkably, nightmarishly, ordinary. He saw a squirrel run across the earth, leap to a lawnchair, and sit up on its haunches to eat something. It seemed curiously human to him – those dark little handlike paws – and when it scampered away behind the house, he looked after it in astonishment, as if its disappearance were a key to what was happening to him.

A few minutes later he sat on Anna's bed, watching her make some last-minute changes to the contents of her suitcase. Her mother called up the stairwell: "Vite, vite, allons-y! Ton père nous attend!"

He helped Anna close the swollen case. They kissed, almost gravely, and with a quick movement she escaped his arms and went out the door. He pulled her heavy bag off the bed and followed. Her parents were already in the car. He put the suitcase in the trunk and closed it, in the sickening gust of the exhaust, while Anna slid into the back seat. Her mother extended a hand from the front window. "You're a good boy," she said. Her remark stung. He did not want to be a boy, did not want to be good. The man Anna had loved had not been good.

Anna had rolled her window down. He was taken aback by her tears, which made the mark on her cheek glisten. His throat tight, he leaned down to her. Their lips brushed – that smell of her, that scent of vanilla that was almost a no-smell, the scent of space itself – and the car began to back up. He walked down to the front sidewalk and stood watching as the Bel Air swung backwards into Banting, then, with the slight jolt of the gear-change, began to slide smoothly forward.

60

LATE AUGUST, and the scream of Alf's tablesaw, bees floating in the towers of goldenrod leaning beside his half-finished steps. Looking up, he saw through an open window of the sweater mill a carousel turning with a load of white bobbins. Swiftly, swiftly, the pale planets fled against the deeper darkness of the hall behind it. Other machines were invisibly at work with a steady brushing clash, like a waterfall, as thousands of needles and small metal parts raced through their tasks, above the deep, organic hum of the drive-belts. Regret lodged a small stone in his chest: he had once been at the heart of that work himself, and though he had never cared as much for knitting as for carpentry, he was alone now, outside the ark of easy purposefulness men and women made when they worked together.

Kneeling, he fit the board into the deck and nailed it home. Already, the fresh pine of the other boards was dirty with the confused prints of his workboots. Descending the stairs, he picked up another board and was about to place it on the tablesaw when he noticed that in the open window of the sweater mill the carousel had stopped. Minutes later it still had not moved. Above idle bobbins, threads belled slightly in the breeze. The knitter in him was instantly alert, critical: no machine should stand idle for long. As he stared up at the high window, he realized he could no longer hear the thrum of work. Suddenly – it was like the uncanny feeling he got when his heart skipped a beat – the mills seemed wrapped in the silence of desertion.

He looked around, the miraculous sole survivor of an event he could not grasp. Nearby, the bees, audible now, flew from frond to frond. A few moments later, he heard a cry. It might have come from a man or a woman – he could not tell which – and it sounded from the depths of the mills like some outburst of pain or alarm of the buildings themselves: as if the thick old beams had yielded up finally a reaction to the saws that had felled them a century before. A little later he heard other voices, shouting and arguing, phones ringing, the sound of breaking glass. The din was coming mainly from the sweater mill, from all six floors, though as he listened it seemed to spread, a contagion of anger or panic that soon echoed from other buildings as well. Standing on the unrailed deck, he looked around in amazement. And then he heard it: the drumming on the stairs that grew louder, and continued to grow louder, as workers streamed into the yard. His first thought was fire.

He saw Lil Hepworth stalk out purposefully, thick legs working under her shapeless skirt. Immediately behind came Jim Corcoran, a spinner, and his cousin Sid Corcoran, gripping the hair on the crown of his head as if he meant to tear it out. Everyone seemed dazed. They stood in the yard, facing the doorways from which yet more workers were streaming. They were coming from all the buildings now: not in a solid mass, as they did when the sirens released them (he looked at his watch to make sure it wasn't noon yet) but more raggedly, in twos and threes, from the door of the dyehouse, the knitting mill, the spinning mill. Some were grim-faced, silent. Others were arguing volubly. A couple were laughing and smiling as if they'd been released on holiday. Behind him now, people came clattering down the plywood ramp he'd rigged at the loading dock. Seeing Joe emerge, he called to him. Joe didn't hear – he was listening to Eddie Baker, who was holding forth with clenched fists – but a woman who was closer to Alf, it was Linda Koch, raised her freckled face and shouted to him, "They're shuttin' the mills!"

Stunned, Alf watched her plump back retreat towards the others gathering in the yard. A man and woman – it was Lottie Connor and Art Freud – were arguing so violently, red faces inches apart, it seemed they must soon fight in earnest. Others were trying to calm them. The growing crowd seethed.

Alf left his perch and stood at the edge of the melee. Beside him, Davy Clark – a tall man of about sixty with a haggard, sour look – blew through his lips in little explosive bursts like the release of steam through a safety valve. Alf realized he was laughing.

When he asked what was going on – he could scarcely believe what Linda Koch had told him – Davy regarded him with bright, dismissive scorn.

"Closing 'er down," he said finally, as if it was an event he had seen coming for weeks, and Alf, like the others, was some kind of ass not to have seen it too.

"What do you mean?"

He still had not grasped, would not let himself grasp, the full truth. There had to be some other explanation: a fire, a burst pipe, short-term layoffs.

"It's over. Finished. They just announced it. They're moving the whole damn thing to Quebec."

"*Quebec?*"

"They say anyone who wants to work down there can apply. They'll get priority. How about it, Alf, you like Quebec?"

There was a viciousness in this – a personal hostility – that added an extra current of confusion to the news that Bannerman's was moving. Disbelief was pounding heavily in his chest, his face. He felt curiously exposed, as though the closing was somehow the result of his own missteps, his own naive miscalculations. He had the same feeling he'd had so often as a child. He could see blame making a wide turn in the far distance, like some kind of winged predator that had seen him on its first pass and now, despite his hopes that he had been overlooked, was returning for the kill.

"When," he said.

"November," Davy said, watching him closely. "Soon as we're finished the fall lines."

Bruce Mason, the new president of the local, had climbed onto the loading dock of the sweater mill now, where he was conferring with two other union officials. Some people in the crowd were watching them expectantly. Others were jeering. By now, Alf understood what had probably happened. The foremen had called the workers together to announce the closing – or perhaps the news had come over the PA system – and the employees had stormed out spontaneously. He'd seen the same thing before, in 1949. But it was one thing to stage a walkout: the question was always what to do next. The workers seemed at a loss. They were jostling about, looking for leadership, and when Bruce finally stood forward with his hands raised to instill calm, he seemed helpless before the milling crowd.

"Brothers and sisters," he began.

"Fuck your brothers and sisters!" someone cried out. New arguments exploded around the perpetrator of this remark. Beside Alf, Davy Clark continued to snort out his silent, bitter laughter. None of this surprised old Davy, it was what the fools deserved.

Bruce said something about "fighting this with everything we've got." He would talk to management – he'd go to Toronto and talk to the president of Intertex himself, if that's what it took. He drew a flutter of weak applause from many, but the sniping of boos and epithets continued. In the windows overhead, a few people leaned on the sills, looking down like casual spectators at some arcane bloodsport. On the sixth floor, Kit Ford coldly observed the proceedings, his glance occasionally shifting to a clipboard on which he was apparently making notes. Across the yard, a fight broke out. Alf heard angry, surprised shouts, the desperate scuffling of feet on gravel. There was sense of a society unravelling at the seams. It seemed that no one knew what to do, or what to expect.

Just then, Alf noticed Lucille, standing with a group of her fellow workers from the sewing department. Instantly, he experienced a surge of the old hunger; she seemed a point of solace – of escape, really – in the dismal confusion of the yard. Since the union picnic, he'd been hoping they might get together again, at least to talk. He watched her tuck in her blouse, watched her hand plunge behind her wide belt, watched the deep, equine curve of her lower back.

A man was approaching the group of women: Bud Reed, from the dye department. He was a well-built fellow of about thirty, with a cockiness in his gait. A tight T-shirt showed his biceps to advantage. He leaned over to say something to Lucille and her friends, then remained beside them, standing so close to Lucille that their arms touched. Alf seemed to come awake as he watched their fingers entwine.

Arriving home at noon, he said nothing to Margaret, but washed his hands and sat at the table, staring over the array of pink Melmac, the ribbed juice glasses she put down with crisp efficiency.

When the phone rang, Margaret answered.

"It's for you."

The voice on the line was male, and toxic with rage. He could not quite tell who it was – half a dozen possibilities flashed through his mind, until there seemed to be not one but several persons there, speaking with a single voice. He heard profanities, a barrage of accusations. The closing of the mills was the union's fault, the voice said. The union had priced itself out of the market. Because of the union they had lost their jobs. "I hope you're happy now, Walker."

"Who is this!" he demanded, and was answered with the clatter of a fumbled hangup.

"Who was that?" Margaret said from the sink.

He barely heard her.

"Alf –"

"They're closing the mills," he said, distracted, the voice on the phone still seething inside him.

"Closing –"

He looked at her sharply.

"Alf, what's going on?"

"The mills," he said. "Intertex – they're shutting them down."

"Who says they are?"

"*I* say!" he cried, furious. He saw Joe standing by the door. His son had simply materialized, and now stood watching them remotely. It had been his mood for weeks, it seemed, ever since his girlfriend had left. Alf had tried to console him – *Plenty more fish in the sea* – but the boy scarcely seemed aware of his existence. Two or three times blue aerogrammes had arrived from France. Joe had hurried them to his room like a prisoner expecting a reprieve.

Margaret turned to Joe.

"Your father says they've closed the mills!"

"For God's *sake*, Margaret," Alf said. Did she trust nothing he told her any more? He stalked down the hall, pausing at the door to the living room, where Jamie and Penny were watching TV. Bud Reed, he thought suddenly. Bud Reed. Wasn't the guy a bit of a jerk? In a trance, he stared at the screen. The Three Stooges were up to their usual tricks: whooping like cranes, poking fingers in each other's eyes, driving each other's heads into trees and parked cars and telephone poles.

61

THAT AFTERNOON, back at work, the idea came to him that he should talk to Prince. He'd demand an explanation, cook up some deal that would keep Bannerman's in town (he had the notion he might somehow reach into the mechanism of power, as if it were an idling car engine, and make some fine adjustment that would stop Intertex in its course). He knew it was a long shot, knew he was a fool to think *he* could change the course of events, but his relationship with Prince gave him hope. He knew he couldn't rest till he'd tried.

After supper, he set out in the Biscayne. At G.O., the Fleetwood was not in its usual place under the willow. He drove to Johnsonville, where the clerk at the Executive told him Prince had given up his room a week ago. He went back to his car and sat behind the wheel, looking out at the wobbling glow of the pool. Children cannon-balled, sending up geysers with their cries. Prince's disappearance seemed the final blow. He and his company had swept in out of the blue, done what they wanted to, and now had flown off with their spoils, into distances where you couldn't get at them. And the thing was, they'd always had the power to do this, whenever they wanted. All the contortions Alf'd put himself through – they'd all put them-selves through – hadn't made a whit of difference. They might just as well as have done nothing.

Driving back into town, he kept looking for the Fleetwood, he couldn't help himself. The hood of a large black car waited at the corner of Shade and Bridge, its body concealed by a store. He was instantly alert, but as it drew away, he saw it was Rick McArthur's Cadillac hearse, the same vehicle Pete had made his last ride in, its long, bonneted cabin decorated with a stylized chrome S, like a baby carriage.

It seemed he hardly slept that night; the next day, punchdrunk, he dragged himself through his eight hours at Bannerman's. Then after supper, feeling a little better, he walked over to the Flats for a special union meeting about the closings. Arriving at the prefab barn near the mills – it had been built by the Lions as a clubhouse – he stood at the back in a press of heat-dampened bodies. Set up in front of the seated, noisily gabbing crowd was a long table where Bruce Mason, the union president, was leaning forward to tap experimentally at a mike. Bert Hatch, an old Bannerman's executive who had grown up in Attawan, sat beside him, his face with its dark jowls looking exaggeratedly mournful. Beside him, Linda Connaught, the secretary of the local, was bent over a three-ring notebook, writing, with her wide face close to the paper, like a schoolgirl.

Just then Bob Prince slipped in from a door at the rear of the stage and took the chair beside Bert Hatch. He was wearing a light-tan summer suit, but no tie. Instantly alert, Alf watched him closely: the slight, superior tilt of his head as he leaned to murmur something to Bert Hatch; the casual rubbing with one finger of a place under his right ear as he gazed coolly over the rows of faces.

"Can everybody hear me?" Bruce Mason said, his disembodied voice suddenly booming from the speakers.

"Unfortunately!" someone barked behind Alf. In the middle of the hall, a heavy woman in a T-shirt – it was Gail Phipps from Number Six sewing – rose to her feet and raised one arm in a kind of salute. She looked around defiantly, shaking her fist as if she were holding aloft a trophy, or perhaps a weapon, as others shouted for her to sit. It took a while for Bruce to get things underway.

Alf had trouble concentrating on the speeches. He kept looking at Prince, while his mind drifted in and out of the proceedings, always returning to some blank, burning space of its own. But when Bert Hatch said he thought that what Intertex was doing was shameful, he heard *that* and joined vigorously in the applause. The workers were not used to hearing terms such as "shameful" from their business leaders. They listened alertly, clearly hoping for more from Bert, some further echoing of their moral claim – maybe even the announcement of some action that might save the situation – but as

Bert droned on it became clear his "shameful" was not leading any-where and they soon grew restless again.

When Bruce invited questions from the floor, Jimmy Quinn popped up, demanding to know if Bannerman's was leaving because the union had come in.

The people at the head table looked at each other, as cries erupted around the floor.

"Answer him!" several people shouted.

"Maybe Mr. Prince could handle that one," Bruce Mason said, looking down the table.

Prince waved aside the mike Bruce pushed towards him. He leaned forward, arms folded on the table (he had taken off his suit jacket and rolled his sleeves artfully halfway up his tanned forearms).

"I'll be as frank as I can," he said, and his rich voice immediately established a calm that had not been in the room before. One or two workers heckled him, but they were quickly silenced. People seemed doubly alert, eager to hear the executive's explanation. "I fought the union coming in. I had orders to fight it, and I lost. Intertex didn't like the result, a lot of people here – probably some of them in this room – didn't like it, but there it was, we had a union." Prince bowed his head a little and frowned as if girding himself for even more painful acts of candour. He looked exhausted, his face pale, bluish shadows under his eyes. At least this has cost the bugger something, Alf thought, if only a few nights' sleep. "Sure," Prince said, "having to pay more in wages, at a time when we were making some expen-sive changes, that didn't help. It was a consideration. But it wasn't the only consideration. I mean, we're not leaving because we're sore losers, or to get back at anybody. This is purely a business decision." Though Prince did not look at Bert Hatch, Alf sensed he was repri-manding the manager for that "shameful."

This was not the simple answer Jimmy Quinn was hoping for, it seemed to cut both ways. The shipper tried again.

"Lemme put it this way, would you stay if we got rid of the union?"

Immediately, a dozen people tried to shout Jimmy down. Others shouted at the shouters. It was another minute before Prince could continue, during which time Jimmy waited patiently, his head with its crude scar hooked over the ear lifted with a kind of moral loftiness. In a life of filling boxes with sweaters, Jimmy, it occurred to Alf, had never enjoyed such public importance, probably never would again.

"No," the executive said finally. "No, we've discussed this, at Intertex, and no it wouldn't be enough."

The silence that answered his announcement had a bruised, stunned quality. The crowd had given Prince authority. And now his authority had rebuked them: delivered a sentence from which there could be no reprieve.

Jimmy said, "What *would* be enough?"

Again Prince frowned before he spoke. He seemed careworn, even troubled. "Look, this wasn't easy for any of us. We didn't take this decision lightly. But hell, the only reason Bannerman's is here is because John Bannerman needed the power from the rivers. Well, we don't use that kind of power any more, we need to be closer to our markets, we need to shed departments that are losing money, we need newer buildings, ones that don't cost so much to keep up. There's no room for sentimentality – we'd soon be dead if we were sentimental – we just have to do it."

Jimmy tried to speak again, but Prince continued. "We all make business decisions. That's what you people did when you decided to ask more for your labour – just like our suppliers sometimes ask more for their wool, or their dyes. Sometimes these decisions are good ones, and sometimes they aren't."

Jimmy sagged reluctantly to his chair. People were shouting at him, telling him what he should have said, what he might still say. He held out his hands and shrugged, saying, "What? what?" Others sat in silence or talked among themselves. When Alf put his hand up, Bruce Mason pointed.

"Another question for Bob Prince," Alf said and heard his voice travel out in the hall like the parody of a voice, nothing to do with him. He watched Prince find him, the executive's face resolving into clarity at the distant table, the blue eyes flashing in recognition.

"When Intertex came in here last year, all the talk was of turning the company around. You said we had the people here to put Bannerman's back on track – people second to none, you said. Well now you're turning your back on us. I'd like to know what made us so second-rate all of a sudden."

"The union did!" someone yelled. "*You* did, Walker!"

Other voices exploded around the room. Alf went on staring at Prince, who gazed down at his papers as order was restored. Finally the executive looked up, speaking with a touch of weariness. "As I said, Alf, it's a business decision . . ."

"Don't patronize us," Alf snapped. "Like those are better decisions than other kinds of decisions. Like we wouldn't understand them, these *business decisions*. Like we have to take it on faith that there's no other way. You're leaving us in the lurch here. We've had this company for a hundred years, a lot of our grandmothers and grandfathers worked for Bannerman's, we feel like it's ours – hell, I think it *is* ours – and you're taking the whole thing out from under us. Why didn't you ever ask us what we think should be done here? You're just running away –"

The hall filled with applause. Even many of the anti-union people applauded, though others sat scowling. Alf, the blood pounding in his head, waited it out by staring at Prince, who stared at his papers.

Finally Prince said, "Look, the decision is made –"

Several people booed.

"I really don't think this gets us anywhere," Prince said, scowling around the room. Each time he tried to speak, the noise erupted.

Bruce Mason, sheltering behind a weak smile, raised his hands. "Brothers, sisters," he said to further boos.

"I think we need to go on," Bruce persisted, leaning into the mike. But an anarchy had been freed in the crowd. Standing up to point accusingly, or sitting in their chairs, people argued across the room while Bruce Mason's loud, hollow, and universally ignored voice boomed overhead. The others at the table looked bleakly around, guests at a family quarrel.

Alf turned away. He no longer believed that Prince had anything for them, no longer believed the man was worth his attention. He pushed through the crowd into the parking lot, walking past the dully shining hoods of cars, until he reached the relative dark of the baseball infield behind the arena. Stopping, he fumbled for his smokes.

"Alf!"

He heard his own name with despair. The young man who slipped to his side on the bench was Lloyd Tindal. Alf had known his father, a drunk with one eye, a breeder of German shepherds, now living somewhere else. He knew everyone in town, it seemed, everyone in town knew him: he wished to God it was otherwise.

Lloyd Tindal's intense eyes met his with the excruciating frankness of youth. "That was great, what you said in there."

Alf went on smoking.

"Alf, look, some friends and me, we've got a plan. We wanta know what you think about it. Maybe you'd help us."

It was then he noticed the others, three or four of them, hanging around at the end of the bleachers like shadows waiting to be asked into the game.

In the Vimy House, their little table was soon crowded with glasses topped with pure, high foam. The television was shouting from its perch above the bar: a woman weeping, her Marine husband dead in a jungle across the world. To Alf, her suffering was just one more irritation. He concentrated on the beer – the loyal, simple beer – and tried to ignore the circle of expectant faces.

They explained – it was mostly Lloyd explaining, calf eyes fixed on Alf's as if his, Lloyd's, life hung on convincing him – that they wanted to take some action. Take over G.O. Or sabotage something, they said. "We wanta burn the place down," Andy Morris said, his flat, smirking face suddenly red. The others looked from him to Alf:

it was suddenly clear to him that this, really, was what they'd been thinking about. "Let them take *that* to Quebec," Andy said.

Alf stubbed out another cigarette. "All you'll do is ruin your lives," he said. "Look at you, you're all young, you can do a hundred other things. You know you'll get caught. It's certain you'll get caught." As he spoke his warnings, their gazes kept meeting his with sudden courage, then dove shyly for the beer. On the TV, Dinah Shore was seeing the U.S.A. in her Chevrolet.

He worried after they'd left. Maybe he should have said more. He lit another cigarette, and wished he was with them, at the beginning of his life. "Yai, yai, yai," the TV cried harshly, and he looked up to see black-eyed dancers whirling: see Spain!

Later, in the street, he stood uncertain as to what he should do next. Distantly, cars were gunning into life: he supposed the meeting was just breaking up. Shouts floated across the river from the Flats.

Walking home, he turned the corner onto Water and saw Jamie – Jamie, in his striped pyjama top and jeans, slowly riding his bike along the sidewalk. It was like something from a dream, scarcely credible. Trotting along ahead of him was Red.

"Jamie!"

Startled, his son stopped abruptly by a street light, hopping on one foot to keep his balance.

"For God's sake, what are you *doing* out here?"

His head down, the boy said something Alf couldn't make out – said it in that queer, flat voice he'd had for several weeks now. Alf supposed he'd snuck out past Margaret, who must have gone to bed early.

"Speak up. I can't hear you."

"You were at Billy's house?"

Taken aback, Alf could only stare. When the boy glanced up, what Alf saw in his face pierced him. "No, no," he said. "No, it's all right. Come on, let's get you home."

They went through the still summer night, with Red trotting beside them in the road, his tail high, past the house where Alf had grown up, under the dim cloud of the maple his father had planted, past other, darkened houses, into the cul-de-sac.

When they got home, Alf made chocolate milk for Jamie, tea for himself. "You can stay up just for a bit," Alf told him. In truth, he felt an urgent need to keep the boy near him. They carried their drinks into the living room, where Alf turned on the TV, flipping the dial and stopping when he recognized an old movie from the Fifties, *Moby Dick*. They sat together on the couch while Alf explained the plot. The great whale swam towards the tiny distant ship (so obviously a model) like a cruising low mound of snow. Then Ahab's peg leg stamped down the decks, while his men crouched below, listening in hatred and fear.

"How big is a whale?" Jamie said.

"Oh, the biggest ones might be over a hundred feet. From here all the way to Olmsteads' over there." His son watched the porch light across the road, where it flickered among leaves.

Something in the boy's expression, the curiosity and trust, moved Alf, and he reached out to squeeze Jamie's knee, feeling with gratitude the little bony knob under the denim. *He wanted to be here*: that was the realization he kept glimpsing. He wanted to be here, in this house. But he didn't feel he *was* here, not entirely: a faint panic was unsettling him. He looked at the stairs in the hall, the white rails leading up into darkness.

Standing up, he went to the kitchen and cut some bread for toast. Billy's house, he thought suddenly. My God, how much did the boy know? From behind came a quiet tap at the door and, turning, he saw a large moth fluttering outside the screen. He watched in a kind of stupor as the insect, so frail and yet so tenacious, banged repeatedly at the mesh, banged out its life, it seemed, with no idea it was harming itself.

When he heard the shattering of glass, he thought immediately it was the television tube. Then came the peel of tires, Red's howling lament from the yard. Racing down the hall, Alf turned the corner and saw Jamie just where he had left him, sitting on the couch in his jeans and pyjama top. The television was still working – in a long shot, Moby Dick was pounding and lifting the little ship with its toothpick masts – but pieces of the shattered window littered the rug like the leavings of an ice storm.

Jamie's face was pale, his eyes glassy, filled with the faraway look of someone listening to the meander of his own thoughts. To the side of his forehead, just starting to bleed, was a rising lump. On the couch beside him, as if he had been playing with it, was a dark, smooth chunk of rock about the size of a lopsided baseball. Bound to it with masking tape was a piece of paper.

It was not until the next morning, returning from the hospital with the police, that Alf read the crudely lettered note. HOPE YOUR HAPPY NOW WALKER THIS IS YOUR DOING FUCK YOU DIE.

62

AT THE HOSPITAL, they had covered Jamie's eyes with gauze, to keep them from drying out, and held the pads in place with strips of tape that masked much of his upper face, giving him the appearance of a bug with bulging eyes – an insect boy, resting against the huge pillow. Three days after the rock had come through the window, he was still unconscious.

Alf sat in a leatherette chair by the bed. It was nearly eleven o'clock. He had been in the room since seven. He watched in a kind of trance, adrift on his own thoughts, at the same time sensitive to every sign – or at least to the possibility of a sign – from the bed. Jamie's mouth was open a little. Alf couldn't hear him breathe in, but the exhalations came in huffs, too brief to be sighs, yet suggesting to

Alf a dangerous weariness, as if the boy were close to giving up. Alf had the impression that Jamie was doing some work – some vast labour, alone, in the dark. He wanted to help, would have given his right arm to go down into that darkness and put his shoulder to the immense weight Jamie was lifting by himself, whatever that weight was, but all he could do was watch helplessly from the sidelines, not even sure what was going on. He thought of a time in the arena, years ago, when Joe had got knocked out during a hockey game. Joe's coach had vaulted over the boards and run slipping across the ice, while the other players had milled around the motionless little body in its purple jersey. Watching from the stands, Alf had not joined them. He didn't want to appear hysterical, didn't want to embarrass Joe, didn't want to break the unspoken masculine code that forbade overreacting to physical danger. And after a minute, Joe had got up, slowly, and skated to the bench grinning at the applause from the other parents while Alf watched in relief and pride. The boy had proved he could take it. Alf tried to wrap himself in the same spirit of resilience now – *his boys could take it* – but Jamie had been un-conscious for so long. It was true, the doctors had reassured them that though it might take time, the chances were good that Jamie would recover. Yet Alf was experiencing a dread unlike anything in his life. He was alert to every movement in the vast bed. If Jamie's breathing paused, he was up in a flash, worrying. If the flow of IV seemed to stop, he was in the hall, looking for a nurse. Everything in his body craved action, the leap over the boards, the slipping run across the ice, but this time he had no choice: all he could do was watch.

Alf smoothed the blanket and touched his son's forehead, which was warm. The bump itself, mostly hidden by the eye patches, had begun to subside, a yellow-purplish swell no worse than many Jamie had sustained before, and yet worse, the doctor said, because the rock had caught him on the temple. The word had turned odd, trai-torous, in Alf's mind. A temple was a place where people prayed (he thought of fluted pillars, like the ones outside the post office in Johnsonville), and at the same time it was part of the forehead, a mysterious, fragile, small spot: an inch either way and Jamie might have been spared. Above the bandages, Jamie's hair flamed in wild tufts.

He smoothed his son's hair and bent to him, whispering for perhaps the hundredth time. "It's Daddy, Jamie. I'm right here." For a moment the breathing paused. It seemed to him that Jamie might be listening. Perhaps he was considering the word "Daddy," down there in the dark. Alf imagined him wandering in a labyrinth, trying to feel his way out. Hearing the word, he might turn in the direction it had come from, and so start up the long passage that slanted towards the light. Then the breathing resumed: perhaps he was coming on the right path now, and perhaps he was heading the other way, confused, into a deeper darkness.

Alf threw himself back in the leatherette chair. Bastards, he thought. Who had done this thing? Someone who blamed him for bringing the union in – for driving Intertex out. Someone with a grudge going back years, who knew? The police, so far, had come up with nothing.

He lurched forward again, thinking he caught a movement from the bed. But the bandaged face lay as still as before. A bubble rose brightly through the throat of the intravenous bottle.

Then Margaret was there, crossing the floor with swift steps.

Alf came awake, sitting upright in his chair. Her gaze had already fixed on the bed. In her arm was a paper bag, which he knew contained things she would need for the night. The hospital was willing to supply an orderly to sit overnight with Jamie, but Margaret insisted on doing it herself. Alf had offered to spell her off, but she'd refused.

He watched her drop her bag on the cot the nurses had set up for her, and bend over Jamie. She touched the boy's hair, murmuring something Alf could not catch, touched the back of his hand.

"Dr. Samuels was in," he said. Samuels was the specialist from Johnsonville who was consulting on the case. Margaret looked at Alf, her eyes hard, bright.

"He still thinks the chances are pretty good."

Margaret kept looking at him, as if she were testing the truth of his words. He flushed and looked away.

After a moment, he stood up.

"I guess I'll go then."

Margaret didn't answer, but went back to ministering to Jamie, feeling his cheek with the back of her hand. She turned to the cot, where she had dropped her bag and purse. Alf went on standing by the bed.

"Well," he said. All he wanted was a word from her, some acknowledgment. But she kept her back to him as she shook out a blanket. Then she turned.

"It's late," she said. "Go and get some rest." She told Alf this in a crisp, factual way, her eyes meeting his only briefly. The weary flatness in her voice unsettled him more than anger might have, for it suggested she wasn't surprised by what had happened to Jamie. It was the sort of thing she might expect to happen now, in the place Alf had brought them to.

He got home to find Joe and Penny in bed. Far from sleep, he sat at the kitchen table, in the dark. From the distant gravel pits, the faint clank of conveyor belts floated intermittently through the screen door. He stared out into the night, across Margaret's garden towards the shadowy bulk of the dyke, the more distant greyness of Lookout Hill where a street lamp dropped an isolated cone of light over the road running past the park. He hardly saw these things.

His gaze was trained on the depth that is more inner than outer, more concerned with the events of the vast invisible world than on the world of things we like to say is the only real one. But there is a place where both worlds mingle, and at one point he became aware that his thoughts were twined with a rushing sound that came from the river, from a place where a lone rock, known to him since boyhood, ploughed stolidly upstream, never getting anywhere, yet never ceasing to progress in the changing water. He let out a long breath and shifted in his chair and when the siren went off, lifted his head a little. The blasts kept coming, at short intervals. In the street, a car suddenly accelerated, as if it had been waiting for just this signal.

Some time after the siren stopped, the phone rang behind him. For a few moments he sat without moving. But then, remembering Joe and Penny asleep upstairs, he rose to silence it.

"Alf, the mills are on fire!" It was Jack Cornish, his foreman on the maintenance crew: his voice narrow and distant, as if calling down a pipe.

Alf flicked on the light and blinked at the calendar. In the square of August 30, Margaret had printed PENNY'S TWELFTH BIRTHDAY! Another life: where people stroked exclamation points in acts of hectic enthusiasm, as if happiness might be commanded.

"Alf, are you there?"

Those buggers, Alf thought, those stupid, goddamn buggers.

"Alf?"

"I'm here."

"The fire department's just come. Johnsonville's sending two trucks. We need more men."

Alf's heart seemed to be punching its way through his ribs.

Through the windshield of the Biscayne he saw at first only roiling smoke, reddening below as it billowed over the mills. The lane off Bridge was blocked with vehicles. Hoses ran everywhere, veining wet asphalt. Several dozen people, many in bathrobes, had gathered under the wall of the arena. Passing the mouth of the lane, he glimpsed the livid windows: storey upon storey of fire, as if a party were going on in the mills, a party of strange, fiery creatures, their laws and language unknown to men, filling the rooms with their dances, their roaring conversations.

There was no place left to park, so he drove around the corner, finally drawing into the parking lot of General Office, across the road from the mills. No flames were visible from here, though getting out of the car, he could hear the hollow, cascading roar of the fire, the small shouts of men calling for hoses. The glowing smoke from the far side of the mill complex rose over the flat rooftops, shedding an eerie light. Everything he looked at – the walls of the mills, even the asphalt roadway – seemed on the verge of exploding into flame. He crossed the deserted street, reaching the fence that bordered the millrace. A stink of mud – the race had recently been emptied, for repairs – mingled with the smell of smoke. Down the street, by a lone fire truck, several men with hoses were shooting water into a building. He began to walk towards them, glancing up from time to time at the darkened windows of the mills. Here and there smoke seeped from under a sash. He was breathing hard.

A voice caught him. It had come from above him, but when he turned and looked at the upper windows, he could make out nothing.

The voice came again. It seemed, almost, to be sounding inside his own head.

"You there! Help me!"

Putting his hands on the fence bordering the race, Alf strained to see.

"Get a ladder here!"

Shouting harshly, trying not to scream: keeping to the last edge before the fall into hysteria.

The voice seemed somehow familiar. But when Alf found the right window, the figure there was half-hidden in a streaming veil of smoke. He could not make out who it was.

"Alf! Bring a ladder!"

He went on staring, spellbound. The man seemed so small and faraway, absurd in the vast, empty buildings. What was he doing there? He seemed to have something to do with the fire itself, was fire's creature; or he was the beleaguered, desperate spirit of the mills them-selves, shouting out a last request for life. *And he knew who Alf was.*

Smoke was pouring around the figure now, he was entirely invisible.

Alf turned at the rail, looking for help. To the south, the hoses were sending thin, ineffectual-looking arcs into the mill. There seemed to be no ladders there. He would have to go around to the back of the mills by Bridge Street. It would take too long. Glancing to his right, he saw the narrow footbridge that crossed the millrace to the base of the building. At the other end of the bridge, a few wisps of smoke coiled gently into the night: the metal door was ajar.

At the truck, Phil Jones gave his place at the nozzle to another man. His hands were stiff, his shirt soaked from a leak spraying from the hose. He'd been in bed with the flu when the siren sounded. Now, feeling both feverish and chilled, and more than a bit sorry for himself, he looked to the north and saw, in the light of flames suddenly leaping above the roof, a figure shrouded in a blanket, crossing the footbridge. Phil watched it lean forward and break into a run – it seemed, under the cowl of the blanket, to be headless – watched it disappear into the smoking side of the mill.

BY MID-SEPTEMBER, the poplars along the Atta had turned yellow. Their leaves trembled with the faintest movement of the air; their inverted reflections, just visible in shadowy water, suggested the presence of another world.

For Joe, there was no question of university. He had failed to win any entrance scholarships, and besides, his mother's new job as a clerk at Millie's Dress Nook didn't bring in enough to support the family, so he had gone to work in the liquor store. He spent his days filling the shelves in the backroom with cartons of Seagram's and

Baby Duck – a task he preferred to serving at the front counter, where he sensed people were watching him. He felt ashamed on account of the events that had befallen his family, as if they were in some way deserved, the punishment for some moral failure, punishment perhaps for having had the father he had had.

The backroom of the store overlooked the iron water of the Shade. On the far shore, past the dyke and the playing fields, the blackened shell of the mills was being knocked down. All day he could hear the faint explosions as the wrecking balls assaulted the thick walls, and bricks fell in showers. Above the ruins, dark flocks of pigeons, like gusts of ash, beat away and frantically returned. One morning he was startled to see that the mills were gone.

They had found his father on an upper storey, his head wrapped in the red tartan blanket. "Smoke was too much for him," Patch Cooper, the fire chief, told Joe one day in his office. He said that one of his men had seen his father enter the mill, but by the time some of the crew had found masks and gone in after him, it was too late. "We don't really know why he went in there. Myself, I think he may have been trying to help someone."

"Maybe that was it," Joe said thickly.

Patch Cooper looked at him for a moment before continuing. "Yes, well, two or three foremen went into Number Six, a little earlier. They were trying to close doors, save records, like. Maybe one of them got into trouble and he tried to help. It could be – course the investigation isn't over yet – it could be he did a brave thing there."

The fire chief avoided his eyes as he said this, and Joe had to wonder what his real opinions were. He knew Patch Cooper had to be aware, as he himself was, of rumours that his father had himself started the fire. He had tried to refuse this possibility, but there was a place in him where he feared it might be true.

The only man who could answer his doubts was no longer there. Joe was still set against his father, as if his dying were one more affront. He'd be walking down the street, and the whole time a voice in him would be going on endlessly, carrying on arguments – *Why did you do it you should never have gone in there why didn't you think of the rest of us why* – that met only a silence deepening like a kind of winter.

A few days after Joe's meeting with Patch Cooper, two provincial police detectives came to the house. They sat on the couch with their notebooks on their knees, interviewing Joe and Margaret. They were trying to piece together Alf's whereabouts after he had left the hospital on the night of the fire. Apparently, someone claimed to have sighted the Biscayne near the mills, an hour or so before the alarm had been turned in.

"What exactly are you implying?" Margaret said, indignant. Joe, seated nearby, watched her draw herself up. She had aged, he thought, her face gone sharp, her eyes too bright in their deepened sockets.

One of the detectives, the softer-spoken one, said they weren't trying to say anything; they just had to tidy up all the loose ends.

"I think I've had enough," she said, standing up abruptly.

"I know it's been hard for you, Mrs. Walker."

"You don't know anything," she said.

When the policemen went on sitting, she left the room.

"I got one more question," the other detective said to Joe. "The night of the fire – after your dad came back from the hospital – were you aware of him leaving the house at any time?"

Frowning, Joe glanced down at the rug. After he'd fallen asleep, he hadn't heard his father come in, but he'd been wakened briefly by the sound of the Biscayne leaving. He had no idea what time that had been.

"I didn't hear anything," he said, looking back at the detective. The man held his gaze for a couple of seconds while Joe, his mouth dry, brazened it out.

Later, he found his mother in her garden, mucking furiously around her tomato plants with a hoe. As Joe approached she looked up at him. "They don't know anything," she cried, her voice full. "Your father –" She broke off and for a moment watched him haplessly, as some new thought rose brimming into her eyes, into features that now looked soft and oddly unformed. He tried to hold her, awkwardly embracing her and the upright hoe together. After a moment she stiffened and pulled back. "All right," she told him. "Let's go in."

Ten days after the fire, Jamie awoke, and in another few days he was well enough to come home. The side of his head bore the shrinking, yellowish traces of his wound, and he seemed slow and abstracted. When Margaret told him what had happened, he went very still, his eyes fixed in deep space. A minute later, he asked if he could watch television.

For some time afterwards, he seemed reluctant to leave the house, even to play. Hoping to rouse his interest, Joe gave his brother his old fibreglass bow and three new arrows, beautifully feathered. One afternoon, glancing out his bedroom window, he saw Jamie standing on the shore of the river, aiming his bow towards the far bank. He wasn't strong enough to pull it back to its full extent, but the arrow he released drifted over the Atta – a flash of orange – and disappeared into the foliage of Lookout Hill. Joe nearly shouted out the window at him – Those arrows were expensive! – but something in the rapt way his brother lowered the bow and stared at the hill held him back, and he watched as Jamie sped the remaining arrows across the water.

Penny took it hard. At the cemetery, she had broken from her mother's side and run to the coffin as Joe and the other pallbearers carried it towards the grave. Lately, she seemed possessed by an extreme urge to *do* something. She was often busy in her room, her table a mess of paper and paints and soap-shavings. She made a papier mâché figure, three feet high, with a black coat and a rather grotesque face, which she told Joe was Johnny North. Joe found it hard to meet her gaze for more than a few seconds because it sometimes seemed his father was looking out at him from her eyes, making some demand – for recognition, maybe, for help – Joe did not know what.

Gradually, by day, a kind of normality settled on the house. But at night came the sudden cries, the drumming of his brother's or sister's feet down the hall to their mother's room. Jamie wouldn't go to sleep unless someone was watching him. To help his mother, Joe often took on that job. One night, while Jamie tossed and kept opening his eyes to check if his brother was still there, Joe sat on the bedroom floor with his back to the wall, rereading Anna's letters by flashlight. In August, she had written to say she was sharing rooms with two English girls, revelling in the fact that each morning they awoke to the smell of fresh bread from the shop below. As for Joe's standing with her, it seemed ambiguous at best. She wrote that she missed him, but her obvious pleasure in her new life made him wonder.

He had written to her about the fire, omitting anything too specific. Of his father he said only that he had died while attempting to save another man. In one way, he was glad to have miseries to report. He felt he had earned the right to her affections. At the same time, these events filled him with shame, and he feared he would lose caste with her.

Two days after he had sent his letter, he had found another of her blue aerogrammes waiting at the post office. Her father, she said, had written her about what had happened. *Oh Joe, my dear Joe, this is terrible!* Immediately the warmth of her sympathy flooded him. She had written him a poem, which, like all her poems, he soon memorized. It was about their last evening together: the churchyard where they'd walked in the wind. She'd been more aware of the poignancy of that moment than he'd realized.

He went to the post office every day. In early October, another letter from her arrived. He took it to the little park, at the end of the main street, where the war memorial was. Sitting on the step behind the monument, his back to the cool stone, he read her news. She was studying German, she told him, and she'd just made a weekend visit to Chartres. After several paragraphs about the cathedral, she mentioned Doug, an American friend. *He's a philosophy major, very interested in Sartre. You know, you can actually see Sartre almost*

*any day here, walking to his favourite café. He looks like a garden
gnome. He has a walleye. It seems to be looking at things no one else
has seen, that have scared one part of him witless. Doug's trying to
get up his nerve to speak to him.*

*I should tell you, Joe, it doesn't look like I'll be able to get to
Attawan for Christmas. We can't afford it, and of course with the
mills gone, my father is making arrangements to come back to
France. They've promised him his old job again. But I want you
to know how much our time together meant to me . . .*

He looked up from the pages, at the scarred side wall of the old
Capitol Theatre, where fading advertisements for long-ago films were
just visible, including the image of an immense tiger with a red
tongue. He had no idea who Sartre was.

That evening after supper, he took a walk along the Atta. Moving
slowly, he reached the dam, and for a while sat on the ancient concrete at its edge, looking out over the thin skim of water racing down
its long, sloping face. Above, the deep water of the millpond
approached the lip with a glassy stillness, before it slipped over. He
had been thinking of Anna. But as he gazed across the pond, where
a late dragonfly skimmed, he had an awareness of his father so
powerful he stopped breathing. This was a place his father had
known – he had swum and skated here as a boy – his father had been
saturated with this place, as Joe himself was. He felt he knew what
his father had seen and felt here, because he was able to see and feel
it too. Spellbound, he looked out over the water.

But then, a cold breeze rising from the Atta, everything changed.
What did he know about his father, really? What could he ever know,
now, about what lay behind his father's eyes, behind his silences? Joe
looked downstream, where the current surged over a rusted weed-
clogged bicycle, and felt the chill of unrecoverable loss.

Over the next few days, a weakness infected his body. He only
wanted to lie in bed, not reading, not listening to the radio, but

drifting in and out of shallow sleep. The yellow trees of Lookout Hill filled most of his window. His gaze kept drifting to a spot of delicate orange-pink – a young oak perhaps – about halfway up the hill. He would look for this tree first thing in the morning, upset if mist hid the hill. In the evening, he watched it with feverish interest as it dissolved in darkness. He had no idea why the tree compelled him so; but when one morning he discovered that a big wind had stripped most of its leaves, he was distraught.

His mother usually came in after work, to give him the news of the day. And Penny liked to bring him his meals – what little he was able to eat. She'd begun to adopt Margaret's manner of brisk cheerfulness and would sit on the edge of his bed chatting about school. One afternoon she brought him a little figure, carved in yellow soap. It was of a young man with a hockey stick in his hand, about three inches high. Joe turned it over in his hands. Penny watched him closely. "It's *you*," she cried finally, piqued that he hadn't guessed. "You remember, when we all went skating above the dam!" And he remembered the hockey game: that day of blue-sky freedom. She had carved him skating alone upstream, his head bowed, his stick held idly upside down. She had caught the stoop of his shoulders, and his old jacket with the torn sleeve, and something else, some indefinable thing that was him. He was astonished – she had just turned twelve – and he remembered Penny and her friends, their chiming voices, as he skated up to the rapids. And again he saw the fox, its long, floating tail.

After a week or so, he began to make small forays around the house. One Sunday morning, when the others were at church, he ventured outside. Everything was strange and bright – almost painful to look at – the green of the yard, reviving after a summer of drought, the sun glinting off the Lions Park footbridge. He still felt frail, unsure of his legs, and also frail in another way, as if what little courage he had for this walk might disappear in a moment. Soon his mind was racing with a nameless panic. It seemed that the future had ceased to exist. When he put out his foot, he half-expected it to fall on nothing. He had to be alert, he had to concentrate, to keep from being swept away.

That first day he got as far as the bandshell in the park, where he sat relaxing, or at least pretending to, before he retreated to the house. Some days later, feeling much stronger, he dared a longer walk. He passed the dam, following the edge of the woods that curved around the fields of the Wiley farm. Though a bit light-headed, he began to move more quickly, lengthening his stride, throwing out his arms. But then, pausing for breath under a grove of pines, he broke into a sweat. All his fear had come back, full force. He glanced around. The sky was too huge, every distance too vast.

He looked up the long hill, to where the fields crested against the sky. *That* was the shortest way home, he realized – straight across the fields and over the hill – much shorter now than retracing his steps by the woods. The fields had not been ploughed for some time, and were covered with wild grasses, with outcrops of goldenrod and chicory and other weeds. As he looked across these fields, thinking he could never cross them (it was too far, too exposed), a wind came down the hill towards him. It pressed over the dry grasses and weeds, making their heads bend, until it reached him. And this wind, to his amazement, was warm. It was a cool day, but a warm wind was coursing over him, touching his face, wrapping him in warmth, moving the plants and branches around him. In his chest, something seemed to break.

He did not know what happened next. In his whole life, thinking of it, he never would understand what happened next. But the next time he was conscious of anything, he was on the hilltop, two hundred yards from where he had just been standing. He had no idea how he had got there. It was as if he had crossed the fields in a dream, or as if some power – the wind itself perhaps – had picked him up and deposited him on the high, bald hilltop, on the grassy edge of an old lane.

He realized he was weeping, gladly and without stint, sobbing like a child. He was sitting with his legs stretched out on the ground, like a child in a sandbox, amazed at everything he saw. Far down by the river, a few isolated poplar leaves glittered. Galleon clouds sailed overhead, a scattered fleet with emblazoned sails, swelling to the west. He saw the erect, white tail of a deer, disappearing over the hill. Normally, he would have been surprised to see a deer, but just now, everything was a miracle equal to it, everything surprised him. A flock of starlings pulsed by with a thrumming of wings he felt in his breastbone. A lone heron launched itself from the water's edge, its wings rowing the deep air as it laboured over the town.

He was rocking, in some ancient, vital movement of self-comforting, though the comfort seemed not to come only from him. Looking down the slope to the river, he knew he was part of it all still. It held him still. He knew he would go on whether he wanted to or not, because he would be carried on, by whatever had carried him onto this hill, by whatever it was that moved the clouds and the birds and the leaves swirling off a nearby tree. But also, he wanted to go on. It was in him again, the desire to go on, however weak or unhappy or afraid he still was, and this was as much grief as joy, because he knew, now, where life was headed. And yet he wanted it anyway, he wanted it because he wanted it, there was no more reason than that. He was alive.

Brian Pickell

John Bemrose's first novel, *The Island Walkers*, was a national best-seller and a finalist for The Giller Prize. Bemrose is also well known as an arts journalist whose articles and profiles have appeared regularly in *Maclean's*, where he is a contributing editor. In the past, he has written for CBC Radio's *Ideas*, for the National Film Board, for the *Globe and Mail*, and for numerous other publications. He has also written a play, *Mother Moon*, produced by the National Arts Centre, and has published two poetry collections. Bemrose grew up in Paris, Ontario, the place that inspired the setting for *The Island Walkers*.

Bemrose has lived in Toronto since 1970. He is at work on his second novel.